I0778759

THE BEST MEDICINE

TEACHERS' LOUNGE
BOOK 5

KRYSTA DEARSON

WWW.SMARTYPANTSROMANCE.COM

COPYRIGHT

DEDICATION

FOREWORD

This book portrays characters living with anxiety disorders as well as discussions regarding barriers to diagnosing and treating mental health disorders. As a physician, I understand that everyone affected by mental health struggles have their own personal experience. The character's journeys in this book reflect my own personal experiences or training as a physician—they do not and should not invalidate or diminish your own experiences with these disorders.

The beginning of each chapter has a quote from a romance novel meant to reflect a book that is being read or listened to by the characters *and* relate to the chapter in some way. Many quotes are from fictional authors that are figments of *this* author's imagination like Lady Jane, Lena Benjamin, Angel Marie and Anne Richter. Most of the quotes are from real books by fabulous authors that I have read and loved. In a way, this book is my love letter to romance authors and readers alike; I love being a part of your community.

PROLOGUE

"I'm coming to get you, Polly Anna Alberton! You can't hide from the evil Queen of Sheeba! Haaa, ha, ha, ha!"

Ducking down behind a bush, I put my hand over my mouth, trying to be quiet. Momma was so funny. She wouldn't think of looking here. I was—

"Ha ha! Foiled! The Queen of Sheeba's found you!"

I screamed in delight as I got up to run, only to slip and fall in the mud. I heard a rip as I fell. Sitting back, I saw a big hole in my corduroy pants, right over the knee. Tears ran down my cheeks. Father would be so angry.

"Oh, baby. It's ok." Momma's arms wrapped around me. I felt so safe and warm. I loved Momma's hugs. "No use crying over a small rip, huh?"

"But," I sniffled, "my new pants are dirty. And there's a hole right here." I pointed at my knee. "What about Father? He's gonna be so mad."

Momma leaned forward, stretched her fingers wide, and sunk her hand into the mud in front of us. I watched in amazement as she pressed a large muddy handprint onto her light-colored pants and giggled as she painted a line of mud down each of our cheeks and dotted our noses.

"There, now we match." She smiled wide and squeezed me tight. She always knew what to say to make me feel better. She traced her fingers over the rip at my knee. "And this rip? Well, it's a memory. Every mistake's a memory. Some of my favorite times have come from mistakes. Don't feel bad if you make a mistake, Polly. Feel bad for people who do everything perfectly the first time, because they're missing out on the fun bits. Those are the bits that make you feel the most alive."

CHAPTER
ONE

JACE

He continued to be surprised by her wit, her radiant power, her hot, wicked mouth. Her pink tongue flashed as she produced the stem from her mouth, revealing a tight knot. Smirking, she dropped the stem onto the table.

"Your turn."

He flushed, his boxers the only thing he had left to take off. He hated losing. She wasn't only tying cherry stems into knots; she was tying his alibi into a knot as well.

"I don't have any truths to tell," he rasped.

Her smile was simpering as she leaned closer. The swells of her breasts pressed against him, her eyes raking down

his body before purring into his ear.

"Drop 'em."

American Tail by Lady Jane
Narrated by Brittney Houston

Deck shorts were a bad choice for a valet uniform. Someone must've complained about being too hot because three weeks ago when I showed up for my usual Sunday shift at the Green Valley Country Club, I was handed a pair of shorts and asked to change. But when your job requires you to sit on the black leather interior of a car that's been baking in the Tennessee summer sun, it's surface-of-the-sun hot.

Torture hot.

Peel-off-a-layer-of-skin hot.

Still, not hot enough for me to change jobs. I liked parking cars, much to my momma's disappointment. Being relatively attractive and polite, I made good tips, and some patrons even asked for me by name. And considering that my sixteen-year-old coworkers looked barely old enough to ride a ten-speed much less drive a stick shift, I was usually asked to drive the more expensive rides.

Today I was working the morning shift, the shift I preferred, when the first golfers arrived. Spotting those first morning golf parties now rounding hole fifteen, I checked my watch, impressed. They were making good time.

"Hey, Tim," I called out to my twenty-year-old valet manager, who was standing at the valet podium under the stone portico. "You mind staying out here while I take my break? The next brunch rush should be coming in half an hour."

Tim spent most of his time inside the air-conditioned clubhouse and looked scared whenever anyone talked to him, despite being, in all actuality, our boss.

He jumped when I said his name, then looked down at his phone, nervously. "Uh, yeah. Sorry, Jace. Shoot, you should've been allowed to go an hour ago."

"No worries, Cal needed a break more than me. I let him go cool off after leaving a layer of his skin on a leather seat earlier this morning."

Tim grimaced. "I guess shorts weren't my best idea."

Chuckling, I shook my head. "Not for leather seats." I lowered my voice. "Not all our ideas can be winners. My advice? Let people choose between shorts and pants. Denice won't mind." I saw Tim swallow at the mention of the Country Club's manager. Denice was known for being a ballbuster. "But if she gives you grief, I'd bring up worker's comp and heatstroke."

Tim nodded in response as I clapped him on the shoulder. I'd just started to turn toward the employee entrance when I heard Tim squeak, "Uh, Jace?"

I quirked an eyebrow.

"Actually, you mind staying out here for a few more minutes? I gotta take a leak."

Dipping my chin, I walked back to the podium as he hurried away. Poor kid. He tried hard. Denice had offered me Tim's job at least once every three months, but I was happy where I was. It was midmorning in early June and the weather was perfect: clear sky, cool breeze, and eighty degrees. I took a deep cleansing breath, the smell of the freshly mowed grass filling my lungs. I loved being outside at this time of day. It beat being cooped up in an office somewhere.

A buzz of my watch alerted me that my buddy Sam had texted me, so I dug my phone out of my pocket.

Sam: Have you ever trapped an armadillo?

Laughing at my best friend's ridiculous question, I typed out my response.

Jace: Not a hobby of mine

Sam: We had a request

Jace: It sounds illegal

Sam: They signed the waiver

Jace: I hear they carry leprosy

Sam: What's leprosy?

Shortly after Sam had finished college, he started a company called Jack of All Trades, with the slogan "We do the DIY jobs you hate." People asked for the typical stuff, cleaning gutters, emptying out a garage, laying mulch. But sometimes, he'd get strange requests. And being his best friend and most frequently used independent contractor, I was privy to the really weird shit. Like wrangling an armadillo.

Sam and I were the same age at twenty-four. Growing up, we both disliked school, but for different reasons. For Sam, it was because of issues with focus and organization; for me, it was because I wasn't a fan of doing things that seemed pointless. But unlike me, Sam actually finished his degree at a local community college. I dropped out after a year of higher education because I never found a career I could picture myself doing for the rest of my life. Why would I waste money on a four-year degree studying something I hated? I would much rather have a handful of small jobs I liked than be miserable in a career that looked good on paper. And yet, I was made to feel, mostly by my momma, and ok, yes, my older brother, and a few folks in town too, that I was going nowhere in life.

But at least I wouldn't be going through a painful, disfiguring disease process.

Jace: Don't find out. Say no

Seeing a black Tesla approach, I pocketed my phone and walked to the other side of the portico. My mind was still preoccupied on saving my friend from himself as I made out the outline of a woman in the driver's seat. Once the car parked, the driver's door opened and I grabbed it by rote, starting my typical spiel.

"Hi, I'm from the valet service. . ."

My words trailed off as a sexy red high heel touched the pavement. My eyes trailed up the bona fide blonde knockout in front of me as she smoothly rose from the driver's seat. She stood tall in heels, only a few inches shorter than my six-two frame. Her clear skin shone in the morning sun, sunglasses hiding her eyes. My hand twitched with a strange urge to remove them, curious to discover the eye color hidden beneath. Suddenly, a ghost of a sound left her lips, and she whipped back around, bending over to lean into the driver's seat.

A sleek black dress covered her from neck to knees. For all intents and purposes, it would be considered conservative. It even had pearl buttons down the back.

But that's not what got my attention.

I was singularly focused on one very prominent asset in front of me. Her dress was tight and stretched with her, highlighting every dip and curve of her truly delectable body as she bent forward into her car.

Remembering I was at my place of employment and staring inappropriately at a patron, I averted my eyes. But they darted back to her quickly as I heard a soft feminine exhale. She'd leaned further into the car, causing her backside to turn up all the more. I tried again not to notice. I mean, I really tried. But then her left heel lifted out of her shoe as she stretched, causing me to reflexively shift closer to her, as if I was going to what? Wrap my hands around her waist and steady her?

Chastising myself, I shuffled two steps away just as she rocked back into her heel and stood. For a moment, it seemed like one of those slow-motion movie montages was playing out in front of me. As she turned, she gave a flick of her head to the left, deftly removing her sunglasses in one go. Her blonde hair waved like a shining curtain in front of her as she quickly snapped her head back to center. Bright green eyes fixed to mine as her silky hair tumbled past her shoulders.

Have mercy.

I had no choice but to stare at the most beautiful woman I'd ever seen. She was older than me. I had no idea how much older, and at that moment, I didn't care. Tall and graceful, full pink lips, I noted a few strands of hair were stuck on her kissable lips. I once again had the reflexive urge to reach for her, to take that lock of hair between my fingers, wondering if it felt as soft as it looked. Her gaze held mine as she gave me a slight smile, making me feel as if I'd been punched in the gut.

I'd always been an unrufflable, easygoing type of guy. But this woman, with her stunning eyes and pretty mouth, was my undoing. Despite clearing my throat, my voice still came out rough.

"I'm Jace, your valet. Would you like to use me?"

Holy shit, man. Get it together.

"I mean us. Use our service, the valet service." I fumbled my words, like a complete fool.

Eyeing me curiously, her small smile grew infinitesimally bigger. I was so focused on her face, I didn't notice she'd been discreetly holding out her keys to me until her gaze dropped to her hand.

"Let me take those for you." I grinned sheepishly, my hand brushing hers as I took the keys. Digging deep and finding some sort of smile to plaster on my face, I held out her valet ticket.

"Thank you." Her reply was deeper than I expected, with a little rasp. I swear to God, I felt that rasp all the way down to my dick.

"Ma'am," I drawled. Good manners had been drilled into me from little on.

Her face dimmed at my words. I frowned when she took my ticket hurriedly and handed me a folded bill. I didn't even have time to say thank you before she abruptly turned to walk toward the club's entrance.

I couldn't move. My eyes were too busy following her as she made her way to the front doors.

She was magnificent. Lithe body. Perfect posture.

I looked down at the tip in my hand.

And loaded. Her tip was twenty bucks. And that was only for dropping off her car.

I glanced back to the front doors, but she was gone.

I wondered what her name was.

It doesn't matter. She's older than you, gorgeous, probably married to the owner or some shit.

I bet her name was just as perfect and polished as she seemed.

You're never going to find out. Quit being a tool.

I got into her car and briefly adjusted the seat back. Then, after turning the car back on, I shifted into drive. I'd just begun driving forward when a deep voice came over the speaker.

"He lapped at her hot, wet pussy, making her moan and thrash, her clit shaking wildly on his tongue. He grabbed her ass, bringing her pussy closer to him still, feasting on her, loving the feel of her."

Words escaped me as I slammed on the brakes. I immediately reached for the volume, turning it all the way down. The console read *American Tail* by Lady Jane.

Huh. Was this some sort of porn podcast? Did they even make those?

I looked in the rearview mirror, then back to the front doors of the club.

Empty.

Hesitantly, curiosity burning in my veins, I slowly turned the volume up again, keeping it quieter this time.

"You like that, baby?" His voice was gravely and deep as she hummed and thrashed, just as into this as he was. "I bet you do, you dirty girl, come for me, princess. Fucking come for me."

Gobsmacked, I leaned back in the seat as I listened to a guy moan in ecstasy through the speakers.

This was low key the dirtiest podcast I'd ever come across.

Laughing in disbelief, I eased off the brake. I drove a few car lengths toward the parking lot when the audio stopped. I looked down to troubleshoot when realization hit me. Whatever she was listening to must've been on her phone, and as I drove away, her Bluetooth cut out.

After parking, I immediately searched on my phone for *American Tail* and Lady Jane. I wanted to know what this siren of a woman, whose perfect composure and elegant grace were completely at odds with her fuck-me heels, was listening to.

Instantly I got hits.

And I'll be damned, it wasn't a podcast. It was a book. An audiobook, to be exact. Lady Jane was a romance novelist, *American Tail* amongst her top-selling books. As a teenager, my sister used to hide books like this under her bed; "Books for the devil" my momma had called 'em.

Curiousity burned in my veins, wondering what else this seemingly proper woman listened to. Was the whole book full of stuff like that?

Before I could think twice, I pulled up the author's page and scrolled to find *American Tail.* The devil on my shoulder grinned as I hit **BUY NOW**.

CHAPTER
TWO

POLLY

There, in the inky black of the shadows, stood Lucian. His ripped chest appearing cut from granite, sweat glistening under the silvery bands of moonlight. As if an internal clock struck, his head strained back, eyes forcefully shut in both agony and ecstasy, a fierce howl letting loose from deep within. His muscles began to pulse as the night filled with the sound of flesh tearing and bones breaking. In a symphony of shadows, moonlight, and magic, his perfect mask was ripped clean, revealing his true self as his magnificent wolf form broke free.

The Seduction of the Shift by Angel Marie
Narrated by Michael Smolton

Four Weeks Later

"I'll have the eggs Benedict."

My father always ordered the eggs Benedict.

This was our fourth country club brunch, making it his fourth eggs Benedict, and the fourth time this year I had to face his judgment. And when your father's a judge, there's plenty to go around.

Meeting for brunch every Sunday was the stipulation he placed prior to me and my two kids moving from Chicago to my vacant childhood home in Green

Valley, Tennessee, one month ago. Wearing his typical dark suit and tie, my father frowned at the menu displeasingly, then folded it and handed it to our server.

"Excellent choice, Judge. And for you?" our sweet server, Kathy, asked me.

"I'll have the egg white omelet with the hash browns." She winked at me as she took my menu. She was my favorite as she always gave me an extra ketchup cup to go with my hashbrowns. Eating hashbrowns without ketchup was like eating pancakes without syrup. A waste of calories.

I also ordered the same thing each time. Maybe one day I'd try something different, but ordering the same thing somehow seemed easier. I knew an egg white omelet and hashbrowns met with my father's approval, as he didn't remark on my choice. So, ordering it felt like the path of least resistance. Growing up the only daughter of the widowed and esteemed Judge Alan Alberton, I've taken this path *a lot*.

"How was your week, sir?"

"Uneventful." My father adjusted his water glass and silverware to be in the exact place he preferred. Fastidiousness, keen observation, and intelligence were my father's MO, and while it made him an excellent judge—his almost encyclopedic knowledge of the law made his courtrooms efficient and his decisions fair and swift—it made growing up under his roof . . . difficult. I'd compare it to *The Sound of Music*, except I had no siblings, Julie Andrews never showed up after my mother died when I was twelve, and my father sure as hell never smiled at me while singing a song about little white flowers.

Looking up from the table, he seemed to inspect me, then cleared his throat. "How was your week?"

I hesitated. Let's observe how I'd have answered if I was being honest: *"Well, exciting week. First, Ryla was kicked out of her swimming lessons at the YMCA because she punched a kid right in the stomach for cutting the line at the diving board. Then I was threatened to be sent to collections for the twenty-two-thousand-dollar bill for Max's intensive outpatient program this past February that my health insurance is refusing to pay despite getting a pre-approval and am now in our third appeal process."*

Instead, I replied, "Great. Work is going well, and Mrs. Simon is wonderful with the kids."

To be fair, that last part wasn't a lie. I'd been incredibly lucky to have found Mrs. Simon, a sweet, retired schoolteacher, to be the nanny for my two kids when we moved back to Green Valley. Since she started with us, I felt like maybe, just maybe, we would finally get back to normal.

Whatever "normal" meant.

I hadn't seen anything approaching normal for almost a year. Ten months ago, my husband of twelve years asked for a divorce, then went off on a yearlong yachting expedition relinquishing all legal and physical custody of our children. It'd been seven months since our longtime au pair, Giselle, moved back to Italy, and five months since I'd had to quit my pediatrician job to home-school my son after severe anxiety made it impossible for him to go to school. Any nest egg I'd had from the sale of our home after the divorce went to health care fees and living expenses, so any hope of buying a new home in Chicago had died a slow and painful death. Moving back to Green Valley was the very last option I had, so I called my father. He lived and worked as a judge in Knoxville, so I knew the country house I grew up in near Green Valley was empty. It'd been empty for twenty years, ever since I'd moved out right after high school.

It was only a brief head nod that let me know he'd heard my reply. His focus remained on the strawberry jelly he meticulously spread across his cut croissant. After a few minutes, he asked, "Does that mean you'll be changing your schedule to full time?"

My father was referring to the bold parenting choice wherein I decided to "shirk" my work duties over, you know, my less important responsibilities, like raising my children. My father would know all about that.

It took all of my willpower to keep up my calm and controlled front, a front solidified with reinforced concrete since I was twelve years old. So, I kept my answer brief.

"No."

"I thought the purpose of working part-time was to watch the children. Now that you have competent childcare, you should be able to work full-time."

No, the point of my slightly reduced-hour contract was to have flexibility and availability for my children and to attend Max's counseling appointments.

The retort was right there on my tongue, but I didn't say it. Neither my father nor my ex-husband understood Max's anxiety disorder. They wrote it off as a choice. Like Max just decided it'd be fun to wake up each day and be terrified to go to school.

Apparently, my father didn't notice my lack of response, as he kept going. "I'll never understand why you choose to work part-time. It's a waste of your education and potential."

Forcing my jaw to relax so I didn't sound like I was speaking through clenched teeth, I replied, "While I appreciate that, I'm still a single parent. I need a flexible job schedule."

I could only blame myself. In a moment of sheer stupidity, I told my father that my new job—I was a pediatrician at a doctor's office called Mercy Health—was part-time. Did I bother explaining to him that it was still thirty-two patient contact hours per week, the same number of outpatient clinic hours I'd worked at my practice in Chicago where that *was* considered full time?

Of course not. The judge didn't like excuses. And the fewer details I gave him about my life, the better.

"You know money isn't an issue. I already offered to pay for what you need," my father added, picking up his spoon and rubbing a spot with his napkin.

That wasn't factually accurate; he would only pay for what he *believed* I needed. Which, as a parent, was technically his right. My only objection was the overt gaslighting in his comment.

I bit back any retort, opting to utilize one of my father's favorite tools to show disappointment: silence.

"Have you made your decision regarding Eagleton?" my father asked after a few minutes of tense quiet.

I took a large gulp of my orange juice, stalling my answer. Yes, I'd made a decision. No, it wasn't going to be an answer he liked.

Eagleton Preparatory Academy was a K through 12 private school, thirty minutes outside Green Valley. It was where I'd gone to school starting in sixth grade, right after my mother died. And last week at brunch, my father unceremoniously informed me that he expected my kids to attend school there as well.

This fall.

That wasn't going to happen.

To some parents, being able to send their kids to Eagleton would seem like a dream come true. The school produced Rhodes scholars, collegiate athletes, and Ivy League graduates. However, at least when I went there, they also produced some of the meanest, stereotypically elitist pricks, who cared more about family status than general goodness.

My ten-year-old son had severe anxiety. He needed acceptance and understanding. And don't even get me started on my youngest. Part girl and part gremlin, my daughter Ryla wouldn't survive a week in that place. Or more accurately, they wouldn't survive a week of *her*. If someone said one wrong thing, I wouldn't be surprised if she burned the place to the ground, then lied to everyone's face despite being found with a used match and lighter fluid.

I'd already researched Green Valley's public schools before I moved the kids here. Sure, the Green Valley School District was small and, like any small town, had limited resources, but the school psychologist I'd spoken to over the phone, a Mr. Sievers, was incredibly nice and curious about Max. He answered every question I had about the 504-plan evaluation process with patience and understanding. When I begrudgingly called Eagleton last week, a snooty woman on the phone told me that they "were not prepared to answer" any of my questions until my kids were enrolled in their school, though they assured me they were committed to "academic excellence."

That was enough of an answer for me.

"I haven't made my decision yet," I lied. I caught myself nervously twisting with my earring, so I quickly moved my hand to my lap. This former defense attorney wouldn't miss a thing.

"Dean Manford is doing me a favor by keeping those spots open at Eagleton." His stern voice belied his annoyance. "They have a two-year wait list. Your hesitancy is not only unwarranted but a reflection upon me."

If I had a nickel for every time that phrase was used growing up. After my mother died, everything from what I wore to how I acted, was carefully constructed to portray the perfect dutiful daughter. If I didn't act according to the judge's standards, there were consequences, like not being allowed to see my friend, Leah, or participate in an after-school activity. By the time I left Green Valley after high school, I was like a hungry rat in a Skinner box;

programmed by my father to act in a certain way, slowly poisoning every life choice and relationship I'd had.

I picked up a croissant from the middle of the table and took an aggressive bite; I'd swear off grain another week.

"I'm aware. I'll let you know soon," I replied roughly after swallowing, knowing that he'd hate the ambiguity of my answer, but not taking the risk of committing to any timelines.

My father wiped his hands, then put both of his elbows on the table. "Those children need a school with solid foundations, not that public school you're planning on sending them to."

How my father managed to keep the gag out of his voice when he said *public school,* I'll never know. I took another bite of my croissant to keep from talking back. Focusing on the buttery goodness melting in my mouth, I recounted the things I was grateful for since moving back to Green Valley.

Number one: I'm living in a house rent-free. Sure, it came with unrelenting memories of a lonely and neglected childhood, but really, was that so bad?

Number two: My kids seemed to be doing better since moving from Chicago. There weren't as many constant reminders of their old life, namely, their father leaving them. We'd even found a pediatric counselor in the area for Max and so far, the two of them seemed to have hit it off. And while my aforementioned daughter had a hairline trigger, she seemed to keep her cool around Mrs. Simon.

Number three: Mrs. Simon. Or maybe I should have made her reasons one and two. I'd been hanging off the side of a cliff from a fraying rope until I found her. She showed up on time every morning, stayed overnight at the house when I was on call, was excellent with my children, and brought baked goods every morning. Not good for my waistline, but who the hell did I have to impress? I had my books, my vibrator, and a door lock. I was all good.

What had my father been asking about? Oh, right. The kids' school. Something he should have *no* say over.

I looked him square in the eye, a tactic I used in high school, on the rare occasion I had to force any bravado.

"We had this discussion last week. I can't commit to any school choices right now."

"All the more reason to send them to Eagleton, Polly." My father's expression looked like he just ate spoiled jelly. "I can't help but say this, your kids need stability. A failed marriage isn't an excuse to drop the ball."

I can't test this theory, but if you could see into my brain at that moment, I'm reasonably certain every single neuron would be *on fucking fire.*

My father had always been strict, but he changed fundamentally after my mother died. He promptly went back to work after three days of bereavement leave when his beloved wife and the mother of his only child, *me*, died after a brief battle with cancer. I didn't realize it at the time, but he shut out practically everything that reminded him of her—effectively turning the house into a graveyard of memories, with me inside of it. And a failed marriage? He was part of the reason it broke. I hadn't realized I'd been so programmed by my upbringing to act perfectly that I fell into similar patterns in my marriage: *always* acting the part of the perfect, obedient wife, *never* advocating my wants and desires. I didn't realize what a mess I'd created for myself, until it was too late.

"I would hardly call what I'm doing dropping the ball." My words sounded weak even to my own ears.

"What would you call sending your children to a public school and not securing something as simple as a full-time job? That's not to mention how wild your children are. The last time I saw Ryla, she growled at me. And Max didn't speak to me at all, then disappeared to his room."

Rage burned just beneath my skin's surface. It was only through a lifetime's worth of practice that I was able to bite back my retort, giving the dutiful daughter's response he expected. "I'll work on that, Father."

Mollified, he nodded stiffly as Kathy delivered our plates. I think she could tell things were tense because she gave me a discrete sympathetic glance before turning to leave.

My father cut into his entrée, the hollandaise sauce and egg yolk spurting yellow liquid onto his plate. I went about putting ketchup on my hashbrowns, but my appetite had disappeared. I used to like eggs Benedict. But watching my father eat it every single Sunday this past month made it look like some sort of sadistic egg sacrifice.

. . .

"You'll be getting an email from Jeffrey soon," he said, referring to his longtime campaign manager and personal assistant. "We have a list of events important to securing my nomination that you and the children need to attend."

I was well aware my father was being considered for a nomination to the Tennessee Supreme Court this year. I'd been going to campaign events for his judgeships my entire life. My attendance at these functions, even once married and fully financially independent from my father, still hadn't felt like a choice even if the emails from Jeffrey had become less threatening and more placating in recent years. Now that I was home and underneath my father's thumb again, I figured my attendance wasn't optional. Still, his words made me pause.

"Did you say, the children?"

Without looking up, my father continued to saw away at his brunch.

"Yes," he said around a mouthful of murdered eggs.

The only thing that made me feel better was picturing twirling my fork in his receding hairline and yanking. Asking me to go to campaign events was one thing, but expecting my kids, the grandkids he'd seen once every other year, if that, for their entire lives . . . parading them around like they're his pride and joy.

No. Just, *no.*

"If you need me for events, that's fine. The kids have had big changes this year and it's not right to thrust them into the spotlight. You're right. They need stability." I nodded, my confidence growing as I used his own words against him. "Let me get them settled and into school first, then we can discuss this again in the fall."

My father opened and closed his mouth, filling me with smug victory that he was utterly stuck by his own words.

"Alan!"

A gray-haired man wearing a sport coat walked toward us along with a woman in an elegant dove gray morning suit.

"John, good to see you." My father's demeanor instantly changed, smiling as he stood to shake the man's outstretched hand.

Poser.

"This is my wife, Elaine," the man, presumably John, said as he gestured to the kind-looking woman beside him. "Elaine, this is Judge Alberton."

"I apologize for keeping your husband so busy on the golf course," my father said as he shook her hand. He pointed to me, and I stood immediately.

"This is my daughter, Polly. She recently moved back to town with my two grandchildren."

Turning on my smile and extending my hand, I gave both of them a firm handshake. "How do you do?"

"A pleasure. Why, I forgot you had a daughter, Alan," John said.

I do my best to forget as well, I wanted to retort, but of course, didn't.

"Polly is a pediatrician who recently started a job with Mercy Health."

"How wonderful. The apple doesn't fall far from the tree. Say Alan, we're suddenly needing a fourth for our golf outing in a few weeks. You interested?"

Elaine turned to me as the men discussed golf. "I can't imagine being a doctor and a mother with two kids. However do you find the time?"

"It's not without difficulty," I answered honestly.

"Your momma must be so proud. I watch our grandchildren once a week and they are the joy of my life. I bet your momma likes watching your kids just as much."

My chest tightened. Elaine's words made me miss my mom with so much acuity, my heart ached. It was a wound that never truly healed. Even though the sting of grief had eased with time, it never truly left. It was dormant, awakening at odd times, forever tinging my life's happy moments, like a photograph in sepia tone.

Polite smile in place, I responded, "My mother passed away when I was young. But she would've been a wonderful grandmother. After all, she was the best mom."

Unlike me, the uncharitable thought floated around me, unbidden.

Thirty minutes of torture later, our brunch was over. I, as always, excused myself to the bathroom so I didn't have to spend more time with my father than necessary.

As I washed my hands, I studied myself in the gilded mirror. Staring back at me was a stranger, someone with blonde hair smoothed into a sleek chignon, polished makeup, and high-necked navy dress. The epitome of demure. Despite the makeup, I could see the traces of dark circles under her eyes and the tightness in the set of her mouth. Like there was someone trapped underneath her perfect mask, just waiting to be set free. Elaine's words came back to me: *Your momma must be so proud.*

This was not who I was supposed to be by the age of thirty-eight.

Stepping to the side, I glanced down, inspecting the aquamarine velvet peep-toe heels I'd worn today. I'd taken note of my father's sneer four weeks ago when I wore my favorite red high heels. But I still couldn't bear to wear ugly shoes today—or any of the other Sundays I'd come here. It was a small sort of rebellion, I suppose. Shoes and books had become my own joy-filled escape. If I could have a secret room that was all books on one side and all shoes on the other, it'd be my own personal heaven.

"Maybe in another life," I whispered to the sad woman in the mirror before walking out.

The humidity of the early July summer enveloped into me as I went outside to collect my car, the large stone portico shading me from the direct sunlight. Glancing at the valet stand, warmth suffused my body. And no, it wasn't the cloying Tennessee heat. There at the podium, not seeing me yet, was Jace.

Four weeks ago, at my first Sunday brunch, I'd used the valet service because I knew my father would expect it. Jeffrey had dropped off the Tesla the night before and told me to use it on Sundays—appearances and all that—as they both felt my Nissan SUV didn't give off the right (and I'm paraphrasing here) "vibe" to his constituency. Then, having forgotten to bring money for a tip, I'd had to dig around the center console praying I'd find cash. I'd found cash alright, two twenty-dollar bills, nothing smaller. After palming one of the twenties, I whipped around to find a young man holding my door open.

Jace, his nametag had read. His black polo highlighted his strong shoulders and defined biceps, making him look like a living, breathing gym advertisement. He flashed a friendly smile at me as strands of his long curly brown hair fluttered in the wind, falling just past his cheekbones. He looked young, early twenties at most, but still young enough that I had no business noticing him. I definitely shouldn't have noticed his bright hazel eyes that danced with humor or the fact that the dimple in his left cheek was deeper than the one on the right.

Then, he called me *ma'am*, breaking me from my spell. Sure, it was the South. Ma'am's were dropped all the time. But that word had the undesired effect of making me realize that I'd been checking out a guy who was possibly *a whole adult person younger than me*—a thought that still made me want to stab a pen in my eye.

So, I unfortunately panicked and gave him all the cash in my hand.

An entire twenty-dollar bill.

Then after brunch, I'd felt obligated to tip Jace my other twenty bucks, the only other cash I had on me, when I picked up my car.

And even more unfortunately, because he kept being here every single Sunday, and I didn't want to make him feel like he'd done a bad job, I kept up the same routine.

If you're counting, that makes the cost of parking my car *forty whole dollars* each week.

But I digress.

I took a deep breath in and started toward the valet stand. Jace's eyes lit when he spotted me.

He's only acting like that because he knows he's going to get another incredible tip, moneybags.

He started walking toward me, his expression set in that laidback way of his, just on the edge of a smile, causing my legs to go all melty. And like they were fourteen-year-old cheerleaders, my hormones started waving poms-poms in the air. I painted on a polite expression and told my body to cool it.

"Y'all set?" His lilted Tennessee accent was liquid honey. Ignoring my suddenly dry mouth, I nodded as I reached into my purse for the valet ticket.

"How was your brunch?" he asked, starting in on what I'd describe as our typical post-brunch conversation. It had been the same conversation every week.

"Good."

"What'd you get?"

"The omelet and hash browns."

After this, he usually smiled, took my ticket, and walked off. But today, his face fell.

"Oh no, didn't anyone tell you?" He leaned closer to me. "It's illegal to order the same thing four times in a row in Tennessee. Some state law. There could be a warrant out for your arrest right now."

I furrowed my brow. "What law is that?"

"A crime against food." Straightening to his full height, a playful grin stretched across his face. "A whole menu right there in front of you, and you order the same thing. It should be against the law."

A startled laugh escaped me, so loud it echoed off the portico. He was teasing me. Or, was this flirting?

Jace crossed his arms. "If it were me, I'd have the avocado toast with sweet corn and chilis. Or the cheese and butter biscuits. No wait, the twice-baked French toast. Please tell me next time you'll eat the twice-baked French toast and report back. I need to eat vicariously through you."

Watching him say this should be illegal. My cheeks warmed as I pictured him sitting across from me, intently watching my mouth as I take a slow bite of the French toast.

Forcing that image out of my mind, I answered, "I've never thought about that."

And no, that wasn't my voice sounding hoarse.

Nope.

Nope on a rope.

I held my valet ticket out to him, but he didn't take it right away. Instead, he tilted his head, curiosity practically another color in his iridescent hazel eyes.

Stop noticing his eyes.

"You ever think about changing it up?"

I shuffled back a few steps, exhaling nervously at his question and held out the valet ticket more insistently.

He took the ticket with a smile and nod, then walked toward the parking lot. I glanced his way surreptitiously, noticing that he'd take a few moments to look up into the sky as he walked, his happy-go-lucky demeanor obvious to anyone watching him. What made him so carefree? What must it be like to feel that way?

Please let him be at least twenty-eight.

I fought the urge to both facepalm and laugh hysterically at the utterly absurd thought that popped into my head, I settled for giving my head a firm shake, as if I needed a physical jerk to clear it. Because I'd clearly lost my mind. First, it didn't matter how old he was, he was still much too young for me. Second, my focus needed to be on my kids. Men were so far off my radar I'd have to take three airplanes, then portage just to find one.

At least real men, that is.

Fictional men were a different story. I couldn't wait for the drive home, thirty blissful minutes of listening to my current book before reality sank back in.

I got out my phone to shoot a quick text to my best friend, Leah. Mrs. Simon wasn't able to stay overnight at the house tonight while I was on call for my pediatric clinic, so Leah had very kindly offered to stay overnight instead. I was able to be at home when I was on call, only needing to keep my phone with me so I could answer any calls that came in from our remote nursing service. I had yet to get called into the hospital for an admission; still, I needed a backup caregiver at home to stay with my kids on the off chance I did get called into the hospital.

Polly: Still on for tonight at 7? I'm sorry again to have asked.

Leah: You need to stop apologizing. Oh no! I have to go to my friend's house and enjoy a night without my kids in a house with an outside stone patio over-looking the mountains and home theater! Whatever shall I do?

Polly: I'll make dinner.

Leah: Not necessary. I'm bringing wine.

Polly: I'm on call.

Leah: It's not for you.

I huffed out a laugh. Leah had been my friend since the second grade, when her family moved to town. We remained close when I'd been forced to attend Eagleton after elementary school. After I moved away for college, we'd drifted apart, only seeing each other on the few occasions I'd come back for the judge's campaign events. We had our first kids around the same time and reconnected over social media, sending funny videos which progressed to text messages and weekly check-ins. Since my divorce, she was the only true friend I had left.

A few minutes later, my car appeared, Jace in the driver's seat.

He held the door open for me. "Thank you," I said as I started to get into the car. On a whim, I suddenly turned and faced him, adding, "Jace."

I'd never referred to him by name before; for some reason, today, it felt wrong not to use it.

Jace's smile deepened and his eyes twinkled as he replied, "You're welcome, Mrs. Alberton."

Rearing back in disgust, I blurted, "I'm a miss! I'm not married. The judge is *not* my husband!" Revulsion slid down my spine at the thought.

Jace held up his hands quickly, eyebrows high on his forehead. "My mistake. I'm just used to the women here being a missus. I'm not sure what judge you're talking about."

Thoroughly mortified, I could only nod lamely in response, wishing for an eject button that shot me directly into space. As he closed the car door and gave me a thumb-up, I realized I hadn't given him my customary tip. Holding up a pathetic finger, I rolled the window down a crack and inched the twenty-dollar bill out the window.

Jace took it, then even used it to give me a little faux hat raise. Flustered, I raised my hands in a weird hand-flapping gesture, then got the hell out of there.

Once out of sight, I pulled over and laid my head on the steering wheel dejectedly. I forced slow, deep breaths in and out of my lungs. Unfortunately, this only made me notice the lingering scent I'd come to recognize as Jace's: fresh and clean, yet with subtle hints of sandalwood and warm vanilla. It made my mouth water. And as I did most of my book listening in the car, I may have . . . ok, very definitely have . . . pictured Jace as the hero in my books, each version of Jace having the same delicious smell.

I groaned. Something was very wrong with me. What I mistook for flirting today was probably mere kindness, or more likely, professionalism. Jace was only doing his job. He called me ma'am, for Pete's sake! I might as well be a hundred years old to someone his age.

I finally sat back and turned on the stereo, waiting for my phone to connect. I was listening to *The Seduction of the Shift* by Angel Marie. It was the first in a shifter romantic fantasy series and I'd had a hard time putting it down. As it came on, I rewound it a minute to get me back to where I'd left off, then shifted into drive, escaping from all the chaos in my life as I began my drive home.

———

An hour later I felt marginally better as I sat at my childhood home's kitchen table—probably because I was inhaling a scone Mrs. Simon had "whipped up" while I was at brunch. It was smothered in her homemade apple butter, which she'd made that weekend and brought over so we could "put a few jars in the pantry for a rainy day."

And did I mention there was sweet tea?

One glass of sweet tea and one and a half scones later, I was approaching something that felt like contentment. Mrs. Simon was literally humming while wiping down the kitchen island, the birds were chirping outside, and I was listening to Ryla's happy chatter from the other room as she played with her stuffed animals.

"Can I have a word, hun?"

I paused mid-bite. Mrs. Simon's anxious expression contrasted with the cheerful afternoon sunlight filtering through the glass patio doors behind me. Unease filled me as I nodded, then roughly swallowed.

"Well, it's the darndest thing, really," she started, making her way around the island to sit beside me. "But every Wednesday when I'm at the Piggly Wiggly, I pick up a ticket to play the Powerball. I've been playin' it for years. It's become a regular joke between my Bob and me, you see, but then a few weeks ago, I played and wouldn't you know it, but I won. First time in thirty years."

The sounds of my daughter's playing from the living room were suddenly drowned out by the pounding of my heart.

"That's . . . great, Mrs. Simon. How much did you win?"

"Well," Mrs. Simon tilted her head side to side, her eyes flitting around the room. "With the total winnings being about twenty-five, my sister's accountant tells us that we should expect about half that."

"Twelve and a half *thousand*?" I hedged.

"Million."

Inhaling sharply, I choked on a few crumbs and coughed violently. Mrs. Simon patted me on the back firmly, as if she didn't just calmly tell me she'd won twelve and a half million dollars.

"Oh dear, I'm so sorry, I should've warned you. Bob did the same thing when I told him—practically choked on the peach cobbler I'd made that night."

Wait. Mrs. Simon had brought us a peach cobbler at least two weeks ago. It'd been the best I'd ever eaten. Did that mean she'd known she was a millionaire for two weeks and was only telling me now?

I struggled to find words. "That's, well. It's a lot of." I paused, collecting my thoughts. "What does this mean?"

"See, that's the thing." Mrs. Simon covered my hand. "With that kind of money, my Bob and I could actually afford to retire down in Arizona and care for my momma. She has the dementia."

The selfish, exhausted, I-just-can't-do-this-anymore part of my brain wanted to shout, *To hell with your momma! I need you!*

Thankfully, the mature part of my brain won and asked, "When do you think you're going to move?"

Mrs. Simon bit her lip, regret in her eyes. "Well, seeing as my momma just broke her hip and is in a state-run nursing home, I'm afraid we'd like to leave as soon as possible."

I wanted to scream and cry. I wanted to get down on my knees and beg her to stay. I wanted to pack our bags and move down to Arizona with her and her Bob, offering myself as the in-home concierge doctor for her mother.

Of course, I did none of those things. I answered exactly as expected, perfect Polly mask in place despite my hopes and dreams plummeting from the side of a cliff now that my frayed rope had finally snapped.

"You have to do what's right for you. I can figure something out. Please don't worry about us."

Mrs. Simon's face brightened, and she clutched my hand. "Well now, that just dills my pickle! I'd been feeling so guilty these past days thinking of leaving y'all in the lurch."

I smiled and nodded, searching for words to pacify her, to put her at ease, but finding none. I had to settle for a fake smile.

Having spent most of my adult life in Chicago, my accent became less Dixie and more Ditka as time went on. But I was back below the Mason-Dixon line, drinking sweet tea, eating homemade scones and apple butter, and sitting across from the woman who just metaphorically lit my last shred of hope on fire.

So, all I could think was hell's fucking bells, what in the world was I gonna do now?

———

"Twelve million dollars?!"

Leah was nursing a glass of wine as we sat on the back patio.

I nodded, staring dejectedly at the Smokey Mountains in the distance, the sun had just set a few minutes earlier. I'd had to break it to my kids before they fell asleep that Mrs. Simon would be leaving us at the end of this week. Ryla, ever one for priorities, had asked if that meant she could still eat cookies every day while Max's crestfallen expression making me fear that he was reliving his dad leaving him all over again.

Leah whistled as she shook her head. "Well, shit. I mean, good for Mrs. Simon, that woman is salt of the earth. When does she have to leave?"

"We settled on the end of this week. Her mom's got "the dementia"," I put finger quotes around that, "and a broken hip. I couldn't ask her to stay."

Leah murmured an agreement then took a sip of her wine. "What are you gonna do?"

I leaned back and rubbed my hands over my face. My force of habit was to say, *I'll be fine,* or *We'll be ok,* but I went for the truth, too exhausted to keep up the polite pretense.

"I have no idea. I'm exhausted. Brunch days with the judge are never good, but this one almost put me over the edge."

"What'd he say this time?"

"I think his exact words were, 'a failed marriage isn't an excuse to drop the ball.'" The persistent sting of that comment made me wish I wasn't drinking water.

Leah made a fist and beat it into her palm. "The divorce wasn't even your fault! You're not the one who packed your bags and left to be a full-time yacht person or yachtsman, or whatever the douche called it. And while we're at it, what self-respecting forty-year-old man has a midlife crisis to be a yachtsman?"

My ex-husband, David, ran a yachting adventure company. His company's brand focused on bringing luxury accommodation to remote locations all over the world. A company *I helped fund* with my entire sign-on bonus, any savings we had in the bank, along with any of my salary that wasn't going toward expenses or repaying my loans.

This was the same yachting company he started when he left his IT job only a year after Ryla was born.

Did he know how to yacht when he told me he was starting this new business? No.

Did he own a yacht? Also, no.

I grinned, remembering when I'd called Leah after David asked for a divorce. Leah and I so rarely talked on the phone, that she'd answered on the first ring, alarm in her voice when she asked, "Polly?! Who's dead?"

A year ago, I'd come home late after work to find my husband of twelve years sitting in our foyer. He'd only just come home from a six-week-long yachting trip a few days prior, so I was surprised to find him a pair of large suitcases next to him, his captain's hat atop them. I was more surprised when he calmly asked me for a divorce, then left for parts unknown.

Leah, upon hearing the story over the phone, called him every name in the book, swore revenge, and offered me an alibi. It was exactly what I needed.

She then proceeded to be there for me, even from a different state, even though she was busy with her own life, teaching third grade and raising two kids. She took time to support me throughout my whole divorce process, where I was essentially cheated out of every figurative penny I had.

Leah narrowed her eyes in question. "What did he tell you that night? Something about it being time?"

"He said it was time for him to take to the seas," I recalled flatly, then swung my eyes to Leah whose lips quirked. "I always thought that husbands left their wives for the nanny or a yoga instructor," I continued on, "but nope, not my husband. My husband wanted to . . ."

"Take to the seas," Leah wheezed out, leaning forward in her chair, covering her mouth with her hand, her shoulders shaking in silent laughter.

"He didn't even have the audacity to be a cliché." My voice was increasing in pitch, the odd hilarity of the situation finally catching up with me. "He hated being married to me so much that he literally sailed away from me . . . on a ship!" I was full-on laughing then, having a hard time getting words out. "Did I tell you that he'd bought a little captain's hat . . ."

"Stop!" Leah was breathless, holding her belly.

"And it was just sitting there," my breaths came in short gasps in between laughs, "on his suitcases."

Leah had tears in her eyes and her hands covered her mouth. I buried my face in my arms to stifle my laughter, not wanting to wake the kids, my stomach aching with each round of laughter.

"I'll be sure to ask around school to see if anyone knows of a good sitter in the area," Leah said when our laughter finally quieted. "And I'll see about getting Max and Ryla into the summer school program at the elementary school. There've been a few kids who've dropped, so there's room in my class. Max can stick tight to me if he wants. I know he'll have some trouble feeling nervous. You know I'll do whatever I can to help y'all."

"I know. And I'm grateful." A tight lump rose in my throat at her words. Her instant understanding. I leaned back in my chair, rubbing my still aching stomach, the laughter easing some of the weight from my shoulders. I felt lighter than I'd had in months. "I think that's the first time I've really and truly laughed since the divorce."

"Come on, you must have laughed some other time. No one goes ten months without laughing at least once."

Her words made me think back to my conversation with Jace at the country club this morning, when I'd laughed in surprise at his teasing. "Other than with my kids, only once that I can remember."

"That's the most pitiful thing I've ever heard." Leah frowned, picking up her wineglass. She wasn't one to beat around the bush, this best friend of mine.

"I unfortunately agree." Because it *was* pitiful—I couldn't recall a single time during my *entire marriage* when I laughed that hard with my now ex-husband. And while laughter wasn't going to help me find a new nanny or tap me out with the kids when my patience was running low, it did feel good to laugh with someone. I glanced at Leah out of the corner of my eye as I reached for my water glass, picking it up to give her a little toast in the air. "But I do feel better."

Leah held up her wineglass in kind. "That's what they say, right? Laughter's the best medicine."

CHAPTER
THREE

JACE

Love Bites by Lena Benjamin

Two Weeks Later

"I'm telling you, the epoxy floor was so simple. It turned out pretty damn good considering I'd never done it before." Sam thrust his phone toward me. We were in the Viking MMA locker room changing into our sparring gear. Scrolling through his camera roll, I was surprised to see there were several photos at the same angle over time.

"Did you set up a time-lapse camera?" I asked, semi-impressed he even knew how to do that.

Sam scratched his forehead with the back of his thumb. "I, uh"—he cleared his throat— "started the top coat for the epoxy the wrong way. I had to sit in the corner of the garage for five hours while it dried before I could leave."

Chuckling, I handed back his phone. Typical Sam. I wasn't surprised. When he started the company, we were a good team. It gave me the freedom to be my own boss, it paid well, and I got to try new things. This worked well for a few years. Sam had the big ideas, and I had the ability to focus and get the jobs done. But saving Sam from lawsuits and bodily harm was becoming a full-time job these days. A full-time *unpaid* job. I was up for adventure, sure, but Sam's focus was on money and had a tendency to say yes when he shouldn't and commit to more jobs then we had time for. Which is what I'd said to him last week when I told him I had to take a big step back from the number of projects I took on.

He shrugged, putting his phone away. "I might add it to the website as a new service we provide."

"We?" I questioned.

"Yeah. I'll teach you. It's a breeze. We could make so much money."

I shook my head as I pulled on my sparring gloves. "I already told you I'm taking on less projects. You gotta find someone else."

I was already busier than I wanted to be lately. Besides the jobs I did for Sam, I valeted on Sundays, helped run the Young Wills program every Tuesday and Thursday night, drove my car for Lyft whenever I could, and volunteered to help out some performing arts classes at both the Green Valley Middle and High School a few days per week during the school year.

My pop always joked I had wanderlust without the desire to wander. And when I was younger, his comments didn't bother me. But lately, I'd become more restless, feeling truly aimless for the first time in my life. On a nice Sunday afternoon like this one, I'd typically stop at one of the county's driving ranges to hit a bucket of balls, then relax at home or go for a hike. Today, I needed to let out some pent-up energy, so I called up Sam, who met me at Viking MMA.

I couldn't get Polly Alberton out of my mind. It'd only gotten worse since I'd found out she was *Miss* Polly Alberton two weeks ago. I also knew she showed up every Sunday at 10:00 a.m. on the dot, always tipped forty bucks, and the only thing hotter than her shoes, was playing on her car's stereo.

For the last six weeks, I'd pathetically spent the best two and half minutes of my week opening her car door, smiling and joking playfully with her, loving her shy smiles as her honeyed floral scent washed over me. Then I'd get in her car, listen to ten seconds of her book, and take a picture of the car's stereo screen so I could remember the title and author. I'd bought and read all the books she'd been listening to, and one thing was for sure: perfect Polly Alberton . . . was anything but proper. Polly's audiobook choice today was about a group of virile young women abducted from Earth, only to crash-land on a planet of giant blue humanoid aliens with huge dicks.

Some guys have all the luck.

Since the first book I'd bought, I'd had a crash course in romance novels. And believe me, it's been an education. These books had some of the straight-up filthiest things I've ever read while also being surprisingly funny and well written. Each book varied widely on how much sex was actually in the book, most of them only had a few chapters. I'm not saying everything that happens is believable; the positions, the angles, the stamina of these guys—they really deserve a round of applause. I'd hit the gym extra hard over the past few weeks because, *shiiit.* I thought I knew how to make sex good for a woman. Cocky for a twenty-four-year-old? Sure. But clearly, I had *no idea.* I'd gone as far as marking pages for the really good moves. I shook my head, thinking about my poor eighteen-year-old self, hell, thinking about my poor twenty-two -year-old self, thinking I was good at sex. Apparently after all these years, all I had to do was read a damn romance novel.

That's not to say I hadn't noticed other things about Polly. Like how she seemed tense over the last two weeks. Or how she visibly steeled herself, rolling her shoulders back as she approached the front doors of the club. Making her laugh two weeks ago had made me feel ten-feet tall. I wanted to hear her laugh again. But after six weeks of Sundays, I'd only learned her name, her shit hot taste in books, and that she was single.

That wasn't close to enough.

Not that knowing more about her would make a difference. Polly was so out of my league that she could be laid out naked on the hood of my car, offering herself to me, and she'd still be off-limits.

Agitated, I picked up my partially unzipped bag causing my current book, *Love Bites*, to fall out. I grabbed for it, but Sam was faster.

"What's—aw, hell. Not another one." Sam grimaced as he picked up the book. He'd laughed his ass off a week ago when he found me in my car reading my last book. "It was kind of funny at first, but now it's just getting out of hand." Sam thumbed the pages causing the scrap of paper I'd been using as a book-mark to flutter to the ground.

"Hey, watch it. I'll lose my place," I complained, retrieving the paper from the floor. When I stood up, Sam eyed me warily, then slowly extended the book out to me.

Ignoring Sam's expression, I plucked the book from his grasp and put it in my locker. Sam had no idea Polly existed, and I wasn't about to tell him. I made it all the way to the locker room door before I realized he wasn't next to me. Turning, I saw he was still standing in the same place, eyes narrowed.

I held my arms out. "You comin'?"

Finally, Sam sighed and walked toward me. "Yeah, alright. Let's get out there before your dick shrivels up into your body."

After warming up on the speed bag, we made our way to the ring. Our trainer, Vick, was on the other side of the gym and gave us a head nod. Sam and I weren't aiming to be professionals, but it'd been fun learning how to box.

"You give any more thought to moving in with me and Owen?" Sam asked as we started to spar. He liked to talk to distract me. It worked some of the time. He could talk a used car salesman into buying one of his own cars, that's how silver-tongued Sam was.

"No." I tried to focus on his movements.

"Come on, our place has three bedrooms, and the clubhouse has a fitness center and a hot tub. We need a roommate. It's practically a palace. You'd be drowning in puss—" He barely dodged my punch as we continued to dance around each other.

"Keep talking, Sammy. You'll make this easy."

He'd told me about the townhouse before. The rent was three times what I was paying my parents in rent and would take a big dent out of my savings.

"You need this, Jace. Just come look at it. I mean, when's the last time you got laid?"

Eight months ago, but I wasn't going to tell him that. I dodged an attack, his punch missing my shoulder by a few inches.

"Nice try," I heckled.

"I'm seriously worried about you. Do you know how good the moon pies you gave last week tasted? I would've gotten down on my knee and proposed to that woman right then and there. That's how good those things were. And instead, you gave them to me—not that I'm complaining. But you're sitting on a golden ticket and not cashing it in. It's almost immoral."

"I've never been a fan of moon pies," I lied.

Since I started helping at the school over a year ago, the interest I got from women, particularly single moms, or aunts, or sisters . . . changed. Women would wait outside school for me to slip their phone numbers in my bag or bring me homemade baked goods. I accepted a few numbers at first, but the few women I'd gone out with never seemed to want me, for *me*. I was never invited over to meet their families, never invited to hang out with their friends. I was a career-less, degree-less young guy in his early twenties. I was "good for a fun time, not a long time"—a direct quote from the last woman I'd taken out whom I'd met at the school. Now when I found their numbers in my bag, I threw them out. And the kids at Young Wills or Sam were always happy to take the homemade food off my hands.

"I mean it," Sam said as we continued circling each other. "You're reading romance books, livin' with your parents, you barely go out. Last time I came over you were keeping score of the Braves' game with your daddy!"

I smiled through my mouthguard. Sam was still dropping his shoulder when he pivoted on his right foot. I could be patient and bide my time. Patience was one of my best virtues.

"I'm saying this because I'm your best friend. You need to move out."

I continued to play cagey, watching his every move. Yeah, I lived with my parents. But I had no need for my own place. I was saving most of what I earned, and despite paying rent plus a third of the utilities and groceries, I still had more savings than most folks my age. Plus, my parents needed help. My pop had rheumatoid arthritis and lived in chronic pain, so I did a lot of the outside work, like mowing the lawn and maintaining the cars, because he couldn't do it anymore. Momma's nerves were getting worse, and she needed a break from caring for him all the time. And while I didn't mind doing any of this, my friends didn't seem to understand. When your parents were the age of most of your friends' grandparents, it felt different.

There, I thought as he dropped his shoulder—*bam!* My fist connected with the guard over his cheek.

"You're still dropping that shoulder, Sam!" Vick called out from across the ring.

Fists up, Sam and I continued to dance around each other, throwing and dodging punches without talking for the next several minutes.

"So, remember that birthday party this weekend? I need a favor," Sam began. He meant *another* favor. He'd already asked me for help with a six-year-old's birthday party this coming weekend when he asked if I could find an affordable traveling petting zoo. Spoiler alert: there were none.

"What's that?" I threw a punch, which Sam barely missed, ducking out of the way.

"I need a clown." He feigned an attack then went for an uppercut, which I easily dodged. "And you used to do all that magic stuff, I thought you might be willing to help me out. Please? One last time?"

"I don't do clowns. And anyway, I can't. It's Pop's birthday. Kent and Sarah are coming into town." I kept my fists up despite feeling winded.

"Sar-aaah," Sam drawled lasciviously, somehow making my sister's name sound suggestive through his mouthguard.

Dickhead.

"She miss me?" Sam continued to shuffle around me as I tried a sloppy attack that he easily sidestepped. Then he got me right on the cheek.

"Don't leave yourself so open, Jace!" Vick yelled. I swear that guy had eyes in the back of his head. I shuffled back and held up my hands for a break.

"The day my older sister thinks of you as anything more than the annoying kid who attacked her with water balloons when she'd come home from college, will be a cold day in hell," I gritted out, grabbing my water at the side of the ring.

"Prepare to buy a scarf. But back to this weekend," Sam said. "The lady whose kid it is requested a clown. Do you know how hard it's been to find one that's not creepy?"

"Why can't you do it? A little face paint, goofy grin. You'd be great," I deadpanned. We both knew Sam would be the worst. In his one and only high school theater performance Sam forgot his only speaking line.

"Funny. Come on, I'm desperate."

I wasn't the worst option he'd have for a clown. I was decent at acting and had spent my entire eighth-grade year perfecting a magician act I still had memorized to this day.

"I don't know . . ." I trailed off, but Sam, of course, sensed an opening.

"You'd be helping me out of a tight spot. I'll get you the costume. You can keep all the profits!"

"If I'm dressing up as a clown, you better believe I'm keeping all the money I make." I huffed out a breath. "Fine. But this is not going on the website. It's a onetime deal, got it?"

Sam saluted. "You got it. I'll even keep your romance reading under wraps, Romeo."

Vick came up behind Sam just then and raised his eyebrows to us.

"I don't want to know."

———

Both of my parents' cars were in the garage when I arrived home that afternoon. My parents' being home wasn't unusual for a Sunday. It wasn't unusual for any day of the week. I could count on one hand the number of times they'd traveled out of the state over the last ten years.

After parking in the driveway, I waved over to our next-door neighbor Mrs. James, who was watering flowers. She and her husband, the now-retired county sheriff, have lived next door to us my entire life. Their son, Jackson James, who was now the current county sheriff, lived across town with his wife, Rae. During my high school years, Jackson had become an older brother figure of sorts to me, more so than my actual older brother had ever been.

I found momma in the kitchen chopping carrots for the roast chicken she made every Sunday. She was a great cook, a trait I unfortunately did not inherit. The kitchen's green floral wallpaper was original to the house, which was built in the seventies, along with the dark wood paneling and green laminate countertops that were the same as in my youth. Momma hadn't changed much either, horn-rimmed glasses, dark pants and a button-down blouse with an apron atop it was how I'd typically seen her growing up. Except for the color of her hair, which was now a light gray, her hair was still in the same style, cut to her chin.

"Smells good." I came over and kissed the top of her head, then teased her by looking all confused at the cutting board. "Whatcha makin'?"

She eyed me over the rims of her glasses. "Roast chicken."

"Can't say I ever had one of those," I joked, sneaking a carrot and backing up as she made a *tsss* noise through her teeth.

"Need any help?"

She paused her chopping to look up at me and smirked. "Not from your smart mouth."

I smiled, loving when she joked around. Momma was typically on the reserved side, with a large helping of anxiety.

I'd always felt different than the rest of my family members. My parents were both retired accountants, my brother was a CPA in Florida who did real estate on the side, and my sister worked as a lawyer in Chicago. They all had stable jobs, content with working in an office their entire lives. I, on the other hand, hated the idea of an office job. I didn't want to do something, just to do something. I wanted to be passionate about it.

"You still picking up Sarah at the airport on Friday?" my momma asked.

The implication being I'd forget. Which irked me because she should know I always follow through on my commitments. Still, I assured my momma I'd pick up my sister.

I really shouldn't complain; my parents were great. Growing up, Pop was busy but attended every home baseball game and theater performance of mine. Momma and I got along for the most part, too, though since I dropped out of college, there'd been an undercurrent of tension between us. I tried to tell myself it stemmed from worry, not disappointment.

"I wish Sarah was coming in earlier. The Front Porch wouldn't make a reservation this early, but I'd like to eat by six. And you know your daddy doesn't like to wait for a table. Maybe we should go out to dinner for a meat and three somewhere in Knoxville instead. . ." Momma trailed off, talking as much to herself as to me. She was the one who didn't like waiting for a table. But as much as I tried to calm her spinning thoughts, nothing seemed to help except lending a listening ear and patience.

"Pop loves the Front Porch steaks. How about Sarah and I get there by five and put our name in, so y'all don't have to wait on a table?"

Frowning, she continued chopping. "I guess I'll think that over. Don't forget, Kent will meet us there, too. He's flying into Knoxville, then driving over. Hired himself some fancy car." Looking up at me, she informed more than asked, "I thought we could all spend some time together as a family on Saturday afternoon since everyone'll be in town and Kent flies back that night."

Who would've known that something good would come out of this clown gig? Because I'd do almost anything to get out of spending time with my older brother, including dressing up like a clown.

"I have some things going on Saturday afternoon, but after that I'll be around."

Momma furrowed her brow at me. "What do you have going on Saturday afternoon?"

"Just a job for Sam."

"You know, with your brother and sister both home, you could ask them some questions about their jobs. Maybe it's time to start school again, now that you're more mature."

And that was my cue. I started to back up toward the hallway leading to the bedrooms. "That's exactly what these past six years were, biding my time so I could major in accounting," I replied. There were only so many comments I could take before they began to chafe.

"You know that's not how I meant it."

I sighed, nodding to agree for agreement's sake, then started to turn.

"Your daddy wants to talk to you. Didn't he stop you on your way in?"

Shaking my head, I snuck another carrot as I walked past her toward the TV room. I found Pop there in his recliner, Braves game on, keeping score per usual.

"Hey Pop, how's the game?" I asked, taking a seat on the couch to his left.

"Not my choice for the lead off." He shook his head, complaining about the batting order. "But I've seen worse."

We were quiet until the inning was over. Putting down the clicker, he ran a hand through his hair. His curly Vargas hair that I inherited had thinned some, but the wild springing curls were still there. Granted, now they had more salt than pepper.

"How's work today, son? You still like working at the club?" He shifted in his recliner, then started pulling at a loose thread on his shirt.

I nodded slowly, confused by his question. Unlike Momma, Pop rarely asked me about my jobs.

"Right, right," he responded, abandoning the loose string to take off his readers, fiddling with the stems in his lap.

"And tomorrow you're driving folks around?"

Frowning, I wondered why he wasn't making eye contact with me. "Yes, I'll be driving for Lyft, just like every other Monday."

He must have found his glasses to be dirty, as he was now cleaning them thoroughly with his shirttail.

"And that theater practice, the one with Jack's wife and that other gal, you still liking that?"

My frown deepened, even though I always found it entertaining how unfazed Pop was by Sienna and Rae—a.k.a. Sienna Diaz and Raquel Ezra, two well-known actresses who lived in Green Valley. Of course, I don't think of them as movie stars, either. I'd met Rae through her husband, Jackson. And I'd known Sienna and her husband Jethro Winston for years, having babysat her kids on occasion. While Rae and Sienna weren't actually my sisters, they'd somehow adopted me over the years, like I was some sort of quasi younger brother they couldn't help but fuss over. So, when they started a program called Young Wills, a theater program for kids in the Green Valley elementary and middle schools, they asked if I was interested in helping run it with them.

"Yup. It's been goin' real good for more than a year now."

"Good, good," he replied almost absently, still cleaning his glasses.

"Things are good, Pop." I leaned forward, putting my elbows on my knees. "Everything alright?" Could it be possible that he and Momma needed money? Why else would he be asking about my jobs? I hadn't seen him this uncomfortable since three Thanksgivings ago when my cousin Patrick announced he was changing his name, moving to Miami, and starring in a burlesque show. It was still one of my favorite memories. My Aunt Midge, his mother, practically choked on her turkey.

"Nah, nothing's wrong. Just that your momma and I are, as you know, retired now and starting to talk about the future. Midge and Rick have wanted us to visit them in Florida a few years now and Kent's been trying to get us down by him, too. Might be better for my arthritis being out of here in the winter, at least avoiding the coldest days."

The game came back on, but he kept the TV muted, a telltale sign that he had more on his mind.

"We were thinking of going down there to visit next week."

This was surprising to say the least, but I recovered quickly. "A vacation in Florida sounds great. You and Momma deserve it. Don't worry about anything here. You know I'll take care of the house."

Shifting again, he palmed the back of his neck. "I know you will, son. You see, a condo has come up for sale right across from your aunt and uncle. When we're there, Kent mentioned checking it out. Told us that the maintenance is all taken care of, and your momma is real keen on that idea. If we like it, we'd have to make an offer on it right quick from what your brother tells us."

Stunned, it was a full minute before I could answer. Maybe Sam had got a stronger hit to my head than I thought, because this wasn't making sense. My parents, who considered going to Nashville a major vacation, wanted to move to Florida.

"Pop," I spoke slowly, eyeing him warily. "If you and Momma want to live in Florida part of the year like Aunt Midge and Uncle Rick, I'd be happy for you." I'd be shocked if they went through with it, but happy for them.

"That's the thing. It costs a bit more than we'd anticipated—"

Well, shoot. They did need money. I knew I had more in the bank than most folks my age, but without a 401(k), I really wanted to save it. But if my parents needed money, I'd obviously try to help them.

"—so, we'd have to make the offer contingent on the sale of this house. We'd be moving there permanently."

I could only sit in silence and stare at the stranger in front of me. They wanted to sell their home. *This* home. My childhood home. It was just so . . . unlike my parents. What's next, a place in the line up beside cousin Patrice in the Miami Meat Burlesque?

"But we'd only do it if you had another place lined up. Your momma and I don't want to spring this on you, son. We know that rent's expensive nowadays."

I shook my head. "I can easily get another place. That's not why I live here."

"Sure, sure. I'm just making sure you know we could help you out with the money from the sale of the house if you need some support for a while."

I literally had never felt lower. I expected this out of Momma, but not Pop. I thought he knew I lived here not only to save money, but to help them out. He'd been having more flare-ups of his arthritis and the last one, a few months back, put him out of commission for weeks.

And now, this. My retired parents didn't want to move to paradise because they were worried about how their adult, twenty-four-year-old son was going to make rent.

A true low point. I shifted in my seat, eyeing him. Hard.

"Pop. If you and Momma want to move to Florida and sell this house, then do it. Don't worry about me. I'll find a place. Sam was begging me just today to move in with him and Owen. In fact, I can call him right now. Really. I'm fine."

"You don't have to make any sudden decisions today—"

I cut him off by standing up, clapping him on the shoulder.

"It's no problem. Probably time I'm out of your hair. I'll see you at supper."

CHAPTER
FOUR

POLLY

It wasn't a monster come to eat me. It was this monster. Who's come to eat me out.

Ruby Dixon, *Ice Planet Barbarians*

It was Monday, and I had just swallowed my last bite of donut before leaving my office for the day, when Vicki—the administrative assistant to the VP of Mercy Health—appeared at my door. I'd met with the VP last week to propose a change to my contract: drop my overnight call requirement but still retain my health insurance. I'd been awaiting their answer.

Since Mrs. Simon left, I'd had horrible luck finding nannies that were willing to do overnights. Clarice, our first trial nanny, started today and she seemed adequate at best. It felt wrong leaving my kids with someone who was merely adequate. My mom guilt pulled hard this morning as I drove to work, leaving both kids in Clarice's care—it took every ounce of resolve not to turn around and go back to them. But I was exhausted. I needed help before I lost what was left of my patience. Every minute I wasn't at work, I was busy doing three things at once. Scheduling interviews for babysitters I barely knew from child-care websites, coordinating counseling appointments, buying new clothes for the upcoming school year, getting our bikes out of our storage container, grocery shopping and food prep, laundry . . . and my actual Pediatrician job.

"Polly, I'm glad I caught you," Vicki said walking into my office.

"Vicki, how nice to see you again. Did you want a donut?" I gestured to the Daisy's bag on my desk. I'd gone to get a salad for lunch only to come back with six donuts, as I strongly felt that I needed a donut, *or six*, to make myself feel better about life.

So far, I was two donuts in with no relief in sight.

Vicki glanced at the bag, then gave me a closed-lip smile. "No, thank you. They reviewed your proposal, and they're willing to drop your call requirement in September *if* you're willing to take over the Green Valley School District Medical Directorship."

Yikes. Try saying that three times fast.

"The current medical director, Dr. Dixon, is retiring next week so the school district asked us to nominate someone to replace him as he is on our staff," Vicki continued. "We thought you'd be a good fit. You'll need school board approval, because it's a joint contract between us and the school district, but that's just a formality. The stipend is nine thousand dollars every six months. I can set up a meeting with Dr. Dixon if you'd like."

"Oh, well. I'd need to learn about the position before officially accepting the position. I don't know very much about what a medical director for a school district does. Do you happen to know how much time per week it would require?"

Vicki's visibly bristled. In an overly patronizing tone, she said, "It would only be four hours per week. And I'm sure with your part time workload, that time requirement shouldn't be too hard, right?"

I stiffened, biting back my retort. I was used to this kind of judgment from men. But from a woman it immediately felt personal. Weren't we all supposed to have each other's backs? Giving her placating smile, I plucked a napkin from the Daisy's bag and wiped my hands, giving me a moment to think. Dropping my call requirement this fall was a win, but taking on a medical directorship of a school district? I had no idea what kind of commitment that really took. But, I needed health insurance. Eighteen thousand dollars a year would put a large dent in Max's therapy bills. I didn't have the luxury of turning down any extra income.

Hiding any discomfort, I stood and extended my hand to Vicki.

"Please send me the contract and put any meetings on my schedule. I'll be in touch."

———

I was about a mile from the country house, when I saw something up ahead.

Someone was walking on the road. A narrow, Tennessee county road, with twists and turns and densely lined trees. Meaning, this was not a road that lent itself to walking.

I turned down my audiobook and made out a small figure—or maybe, was it a kid? Who'd let their kid walk on a road like this? I got closer, squinting . . .

Panic flooded me as recognition hit.

Because the young kid who was walking determinedly toward me, little hands fisted on her backpack straps, blonde hair high up in a ponytail, wearing the same sequined rainbow shirt I'd set out for her this morning, was *my kid.*

Sucking in a breath, I pulled over and hopped out of the car, sprinting toward her. "Ryla!" I shouted coming to a stop in front of my almost six-year-old. "What in the world are you doing?"

"Running AWAY!" she yelled, continuing to walk at her steady pace, little face furious.

I grabbed my phone with a sweat-soaked palm. No missed calls. Did Clarice, our nanny of one day, even know Ryla was gone? We were a good three-quarters of a mile from the house. Granted, Ryla appeared significantly more prepared than her last runaway attempt in February, where she'd left the house in the middle of winter dressed in a t-shirt, leggings, and Crocs with her favorite stuffed animal goat under her arm. This time, she was significantly better prepared, wearing socks and tennis shoes as well as a backpack complete with her flamingo thermos tucked in the side pocket. If I hadn't been so blinded by rage, I might've actually been proud.

Because how far would Ryla have gotten if I hadn't found her? I mean, these were the rural woods of Tennessee. Mountain territory. She could have been hit by a car, eaten by a bear, or have gotten *fucking kidnapped.*

"Ryla." My tone was firm, but I dug deep to remain calm. Ryla wasn't one to be wrangled easily. Even though I wanted to simultaneously hug her tight and scream at her for putting herself in such danger, I had to get her off the road without her bolting.

"Ryla, please stop." I crouched down to her level before she passed me. Surprisingly, I was able to stop her easily; she came to a halt as soon as my hand came in contact with her arm. "What are you doing?"

"I'm gonna go live with Giselle!" she cried, eyes welling with tears. And like every other time she's said this during the last seven months, telling me flat-out that she'd rather be with our former au pair than with me, my heart broke a tiny bit more.

"I promise we can talk about that. Right now, we're on the side of a road. It's not safe."

I waited fifteen seconds. Ryla didn't fold, not giving an inch.

"Does Clarice know you left?" That only earned me a scowl.

After another long moment of silence, I'd had enough. Angry, tired, and hot, I resorted to a low-down parenting trick. A lazy one, but incredibly effective.

"I have Daisy's donuts in the car. If you come with me right now, I'll let you have the chocolate one with sprinkles."

Like everyone else with a soul, Ryla was a sucker for chocolate. As a rule, I didn't trust anyone who didn't like chocolate. It seemed unnatural.

"Fi-nah," Ryla whined, overly enunciating the word *fine* and stomping to the car. As I began to help her up into her booster seat, she whipped her head to me, eyes flashing with impressive vitriol. I held my hands up, letting her do it by herself.

Biting my tongue, I closed her door and got into the driver's seat; the relief that she was safely in the car warred with the intense anger that she'd been on the road in the first place.

She was sullen in her booster seat on the short trip to the house, arms crossed, stonily looking out the window. I had to give her time. She had big emotions. After a blowup, she would eventually apologize, usually with a dramatic flair. I knew that my daughter seemed, to most everyone else, like a spoiled brat. I'd already heard this enough from my ex-husband and even my father, on the few occasions he'd spent any time with her. Never mind that in between blowups, she was a smart, funny, and charismatic delight.

Never mind that she was still five for another week and it was my job to help her process her big emotions rather than belittle and yell at her for having them.

Just over a minute later, I parked in the three-car garage, anxious to find Clarice and figure out what the hell was going on. I knew my mother's intuition was tingling this morning for a reason.

"Hello? Clarice? Max?" I shouted as Ryla and I walked through the garage entrance, which was situated in the west wing of the house. I didn't realize that other families didn't have things like "wings" in their homes until eight-year-old Leah discovered our house had a west wing and a library and literally spent the entire day searching our home for a talking candlestick, mantel clock, and teapot.

I walked down the hallway, past the small laundry room and library, to the middle of the house, which opened into a large kitchen overlooking the backyard.

"Max?" I called out, dropping my purse on the island countertop, then past the kitchen table and looked through the sliding glass patio doors, seeing the stone patio and pool beyond.

Empty.

Now, yes, this house was big. About two times bigger than the house we had in Chicago. But not so big that Max wouldn't be able to hear me yelling for him. Or Clarice, for that matter.

Fear made my heart race as I dropped the bag of donuts on the table, told Ryla to help herself, then moved through the kitchen's arched open door to the living room. The living room was beautiful, which had a huge floor-to-ceiling picture window showcasing the mountains in the distance, but it was also, infuriatingly, empty.

"Max!" I yelled again, turning away from the windows. There was a large open staircase on my left, leading upstairs to our bedrooms. To my right, a darkened hallway led to the east wing. I didn't go down that way often, as it led to my parents' old bedroom, and I doubted Max would go down there either. If I went straight back from the living room, I'd find a small study, a formal dining area, and foyer.

I flew up the stairs, the most likely place to find Max was his room.

I burst through my son's bedroom door, exhaling in relief as I saw my ten-year-old lying on his bed, living his best life—still in his pajamas at five thirty in the afternoon. Headphones on, snack wrappers strewn around him, he looked like he'd been in here all day. While this is what I would expect a college freshman to look like in their first year of freedom; it was absolutely not something I allowed for my son. Frank, his therapist, emphasized the importance of limiting screen time and varying his activities, which I explicitly discussed with Clarice yesterday and reviewed this morning.

Max didn't appear concerned by me finding him out. Cheeks upturning, happy to see me, he took off his headphones. "Hi, Mom! Want to watch this video with me?"

My brewing panic and anger at the situation bypassed all reason, completely blinding me to his little bid for my attention. I put my hands on my hips. "I've been calling your name! I can't find Clarice anywhere. Do you know where I just found Ryla?"

Max started to shrink back on his bed.

"She was walking down the side of the road. Clarice is nowhere to be found, and you look like you haven't left your room all day."

Max's eyes started to water and whispered, "Is Ryla ok?"

Instant remorse filled me at the sight of his tears. This wasn't his fault, and he certainly didn't deserve how I'd taken my anger out on him. Inhaling, I aimed for something more controlled. "I'm sorry. Ryla's fine. She's eating a donut downstairs, but I can't find Clarice. Do you know where she is?"

"I-I heard yelling. Clarice gave Ryla a time-out, I think." Shame continued to fill me as I heard the smallness of his voice. "And then I think she might have gone outside."

I went to him, giving him a hug and kiss on the head. "Thank you, Max. But maybe, pick up the garbage and get dressed in regular clothes? I'll find Clarice and take care of it. Your sister is at the table with a large bag of donuts if you want to keep her company."

As I walked back into the kitchen, I glanced into the backyard and did a double take. Whisps of smoke were curling into the air, like someone was on fire. Rushing to the patio doors, I *did* spot something on fire. Because laying down on one of the lounge chairs by the pool was our new nanny . . . smoking what looked to be a joint.

Sweet baby Jesus smoking the wacky tobacky. Was this really happening? I blinked thrice, but the image in front of me remained.

"Ryla?" I asked. She was currently sitting at the table, legs swinging, happily munching on her donut. "Whatever you do just . . . stay inside. Ok, sweetie?"

"Ok, Mommy."

I rolled my shoulders back and opened the patio door to walk outside, making sure to close it tight behind me.

The distinctive smell of pot lingered in the air as I approached Clarice. She was laying on a chaise, eyes closed—not moving as I walked toward her. Perhaps she was too stoned to hear my footsteps on the stone pavers. Or too stupid.

"What in the hell are you doing?" I thundered down at her.

"Ms. Alberton! I was taking a little break!" Jolting upright, she dropped the joint on the front of her shirt. Letting out a muffled curse, she picked it up hastily and brushed the ash from her shirt.

My voice became deadly calm. "Is that your explanation for why you're smoking weed on my back patio when you're supposed to be watching my children?"

"I can explain. This isn't what it looks like!"

Clarice stuck two fingers in her mouth, pinched off the lit end of her joint, lifted the collar of her shirt, and stuffed it inside, what I presumed to be, her bra.

Classy.

I snorted. "Oh really? Because it looks like the nanny I hired to start *today* is smoking a J as my five-year-old ran away from home. You remember Ryla, right? I just found her more than half a mile down the road with her backpack strapped to her back. You're lucky she didn't get lost or picked up by some stranger or . . ." I paused, emotion clogging my throat. I pinched my nose to stop any tears, finally looking back to Clarice when I felt them pass.

"It was for stress!" Clarice implored. "I've never been treated that way by any kid in all my years of working as a nanny. Your daughter—" Clarice had the nerve to start, but I cut her off by holding up my hand, eyes burning with rage. Yes, I knew Ryla was difficult. Yes, I was primed and defensive when it came to her, but Clarice couldn't seriously be trying to blame her behavior on my daughter.

"Allow me to ease your stress level. You will no longer be needed here. Please leave. *Now.*" I pointed to the side of the house. I didn't want her to step one more toe inside my home.

"But, my bag!" Clarice sputtered.

"I will meet you at your car with your things."

Scoffing and grumbling nasty things under her breath, she started around the side of the house. I hurried back inside, fisting my shaking hands after shutting and locking the patio door.

I glanced at Ryla. "Everything ok?"

Chocolate smeared across her face, Ryla nodded silently, her eyes watching me warily. I smiled brightly at her in what I hoped to be taken as reassurance, causing her to resume eating her last few bites of a donut. I had never been more grateful that she ate at sloth speed. I found what looked to be Clarice's purse and went outside. Neither of us spoke as I held out her bag to her. But Clarice did give me one last grumbled salutation before leaving: "Good luck, frosty bitch."

I stood outside long after her car drove down the driveway, past the gates and out of sight, feeling pressure behind my eyes for the second time today. But I wasn't going to do it. I wasn't going to cry.

My kids were inside the house, hurting, and looking to me to fix it. I had to pull myself together to have a chance at keeping everyone and everything together.

Even if I was more broken than they'd ever be.

———

"Mom?" Max was drawing with his favorite colored pencils at the island as I made dinner.

"Yeah, bud?"

"Does this mean we have to keep going to summer school?"

Leah had indeed worked her magic, and Ryla and Max were able to attend the Green Valley summer school day camps a few days per week since Mrs. Simon left. Leah's plan to have Max stick close to her all day to help him with his anxiety was working well, all things considered.

This February, Max developed panic attacks anytime he, Ryla, or I left our apartment. It became so severe I ultimately pursued a pediatric intensive outpatient behavioral program for him. He'd made significant progress, but he still had trouble with leaving the house and finding the words to express himself. If I was being honest, I suspected there was something else underlying the anxiety, like autism spectrum disorder. But at the time of his testing, anxiety was his main problem, so it was hard to determine anything else that may be contributing to his symptoms.

"I know I said you wouldn't have to start school until this fall. But I'm so proud of you and how brave you are being every day," I told Max.

Never one to take compliments, he continued looking down at his picture as his cheeks warmed. I put the meal in the oven to cook, then stood up and glanced around. Max was still coloring intently but Ryla, who was at the table last I checked, was missing. Max shook his head when I asked if he'd seen where his sister went. I still needed to talk to Ryla about what happened with Clarice today. I glanced at my watch. Dinner took forty minutes to cook. Then after dinner I had another hour of charting to finish on my computer, which consisted of finishing any medical notes, answering messages, reviewing results, and answering any staff messages that had come in. Once I finished that, I had my own personal emails to check, a few bills to pay, and a new weighted blanket to order for Max; his current one was too warm, so he'd begun kicking it off at night and wasn't sleeping as well.

"Mom? Is it ok if I watch my tablet?" Max asked. Being on their tablets had become an unfortunate habit for both kids when I needed time at night to collect my sanity and get things done.

"Sure, just for a little while. I'm going to go talk to Ryla."

I finally found the absconder in the basement theater room, which she had transformed into a couch cushion fort.

"Ryla?" She popped up from a hole in the middle of the cushions. "We need to talk about this afternoon."

"I'm sorry," she said quickly.

"I appreciate that, but we still need to talk about why it happened."

Ryla threw her head back dramatically then disappeared like a gopher into her hidey-hole.

"It's dangerous to leave the house without telling someone," I yelled out. "You could get hurt or lost."

"I didn't do anything!" Her little voice came out muffled. "She was always looking at her phone and didn't play and yelled at me and let Max be in his room all day!"

"What happened that made Clarice yell?"

Silence.

I paused. "Did she do something you didn't like?"

More silence. Or maybe it was muttering.

"What was that?"

Ryla's head suddenly appeared. "I SAID, she called me A STUPID BRAT!"

"She what?!" I shouted, my fury at Clarice brimming over any control I had in that moment. My hands went to my chest absently due to how tight it'd suddenly become.

"Uh-huh. She found her phone under the couch and then her watch in the oven and then she yelled."

Wait. What?

"Ryla, how did her watch end up in the oven?"

My daughter merely crossed her arms. "I put it there."

Aaaand, now things made a little more sense. Still, a child hiding your watch and phone was not a reason to call any kid a stupid brat nor smoke marijuana in their home.

"And while it wasn't right for Clarice to call you that, you also can't hide someone else's property. If you do that again, you will lose any tablet-time privileges for a week."

Ryla's face went molten. "I'm going to take *your* tablet time away for a week!" Her little face started to crumple, pain slicing through me at her next words, "I want Giselle!"

The tears I'd been trying to hold back all day blurred my vision as Ryla scampered away and ran up the stairs. After a minute, I heard the sound of footsteps running through the house followed by a very faint door slamming—likely her bedroom door, a sound I'd been hearing a lot since we moved here.

Bone weary and drained, I put away the cushions, then went upstairs to check on dinner. As I shut the oven door and stood up straight, my muscles screamed against the pull, the tension in my body refusing to melt away, not allowing me to take in a full, deep breath. Sighing, I walked to the island and pulled up the tablet I used to track everything from the daily menu, our to-do list, and the kids' schedule and goals for the day. The box beside Max's reading and journal time was unmarked.

"Max!" I called out, walking into the living room to find him on the couch with his tablet. "Did you read any of your book today? Or do your journal entry? Remember Frank wants you to write in it every day."

Max opened and closed his mouth silently, answering without speaking.

I narrowed my eyes and crossed my arms. "Tablet time is over. Go upstairs and start reading. Now."

Eyes wide and sorrowful, Max tentatively walked past me on his way to the stairs. I wanted to reach for him and hug him, not liking the chasm between us that I couldn't cross. Once he was out of sight, I turned to stare out the windows, seeing the mountains that stood deep purple in the distance beyond. They looked cold. Distant. Unapproachable.

Like me.

I dropped my head into my hands, heart aching. How the hell did I get here? My daughter hated me so much, she wanted to run away. I was snapping at my anxiety-ridden son. And somehow, despite moving away twenty years ago, I've ended up back in a home I never wanted to live in again, finding that I'd turned into the person whose mask I wore: perfect Polly Alberton, the Stepford daughter who turned Stepford wife who was now a Stepford mother.

The problem was, I had no idea how to unmake her.

54

CHAPTER
FIVE
POLLY

I told Georgie and the others that for a cheeseburger, I'd do just about anything. But having an alien lay claim to me feels . . . weird. I don't even get a choice? This is like me saying "I want a cheeseburger" and someone slapping a pickle into my hand and saying, "Fuck you, you get a pickle."

Ruby Dixon, *Barbarian Alien*

Dr. Alberton,

Attached is a list of the events pertaining to the Judge's bid for the Supreme Court nomination to which he requests the attendance of you and/or your children. Please let me know at your earliest convenience if you have any conflicts so we can remedy the situation.

It has also come to the Judge's attention that Mrs. Gloria Simon is no longer in your employ. I have taken the liberty of finding suitable nanny replacements. Please review the enclosed information and let us know your choice or one will be chosen for you. If they don't meet your standards, I am also including information on the boarding options for Eagleton Preparatory Academy so that you would be free to attend the following events as requested, preserve a full-time work schedule, and retain your current living quarters.

Regards,

Jeffrey Savient

. . .

I rubbed the suddenly spasming muscles at the base of my neck. I was in between patients, midmorning on Tuesday, and I already felt a migraine coming on. There really was no circle of hell suitable for "Regards Jeffrey" and his patronizing emails. If he thought for one minute that I'd ever send my kids to a boarding school, then he was obviously smoking the same thing as Clarice.

I debated making a voodoo doll of him with Ryla later and calling it a craft.

As expected, a headache pounded in my temples the rest of the morning. The threat was clear: attend these events or we'll kick you out of your home. A brief review of the nanny "options" revealed militant older women who looked ready to whack a kid with a ruler if they stepped out of line. I wouldn't let them watch a snake I didn't like, much less my children.

During a break between patients, I searched in vain for homes for sale in Green Valley, something I'd been doing for months, still finding none that were within my budget. The houses in my budget looked like they came with three bedrooms, two bathrooms, and a family of raccoons in the kitchen.

My clinic day ended early at one o'clock, so I made a stop at the Donner Bakery before heading to pick up the kids from their summer school program. I desperately needed caffeine. Seeing something called a dill pickle cupcake, I picked one up for Leah as a thank-you for helping us out and headed to the school.

The Green Valley Elementary School didn't look much different from twenty-five years ago. It had the same red brick siding and rectangular veranda leading out from the front doors. As I walked inside, I gave a head nod to the nice administrative assistant I'd met with Leah when Max and Ryla had started summer school, holding up the iced coffees and white bakery bag, explaining that I was taking them to Leah.

"Oh, isn't that sweet. You go ahead sugar," she said, buzzing me in.

The smell of crayons, cleaning supplies, and rubber permeated the air as I made my way to Leah's third grade classroom. Her room was cheery and busy, just like her, with solar system posters, a reading corner, and plants covered with different colored cellophanes spaced evenly apart on the window ledges.

Leah was at her desk, dark wavy hair up in a bun, wearing a T-shirt and shorts along with Tinkerbell earrings. She'd been obsessed with Disney for as long as I could remember and actually named her eleven-year-old daughter and seven-year-old son, Belle and Eric, respectively. Her husband, Kyle, was a very understanding man.

"Knock, knock," I called out, entering her classroom. "I thought I'd bring you an afternoon snack."

"For me?" Leah exclaimed excitedly, getting up from her desk.

"Is Max around?" I handed Leah the bag and one of the iced coffees from the carrier.

Leah's eyes closed slowly as she took a sip of the coffee. "You're a stallion in a field of donkeys. Let no one convince you otherwise." She took another fortifying sip, then smiled proudly. "*Max* is in the auditorium with the other kids."

"What?"

Leah nodded. "He's been pretty tight to me, but then today, he just wanted to go. All by himself. I checked on him a few minutes ago and he seemed fine."

Pride filled me. After all, that was the goal. Yet at the same time, I was nervous. What if he got scared? What would he do? Pushing against the urge to go check on him myself, I followed Leah toward her desk and sat next to her on a too-small-for-an-adult chair.

"You didn't have to bring me anything." Leah's protest was at odds with how eagerly she peered into the bag.

"You've been a lifesaver. It's the least I could do."

"I'd happily help you for free—" Leah stopped and gasped, pulling out the clear plastic container housing a white-and-green cupcake. Excitement filled her eyes as she pried open the lid and gave it a small sniff.

"It's a dill pickle cupcake, so if it's terrible, don't blame me. I know how much you like—"

I was interrupted by the sight of Leah practically attacking the cupcake with her mouth like a feral cat, face-first into the green-and-white confection.

"—pickles."

Wow. She'd really gone for it. Just dove right in, not caring how much frosting could get on her face. Wolfing it down happily, white frosting from nose to chin, she finally swallowed and let out a contented sigh.

"I thought these were an urban legend. I've heard of 'em, but I've never seen them sold."

She went back in for the last few bites. I couldn't keep the smile off my face as I leaned forward to grab a napkin from the bag, handing it to her after she finished off the last of the cupcake.

I glanced at my watch. "You ate that entire thing in less than a minute."

"I'm like a pelican with carb," Leah explained, wiping frosting from her face. Balling up the napkin, she lined up her shot, then pitched the napkin into a garbage can from ten feet away.

"Woohoo!" Leah hollered, throwing up her hands as she sank it on the first try. I marveled at her obvious ease in her own body. How she seemed light and happy. No stressors stacked on top of each other to weigh her down.

"Hey," I asked Leah, "do you know anything about the school district's medical director?"

Leah tipped back, balancing on two legs of her desk chair. "Why?"

"Mercy Health agreed to drop my call requirement, but not until September, and in order to keep my benefits, I have to take on the medical directorship of the school district."

She wrinkled her nose. "Why do you have to—Hey!" she exclaimed, interrupting herself. She brought her chair down and pointed at me. "You need to talk to my friend Rose!" Leah looked at her watch, then up to the clock, then back down to her watch. Suddenly, she bolted up and across the classroom, closing the door, then dashed back to sit right across from me in her own little chair.

"My friend Rose is the school's special ed coordinator," Leah began, the enthusiastic glean in her eyes making me strangely wary. "She and a few others have been working on getting more funding to improve special ed resources for the school. This spring she won this long-shot grant specifically to aid the special ed program. We were all pretty shocked. But now, Rose has been pulling her hair out working with the school board and needs help. The school board president wants to use the grant money for sports rather than special education. I know the school's medical director hasn't been helpin' much and was leavin'. But I never thought about asking you—of course you'd be the perfect choice! She's gonna be happier than a pig in mud!"

I couldn't help the amused grin that spread across my face. Whenever Leah got excited or angry, her Southern gene activated.

I gestured to the closed classroom door. "What's with the cloak and dagger act? Is it really that contentious?"

"Yes. And the rumor mill is that the grant was funded through an anonymous *local* donor."

I tilted my head, not understanding. "If they're local, why not just anonymously donate the money to the school? Why do it through a grant?"

Leah shrugged. "Who knows why rich people do the things they do? Anyway, you and Rose will get along great. She's sweet as pie and equally obsessed with Disney, so you know she's good people. Where's your phone? Her number's 555-6028." Leah recited this rapid fire from the top of her head, not surprising to me, her ability to recall numbers and dates rivaled an internet search engine.

I patted Leah's hand. "I'll need that number repeated again later. It's not a done deal. And I don't have time. I still need to find a nanny and then with Ryla's birthday party this weekend . . ." I sighed. "I told you she invited every kid in her summer school class last week without asking me first, right?"

"I still can't believe you hired a petting zoo."

I groaned. Not only could everyone attend, but in a moment of sheer brilliance, Ryla had also asked for a petting zoo. And in a moment of true stupidity, I said yes. Thank God I found a local party planning company to help.

"Do you need any help?" Leah held up her hand, stopping me before I could reply. "Wait, I'm staying over Friday night when you're on call, so I'll already be there bright and early on Saturday to help. Easy peasy."

I shook my head. "You really don't have to. I don't have much left to do. Just a few party favors. And picking up the cake. And putting up the decorations." I winced, feeling more overwhelmed as I recalled everything I had left on my list for Saturday. "And the treat bags. Why did I do this to myself again?"

"You wanted to make up for the fact that your kid's daddy is a level one *prick*." You could tell Leah was happy with herself as she leaned into that last word. "And you wanted to make your kids happy."

Leah jerked her head up at the clock. "Shoot! It's quarter past. We need to get to the gym." Not sparing me an explanation, Leah grabbed her iced coffee and sped out of the room.

I had to jog to catch up.

"Why are we going to the gym?" I asked, breathless. The kids didn't get done with their day until 3 p.m.

"The puppet show started one minute ago."

"Did you say puppet show?"

Her eyes lit. "You have to see it. A guy who helps out with theater classes at the middle and high schools performs a full-on puppet show twice a year for the kids. He lets them try it too. And I'm not talking sock puppets. I mean honest-to-goodness string puppets. He's great with the kids and they all adore him. I think half of Belle's class is in love with him."

"As long as it's puppets and not clowns. You know how I feel about clowns." I fought off a shiver.

Leah laughed. "That might be my favorite memory of the fourth grade."

We linked arms, continuing down the hallway until we reached the gym. In the middle of the court sat a large rectangular wooden frame at least thirty feet wide and fifteen feet tall, with red curtains and, as Leah promised, two marionettes. On the left was a monkey, and on the right was a puppet that looked like Bert from Sesame Street.

And there were at least fifty kids sitting in front of it with rapt attention, giggling at the puppets' antics. I spotted Ryla near the front, Leah's son, Eric, to her right and Max to her left, a happy smile on his face.

"Oh!" exclaimed the Bert puppet. "Oh, how dare you! You sneaky little monkey. That was supposed to be my lunch, and you ate it!"

"Ooo-ooo-ooo, AH! AH! AH!" replied the tiny monkey, causing the kids to erupt into laughter.

"No! You can't have more!" the Bert puppet announced in outrage, again causing giggles throughout the crowd.

"Ooo-ooo-ooo, ah?" The monkey's sounds were quiet, almost conversational.

"Especially not the peanut butter!" The Bert puppet hollered. I craned my neck but still couldn't tell where the person controlling the puppets was standing.

For the next twenty minutes the kids ate up the hilarious performance, which ended in Bert and the monkey dancing the tango. I enjoyed the puppet show almost as much as I enjoyed my kid's laughter—because there was nothing better than the sound of your child laughing.

Robust clapping and cheers erupted at the end as a teacher from the audience walked up to the puppet show frame. "How about that, everyone! Let's give it up for our puppet master!"

The clapping continued, but all sounds faded away as a young man appeared. Dressed in all black, he was wearing a microphone headset over his mop of curly brown hair. He had the monkey puppet under his arm as he waved jovially down to the kids.

A very familiar, very handsome, young man.

A man I'd only ever seen in a black polo, driving my car.

Jace.

CHAPTER SIX

JACE

Ruby Dixon, *Ice Planet Barbarians*

"Nice show today, Jace. You should really think about getting a teaching degree," Mr. Nichols said as I was packing up my puppet show props.

I knew Mr. Nichols meant well. Everyone in town meant well. But it was hard not to take their comments as judgment after a while. Like how I spent my time, volunteering at the school here and running Young Wills weren't worthy pursuits because it wasn't a formal career.

"Thanks, but I'm happy with what I'm doing."

"If you ever change your mind, I know some faculty at UT Knoxville in their education program. I'd be happy to introduce you. See you Thursday."

I continued to pack up my rolling suitcases, recalling when Sienna, too, offered to arrange a meeting with a professor who ran the performing arts education program at a local liberal arts college. She didn't judge me when I declined, but if I was being honest with myself, I've tossed around the idea of teaching more seriously since then. I loved working with kids, particularly in the theater, seeing them shine in their own ways, finding their confidence. Yet, a part of me was scared that if I formalized it by making it a career, it'd take some of the magic away.

I was on my way out, heading around the corner toward the main hallway, when a familiar voice made me pause. It was the voice I looked forward to hearing every Sunday, the little rasp once again causing a throb at the base of my spine.

I peered around the corner, and there she was. Polly Alberton.

She looked upset, pacing back and forth, speaking rapidly into her phone. "I understand that. But I'm sure you can also understand how alarming it was to come home to find my nanny, the one I hired from your service, smoking *marijuana* in my home when she was supposed to be watching my children." She paused. "Uh-huh. Yes. But I need someone to watch my kids overnight when I'm on hospital call, not just during the day."

Hospital call. Was she a nurse? And watch her kids? She must be a mom. My eyes moved over her upswept hair, sunglasses sitting on top of her head, then moved down her body. She wore a short black blazer, and tight, dark blue jeans molded to her incredible ass.

A *hot* mom.

A mom I'd like to—

"Fine," Polly snapped. "Yes. I'll look for your email. But I will expect this month and next month's fee to be refunded."

Jesus, this woman was sexy when she was direct.

I turned back around, hiding behind the corner. Listening. Waiting. Holding my breath. I heard a couple soft footsteps, followed by a sigh. What in the hell was I doing? Hiding? And why? I wasn't one to hesitate. I took a step forward just as Polly whipped around the corner, causing us to practically collide.

"Oh!" she cried as I reflexively grasped her shoulders, stopping us from crashing headfirst into one another. A look of shock crossed her face, so I automatically stepped back and dropped my hands, missing the soft feel of her body under them instantly. I'd been close to her before, on many occasions. Except today her makeup was fresh and light, splashes of freckles were visible across her cheeks and nose.

"*Miss* Alberton, pleasure to see you again." I laid on the Southern charm on thick as I could, taking my time, letting the *s* from the *Miss* drag on a little longer than usual.

"It's just Polly." She stiffened and backed up a step. "I saw your puppet show. You're very talented." Her expression was polite, face still unreadable. But her vivid green eyes were running all over me, despite her rigid posture. Like they were the only thing not buttoned up about her.

"Thank you." I couldn't help the wide grin that came over my face, loving the glimpse of another side of Polly Alberton.

"Do you work here?"

"At the school? No. I assist the theater classes throughout the school year and there's an after-school theater program I help out with, too. I picked up the puppet show gig after a friend of mine gave me the idea. Her husband helped me build the stage. How old are your kids?"

She widened her eyes at my question, then bristled, narrowing her eyes suspiciously. "How do you know I have kids?"

Hell, but she was a live wire. I didn't want her to know I'd been listening to her phone call, so I shrugged. "I'm only assuming, since it's almost pickup time. It's why most folks come here about now."

"I guess that makes sense." Polly seemed to hesitate. "I have two kids: Max is ten and Ryla's five."

I remembered the new kids I met today, a brother and sister with blond hair and green eyes. Of course they were Polly's kids, they looked just like their momma.

"Do your kids go to a different school during the year?"

"No." Polly crossed her arms. "We just moved here in June. I grew up around here."

I'd been cataloging everything she was saying. Moved here last month, check. Grew up here, but no accent, check. Single. Two kids. On call for the hospital. Check, check, and check.

"Did you move back here for work?"

She opened her mouth, then shook her head and snapped it shut. "Yes."

Her reply was simple, yet I had a feeling that the story was anything but. I didn't get the impression that a follow-up question was going to get me anywhere, so I pivoted. "Your daughter's a real hoot and a half. She had the entire group in stitches when it was her turn with the puppets, pretending the monkey was in love with Bert. It was brilliant. I honestly wish I'd thought of it."

Polly's lips slowly curved into a smile as I recounted the story.

"My Ryla?" Polly's voice was gentle as she took a step forward. It seemed unconscious, though, like she wasn't aware she'd moved closer to me.

"Yup." I nodded. "She was the first volunteer. In the middle of her act, she couldn't figure out how to move one of the mechanisms for the puppets and looked like she was either gonna cry or throw it on the ground." I raised my eyebrows. "I'm still not sure which. Then a boy who must be your son came and whispered in her ear, calming her down instantly."

Polly shifted, looking down briefly. "Ryla has a bit of a temper, but my son, Max, is incredibly patient with her." The melancholy in her tone confused me, as did the strong urge that came over me to take away her sadness.

"She's a natural onstage," I continued. My words were true, but I picked them carefully, wanting to see Polly smile again. "You can't teach that kind of comedic timing. You should think about having her join Young Wills. It's a theater program for elementary and middle school kids that live in the Green Valley School District. They meet every Tuesday and Thursday evening at the high school auditorium during the summers."

I could have explained more definitively that I was one of the three instructors, but I didn't.

"Ryla would love that. Is the program open to new kids right now?"

"Absolutely!" . . . *not.* "I know the women who run it. If you're interested, just give me a call and I can reach out to them."

Polly's head tilted to one side. "I'd need your number for that."

"Are you asking for my number? It's a little forward of you, but I guess that's alright," I teased, making a big show of looking down and patting my hands over my pockets. I peeked up at Polly to find she was grinning, making me feel ten feet tall, pleased I'd put a smile on her face. More than pleased if I was being honest. I was playing a losing game, asking for her number, counting her smiles, knowing this would never lead anywhere. And yet, I couldn't help myself.

"Young Wills is always looking for stage crew, too. If your son wanted to join, he'd be welcome. I get the impression he prefers to be out of the spotlight."

Polly's eyes softened a touch. Not taking her eyes off mine, she took her phone out of her pocket, holding it up. "What's your number?"

Caught by her gaze, feeling like we were in our own world, I only started to recite my number when a short blonde head blurred past me, breaking the spell.

"Mommy!" The aforementioned hoot and a half practically tackled Polly, holding tight around her momma's waist. The force of Polly's full wattage smile was blinding when she looked down at her daughter. Never mind hoping for Polly's small smiles. I wanted *that* smile. The one paired with pure happiness on Polly's face. And I wanted it aimed at me.

"Hi Ryla, sweetie, did you have a fun day?" Polly asked as Ryla bounced up and down, still holding on to her momma.

"Yes! Yes, yes, yes, yes, yes—" Ryla's chant cut off abruptly as she turned and saw me. Her eyes popped wide in recognition at the same time a few kids walked past us, calling out, "Bye, Mr. Jace! See you at Young Wills tonight!"

Polly's head snapped in my direction at their words. Sheepish grin in place, I came clean. "I might help out with the Young Wills program from time to time." As in *every* time.

Movement directed Polly's attention down the hallway. Her son was walking behind a group of kids, eyes downcast, but looking up every once in a while. His face lit up when he saw his momma. As Max reached them, he gave his mom a side hug then shifted his eyes to mine curiously for a beat, then flitted away.

"Mom, mom, mom, mom, mom, moooooom," Ryla chanted again, demanding Polly's attention.

"Ryla. I hear you," Polly replied calmly, looking to her daughter. "What is it?"

Pointing a little finger at me, Ryla announced, "He has the puppets. Mr. Jace! Can I show my mom the puppets?"

Polly's head was shaking before her daughter could get the full question out. "You know Max has an appointment this afternoon. We can't be late."

"I don't wanna go there. It's boring. I want to see puppets!" Ryla's little face scowled as Max's blanched.

Reaching in and out of my pocket discreetly, I knelt down in front of Ryla. "It's Ryla, right? I'm sorry, but I don't have time to show you the puppets again today. Besides, they're all packed up." I gestured to the suitcases beside me. "But I'll tell you what. I'll be back on Thursday. You can take another crack at 'em then."

As Ryla's green eyes lit up, I felt Polly's on me.

I tilted my head and pointed to Ryla's ear. "Hey, what's that?"

"What?" Ryla looked confused.

"Behind your ear," I explained, reaching behind her ear with my right hand. "I swear I saw something."

Doing the first magic trick I ever taught myself, I moved the quarter from where it'd been hidden in the soft web between my thumb and palm and pretended to find it behind Ryla's ear.

"You better keep track of that." I handed Ryla the quarter, her little body practically vibrating with amazement.

"Holy moly!" Ryla screeched, scratching wildly behind her little ears, looking for more coins. "How'd you do that?" Ryla grabbed my hand, turning it over in earnest.

I spread my fingers wide and held them up. "Magic!"

It was only then that I glanced at Polly and Max, who had twin expressions of guarded amusement: cheeks upturned in a smile, but eyebrows knitted together. I slyly reached into my pocket again.

"You're Max, right? I'm Jace." At my greeting, Max moved closer to his mom. I played it off and pointed at him. "Wait a minute, do you?" Extending my hand behind his ear, I produced a second quarter.

I wanted to puff out my chest at the look of wonder on Max's face and the small step he took toward me.

Placing the quarter in his hand I teased, "You two need to do a better job of keeping track of your money."

"I keep mine in Totes *Baa*-goats." My head swung to Ryla at her comment, swearing she'd just made a little bleating noise. She jerked a thumb at her brother. "He spends all his on video games," she said, making me laugh and Polly hiss, "Ryla."

"What?" Ryla's expression was pure innocence, though I got the impression she knew exactly what she was doing.

Polly rolled her eyes. "Alright, kids. Thank, uh, Mr. Jace here," she said, stumbling over my name. "It was nice to see you again." Polly began to corral her kids down the hallway, so I grabbed my suitcases to walk with them. Once we got to the front entrance, I walked briskly ahead and held the first double door open.

"Allow me."

Polly gave me a curt nod as she and Max moved through the doorway. Ryla shot past them reaching the outer door first, pushing against it with all of her might.

"UUUnnnnggghhh," Ryla grunted as she pushed the door open, holding it for us. "Quick! Before I lose it!"

Once we all dashed through the door, Ryla let go and her little chest heaved with her effort.

"Thank you for holding the door open. My arms are so tired from the puppet show, I don't know if I'd have ever gotten that open."

"But you have such big muscles."

I guffawed as Polly chided, "Ryla!"

"Look at his arms, Mom!" Ryla accompanied this by pointing at my arms.

Admittedly today, I was wearing a T-shirt that was on the snug side. "Can I feel 'em?"

Closing her eyes, cheeks flushed red, Polly shook her head slowly at her daughter's request. I was trying not to preen like a peacock whose feathers were just complimented, even if it had been by a five-year-old.

I moved the lighter of the two spinner suitcases toward Ryla, gesturing to the parking lot behind her. "I'm parked just down the row there. If it's ok with your momma, want to help me get this to the car?"

Ryla glanced at Polly, who nodded. Then with a determined look on her face, Ryla was off, practically sprinting down the veranda, pushing the suitcase in front of her. For a little thing, she was actually pretty fast. "Come on slow pokes!" Ryla called out behind her.

I fought back a chuckle, starting after her. Polly certainly had her hands full. I wondered if their daddy was in the picture. Glancing to my right, I noticed Polly wasn't following us. Glancing behind me, I saw her kneeling in front of her son. Max was stock-still, face stricken, chest moving quickly up and down as he clutched at his momma's hands. Polly was crouched down, murmuring and looking intently at her son's glassy eyes.

Shoot, I hadn't even noticed he was having a hard time. I'd never had a panic attack, but my own mother had them on occasion. From the way Polly was reacting, my guess was this wasn't his first one. Opting to give them some time and seeing that Ryla was almost to the parking lot, I jogged after her. Thankfully, she stopped at the juncture where the veranda met the parking lot. After catching up with her, I noticed she was looking back at Max and Polly. I briefly wondered if I was doing the right thing, giving them space.

"He has more butterflies in his belly than other kids. He just needs time to calm them down."

I turned my head back to Ryla, who apparently had the wisdom of someone ten times her age. She was just as much of an enigma as her mother.

After looking down the road both ways, Ryla pushed the suitcase ahead of her and I walked beside her. Confidence blaring, she led me down the rows of cars even though she didn't know which car was mine.

"Do you have kids?" she asked out of the blue.

"Nope."

"Do you have a wife?"

"Not one of those, either." I answered easily.

She slowed, eyeing me up and down, *real* squinty. I felt like I was in a lineup.

"How old are you?" she asked. I glanced back to Polly and Max before turning my attention back to the short Sherlock Holmes.

"Twenty-four. Why, how old are you?"

She began to walk at a normal pace again, nose in the air. "Almost six. Do you like kids?"

I chuckled. "Did my momma put you up to this?

In response, Ryla gave me a fairly harsh "you're a moron" expression—one I hadn't been on the receiving end of since the sixth grade. She followed this up with, "No. I don't even know your mom."

Fair point. "Sure, I like kids," I answered, moving on. "Sometimes I like them more than adults—Hey, there's my car!" I tried to distract her by making a big show of opening my trunk with a button and yelling, "Abracadabra!"

Ryla was unimpressed. "You just pressed the button," she said flatly.

I shrugged and glanced at Polly and Max who were now at least hugging.

"You can be our new Giselle!" I jerked my head to Ryla whose green eyes were wide with delight.

"Uh, who?" I asked, putting down the suitcase handles.

"Our Giselle! She's in Italy so we need someone to watch us even though we're not babies. Miss Simon made good cookies but won a lot of money and then we had one that was really mean but only for a day and now we have to find a new one."

I had no idea what she just said or what a Giselle was, but from Polly's conversation earlier, I had a feeling I knew where she was going with this.

They were in the market for a babysitter.

Which meant Ryla was looking to buy me.

"Well . . ." I searched for a segue when inspiration struck. I lifted the suitcase, but pretended it was too heavy. I tugged on it a few more times, not letting it budge.

"Oof." I pretended to wipe sweat off my forehead. "Say, did you add weights to this? It's too heavy!"

Ryla giggled as I tried and failed to lift the suitcase again.

"It's not heavy!" She laughed as she grabbed the handle with both hands and lifted it straight up in the air, then slammed it back to the ground.

We played this game a few more times, Ryla laughing harder with each of my failed attempts. Sighing, I dramatically wiped my non-sweaty forehead again, then put my hands on my hips. "I think you better help me."

Ryla went to pick up the suitcase, and I made a big show of grunting and talking under my breath as we both lifted it into the trunk. After both of the suitcases were in the back, I dusted off my palms.

"Well, little miss Ryla. I am so glad you helped me with those heavy suitcases. I don't think I'd ever have gotten them in there!"

Ryla clapped, jumping up and down and shouted, "Now you have to be our new Giselle!" at the same time as Polly and Max came up behind us.

And judging by her slightly open mouth, Polly definitely heard what Ryla said. Head whipping back and forth between her daughter and me, Polly shouted, "What in the world? Ryla! Did you just ask him what I think you just asked him?"

Nonplused, Ryla merely looked at her momma and shrugged. "What? He said he likes kids more than grown-ups."

Oh, *shit*.

I opened my mouth and held up my hands just as Polly gave me a sharp, disgusted look and moved closer to Ryla protectively, Max mirroring Polly's every step.

"Whoa, that is not how I meant it—"

Polly cut me off with an incredulous look, her eyes silently saying, *I'm sure*. She jerked her head to Ryla. "We have to go."

"But, Mom—"

"NOW." Polly's stern command was accompanied by a sharp finger snap. Ryla went immediately to her mother's side as Polly led her kids past me without another word.

I watched her walk away, head held high, her long legs eating up the ground in front of her.

Damn, but she was sexy as hell.

It's a shame she thought I was a pervert.

CHAPTER
SEVEN

POLLY

The company didn't just fuck me over. They fucked me sideways, upside down, every which way to Sunday, and everywhere in between.

American Tie by Lady Jane
Narrated by Brittney Houston

I didn't get Jace's number. Probably for the best, even though Ryla was able to piece together an explanation that assured me he wasn't a pedophile. I had a meeting with Dr. Dixon on Thursday afternoon, so Leah agreed to take the kids to her house after school. I conveniently forgot to tell her about my encounter with Jace on Tuesday. I'd barely let myself think about it. Every time I thought of being interrupted before I could get his phone number, I chided myself for feeling disappointed. I should not be thinking of a twenty-four-year-old guy that way.

Yes, I'd learned his age from Ryla, too. Something else I'd thought about too much over the past forty-eight hours.

Dr. Dixon, who served as the school district's medical director for the past twenty plus years, was nice, for a dinosaur. At seventy-nine, he'd been working at Mercy Health since its inception in 1983. I'd been taught by plenty of doctors that were older. One of my favorite med school professors was in his eighties. But Dr. Dixon had a white lab coat buttoned with the wrong buttons and had so much dry skin flaking off his ear that when he adjusted his hearing aid, it looked like a thin layer of salt was covering his desk.

Shudder.

He wasn't a wealth of knowledge about the school district position either. I got the impression that he was a medical director in name only when he pulled out a dusty binder when I asked what he used to look up school policy. At least I'd been emailed a copy of the contract that outlined my responsibilities in detail. Once I read the twelfth bullet point, I'd rubbed my forehead harder than normal. Four hours per week, I think not. It would take all the extra time I saved by working reduced hours at the clinic, but I'd have to deal with it. I couldn't do overnights on call anymore; it was too hard to find help. And even though I'd just gotten a response from my insurance saying that I won my appeal to cover Max's IOP bills from earlier this year, I still needed health insurance. Max's therapist had recommended DBT therapy. He also placed a referral for an updated neuropsychology evaluation after agreeing with me Max should be evaluated for autism spectrum disorder. Should he need it, he could only receive school accommodations for this if he had an official diagnosis. In a stroke of luck, Max's therapist was able to get us an expedited appointment with a pediatric neuropsychologist in Knoxville in three months.

How did a child without connections, without parental buy-in, afford and receive that kind of help? Perhaps being the medical director of the school district would be an opportunity for change.

With all of that swimming in my head, it was no wonder I couldn't concentrate on my audiobook, rewinding the same part three times before I pulled into Leah's driveway. As I walked into her house, I rolled my neck to release some of the tension that had taken up permanent residence in my upper back and shoulders.

"Hey," Leah whispered when I found her in the kitchen. She waved me down the hall, and I poked my head into their family room, seeing Ryla asleep on the couch. She was using their Bernese mountain dog, Bernie, as a pillow.

Asleep, Ryla looked like the five-year-old she still was for a few more days. Her cute, rounded cheeks and pursed mouth reminding me of Max before he lost all his baby fat. Leaving the door open a crack, I followed Leah to her kitchen.

"Where's Max?"

"He's downstairs, playing video games with Belle and Kyle."

"Really?" After his panic attack two days ago, I was living with the constant worry that he was going to relapse. But the next day he got up and went to summer school without significant fuss.

Leah winked. "It surprised me, too. But when Belle offered him the controller, he took it and sat next to her, like it was no big deal." She opened the fridge. "You want to stay for dinner? I'm making spaghetti."

I hesitated. Staying for dinner was tempting. Waking Ryla early from a nap was a guaranteed screaming match, then I'd have to get us all home, make dinner, do two nanny interviews on the phone, then get everyone settled into bed. I felt exhausted just thinking about it. But, Max was an incredibly picky eater. Unless Leah had a specific brand of dino nuggets, he wasn't going to eat anything here.

"You don't happen to have dino nuggets from the Pig, do you?" I joked humorlessly, mentally preparing to wake the sleeping dragon that was Ryla.

"Do I have dino nuggets?" Leah pulled out her freezer drawer with a flourish, displaying several boxes of the exact brand Max ate. "I saw them in your freezer and was intrigued. Eric's hooked. He's really into dinosaurs."

I almost gave her a hug. "Yes! We can stay. How can I help?"

Leah pointed to a cutting board and strainer with freshly washed strawberries on the counter. I got to work cutting them up as Leah offered me a glass of wine.

"No thanks, but I'd love an iced coffee."

Leah glanced at her watch. "This late?"

"It's going to be a long night. I have phone interviews with two nanny candidates later tonight. If they're even decently good, I'll have to beg them to start next Monday."

"How'd your meeting with Dr. Dixon go?" Leah's voice was muffled as she dug through a lower cabinet, presumably looking for a pot.

I laughed humorlessly, continuing to slice the stems off the berries, the monotonous task somehow soothing. "The most eventful part of our meeting was when the batteries for his hearing aids died, and I spent the latter half of the interview practically shouting at him. Not that he was a fountain of knowl-edge before that."

Snorting, Leah stood up, pot in hand. "Did I tell you that he was Kyle's doctor as a kid? Kyle said he seemed ancient even back then, bless his heart."

"I'm not surprised. I don't think he does much for the district."

"Do you think you're going to do it?" Leah asked while filling up the pot with water.

I shrugged. "Probably. And who knows, maybe something good can even come out of it. There were so many barriers when I tried to set up a 504 plan with Max's school in Chicago."

Leah was well aware of this as she was my main sounding board during that time. In February, when Max was ready to be discharged from his intensive outpatient program, his school told me that they wouldn't be able to determine if he was even eligible for services for two months—by which time school would almost be done for the year. And let me be clear, I wasn't worried about how he would do academically. Max was incredibly smart; his actual school-work was not a challenge for him. I worried about how he'd suffer socially with his teachers and his peers who didn't understand anxiety. Who didn't ask the questions or take the time to understand *Max*.

"That reminds me!" Leah eyes were bright as she brought the pot to the stove. "I saw Rose at school today, my friend and special ed coordinator I told you about? When I told her about you, well, if she were a dog, she'd have peed all over the floor."

I stopped cutting strawberries to look at her, "Is that a saying?"

"It could be. Too much?"

"You're right at the line."

"She'd love to talk to you. Can I give you her email? Or phone number?"

I nodded, returning to cutting the berries. "I'll talk to her."

"Great! Where's your phone?"

My hands were full of strawberry juice, so I nodded toward my purse, giving Leah my phone's passcode so she could enter Rose's contact info. I was busy chopping when I heard Leah ask, "Hey, Polly? What's this?"

"What's what?" I asked, still looking down, when I heard a voice.

"buck and groan and curse and finally, I was over, over, over that glorious edge—"

My head sprang up to see Leah gaping at my phone in her hands, the audiobook I'd been listening to earlier blaring out loud. Leah shifted to stare at me, one hand going to her mouth.

"Shit!" I cried, dropping the knife, frantically searching for something to wipe my hands on as I rounded the island hastily, but Leah held my phone out of my reach and ran around the island *in the opposite direction.*

"Turn that off!" I hissed from across the island.

There was no other word to describe Leah's expression other than gleeful as the phone continued to play.

"shaking and gasping my release, his fingers still inside of me, his lips over that bundle of nerves, his tongue wicked."

I practically threw myself across the island, grabbed the phone from Leah—strawberry hands and all—and turned it off. I considered hurling it against the wall for good measure, but settled for pressing it against my chest.

Cheeky delight filled Leah's face. "What was THAT?!" she whisper-shouted.

"It was *nothing*!" I hissed. "You heard *nothing*!" Mortified, I looked around wildly, then, spotting a roll of paper towels, I grabbed a few and wiped off my hands and phone.

"That was not nothing, that was *hot*! I didn't know you listened to books like that. How long have you been reading romance?" Leah came around the island to stand next to me.

"This is my first one," I lied, throwing the paper towels away. Leah began to bounce up and down beside me with presumed elation.

"I'm just. So. PROUD!" Leah suddenly hugged me, rocking me from side to side, like we were in the middle school bathroom after hearing a rumor that a crush had asked about us. Not that I'd had an experience like that, but I surmise that's what happened when one was in the seventh grade and actually had friends at school.

Pulling back, Leah held onto my shoulders. "Welcome."

I darted my eyes from side to side, then back to Leah, my confusion stymieing my embarrassment for a moment. "To where?"

"To the romance book club sisterhood."

"What are you talking about?"

"Women who read romance? And I'm not talking your grocery store bodice ripper, five-dollar types, though I'm not opposed to a good bodice ripping. I mean all genres of romance. Open-door, closed-door, morally gray, fantasy, rom-com. I'm here for all of it. But I didn't know *you* would be!"

She started to dance what looked to be a mix between the running man and cabbage patch. Noticing my wary expression, she stopped. "Unless . . . you're really telling me the truth? *Is* this your first one?" Leah almost sounded disappointed.

I glanced over my shoulder, making sure we were alone. "Of course it's not my first one," I whispered. "But I don't *talk* to anyone about it!"

This had Leah dancing around me all over again. "Well butter my butt and call me a biscuit! This is the best surprise ever. I never knew you liked reading romance, like the rest of us enlightened ones. There's so few of us." She said that last part to herself, solemnly, then held out her hand to me.

"Alright, let me see it."

"What?"

"Your Kindle library. And Audible library. Are you a Kobo girl? Google Play? Oh! Do you Hoopla! Or Libby? Our library is getting really good, we have an in with one of the librarians." Leah clapped her hands again. "I've been reading romance for years! When did you start? I can't wait to talk about it with you!"

Leah was talking so fast, like she usually did when she got excited, that it took me a minute to process. "I've been reading romance since I was pregnant with Ryla. There was a *Twilight* marathon on TV, and I couldn't sleep. I was curious what all the fuss was about."

Leah nodded, her tone becoming reverent. "*Twilight*. It paved the way for so many of us." She tilted her head to the side, her expression turning sad. "Have you really never talked to anyone about what you read? Talking about books is half the fun of reading."

I opened my mouth, but she cut me off before I could answer.

"Forget I asked that, stupid question. Of course you haven't told anyone. Not that I don't understand. We're conditioned to think that reading romance is shameful and dirty and just for us lonely mommas," she said with a roll of her eyes.

While her comment stung a bit, she wasn't wrong. It's why I hadn't told anyone about reading romance. The appearance of impropriety was something I'd been strictly programmed to protect against. And not only that, I feared no one would take me seriously if they knew I read romance. It became a dirty secret; or at least, a secret part of me I didn't share with anyone.

But this was Leah, my best friend, and although it was hard for me to trust anyone, I trusted her. Sighing, I pulled up my Kindle app and handed her my phone.

"Have at it."

Exclaiming gleefully, Leah plopped herself down on a stool as I finished slicing the last of the strawberries. Leah was smiling and talking quietly to herself as she scrolled through my collection. "You have such a great taste in books! You'll have to send me screenshots of your library."

Leah put down my phone and went to the stove, turning on the burner to let the water boil before she spoke again.

"You should come to my book club. We try to get together once a month. Now that I know that you read the same stuff, you'd be the perfect addition."

Apprehension coiled its way around my body. I knew I'd regret talking about this. The thought of talking to women I've never met before, and about romance novels no less, made my palms sweat.

At my silence, she asked. "What's going on in that brilliant brain of yours?"

I shrugged. "I've never been great at making girlfriends."

Leah scowled. "I blame your daddy and the lack of sleepovers. But what about friends in college?"

For some reason, my reply was hesitant, trusting Leah . . . but still finding it hard to tell her the truth.

"I didn't have many." *Any.* "I was in a single dorm room and studying took up most of my time so I could graduate in three years. I rarely went to parties." *Never.* "Then in medical school, I met David. Any friends I made after that were *our* friends, never mine. And he kept them all in the divorce." *Not that they really knew the real me.*

Giving me a determined look, Leah crossed her arms. "Alright. Our next book club is next week, Saturday, and you're coming."

"But—" I started.

Leah shook her head. There was no compromising with her. "It's done. Kyle can watch the kids. It won't be a tough sell to get my kids to your house anyway. They found out you had an inground pool from Ryla this week."

"What if I don't want to go?" I hedged.

"You'll love the book! I picked one of my all-time favorites. It's a slow burn grumpy sunshine about a vegan professional football player who pays his ex-assistant to marry him so he can stay in the country. He's from Canada." Leah snapped her finger. "Ha! You're already intrigued, I can tell. Come on, you can bring all the iced coffee you can drink, what do you say?"

I sent her a reproachful glare. "You could charm the skin off a snake."

"Attagirl! You can take the girl out of the South, but not the South out of the girl. You're just one y'all away from eatin' grits in the mornin'!"

I groaned. "I'm going to regret this, aren't I?"

"Nothing ventured, and all that. Now let's talk about that book you were listening to . . ."

CHAPTER
EIGHT

JACE

Talking about my love life with my mother was as helpful as googling symptoms when feeling sick. I'd only end up feeling worse.

Piper Sheldon, *Stranger Than Fan Fiction*

"Aww, look at you, baby brother. You look like an actual man!" I swung my head from where I'd been sitting at the bar and did a double take. My sister, Sarah, was walking toward me. Her hair had always been a longer version of mine, down past her shoulders, but now there were large sections of bright pink scattered amongst her dark brown curls.

"I've always been a man," I grumbled as I got up from my chair to give her a hug.

I'd been ready to pick her up from the airport when she'd texted me that she was getting her own ride and would meet me at the Front Porch to keep me company when I waited for a table.

Sarah grabbed my cheeks and smushed them together, moving my head back and forth. "Of course you are."

I scowled then scooped her up, spinning her around. "Could a teenager do this?" I grinned down at her after putting her back on her feet. "It's good to see you, Sarah. You look beautiful."

"Always the charmer," she said as she took the seat next to mine. "I'm sure you've heard about the absurd idea of Momma and Daddy moving to Florida?"

"I've been so informed."

"This is all Kent's doing. I heard he's struggling to get sales. It's not gonna happen. There is no way. I love him, but Daddy moves slower than molasses. It took them ages just to get cell phones."

I inwardly shuddered as I took a pull of my beer. My unofficial role at home was also helping my parents with every single piece of technology in the house, including setting up their Wi-Fi. It's a lesson in patience each time. Pop still thanked Alexa whenever he asked her a question and he frequently asks how she's been.

"What are you gonna do if they move?"

I glanced at her out of the corner of my eye. "Do you mean, am I going to stay in Green Valley?"

"Come on, Jace. You're so young. Don't you want to travel, see the world? You don't have a career, or strings, to hold you here anymore. You're free!"

"If I wanted to travel, Sarah, that's what I'd be doing."

As a rule, I'm not against travel. I went on a handful of trips with Sam and our buddy Owen over the last few years, but it never caught my interest. Give me the clean, sweet mountain air of the Smokies and I'm happy.

"Are Momma and Daddy still giving you shit about not having a job?"

I covered my heart. "You wound me. I have several jobs."

"I mean a "real job"," she explained, making finger quotes as she spoke.

"Golly, gee, Sarah. Do ya mean one of them fancy jobs that pays you in real money?"

"I mean a career, smart-ass."

"I'm happy where I am. You know I don't want to spend my time and money studying for a career I don't want. I just haven't found it yet."

"I'm not here to judge." Sarah held up her hands. "I only want you to be happy."

"I am happy."

Though, this was starting to feel untrue. And yet, this was not something Sarah needed to know.

"Then I'm happy." We were quiet for a minute, until she turned her head toward me again. "Soooo, any girls in the picture?"

I glanced at my watch. "You made it a whole five minutes. It might be a record."

"Come on. Look at you! Look at your hair! I bet you have girls offering themselves to you right and left."

I mean, she wasn't wrong. There was a lot of interest. But none of the women felt right. I was waiting for a woman who wanted the real me. I was waiting for a woman who felt necessary—essential to my survival. Because that's what I wanted. It's just like with a career. Once I found what I wanted, whether it be a career or a woman, there would be no going back for me. Once I'm in, I'm in, one hundred percent.

But again, Sarah didn't need to know that.

"No one that's caught my interest enough to date seriously." As I said it, I recognized the lie for what it was. There was a woman who'd caught my interest, more than caught if I was being truthful. A sexy blonde with long legs, a sharp tongue, and an ass I'd like to—

"Sure, Romeo. Tell that to your eyes that just went all hazy." Sarah rubbed her hands together. "Please? I won't say anything to Momma, I swear."

"Tell you what, Sarah. I promise to text you the minute I like a woman, and she likes me back. That enough to calm your britches?"

"Deal."

———

The Front Porch's steak was good. The grilling of my sister was even better. I loved my sister, but seeing the shock on my momma's face when she and Pop arrived warmed my heart.

They were in a standoff now, sitting across from one another at our table, identical stubborn looks on their faces.

"Did you have to go with bright pink?" Momma asked, lips pursed.

I swallowed a chuckle by taking a pull from my beer. Maybe I'd even order a whiskey next. After all, the heat was off me for one evening, the medium rare steak I'd ordered was melting in my mouth, and my brother, was late.

"Momma. I'm thirty-four years old. I am financially independent, live in a fabulous condo, and am thoroughly happy in my career."

"But, your law partners. What must they think?"

Sarah leaned forward, not giving an inch, staring Momma down. "They think I'm a talented lawyer who doesn't do trial work and makes them a lot of money. It doesn't make one bit of difference what color my hair is."

"Nick, say something."

Pop, who was clearly avoiding the conversation, jerked at the mention of his name. Turning to my sister, he cleared his throat. "I think you look lovely, sugar, as always."

I couldn't hold back my guffaw.

"Thank you, Daddy." Sarah fluttered her eyelashes as Momma looked up to the ceiling in exasperation.

"The prodigal son has arrived!" My stomach sank as Kent came in, announcing himself with arms stretched wide.

I wanted to say, *It's returned*, but cut off a large piece of steak instead.

"Kent!" Momma stood, eyes beaming as Kent gave her a hug and kiss on the cheek.

Kent and I weren't close on account of him being fourteen years older than me and a complete horse's ass. Kent and Sarah were also like oil and water. They had an intense sibling rivalry growing up.

Kent surveyed the rest of the lowly people—his siblings—at the table.

"Fucking hell," he shouted, doing a double take at Sarah.

"Kent!" Momma exclaimed, and my sister barred her teeth like she was about to spring across the table and attack him.

"Easy," I murmured, putting my hand on Sarah's arm. Not that I wouldn't be on Sarah's side.

"I'm so sorry, Momma," Kent crooned, apologizing to the wrong person. "Sarah. Your hair's different, I almost didn't recognize you."

"Yeah, doesn't she look great?" I raised my eyebrows.

"Yeah, like I said, different." He took the seat next to Momma, which put him directly across from me.

"Little brother. Look at you. You old enough for that beer?" He smiled disingenuously, or maybe that was his normal smile.

I made a show of looking at my watch. "Did your flight get in late, Kent? Or maybe your driver took a wrong turn?"

Smile flattening, he narrowed his eyes on me. "There was traffic in Knoxville. Something you'd know if you lived anywhere else but this podunk town."

Kent flagged down a server who happened to be walking by. "I'd like a pour of Blanton's, neat, in a Glencairn."

The server hesitated, glancing at our table briefly, then back to the self-proclaimed prodigal son. "Sure, I'll just . . . find your server."

"So." Kent looked between our parents. "Did either of you tell them the news?"

"We wanted to wait for you to share the happy news," my momma replied.

"What news are you talking about, Momma?" Sarah's face mirrored how I felt on the inside. Uneasy.

"I put in their offer on the condo in Florida, and it was accepted. It's move in ready. Which means, once everything's final, Mom and Dad are moving to sunny Florida!"

Sarah and I didn't speak—shock tended to do that to a person.

"Oops," my brother said, leaning forward and rummaging around the bread-basket, touching every single roll before taking the first one he'd touched. "Did you two not know? I know they were worried about their little boy. Didn't want to move away and leave you here all alone."

Momma's smile was stiff, and Pop looked at Kent a little sharply.

Plastering an easy smile on my face, I leaned back, not wanting him to get the best of me.

"Pop and I talked about it. In fact, I have a place all lined up. Signed the lease this morning and move in on Monday." It was a complete and utter falsehood, but I'd sleep on the couch in Sam's pussy palace if it meant saving face in front of Kent.

"Son, there's no need to do that. We haven't even put the house up for sale yet. There's plenty of time to—"

"No, it's time. But still count me in on whatever help you need. I'm only a few minutes' drive away, until you move to Florida, that is." I could see the worry in my momma's eyes. We had a complicated relationship, sure, but it was mostly good. So, I took a breath and held up my beer for a toast. "I'm happy for y'all, really. This is supposed to be a celebration, right? Pop, congrats on another trip around the sun. You made seventy-four look great, but here's to seventy-five." Saluting my pop, I then raised my beer to Kent and gave him a stiff nod.

"I'm sure Kent will have your back in Florida, same as I have here."

The threat in my eyes was clear: He better not fuck with them.

CHAPTER
NINE

POLLY

"It's a bird!"

"It's a plane!"

Jenny rolled her eyes. "It's a penis, you morons."

Drags to Riches by Ann Richter
Narrated by Nikki Martin

"Mommyyyyy! The goat's chasing me!"

I charged after the little goat who was chasing Ryla around our backyard, nipping at her pretty rainbow birthday dress.

"Shoo! Shoo!" I grabbed the little menace and carried it over to the makeshift pen, plunking it down with the rest of the escape artists. It bleated, displeased with being recaptured.

Ryla's birthday party had been going well, until the goats from the petting zoo started escaping like tiny Houdinis. How they were getting out, I had no idea. It was bad enough that they pooped little pellets all over our backyard, but every time the kids got near them, they'd not only eaten the corn feed the kids held out, but tried to inhale the kids' shirts as well.

"Everyone!" I shouted to the party guests that were mingling on the stone patio and around the pool. "Until we have the goat situation under control, please move inside the house!"

I strode over to the guy in charge of the petting zoo. "I don't know what you have to do, but if these goats manage to get out again and eat any of my guests' clothing, not only will you reimburse them for the damage, but I will be getting a full refund, you hear me?"

The punk, who was wearing earbuds, continued looking at his phone like I wasn't even talking.

"Do you hear me?" I snapped my fingers in front of his face, feeling like I was ninety-five and poking him with a cane.

He finally glanced up at me, eyes hazy. "Bet." I caught a vague whiff of marijuana.

Huh. Perhaps he knew Clarice.

At least Ryla looked like she was having a good time. We started the day on the right foot when she actually let me wrangle her hair into two French braids without any screaming. She skyped with Giselle without any tears, and Max didn't immediately go to his room once the guests arrived, even though I'd made the rule that he was allowed to go into his room during the party if he needed a break. Leah had awoken bright and early and was my saving grace all day. She offered to keep an eye on my kids during the party so I could manage the guests, taking that worry off my mental plate. About a half hour before the party started, Sam from the Jack of All Trades company I'd hired to organize the party's entertainment arrived with the petting zoo . . . and that's when things started to unravel.

Just as the first guests arrived, Sam got an emergency call and had to leave. Then, the unseasonably hot summer weather started to make everything melt, so we had to move all the food inside. After that, a cry erupted from a little girl near the games area when a little goat started nipping at her untucked shirt from behind. Within the next five minutes, all the goats began to make their move, acting like convicts in a jailbreak, looking for any fence weaknesses.

Ensuring that no one except the goats and their wrangler were outside, I shut the sliding porch door and turned around . . . to absolute chaos.

I had planned for an outdoor party, and now the kids were running around the kitchen as though they'd never been inside a house before. Walking into the living room, things just got worse. The kids were using the toys I'd intended for outside use—large bouncy balls, foam airplanes, Hula-Hoops—like they were in a rage room.

Ding-dong! I heard the doorbell chime as Ryla shouted, "Mom! Can we open the Silly String?" from across the room.

"No!" I shouted back over the chaos, then heard the doorbell again.

Rushing to the front door, hoping against hope it was the magician coming to salvage this party, I opened the door and gasped, jumping back and slamming it shut. Heart thundering in my chest, I hesitantly opened the door and peered outside, half wondering if it was a figment of my imagination.

Nope. Not my imagination. There, standing in between the stone pillars of the front porch, was a clown.

He looked like every other clown that haunted my dreams: white face paint, creepy ruby-red smile, red ball nose, and rainbow wig. The clown wore a yellow suit with white polka dots and looking down, I saw the ensemble was complete with large red clown shoes. He wasn't speaking, just staring at me with wide eyes.

I leaned slightly to the side, peering around him, then looked behind me—we were alone. This didn't appear to be a prank.

"Are you here for . . . the party?" I held my breath, fearing the answer. I distinctly remembered emailing Sam and asking for a magician—*no clowns*. I think I'd even underlined it.

The clown didn't reply. Was this one of those creepy clown mimes?

Frowning, I tried again. "I'm Polly Alberton. My daughter's sixth birthday party is today. I had requested a magician. Were you hired by Jack of All Trades?"

After one more pause, as if I'd chugged a quarter into a game slot, the clown opened their mouth and pointed at me.

"Right you are! Nice to meet you. I am Kent the Clown!" His voice was exaggerated, like a DJ of olde. "And I'm ready to amaze the birthday girl and all of your guests. I'm the master of magic tricks, the bringer of balloon animals, and the maker of your child's dreams come true!"

And then he did a little pose, complete with spirit fingers.

So, not a clown mime, then.

Though, perhaps someone I shouldn't bring near children . . . at least not until I asked for ID.

I'd just opened my mouth to ask for said ID, when an authoritative voice came from my left, up the front walkway.

"Polly?"

In horror, I turned to see my father, Judge Alan Alberton himself, walking toward us. Wearing a crisp shirt and black slacks, he was eyeing me and the clown. Hard.

"Father!" I exclaimed, painting on a smile wider than the clown's. "I didn't know you were coming!"

He stopped a few feet from the clown, giving him one more long look, then turned to me. "I received an invitation in the mail."

He had? How could he have . . . *Jeffrey.* I'd sent him a mock-up of the invitation last week to ask if I could have a petting zoo in the backyard. He must have sent it to the judge.

My father's gaze continued to move between me and the clown. "The invitation didn't say anything about clowns."

Yeah. No shit.

"Didn't it?" My voice was high and tight. "This is Ryla's birthday surprise. She LOVES clowns. Carlos here"—

"Kent," not-Carlos murmured.

—"KENT!" I said loudly, correcting myself, "is the uh, minister of magic and the baker of balloons!"

Nope. That wasn't it.

"The kids are going to love him!"

Keep going, Polly! In for a penny, in for a pound!

"Ryla will be thrilled to see you!" I lied. "Please, come inside." Realizing I'd been twisting my earring, I dropped my hand to my side and stepped back, waving my father inside. It should be troubling how easy the lies came to me, but I'd spent a lifetime lying to this man. He practically harrumphed and strode past me.

"The refreshments are in the kitchen!" I shouted after him, wide smile in place. My smile fell immediately after turning to find that the clown had also begun to make his way inside.

"Not so fast!" I hissed, stepping in front of him as he was about to cross the threshold. I put my hand to his stomach, effectively blocking him. I almost reared back because his abs were *rock hard.*

Apparently, this clown went to the gym.

Shaking off the weird thought, I took a quick glance behind me to make sure the coast was clear, then glared at Carlos the Creeper, lowering my voice.

"Look, Carlos," I started, then seeing the clown open his mouth, I shook my head. "I mean Kent. Whatever your name is. If you were hired by the company, great. I wanted a magician, but who the hell cares. I'm only letting you in the house to save face with my father. If you scare or hurt anyone, including but not limited to my children or any other child here, I will cut your balls off with a razor and feed them to the goats out back, you got me?"

The clown's face went slack. Satisfied, I stepped back, removing my hand from his washboard abs, and nodded.

"Fantastic." I hooked a thumb over my shoulder. "Party's through here."

CHAPTER TEN

JACE

L.H. Cosway, *Painted Faces*

Sweat poured down my body underneath my neon yellow clown costume. It was over a hundred degrees outside, the sun mercilessly beating down on me as I set up my clown show in the backyard of Polly freaking Alberton's house. The sweatband I wore under the rainbow wig was already soaked. My skin had begun to itch a few minutes ago. What the hell was in this makeup?

These were only some of the reasons that Sam, was now a dead man.

Polly already thought I was a pervert before I showed up at her daughter's birthday party dressed as a clown. If she found out it was me underneath this neon yellow monstrosity, I was almost certainly going to end up in jail. I could only hope Jackson was the officer who was called to the scene. On second thought, I hoped it was anyone but Jackson. He'd be all business, taking my mugshot, fingerprints, the whole deal, and then he'd tell Rae, who'd tell Sienna, and I'd never live it down.

"Are you my magician?"

Turning at the clear, high-pitched voice behind me, I saw Ryla, wearing a giant birthday crown and rainbow dress, complete with rainbows drawn on her cheeks. I took a look around, but besides the imprisoned baby goats, bleating for their lives, no one else seemed to be out here.

I still took a wide step back from Ryla, making it clear to anyone watching that nothing inappropriate was happening.

"You must be the birthday girl! Yes! I'm Kent the Clown, here to amaze you with magic and wonder!"

Unconvinced, the tiny birthday girl in front of me narrowed her eyes. "Prove it."

I attempted to swallow, though my mouth was already bone-dry after the interaction with her momma earlier.

"Your wish is my command." I kneeled down as I tried to hide the tiny adjustment I made to my sleeve. "But first, a little present for the birthday girl!" I made a faux flower bouquet appear from my sleeve. I looked at the bouquet, then to Ryla, like, *ta-da!*

She'd jumped back when the bouquet first appeared, then hesitantly took a step forward to accept it. Tilting her head, she assessed me dubiously, correctly sizing me up as the clown imposter I was.

"Not bad. But can you do real magic?"

I put a hand over my heart. "That was real magic, of course! But yes, only the best tricks for you today. But first, hey! What's that?"

As soon as I pulled the coin from behind her ear, the next trick in my arsenal, I remembered that I'd done this for her a few days ago. But it was too late. Ryla's face lit when she first saw the coin, but then her expression turned quickly from suspicious to *elated.* Her mouth fell open and her eyes went comically wide, like my makeup and wig were stripped off.

"Mr. Jace?" she whispered.

Nervously, I ducked down, darting my head back and forth to check around us, and decided to come clean.

"Yeah, it's me. I wanted to surprise you on your big day," I whispered, thankful no one else was around when she launched herself at me, hugging me.

She was sturdy for a little thing. I was kneeling and almost fell over. Hugging her back, more to help steady us both, I quickly set her away from me.

"But no one else knows it's me. I'm tryin' to break into the clown business," I lied, feeling horrible. "So if you wouldn't mind *not* telling your momma—"

I heard the patio door open, and my eyes locked with Leah Michaels, who taught third grade at the elementary school. And boy oh boy did she eye me *hard*. Ryla looked over and waved at Leah, whose face instantly transformed into a sweet smile.

"—or your Auntie Leah," I added under my breath, "I'd appreciate it."

Ryla shook her head, laughing. "That's mommy's friend, Leah. She's not my aunt!"

I kept my tone hushed. "Still, if you could keep this between you and me, just for now, I promise I'll make this the best show ever!"

She made a zipping motion of her lips then ran up the stairs and into the house. Leah gave Ryla a warm smile as she ran past her, then looked at me, her smile dropping instantly. She pointed two fingers to her eyes, then pointed them to me; the *I'm watching you* message was received loud and clear.

If my mouth hadn't already been bone-dry, I'd have gulped. I was definitely going to jail.

———

"Hiya, kids! I'm Kent the Clown! And I hear there's a very special birthday today, and I'm here to celebrate with you!"

Crickets.

No wait, bleating. All I could hear was the bleating of the tiny goats who were all staring at me from inside their pen on the lawn.

Shaving his head. Gluing his socks together. Putting water in his gas tank.

All of these retribution options were too tame for my former best friend, the one I texted quickly after finding Sam was missing from the party.

The kids sat silently on the stone stairs in front of me, their parents behind them. All of whom were staring blankly at me. Because people, as a rule, do not like clowns. When Polly first led me through the house to the backyard, one girl screamed and ran away, crying for her momma.

Polly was standing in the back, arms crossed. Her daddy stood to her left, arms also crossed. I stood up straighter. I had a job to do. And I didn't want to ruin Ryla's birthday. The show must go on.

"What do I have here?" I held up three raw eggs. The two prop eggs I'd need later were hidden safely in the pouch at my waist. Two hands shot up.

"What do you think, little lady?" I pointed to a girl in a green dress.

"Eggs."

"Right you are. Here, pass these around, but make sure not to crack them. I want everyone to feel 'em and verify that they are, indeed, real eggs."

As the eggs were being passed around, I addressed the audience again. "Now can anyone tell me, what we do with eggs?"

A few hands went up. Maybe this wouldn't be too bad after all. I pointed at another kid. "Eat them!" was his reply as all three eggs were passed back to me.

Nodding I shouted, "That's right, juggling them!"

A few giggles and startled shouts came from the kids in the front as I began juggling the eggs practically over their heads. They squealed and laughed as I pretended to bobble them.

But I wouldn't drop them. I'd practiced this bit for over a year starting at age twelve. It didn't make me many friends, but I could still juggle in my sleep.

I stopped juggling the eggs and held my hand to my ear. "What's that? Y'all *eat* your eggs? Well, shoot. I forgot you can eat 'em too. Now, who here thinks these eggs are real?"

Almost every hand shot up, but I pretended not to see them.

"None of you? Really? Alright then, I guess it's ok for me to do this!" I heard a collective gasp as I brought an egg up high over my head, then quickly smashed it over my little clown cap I'd put on over my wig. The yolk and slimy egg white dripped down my wig and onto the ground.

Actually, the wig came in handy. When I used to do this in my magic show, I did it on my forehead, and the egg would run down my face.

I was delighted at the kids' happy squeals. Going on with the show, I made a disgusted face.

"Who put a real egg in here?" I pointed at a few kids. "You?" A little girl shook her head furiously, then pointed to a little boy next to her who shook his head, too.

"I guess these *are* real eggs! Darn it all, now I only have two." I made a big show of holding up the remaining two eggs for all to see, then exaggeratedly snapped my fingers.

"Hang on a sec, I remember puttin' a spare somewhere . . . here it is!"

I retrieved one of the two prop eggs from my waist pouch, now holding two real eggs and one prop egg in my hands. As soon as I brought the fake prop egg out, I started to juggle the eggs again, walking near the kids and juggling almost over their heads again. It was then that I noticed the patio door slide open, and a bright blonde head with green eyes peeked out, watching intently.

"Now, where's the birthday girl?" I asked the crowd, stopping my juggling and making a big show of searching the crowd, even though Ryla was sitting front and center.

"She's here! Ryla's right here!" A kid I recognized as Eric stood up and pointed at Ryla excitedly from his spot next to her.

"Come on up here, little lady."

Smiling, Ryla scrambled up. Her crown had gone a little crooked since I'd last seen her. When she got close to me, she gave me a small wink. I put the two real eggs in my waist pouch and held up the empty prop egg.

"Listen up, folks. For Ryla's special birthday surprise, we need the contents of this egg to turn into a chick. And you have to help me do it. So, on the count of three, I need you to shout, 'OOGALY BOOGALY!'"

I had them practice a few times, the kids getting more and more into it with each try.

Glancing at the parents, I saw there weren't as many frowns, and Polly's arms were no longer crossed, which I was taking as an absolute win.

I gestured to Ryla. "Now, little miss, you have special birthday magic. On the count of three, I want you to shout, 'Oogaly boogaly!' along with everyone else. And you'll need to wiggle your fingers right at the egg. Can you do that?"

She nodded.

"Alright. One, two, three—"

"Oogaly boogaly!"

As everyone screamed, I noticed Max, who had started watching us from the patio door earlier, was now standing fully outside, back up against the door.

I shook the egg, pretending that it had worked and was now ready.

"Magnificent!" I cried. "Now, let's crack this open to see if it worked!"

Gasps filled the crowd as I cracked the prop egg over Ryla's crown. Then, the gasps turned to clapping and impressed shouts as everyone realized the egg was empty and there were only a few little pieces of shell falling to the ground.

I put on a puzzled expression, eating up the kid's amazed reactions.

"Huh. That's funny, I swore I heard fluttering inside this egg." And then I snapped my fingers and grabbed the other prop egg from my waist pouch, which, unbeknownst to everyone, came complete with a wind-up chick inside.

"Alright, let's try this again. One, two, three! Oogaly boogaly!"

After I cracked the egg and held up the wind-up chick, Ryla beamed, the crowd clapped, and thank you Jesus and the Holy Goats, Polly was smiling.

———

I was zipping my duffel closed as I used the back of my thumb to scratch beneath my wig. My skin had gone past itching to burning before the clown show started. Of course, I'd then stayed to sing 'Happy Birthday' to Ryla, who also asked if Kent the Clown would stick around for cake. My eyes had started to water so badly, I was going to have trouble seeing the road; but I wasn't going to risk taking off my makeup here.

"Hi! I wanted to catch you before . . . are you alright?" I squinted to see a blurry Leah Michaels in front of me.

I waved her off. "This is my last bag so I'll be out of here soon. I'll be alright." If me being five minutes from having the skin melt off my face was considered alright, so be it.

Leah took a step closer to me. "Jace? Is that you?"

Damn. I'd forgotten to use my clown voice. Ducking my head as I hoisted the bag over my shoulder, I gave a sheepish smile in her direction. "Oh, uh, yeah. Hi, Leah. Just doing a favor for a friend."

I didn't want to be rude, but I needed to go or else I was going to start scratching my face so hard it was going to bleed. "I think I'm having a little reaction to the face paint. If you'll excuse me." I started to walk off, desperate to get some relief, when Leah jumped in front of me.

"I had no idea it was you! You sure outdid yourself." Leah paused. "Do you need a bathroom? Or like, a doctor?"

Probably. I shook my head, just wanting to get out of there. "Eh, I'm fine. It could be worse."

Leah crossed her arms, I think. I was having a hard time seeing her.

"Sure thing, I'll let you go. But only if you can tell me how many fingers I'm holding up."

I squinted at her fingers.

"Three?" I guessed.

"Four." She grabbed my forearm and started to pull me toward the house. "Come on, Kent. I'll show you to a bathroom no one uses. Then you can make a quick getaway in your clown car."

CHAPTER
ELEVEN

POLLY

Rock bottom is the only bottom I've touched in over a year. So, yeah. It's been quite a dry spell.

Drags to Riches by Ann Richter
Narrated by Nikki Martin

After the clown show came cake and presents, after which the party wound down. In the biggest surprise of the day, Kent the Clown's act wasn't creepy. He had the kids eating out of his hand, and even the adults were entertained. There was one bit near the end when he started to do a soft shoe dance routine with a broom and coat that had the kids cracking up whereas I, on the other hand, appreciated it due to something else. By that point Kent's yellow costume had started to stick to him, unsurprisingly due to the heat, but it showed off his toned body underneath as he swayed and dipped the broom. I didn't think I'd ever be attracted to a clown, but perhaps this was a new low. I'd become so sex deprived that I was now lusting after clowns.

I was saying goodbye and handing out treat bags to the kids when the one person I'd managed to avoid for most of the day came up to me.

"Polly, if I could have a word."

I gave my father a stiff nod, then handed off the last treat bag to a little boy and waved goodbye at his mother, then shut the front door.

"Where would you like to talk?" I asked the judge.

He turned silently, so I followed him into the small study near the entrance.

"A few things," he began. "First, I can't make brunch tomorrow. I was invited to a golf outing with some important people. We will resume the regular brunch schedule next week."

My giddy relief at having Sunday brunch cancelled was short-lived as he continued on.

"Second, Jeffrey hasn't heard from you regarding the email he sent this week. As I was coming here, I told him I would verify your choice of nanny with you."

He took a folded paper from his pocket and handed it to me. Opening it revealed pictures and short bios for the nannies I remembered seeing in Jeffrey's email.

"All of these nannies are able to relocate here for one year. I will pay their salary. They will report to both you and I. If they are found to be insufficient, a replacement will be sent."

I continued to stare at the paper, but fury interfered with my ability to process any information. Perhaps any other single mother would jump at this chance. Perhaps I was being ungrateful?

I looked up at my father silently. His expression was predictably stoic.

"And if I may be frank, Polly, I can't help but say how disappointed I am. The party today was in poor taste. My granddaughter was running around wildly and barely acknowledged me in my own home. I rarely saw Max and when I did, he didn't say a word to me. From the way you and your children behaved to how they were dressed, it was completely inappropriate. Our family is to be held to a higher standard. My nomination to the Tennessee Supreme Court is on the line. You should be instilling your children with decorum and discipline. Maybe then, they would be normal."

Nope. I wasn't being ungrateful.

I was becoming *unglued*. I jerkily folded the paper and thrust it back to him.

"If you cannot choose a nanny, then I will be forced—" He was still talking when I uncharacteristically cut him off.

"I already hired a nanny."

He stilled, clearly caught off guard.

"And I'm signing a new contract with Mercy Health next week. A full-time position. So, while I appreciate your help," I had to practically spit the words out of my mouth, they tasted so bitter, "I will not be needing any additional assistance."

The rigidity in my spine increased as I layered lie upon lie. My chest ached with pressure and tears burned behind my eyes. I was two point six seconds from seriously losing my shit.

"Excuse me." I brushed past him and retreated blindly down the hallway, somehow ending up in my parent's old bedroom. I'd only come in here a handful of times since we'd moved in—mostly to drop off clean towels when Mrs. Simon had stayed overnight. Leah found it too unsettling to sleep in here, opting to sleep on the couch in the living room instead.

It was dark, so I couldn't see much. It smelled of dust and like any room left long undisturbed, there was a certain stillness about the air. As my eyes adjusted to the dark, I took in the familiar layout of the room. It hadn't changed in thirty-eight years. An antique four poster bed was on the left side of the room, headboard against the wall. The bathroom and closet were off to my right, opposite the bed. Straight ahead, on the far side of the room, was an ornate fireplace and sitting area. My father had kept my mother's shrine well preserved. Everything was precisely how it had been when my mother was alive and yet, nothing was the same.

Keeping the lights off, I leaned back against the closed door and dropped my face in my hands, finally able to let out a stifled scream.

Wiping my hands down my face, I stared unseeingly in front of me, my mind going a mile a minute. How dare my father do this? How dare I *let* my father do this? Did I really need his help so much? What was I going to do? I either needed to pick a nanny or move out. If it were only me to think about, I'd gladly move out and stay in a rusted tin can to spite him. But moving my kids again, after all the changes they've had this year?

How did I let myself get into this situation?

My eyes had now fully adjusted to the dark, letting me take in the familiar wainscoting, the white marble of the unused fireplace, and the floor-to-ceiling windows on either side of the fireplace; their rose window valences and thick curtains were pulled tight, a thin line of sunlight hinting at the edges.

"Actually, Father," I said aloud, no one around to hear me except the ghost of my mother, "thanks, but no thanks. I'd rather live on peanut butter and moldy bread than take one more cent from you. Not only are you a terrible father, but somehow, you've managed to be an even worse grandfather. Congratulations! And while I'm at it, thank you for screwing me up so much, that I married the first person who showed me a pale impression of love, thinking it was the real thing until, surprise! I acted however he wanted me to act, thinking it was the only way he'd love me, twisting myself up into a pretzel so tightly, I don't even know who I am anymore!"

I bent forward and rested my hands on my knees, sucking in air, gripping them tight. I did feel marginally better. Not good, but less unhinged. Maybe I'd have to come in here to rage more often.

I was about to turn and leave when the door to the ensuite bathroom suddenly opened. Jumping back, I rammed my head and back into the door and shouted. I had no idea what I said, I was too focused on not getting murdered by the murderer that came through the door.

But it wasn't a murderer.

There, looking equally stunned, hair wet, face red and blotchy, was Jace Vargas. He held a black shirt to his bare, ripped chest, and a yellow clown costume was tied at his waist.

Fucking hell!

Jace was Kent the Clown!

Sidenote: He had a six pack.

Second sidenote: I wanted to touch it.

"What the hell are you doing in here?!" I shrieked.

Jace opened his mouth as the doorknob to the bedroom turned, causing me to stumble forward allowing the door to open to reveal . . . my father.

Because this day couldn't get any worse.

My father's head jerked back and forth between the shirtless Jace and me, finally settling on me.

"Polly? What is going on in here?"

Pointing at Jace, I blurted the first thing that popped into my head.

"He's our new nanny!"

CHAPTER
TWELVE

JACE

I would say it was nice to meet you, but I was naked so . . . it wasn't.

Samantha Young, *On Dublin Street*

After Leah showed me to a bathroom, I'd quickly washed off the makeup to reveal a nasty red rash on my face and neck. I filled up the sink with cold water and began submerging my head for as long as I could hold my breath with palpable relief. I'd just gone for my last dip when I thought I heard something from the next room. Taking my head out of the water, I waited for another noise but heard nothing. Feeling like I'd been in here too long, I grabbed a towel, my skin burning at the touch as I pressed it to my face to dry off. I'd also rinsed my shirt as it had been soaked with sweat, so I wrung it out and shook it, not looking forward to the burn I'd feel pulling it over my head. Slinging the shirt over my bare shoulder to delay the inevitable, I opened the bathroom door.

"Fucking molasses!"

Startling hard, I pressed my shirt to my chest and stumbled backward. My mouth went slack as I stared at Polly Alberton, who was standing against the door, green eyes livid.

"What the hell are you doing in here?" she yelled—and I mean, *yelled*—but not before I noticed her eyes rake up and down my shirtless chest.

I honestly had no words. Probably the reason why I was standing in her house shirtless with a clown suit tied at my waist would be a good start, but before I got the chance, her daddy burst into the room.

He also had a great question. What was going on here, indeed? I was debating if I could make a run for it in these shoes, when Polly pointed at me.

"He's our new nanny!"

Shock froze my body. What did she just say?

"What do you mean, he's your nanny?" Face furious, Polly's father continued to look between us. I remained motionless.

Polly clasped her hands behind her back and took a step to the side, like a soldier at ease. "He's the nanny I hired to watch Ryla and Max. We met when he was working with the school summer program. He also runs a theater program here in Green Valley for kids and offered to do the clown bit for Ryla as a surprise for her birthday."

I did a double take because Polly just lied like a pro, her entire demeanor morphing from startled, to angry, to calm faster than I could juggle three eggs.

And I was an excellent juggler.

Polly's father looked me up and down, as if judging the veracity of Polly's words. I smiled hesitantly.

"He looks familiar. Who are you?" he barked.

Spurred into action, I piped up, my voice squeaking for the first time in ten years. "Jace. Jace Vargas, sir," I added, holding out my hand that he *didn't* come forward to shake.

Moving his gaze from me, he glared at Polly with hard eyes. I instinctively took a step closer to her.

"This is my father, Judge Alan Alberton," Polly explained calmly to me, still acting as if everything was normal.

Oh, my fuck. Her daddy was a judge? I bet he was good at his job, because I'd never felt more judged in my entire life. A prickling sensation came over my body at his calculating stare. Or maybe that was the rash.

From what I'd heard, a county jail was very different from prison. Local cops. Interesting company. Someone new always coming and going. Sure, there was probably only one toilet and a dirty blanket stiff from someone else's urine, but you didn't have to be anyone's bitch to survive.

At least I hoped not, because jail was definitely in my future guessing by the way the judge was glowering at me.

"As you can see, Jace had an allergic reaction to his clown makeup. These will be his rooms—"

Oh, the judge didn't like that. His head snapped from Polly, to me, then back to her, his face turning beet-red with anger.

"—when he moves his things in tomorrow."

Honestly, if I didn't know any better, I'd think Polly was an actress in another life. She was even making me start to believe her.

"He can't be your nanny. He's a boy." The judge's words made me stand up straighter and puff out my chest, forgetting I was naked from the waist up and clown from the waist down.

"You've really gone and made a mess of things, Polly. First with the divorce, then the party today, and that's not to mention the kids' schooling. Now you bring this boy into my home to watch your children. What are people to think of a mother who—"

"Who brings someone reliable into their home to watch their kids?" Polly cut him off with a sharp voice, eyes hard and even. Her retort seemed to surprise the judge because his eyebrows hit his hairline.

"Jace is an adult with more experience with kids than most people his age. He has glowing recommendations, an impeccable driving record, and most importantly, he's kind—a trait I value in anyone who cares for my children. Now, unless you're telling me that men and women can't do the same jobs equally, a fact I don't think you'd want anyone in the public to catch wind of, I think we're done here."

Polly crossed her arms as she glared at her father, reminding me of the woman who had threatened me at the front door earlier today. Hot damn. I'd never been more attracted to a woman in all my life.

"I will email Jeffrey tomorrow to inform him that a nanny is no longer needed," Polly said stiffly. For a moment, I thought I heard a small shake in her voice, but she was still standing tall and proud.

"I'll take care of it," the judge replied gruffly. "I will see myself out." Giving me one final glare, he stalked out of the room.

As his footsteps faded down the hallway, Polly moved to the door and shut it quietly. She put her ear to the door and paused, her body sagging with obvious relief after a few moments. She slowly turned around, eyes closed, and leaned back against the door.

Her eyes immediately locked with mine as she opened them, flashing despite the shadows of the dark room. Standing there, all assessing green eyes, pretty pink mouth, and silky blonde hair, I felt that tingling all over my skin again. It was definitely not from the rash.

Polly's voice was a whisper. "How much of that did you hear?"

Confused, I hesitated. "Uh . . . I heard everything you said to your daddy."

My response must've frustrated her because she shook her head quickly, squeezing her eyes shut, then opened them. "No, not what I said to my father. Before that. When you were still in the bathroom."

Anyone could see Polly was agitated. So even though I was confused as hell, I tried to keep an easy smile on my face to put her at ease.

"My head was dunked underwater in the sink to stop the itching. So, I didn't hear much of anything until I came through that door."

Polly's entire posture melted, visibly relieved to hear this news. "I'm sure you have questions."

"Maybe a few."

"It's complicated between me and my father. We're not close. This is his house. My kids and I are only staying here because he's allowing it. I need a nanny until the end of summer who can live here and stay with the kids overnight in case I get called into the hospital on the days I'm on call. The call requirement for my job is ending by September first so by then I think I'll be able to get by with only after school care. I haven't been able to find a reliable nanny yet and my father keeps threatening to hire one for me that looks like —" Polly's words stopped suddenly, her posture straightening. She turned woodenly and painted what I think was supposed to be an apologetic smile on her face.

Not her real smile. Her expression looked like this house felt: cold.

I hated it.

"I'm sorry," she said. "I'm sure you have better things to do than listen to my family drama. I'm sure I sound like a pampered rich girl, complaining about the thread count in her sheets."

"Family's complicated. And I don't mind. I've got nowhere important to be."

Polly's civil expression remained. I wanted to banish all insincerity from her face. I wanted her to look at me with one of her blinding smiles, hell I'd even take her rage over this.

"You can trust me with your secrets, Polly," I said softly, not even knowing I was going to say it until they left my mouth.

Polly did a double take, her perfect mask cracking at my words, her shoulders relaxing. Silence hung between us until she flicked her eyes once more down the length of my body and back up. Nodding to herself, as if a decision had just been made, Polly took a deep breath in and started to pace back and forth in front of me.

"Ok. Well. How could this work? You'd have to go along with telling people you're our nanny. Or maybe just don't say no if people ask." Polly was looking between me and the ground, talking more to herself than to me. "Or only at the club. Just so my father isn't suspicious. That would give me time to find someone else . . ."

A plan took shape in front of me as she spoke.

Going for nonchalance to cover the sudden thrum of anticipation in my chest, I placed one hand in the waist pocket of my clown costume, my other hand still held my damp shirt to my chest. It almost seemed too perfect. She needed a nanny. I needed a place to live. I liked her kids. And I'd be getting paid to see Polly, every day.

My mind wandered to what she might look like in the morning. Was she an early riser? Or did she wake up slow, all sleep rumpled and soft, yawning as she said good morning with a lazy smile? A wave of profound want swept over me, the desire to know her, the real Polly Alberton, becoming irresistible in that instance. But in the back corner of my mind, a small voice warned this job would only make her more off-limits.

"I have an impeccable driving record," I blurted out, apparently deciding to hell with warnings.

Polly's head snapped in my direction. "What did you say?"

"I've never been in trouble with the law, I have tons of experience with kids, and I could give you glowing references."

"But"—she paused, disbelief in her tone— "there's no way a twenty-four-year-old guy would be interested in being our nanny."

I didn't recall telling her my age, so the fact she knew it made me stand up a hair taller. I raised my eyebrows. "A guy can't be a nanny?"

She sucked in a breath, then released it. "That's not what I meant. But I don't know anything about you other than you valet at the country club and work with kids at the school during the week. How do I know you're not a murderer that preys on small families while dressed as a clown?"

I chuckled, looking down as I shifted my ridiculous shoes. "I was born and raised in Green Valley. The house I've been living in is being sold, so I've been looking for a new place. Besides working for the school, I valet on Sundays, drive for Lyft most days of the week, and the rest of the time I work jobs that my buddy needs help with. I've lived next door to the county sheriff for years. I don't know how to do a background check, but I know he'd vouch for me."

Polly still didn't look convinced. "The kids have summer school a few days per week, but otherwise you'd have to be with them all day. I'd need you Monday through Friday, about seven to five, sometimes earlier. And I have overnight hospital call every five days. I usually only get calls I can answer from home, but if I'm called in, I need someone here just in case. I would only need you through August. I'm a doctor, a pediatrician. I started with Mercy Health at the beginning of June."

A doctor. The pieces were making more sense now. I shifted my weight, switching the hands that were holding my shirt to my chest as I remained quiet, sensing she had more to say.

"Does that really sound like a job you want?" I could hear the tension in her voice, so I gentled mine.

"I'd already figured it was a live-in nanny job, and as I'm looking for a place to live, that'd work out just fine for me. And I assumed that watching the kids means helping them get ready, picking them up from school and stuff, and playing with 'em would all be part of it. I've babysat kids plenty in the past, this doesn't sound too different. My other jobs are flexible. The only thing I can't miss would be the Young Wills nights on Tuesdays and Thursdays. I'm sure the two women who run it with me would be more than happy to have Ryla or Max there, too."

Polly wasn't smiling, but if I had to put a label on her expression, I'd say she looked more curious than angry. "Don't you want to know the pay?"

"Alright, what's the pay?"

"Twenty-five dollars an hour."

Hot damn! Why hadn't I become a nanny years ago? I merely nodded as if I was calmly mulling that over. "I can work with that."

Polly went back to pacing, obviously thinking over what I'd just offered so I took the opportunity to shake out my still damp shirt. My skin itched just looking at it.

To hell with it.

I pulled it over my head, my burning skin protesting. After tugging it down, I looked back to Polly.

She was staring at me, then gave her head a little shake. Her voice was quiet, the low rasp driving me wild. "It's a very tempting offer. But really, Jace, why would you want to work for us?"

Her expression was surprisingly unguarded. There was a sadness in the curve of her mouth and exhaustion in her posture. But in her eyes, I saw the flash of reluctant hope.

"Are you offering me the job?" I asked.

Taking a deep breath in and out, she nodded. "Yes."

"Then I'm in. When do you need me to start?"

"When *can* you start?"

"I could start tomorrow."

"Tomorrow?!"

"Tomorrow."

She bit her lip. She wanted to accept, I could tell, but something was holding her back.

I bent my knees a bit, tilting my head to the side to catch her gaze, which had been downcast toward the floor.

"Isn't that what you're saying you need, Polly?"

I could tell my question threw her for a minute. Like it took something for her to accept help, even though she was the one asking for it.

"Yes."

I was a little surprised she agreed so quickly, but I wasn't going to argue. "Great. I'll plan on coming over tomorrow afternoon with my things. You want my number?" I grinned as Polly got her phone from her pocket and thrust it at me, her floral scent drifting over me. Plugging in my number and sending myself a text, I held out the phone to her. Taking her hand down from twisting her earring, she accepted her phone.

"Can't say I ever thought I'd do an interview shirtless," I teased. I gave a cursory look down at my now-covered chest, then back up to Polly, quirking one eyebrow. "Mostly."

A laugh burst out of her as a shout sounded through the door. "Polly? Where are you?"

"Crap!" Hastily walking toward the door, she wrenched it open. "Coming!" she shouted down the hall.

Polly closed the door again, glanced over her shoulder at me. "OK. I guess we're doing this." Her eyes moved down to my neck, and she winced. "One percent hydrocortisone cream, Loradatine, and a cool compress. Don't scratch that."

And then she was gone.

I watched the door long after she left.

CHAPTER
THIRTEEN
POLLY

To quote a great poet of yore, "The shit hath hitith the fan."

Drags to Riches by Ann Richter
Narrated by Nikki Martin

Between Ryla's party, the interaction with my father, and hiring Jace, today couldn't have been more surreal.

As I loaded the dishwasher, my mind kept replaying Jace's Kent the Clown act. He was phenomenal. After a few minutes, he'd had everyone completely absorbed by his performance. I'd had a rare mental image of my mother at one point, as if she was standing and laughing alongside me, nudging me with her elbow, equally impressed.

"What's that smile for?" Leah asked me, coming into the kitchen.

"Just the day. Thank you so much for helping. And staying overnight. I wish you'd let me pay you, you really don't have to stay longer," I told her as I placed the last of the dishes into the washer.

"You can pay me in books!" She turned on the faucet to rinse some dirty plates. "I saw the door to the basement was open and went down there. You must have had some rogue partygoers. I picked up this contraband." Leah gestured to her hand where she was washing the remains of frosting from a plate. "I'd check the rest of the house just in case."

"Little hoodlums," I teased. "Hey, I have a meeting with your friend Rose next week."

"Already?" Leah asked.

"Yep. I emailed the school district superintendent on Friday with more than a dozen questions. Rose was cc'd on the reply I got back from him. No less than half an hour later I got an email from Rose, herself. It was ten paragraphs long. We set up a meeting for Monday." I eyed Leah with trepidation. "Her enthusiasm really jumped off the page."

"That's Rose for you. You're gonna love her." Leah rinsed a dishcloth in the sink. "You kind of disappeared for a little while there at the end. You seemed pretty frazzled when you came back. Everything alright?"

I shut the dishwasher and grabbed the dishrag from her to start wiping down the counters. I had yet to tell Leah about what happened with Jace and my father. "Oh, uh, yeah. I had to tell my father that I hired a nanny which was right after he offered me a mail-order nanny straight from the Tower of London. Words were exchanged."

"What? You found a nanny! When? Who is it?" Leah asked excitedly.

"Oh, um. Yeah. It's actually that guy who did the puppet show at the school. Jace Vargas? He was the clown today, too, if you can believe it." I was too much of a chicken to look at her as I said it. Her answering silence was louder than anything she could shout.

"Did you just say Jace Vargas?" Leah took a step closer to me, pressing into my side.

"Yep!" I continued to avoid her eye contact as I wiped down the counter.

"How do you know *Jace Vargas*?"

"Why do you keep saying his full name like that?" I played dumb, which was incredibly stupid of me. You don't play dumb with Leah. She's like a shark. Once there's blood in the water, you get out of the water, fast, or prepare to be eaten.

She eyed me hard, crossing her arms.

I glanced toward the living room where our two youngest kids and Max were happily playing a video game; her husband and daughter had gone home when the party ended. Sighing, I grabbed a towel to dry my hands, knowing I needed to come clean about how I met Jace.

"Look, I didn't say anything when we were at the puppet show, but I'd met Jace before. He's been valeting my car at the country club when I had brunch with my father. When I was waiting for Ryla and Max at school this week, I ran into him again and we talked. Then he showed up as the clown today, but I had no idea it was him until I found him in my parents' old bedroom."

Leah's jaw got progressively more slack as my story unfolded.

"Then my father walked in and saw Jace shirtless, and I panicked and shouted that Jace was our new nanny, and now, he's our nanny."

Once I was done speaking, she grabbed me by my shoulders and pushed me backward.

"What are you—" I started to ask as she shoved me into the kitchen pantry and shut the door. Crossing her arms, she stared me down from only three inches away.

"Why did you just shove me into the pantry?"

Leah didn't seem to register my question, suspicion oozed out of her every pore. "Why was Jace shirtless?"

"I don't know! I found him like that. I'm assuming it's because his face paint gave him a flesh-eating bacteria," I deflected.

Leah refused to be derailed. "Who talked to whom first?"

"Today?" I asked, confused.

"No, at the school," Leah said impatiently, like I was the one not making sense here.

I crossed my arms. "I don't remember. I think he did."

"With or without the kids?"

"At first without the kids, then with the kids. He walked with Ryla when Max had a panic attack. He was really good with Ry—hey!" I sputtered as Leah reached out to grab my shoulders.

"Spill it."

"There is nothing to spill! He was wheeling out his suitcases of puppets, and I talked to him for like five minutes. He was great with the kids and then we all walked out to the parking lot together. I really didn't know he was the clown until after the party today. That's it."

"There's really nothing going on?" Leah didn't look convinced.

Scoffing, I shrugged out of her hold. "No!"

Leah raised one eyebrow. "Why didn't you tell me about knowing him, then, if nothing is going on?"

It was a fair question, but I still looked to the side, adjusting an off center box of noodles to delay my answer. A part of me didn't want to say anything because I knew she'd know, in that sneaky soothsayer way of hers, that I was attracted to Jace, even though I really didn't want to be attracted to him. Even though I knew Leah had never given me a reason to think she'd judge me for being attracted to Jace, I still feared her response. Guilt battled with my fear of judgment, halting my explanation, making me open and close my mouth without words.

An understanding expression overcame Leah's face as she took in my obvious emotional wreck of a state. "It's ok that you didn't tell me. I'm your best friend and as your best friend, I will continue to abide by the best friend code. You'll tell me when you're ready."

"What's the best friend code?"

"It's the code wherein I know and accept you no matter what. Like, I know you grew up in an emotionally stunted state where your father held affection for ransom in exchange for appropriate behavior, making you hide your real feelings. It's why you're always apologizing, always wanting to give me things in exchange for my help. I know how hard it is for you to show your true self to people. Even to me."

While Leah's candor wasn't atypical, the truth of her words knocked the metaphorical wind out of me. She was right. I've held people at arm's length my entire life. I'd only started to find the courage to be myself in small ways these last few years, which made it all the more difficult to come home and be under my father's thumb, yet again.

Yet, I never stopped to think what that must be like for Leah, feeling like I was holding her at arm's length.

"I'm sorry I hurt you, Leah."

She knew what I was apologizing for. I was sorry I kept a part of myself locked away. I'm sorry I didn't trust our friendship enough to tell her the truth.

No wonder I didn't have any other friends.

"Please, I'm far from perfect. You still love me even when I forget to text you back for weeks. We're friendship goals. Not perfect. Not neat and pretty. But the kind that's real. The kind that shows up with a shovel if you need it, kind of friendship."

"I don't know what it is about you Green Valley people that keep threatening to kill for one another . . . but I'm kind of here for it."

"You're from here too, lest you forget. It's our way of showing love."

I quirked my lips to the side. "I love you, too. Can we get out of the pantry now?"

Leah shook her head, giving a high snickering laugh. "Dear, sweet, innocent Pollyanna." I glowered at my least favorite nickname, putting my first and second name together—a fact Leah fully knew. "No. I didn't only bring you in here to interrogate you. You haven't lived in Green Valley since another life-time ago, so I'm going to give you the tea, the gossip, *and* the dirty details."

Leah was enjoying whatever this was way too much.

"Since all the Winston men went off the market years ago, Jace Vargas has become the town's new Billy Winston."

I furrowed my eyebrows. "Who's Billy Winston?"

Leah waved her hand. "Never mind. My point is, Jace is the unicorn of all the young, single men in town. He's a gentleman, great with kids of all ages, helps out his parents, and is easy on the eyes."

I opened my mouth in disgust. "Are you telling me I hired the community bicycle to watch my kids?" I was more upset about this news than I had any right to be. I turned away, absently straightening cans of soup as Leah kept talking.

"Calm down. He doesn't sleep around. I said he's a unicorn, not a stud stallion. He's like . . . the ungettable get. He's always nice as can be to the kids at school and their parents, but when it comes to single women, particularly the single mommas in town, he's friendly, but keeps his distance. He had to get permission to come and go through the back doors of school for a time because all the single moms would be out in the front of school, holding casserole dishes or baked goods, trying to get his number."

Snorting, I looked back at Leah. "You must be joking. Single moms don't have time for that. Speaking as one, we barely have time to cook for ourselves. We should be cooking food for each other, not for the single men in town."

Leah laughed and started to straighten the pantry items with me. "I love you and can't fault you there."

"How do you know all this?"

"I work in a school. Gossip comes to me like osmosis."

"I still don't understand what this has to do with me?"

She lowered her voice unnecessarily. We were in a pantry; our kids would never hear us. They have trouble hearing me when I'm standing directly beside them. "People are going to talk. Jace is nice, but he's laid back. He's never shown . . . preference, best I can tell."

Well, color me offended.

"If people think I'm an ogre just because the town's unicorn doesn't want me, then good riddance! I'm not interested in a relationship, either. Ever again! I didn't get divorced just to hitch my wagon to another dead horse."

I was panting by the time I was done.

Leah burst out laughing, knocking her elbow into mine. "You are on fire today. I love you and how smart you are, but sometimes you can be really obtuse."

"Maybe I think you're obtuse," I retorted in a Ryla-like manner.

"People are going to assume something *is* going on between you two, not think you're an ogre. *That's* what I'm saying. You're an insanely attractive, single mother. And he's going to be living here—"

"Mooooommmmmaaaa! Where are you?"

Leah popped her head out of the pantry door. "It's mine," she called out.

As she was walking away, I whisper shouted after her. "If you think that the entire town is going to think that there's something happening between us, just because I hired him to watch my kids . . ."

Leah was no longer in the kitchen.

". . . then I feel sad for the town!" I finished, whisper shouting to myself.

The thought that Jace would be interested in me—a thirty-eight-year-old, divorced, single mother—was laughable. Which made my reaction to him all the more ridiculous. Take today for instance. He had a red rash all over his face and my body still wanted to mount him like a gazelle in the middle of mating season in the savanna. Sure, he'd been shirtless, but that was no excuse. It made me no different than the single mothers who preyed upon him at the school, like some sort of she-cougar.

Maybe Jace being the kid's nanny will be for the best. It sets a clear and definite boundary. Like with a patient's parent, I can notice if they are attractive but never be tempted to pursue anything.

Giving myself a firm nod, I realized I could do this. Attraction was a mere biological response, and I was an expert in controlling my reactions, even if my desires were in direct opposition. Hell, I majored in that. A pure, involuntary, biologically programmed response had nothing on me.

I had my books to keep me warm and satisfied. And I got the job done, *every single time.*

Take that, National Geographic.

CHAPTER
FOURTEEN

JACE

"I get paid for my time, not sex, but if she's hot and wants it, I say why not? I'll throw it in as a freebie."

"And if she's not hot?"

"I'll probably still throw it in. My standards aren't real high."

J. Bengtsson, *Fiercely Emma*

Sam: If you ask me the rash improves your face

Sam: No problem on covering your shift. Denice probably misses me anyway.

Sam: That mom is pissed. I got a really angry email about the petting zoo going to hell. Remind me never to use my cousin Fletch for anything again

Sam: Has Denice always been this hot? She's already snapped at me twice. I think she likes me

I had several texts from Sam when I woke up the next morning that I promptly ignored. Late last night, I sent him several pictures of my face along with a text:

Jace: The client asked for a magician, not a clown. The face paint you

125

provided gave me leprosy. I need you to cover my shift at the valet tomorrow. I already messaged Denice. You owe me.

Sam had previously valeted at the country club, occasionally pitching in during large events. Denice acted like she hated him, but he's great with the customers so I knew she'd be fine with it.

After a cold shower that morning, the ghost of itching past didn't return, and I counted myself lucky. I received a few sidelong glances at the drugstore yesterday, apparently no one had ever seen someone dressed as part man/part clown/part rash before, but the cream and medicine Polly suggested worked like a charm. I'd always been sensitive to certain shampoos, but I hadn't had a reaction like this in years.

A few hours later, I was finishing packing up my stuff when I texted Sam back. I already texted Polly to confirm that I'd be over around three when Sam actually called me back. I answered on speaker, continuing to pack up my clothes.

"What does 'I'm moving out of my parents' house, and I need to store my stuff at your place' mean?" Sam's voice greeted me, reciting the text I'd just sent him aloud.

"Exactly what it sounds like."

"What brought this on?"

"I got a job working with a family who needs a nanny for the summer. I sent in references, did an interview—" of sorts, Sam didn't need to know the shirtless details— "and met the kids, who are pretty great. It pays well, and my parents might be selling their house, so I needed to move."

My explanation was met with silence, so I continued to go through my closet to finish packing.

Ten seconds later, Sam replied, "You're telling me that you're some kids' nanny and are moving in with the entire family?"

"Yup."

"And your parents are moving?"

"Seems that way."

He snorted. He knew my parents well. "To where?"

"Florida. I was just as surprised as you."

After another long, presumably stunned, silence, I asked, "Can I ditch some stuff at your place for now? If my parents ask, that's where I'm living. My parents think my lease starts tomorrow."

"Jace, if that even is your real name anymore, this isn't the way to move in with us. You should *actually* be living with us. Not pretend living with us."

I switched the phone from speaker, holding it to my ear. "You dressed me up like a clown and sent me to a kid's birthday party where the mother wanted a magician. You're lucky my balls are still attached to my body. You'll be owing me for the next twenty years."

He didn't need to know it'd worked out in my favor.

Sam grumbled in agreement. "Yeah, I got you. You need any help with your stuff?"

"Nah. But can I come over in an hour to drop off some boxes?"

"Sure, I'll be around."

While I may want to ring his neck sometimes, Sam was a good friend.

———

I was pulling away from Sam's townhouse, on the way to Polly's, when I got another call. I expected it to be my parents. Momma had cried when I left, giving me two hugs and a large picnic basket filled with food. Not wanting to show up at Polly's house with a basket of food from my mother, Sam was all too happy to take it off my hands. Pop seemed sad when I left, too. More than I expected. So much so I insisted several times I'd be checking on their house when they went to Florida this week, just to take the worried look out of his eyes.

"Hello?"

"Jace? It's Jackson James."

"Hey Jackson. Thanks again for being willing to give me a reference."

I heard a cough. "Sure thing. I wanted to make sure I understand this correctly," Jackson spoke cagily. This was followed by another cough. Or maybe it was a throat clearing. "You really took a job as a live-in nanny?"

"Yup. I needed a place to stay. It seemed like a mutually beneficial option."

"A place to stay? Is everything ok? Are Nick and Susan alright?" He used his stern cop voice, which made me grip the steering wheel harder.

"My parents' are fine. They're thinking of moving to Florida soon . . . permanently."

"I wasn't aware of that."

"It's a recent thing."

I heard some murmuring in the background. After a pause, Jackson responded, "You know you can always stay with Rae and me. You're always welcome."

"I appreciate that."

Jackson cleared his throat. "I wanted to call you and say that I already talked to your, um, new employer. In case she asks, we gave you a great reference."

I paused a beat. "We?"

"It's possible Rae might have gotten on the call with me."

Well, shit. Stopping at a red light, I laid my head against the headrest. I liked Rae. Loved her, really. Like a sister. But I did not want to talk to Rae, or Sienna for that matter, about Polly. Not yet. They'd be about as bad as my sister if they found out. Worse maybe. Like the two bamboozling aunts I never wanted.

Resigned, I blew out a breath. She was clearly listening. Might as well get it over with. "Put her on," I deadpanned.

"Oh, uh, Rae's not—"

"Jackson."

"Yeah, one sec."

I heard a little mumbling, followed by an audio change, like I was being put on speakerphone, and then Rae's voice.

"Jace, honey! We just got off the phone with Polly Alberton. She sounded very . . . put together. I told Jackson we needed to call you as this is the first I've heard about you being a manny."

"Nanny," I clarified as I heard a snort in the background followed by a little thump.

"Right, right. How did this come about?"

I ran my hand through my hair. "It sort of fell in my lap. I'd met Polly on a few occasions when I valeted for her at the country club. And then I talked to her at the elementary school last week. She has two great kids and she's new to town. I mean, newer. She's actually Judge Alberton's daughter. Do you know him?"

Jackon piped up. "Judge Alberton?"

"Yeah."

"No."

The light turned green and I eased my car forward. "Anyway," I continued, "her kids needed a nanny for the rest of the summer. We kept running into each other and got to talking . . ."

Stop talking about her so much.

"It's good money, and I said yes."

It was silent for so long I thought the call had dropped, but it still read as active on my car's screen. Unease prompted me to fill in the silence.

"I thought I could bring the kids to Young Wills. You should see the youngest, Ryla. She's only six but I bet she'd be a natural onstage. Max is ten, but he's real shy, so he might only sit in the audience. Then again, we're always needing stage crew, maybe I could get him to join in eventually. I wouldn't think you'd need to do any background checks on her or the kids before they join Young Wills. But feel free to do a background check on me if Polly wants one." I paused. "Not that I need to tell you how to do your job."

That was more words than I'd ever uttered, in one go, to Jackson. Or Rae.

I braked before an upcoming turn, flipping on my blinker. The steady ticking was probably the loudest sound on the call.

"Well, Jace," I could practically hear Rae's smile as she finally spoke up, "we certainly appreciate *all* that information. And I can't speak for Sienna, but I bet she'll be thrilled to have you bring the kids along."

Damn it. I didn't think this all the way through.

"See, nothing's set in stone. I don't know if—"

"Good luck! We'll see you and the kids on Tuesday. Can't wait!"

"Bye," I muttered, but she'd already hung up.

Bamboozled.

CHAPTER
FIFTEEN
POLLY

I'll stay home with my Kindle and my cat. They never disappoint.

Melanie Harlow, *Man Candy*

I've never been asked to do this, but if I was asked to find a needle in a haystack, my guess is that even if I went through it one piece of hay at a time, it would still be faster than brushing my daughter's hair.

"Oww! You're pulling!" Ryla yelped, scooting forward on her bed and out of my reach, as I painstakingly teased apart the world's biggest rat's nest in her hair. I was literally pulling it apart hair by hair. My daughter had a sensitive head. My daughter had a sensitive *everything*.

"This is why we need to brush it every night, sweetie," I explained, trying to keep my voice gentle.

"I brushed it last night!" Ryla lied, tone indignant. She absolutely didn't brush it last night. Getting her to brush her hair was akin to giving a cat a bath.

"Ryla. You know it won't hurt as much if we brush it every night. New rule, we have to brush your hair after your nighttime snack, just like with your teeth."

Ryla merely harrumphed.

"I guess you don't like eating chocolate then," I replied.

"THAT MAKES ME EVEN MADDER!"

I sighed, turning quiet as my emotionally reactive volcano erupted. I knew better than to threaten her. Even if it was in a teasing way, it never worked. She always exploded. I knew the best thing would be to let her calm down first. Or make her laugh, because there would be no brushing her hair until that tiny Tasmanian devil inside of her calmed down.

But, today, I was on a time crunch.

"Please sit back and let me brush your hair." I tried to keep my tone soothing. "Mr. Jace will be here soon, and we need to make sure you and Max look nice when he gets here."

"Why? He knows what I look like." Ryla's tone was still angry, but she did scoot back.

"It never hurts to make a good impression," I said as I resumed the painstaking task of brushing her hair and shouted for my son.

"Max? Did you get dressed, yet? Mr. Jace will be here soon!"

I heard a muffled shout from Max's room next door, which I took as tacit agreement.

"Mom?" Ryla piped up a few minutes later.

"Yeah?"

"Is Mr. Jace really gonna, like, live here and take care of us like Giselle did?"

"Yes, just like we talked about last night. You and Max were all for it. Remember?"

"Do I have to call him Mr. Jace?"

"We can ask him when he gets here." I looked at my watch. Never has an hour passed so quickly. Jace would be here any minute. I'd been madly picking up around the house for the last hour, only to realize that Ryla's hair was a snarly mess and Max had never changed out of his pajamas.

"There! Done," I said after another minute, giving the back of her head a kiss. "Now, I need to go change."

I bolted across the hall to my room, quickly changing out of my leggings and tank top and into more appropriate white capris. I grabbed a black T-shirt from the top of my dresser and started slipping it on when the doorbell rang. As I dashed down the stairs, I vaguely registered that the shirt was tighter than I'd remembered. The hem barely reached the top of my pants. I made a mental note to start drying our clothes on low heat.

Pausing for a brief moment, I inhaled quickly, then opened the front door to reveal Jace, sans rash. He wore a soft looking navy T-shirt and easygoing smile —a stark difference from yesterday, when he'd come to the door wearing his Kent the Clown costume. The memory made a smile play on my lips and as if reading my mind, he smiled knowingly back at me.

"Hi," I breathed out. My breath stuttered as I watched a few curly strands of his chocolate brown hair catch in the breeze.

I wanted to run my hands through it.

Inwardly, I winced.

Involuntary Biologically Programmed Response: 1

Polly: 0

"Hiya, little miss," Jace greeted Ryla as she skipped up next to me.

"Do I have to call you Mr. Jace?" Ryla blurted.

"Most of my friends call me Jace. Why don't we go with that?" He turned his cute, dimpled smile back to me. "Hiya, Polly."

Nodding, I averted my eyes from the dimples, but that meant I was now staring at his chest, which of course made me think about his abs.

Don't think about his washboard abs under that shirt!

. . .

Ok. Don't think about his washboard abs, **again**.

"Are we friends?" Ryla asked Jace from where she was standing three inches in front of him. Personal space was not really a concept she grasped yet.

"Sure, we are." Jace placed a knee on the ground, his focus completely centered on Ryla. "We even have a secret handshake."

Ryla's eyes bugged out. "We do?"

Jace put his hand over his heart. "You don't remember our secret handshake?"

"No." Ryla shook her head vigorously.

"Here, make a fist." Jace demonstrated. "It starts like this." He knocked his fist over and under hers. "Then like this." He gave her fist a little bump. "And for the ending." Jace flared his fingers out, brought his thumb to his nose, and blew a raspberry, making Ryla jump up and down, utterly charmed.

She wasn't the only one.

"I want to try!" Ryla mimicked the handshake back to him, then blew her own raspberry with relish.

"Great job!" Jace popped up at the same time Ryla asked, "Do you and Mommy have a secret handshake?"

Exhaling a small tittering laugh, a sound I have never made before in my entire lifetime, I waved Ryla's question away with a fluttering shake of my hand.

"Nah, we shake like adults do." Jace bestowed a bemused smile to Ryla, then shifted it to me as he held out his hand.

It's funny how you can shake someone's hand and think nothing of it; it's just a simple handshake and then you move on with your day. But when my hand slid into Jace's warm, strong grasp, a buzzing awareness spread through my body. I instinctively moved a step closer to him, craving more, unable to stop myself. It was like he was the edge of a cliff, something that's risky to be near, but you can't stop yourself from looking over the edge.

"Why are you wearing Max's shirt?" Ryla announced loudly, breaking me out of my trance.

I dropped Jace's hand like a hot potato, looking down at my shirt in horror. Stretched tight across my chest were the words 'Friday Night Funkin', my son's favorite computer game. Both f's were unfortunately placed over the swell of each breast, accentuating them loud and proud. I knew this shirt was too tight! It must have gotten mixed up with my clothes somehow.

"Shoot!" I exclaimed, mortified. I quickly crossed my arms over my chest, which caused the shirt to ride up over the waistband of my capris, exposing my stomach like I was a coed pledging a sorority. I pulled the shirt down, but that accentuated the f's even more.

Doing a weird self-hug, I laughed nervously and excused myself, running up the stairs and cursing this day to hell.

I changed into my originally intended black shirt whilst busy mentally chastising myself.

Remember what you told yourself last night? You can think he's attractive. It's an empiric fact. A nun would revoke her chastity vows at the sight of him! But you are a mature, thirty-eight-year-old, mother of two. You will not be felled by a man with cute dimples and slabs of abs who is fourteen years your junior. Get it together!

"Where's Max?" Jace was asking Ryla when I returned to the foyer.

"He's in the playroom reading," Ryla explained, grabbing Jace's hand. "Wanna see my room?"

"Ryla!" I admonished. "You can't ask a strange man to see your room."

She eyed Jace, then me. "You think he's strange?"

Twin circles of red permanently took up residence on my cheeks. "Strangers. I meant strangers. Any stranger in general, male or female. Unless I give them permission."

"Is Jace a stranger?" Ryla cocked her head, appearing confused. As she should be, I wasn't making sense. I'd lost any functioning brain cells somewhere between the f's of Max's Friday Night Funkin' shirt.

"No," I said weakly.

"Then why can't I show him my room?"

I looked down to the ground in defeat. So much for getting it together.

Jace merely looked down at Ryla. "I'd love to see your room. But I think your momma wants to give me a tour first. How about we start down here and work our way up?"

Grateful to Jace for putting together an actual intelligible sentence to end this mortifying back and forth, I gestured toward the living room.

"OK." Ryla shrugged and skipped off toward the living room. I glanced at Jace and saw that his lips were pursed together, fighting a smile.

"You scared off yet?"

His hazel eyes danced. "Not in the slightest."

———

"And this is the kitchen!" Ryla was having a great time on this tour, announcing each room with jazz hands, interjecting commentary here and there. Once I spent too long explaining something so she'd flounced off to the next room yelling, "You coming this century, slowpokes?"

Jace was attentive and curious, quietly asking a few questions to me or Ryla. We started off the tour by showing him the basement theater room, then returning to the first floor, starting at the library and moving down the hall to the kitchen.

"This is where I put the meal plan and daily schedule." I powered on the tablet on the island as Jace came to stand beside me. "This also has a calendar, important information for the kids, those kinds of things. We've been using it since our previous au pair, Giselle, was with us."

"His name's Barry!" Ryla chirped, nudging me out of the way so she could stand between us.

"Oh yeah? Why'd you name him Barry?" Jace drawled.

"Because that's what he looked like." Ryla's tone was matter-of-fact, but I still winced, peeking over at Jace who was nodding as if she made sense.

"What does Barry do?"

"Mommy puts the menu in him and lists and not fun stuff like going to therapy and I have to mark it off like this." Ryla demonstrated how each of the kids tapped the screen to check off the scheduled tasks for the day.

I took over from Ryla and went through how to navigate the app. "Here's how you get to the home calendar and here's where you press to get to the to-do lists and meal plan. Giselle loved to cook, so she helped plan out the meals and I've kept a lot of the recipes the same. If you don't know how to make something, the recipe pops up like this. I usually plan everything out a week or two in advance. At least, that's what I did for our previous au pair—"

"Giselle?" Jace grinned, tone playful.

I let out a light laugh, then squinted one eye. "Have I mentioned her name before?"

Chuckling quietly, Jace glanced down at Barry again, his grin falling slightly.

I hesitated. "Do you know how to cook?"

Jace glanced up, a reassuring smile on his face. "Sure. Not a problem."

"I can help! I have an apron, and my name is on it, see?" Ryla emerged from the pantry wearing her apron proudly showing off her name that had been stitched onto it.

"I see. Did your momma help you do that?"

"Giselle did it! She cooked with me and played with me and one day when I'm really old, like sixteen, I'm gonna go live with her in Italy for real!"

For the first months after Giselle left, I'd heard these types of comments daily. Luckily it had been happening less often now, but each time she said it, that old wound got pressed, a bruise that's never been allowed to heal. Gratefully, Jace asked Ryla a question about cooking so I was able to collect myself. After Ryla put her apron away, I slowly began to back out of the kitchen, gesturing to them both. "I can show you your room, Jace, and then we can go upstairs."

Jace and I were walking under the arched open doorway separating the kitchen from the living room, which was easily wide enough for two people when Ryla scurried past me and the wall, shooting off toward the living room. I side-stepped toward Jace, accidentally knocking into him. It really could have stopped there, but I jerked to the right, resulting in my feet and body turning in opposite directions. Losing my balance, I was horrified as I began to fall, but Jace caught me, bringing his arms around me and pressing me into his chest.

"Sorry!" I wheezed, inadvertently catching a lungful of his cologne.

"Don't apologize. Are you alright?" he asked, helping me stand upright.

"I'm fine, really. Thank you." I stepped back as soon as I gained my bearings. His hands, however, trailed down my arms to my wrists. Goosebumps that I hoped he wouldn't notice erupted over my skin. He let go of me almost reluc-tantly, watching me with a wary expression, not letting me go completely until he was certain I was fine.

Which I certainly was *not*. Mentally, that is.

Not in any way.

Cheeks fire engine red, I spun and walked toward my parents' old bedroom, extra aware of Jace's presence beside me. Leah's words from yesterday kept playing in my head, that he was hands off with single mothers, showing them no interest. Yet that was contrary to every interaction I'd ever had with him. Including today. He was easygoing, yes, but he was also flirtatious. He showed keen interest throughout the entire tour, asking thoughtful questions. He didn't seem like someone disinterested in me or my kids. Was it all just an act?

"You might remember this room." I half turned to Jace as we walked down the hall.

"I do, but not with regular shoes on," Jace smirked.

We found Ryla jumping on the bed. The very old, antique, four-poster bed that would cost a fortune to repair.

"Ryla! You're not allowed to do that! Get down!"

Ryla landed on her butt. "Giselle let me jump on the bed."

"Not this bed. And she's not here." At my firm tone, Ryla's face scrunched into a mask of fury. She slid off the bed, then stomped past me, huffing all the way down the hallway and up the stairs, until I heard the familiar faraway slam of her door.

I glanced at Jace to explain away or apologize for what happened, but I found I didn't quite have the words. It was embarrassing. And disheartening. My own daughter preferring an au pair to her own mother. My complete inability to control her. I opted to ignore what happened, straightening my spine and fixing a too-bright smile across my face. I purposefully didn't meet his eyes, not wanting to see his expression, which was likely full of regret at taking this job, or worse, sympathy.

"This was my parents' room. My room's upstairs across from the kids so I can be closer to them."

And to avoid the hazard of repressed memories that come with this room.

Jace was quiet as I continued to point out things around the room. "I don't know the last time this actually held a fire, so I'd probably avoid that," I explained when we got to the fireplace. My attention snagged on the rose window treatments my mom had loved, which were still draped from floor to ceiling. I reverently stroked one of the gauzy curtains, remembering hiding behind them, giggling while my mom looked for me. I felt tears threaten suddenly; since I'd come back to live here, the memories of my mother were harder to avoid, like they'd transformed themselves into gaping black holes, their gravitational pull threatening to suck me in.

"Polly?"

I blinked to see that Jace was leaning against a bedpost, watching me warily.

I pointed to the windows, trying to play off my tears. "You can keep the windows open or closed, whatever you like." I started to walk back toward the bed, gesturing around the room. "Feel free to put your stuff anywhere."

"Are you ok?" I could hear the concern in Jace's voice. Unable to stop myself, I turned to face him and took in his expression. Kindness radiated from him. And I didn't deserve it. I was a mess of guilt and anger and sadness, bone-deep tiredness, a thousand spinning thoughts, and it was my own stupid spineless making.

"Look," I began, crossed my arms.

"Uh-oh." Jace smirked, his teasing in his tone tempering some of my distress.

"What?"

"Whenever someone starts a sentence with *'Look'*, in that way it's never followed by anything good."

"I don't follow."

"It's never a, 'Look, I've inherited a billion dollars but can only spend half of it so I'm giving you the other half,' kind of conversation. It's always a, 'Look, your buddy's in jail and you need to bail him out, so give us all your money,' type of conversation."

I don't know what kind of magic Jace possessed to diffuse the tension in my body in seconds, but he did. The stereotype of what I thought a young, twenty-something guy would be like was completely at odds with his calm demeanor, his patient concern.

Leah was absolutely right. He really was a unicorn.

Huffing a resigned laugh, I shook my head. He didn't deserve this. I had to give him an out that I honestly hoped he wouldn't take. But it would be borderline irresponsible to let Jace get mixed up in all of this chaos unknowingly.

"It's nothing like that. Before you officially start, I feel compelled to lay it all out, all the crazy complicatedness of my life, and if you want to leave, I under-stand. No questions asked."

Jace shrugged, looking almost amused.

I sat down in one of the fireplace chairs. "We moved here from Chicago at the beginning of June. My husband and I divorced last fall, after which he gave up all custody of the kids."

Jace sat down as I talked, eyes narrowing, all amusement gone from his expression.

"Giselle had been with us for almost two years at that point. She was willing to stay on another year, but her mom got sick, so she had to go back to Italy shortly after the first of this year. It broke Ryla's heart."

I tried not to get stuck on the mental image of Ryla clinging to Giselle when she left for the airport, her little face crumpled and tear-stained.

"Two months after Giselle left, I had to quit my job to homeschool Max. His anxiety became so severe, he'd have panic attacks leaving the apartment and needed to go to an IOP, an intensive outpatient program, to receive the care he needed. All the money I had left, that money I'd hoped would eventually go toward a downpayment for a new house, needed to be used for therapy bills or monthly expenses. The child support payments I received were nowhere near the cost of Max's health care expenses. Yes, I could have forced the courts to make my ex-husband split the medical costs, but my ex, David, was never supportive of Max seeking help for mental health issues. I didn't want to risk David fighting me on it, so I didn't even ask. Don't get me wrong, I'd gladly do it all again. Max is much better, but I fear he'll relapse at any point. And Ryla's gone completely off the rails with all this change."

I'd been looking down as I spoke, so I snuck a glance at him after this last revelation. I wanted a hint at how he was taking this, wondering if he was going to bolt.

But his attention was steady. Giving me time. Giving me the courage to continue. So, I did.

"The only reason we're here is because my father offered us this house rent-free, in exchange for having brunch with him once per week. But he keeps piling up new demands. And now that I'm working again, the spousal support payments I'm required to pay are essentially canceling out any money coming in from child support. Yesterday, just before I came in here, my father pulled me aside and told me that he was bringing in a militant-looking nanny and I panicked, thinking that if I refused, he'd kick us out and we'd be homeless. And you know what happened next."

I gentled my tone, feeling strangely shy now that I'd laid the good, the bad, and the ugly all out for him to see. "So, knowing all that, there're no hard feelings if this isn't for you."

Jace leaned forward, resting his forearms on his knees.

"What's next on the tour?"

CHAPTER
SIXTEEN

JACE

From the moment perfect Polly Alberton came into my life, I knew I was in trouble. With each meeting, she kept layering wit and sweetness and humility into the body of a bombshell. I didn't think it could get any worse than yesterday, when she'd put her hand on my stomach, nearly causing me to get bricked up in my clown costume. But when she came to the door this afternoon in that tight black T-shirt, her tits pointing toward me like the green flag of a goddamn NASCAR race, I had to think about accidentally walking in on my father in the shower so that Captain J didn't salute at full attention.

At least Polly seemed completely unaware of the effect she had on me. When she lost her balance on the way out of the kitchen and I caught her, finally having her supple skin underneath my hands . . . I didn't want to let her go.

After leaving her parents' room, Polly took me on a tour upstairs. All afternoon she'd been giving me guarded looks, nervous energy radiating from her, giving me unnecessary warnings like I wasn't already committed before I walked through her front door.

"This is my room." Polly pointed to a doorway on the right, just at the top of the stairs. "Ryla and Max's rooms are on the other side," Polly pointed to the two doors across the hall from hers, "and a Jack and Jill bathroom connects them."

"This is the playroom." Polly opened a door further down the hallway revealing a room with three large windows on the far side, with shelves of toys along two walls. Max was sitting on the floor in the far corner of the room reading a book on top of layers of blankets with piles of pillows around him. Gauzy curtains hung above him, and fairy lights were strung along rounded edges of the curtains, giving the space a cozy feel.

"We made a reading nook over there," Polly said, pointing toward Max. "Hey Max, Jace is here. We're doing a tour."

We walked a few steps into the room as Max sat up, eyes glancing between me and his momma, then back down to his book.

"This is one heck of a reading nook." I stopped at least ten feet away from Max. "Whatcha readin'?"

"*Wings of Fire*," Polly answered for Max, coming up beside me. "He's almost to the fifth book in the series and finished up a graphic novel version recently. Isn't that right Max?"

Ryla suddenly burst between Polly and I, the tantrum from downstairs clearly forgotten.

"I can make the lights change color!" Ryla plopped down next to Max, grabbing a small black remote to demonstrate the color-changing options of the fairy lights. After oohing and aahing over the lights, I shuffled closer to the reading nook and crouched down on the balls of my feet.

"*Wings of Fire* sounds pretty cool. You'll have to tell me about it," I said to Max, then looked over at Ryla. "What do you like to read?"

"I want to start Harry Potter, but *she*," Ryla pointed derisively at Polly, "won't let me start it until I'm seven."

I heard Polly sigh, obviously trying to approach Ryla with patience, but the strain was evident in her voice. "It's too scary, Ryla. I already told you. Your brother was scared of that book when he was your age. I don't think it's a good idea right now. I'm so proud of how well you're reading, but just because you're able to read something, doesn't mean you're ready."

Ryla crossed her arms, put out. It seems put out might be her default state.

"Hey, little miss. Your momma has your best interest at heart. Those books were scary even when I read 'em for the first time and I was older than Max was now, so how about we give her some slack. There's plenty of books out there to read and we have a pretty cool library in town. My momma is friends with one of the librarians. I'm sure she'd be able to find some books for you."

Ryla looked slightly less miffed at my suggestion. I pointed over at the doll-house in the corner which I assumed was hers. "I've never seen a dollhouse like that. Want to show it to me?"

Those were definitely the magic words. Eyes brightening, Ryla popped up. "That's *my* dollhouse! It used to be mom's, but now it's mine. Want to see the toilet?"

I kept a straight face. "Absolutely."

Ryla proceeded to show me a three-inch-tall porcelain toilet that made a real flushing noise when you pushed the tiny handle.

"Can I try it?" I asked.

"Only if you're careful, *it's vintage.*" Ryla whispered that last part. A small snort from behind me had me betting it was Polly who'd given her daughter the same instructions in the past.

My attention snagged on an open toy bin next to the dollhouse that had a feather boa looped over the edge.

"What's in there?" No sooner had I asked, than Ryla was up and heading to the chest, grabbing the boa and what looked like a pirate hat and a foam sword.

"Wanna play dress-up with me?"

I tapped my chin, making it seem like I was hesitating when really, this was right up my alley.

"I'll play on two conditions: I get to be a pirate, and Max has to play, too."

———

Fifteen minutes later, I was on my knees, palms up, begging for my life as Ryla the Terrible held a foam sword to my throat. My first mate, Max, stood begrudgingly at my side as Polly straightened up the room, watching us out of the corner of her eye with a smile.

"If you please, sir, I am but a lowly pirate, sailing the seven seas since me birth. Have mercy!" I pleaded in my best pirate accent. "At least save my pet snake, Slither-me-Timbers is innocent!" I added, stroking the feather boa looped around my neck.

Ryla narrowed her eyes as she looked down the sight of her sword. "Quiet! Or you walk the plank!"

I was ten shades of impressed at her acting prowess. Sienna and Rae were going to get a huge kick out of her.

"What in the world is that?" I pointed behind Ryla, who, being six, fell for the oldest trick in the book. After looking behind her, I popped to my feet and retrieved the foam sword I'd "dropped" on the floor earlier.

"Ah-ha!" I cried, swiping the sword left and right as Ryla whipped her head back to me, her expression filling with outrage. We weaved around each other, Max jumping out of the way as our foam blades bopped against each other. In a solid move, my swashbuckling opponent feigned left, making me weave right just as she stabbed me through the chest (or in this case, my armpit) screaming, "Die, pirate scum!"

I heard a choked gasp from the reading nook, but I didn't look over to Polly. I was giving it my all, clutching at the boa around my neck, making choking and gasping noises as I fell to the floor.

"Avenge me!" I cried out to Max, who, if I didn't know any better, was fighting a smile.

My head and arms went slack, and I closed my eyes. After a few seconds, I felt a light kick to my foot. I snapped my eyes open. "Hey, no fair! Kickin' a man when they're down!" I teased, making Ryla and Max erupt into giggles.

After I got up, Ryla, Max, and I were greeted by clapping from our audience of one, who bestowed us with one of her real smiles.

We all took turns giving a bow. After bringing my hat to my chest and bending over low, I snuck a glance at the still cheering Polly. She wasn't looking at me like I was a kid. Like I was some aimless, career-less guy, good for a fun time, not a long time.

She was looking at me like I was good enough, just being myself.

CHAPTER
SEVENTEEN

POLLY

"Compromise is a way for both sides to lose politely. I do not lose, and if I do, it's never polite."

Her eyes were smoke and intrigue in the rearview mirror.

"So, in answer to your question, no. I won't be taking off your handcuffs."

American Thighs by Lady Jane
Narrated by Brittney Houston

"**A**re you dusting?"

A sudden voice made me drop my dust rag and yelp as I flattened myself against the bookshelf I'd been dusting.

Jace was standing in the doorway of the library, a curious look on his face.

"What are you doing here?" I rasped as I took out my earbuds.

"Do you always clean at—" he made a big show of looking at his bare wrist—"zero dark thirty?"

I bent to retrieve my rag and collect my thoughts. My heart was still racing in my chest. Mostly because Jace was wearing the hell out of a white T-shirt and black sweatpants.

Tonight, after the kids and I helped Jace carry his things into the house, we had dinner together. Ryla peppered him with questions, practically forcing Jace to fill us in on how many jobs he had (*more than a handful*) which was his favorite (*Young Wills*), and his position on chocolate (*pro*). This led to a discussion of Ryla and Max attending Young Wills. Ryla's position being definitively pro whereas Max's expression made me think he fell somewhere between the 'no' and 'hell no' range. After Jace went to his room for the night and I got the kids wrangled into bed, I laid awake, my mind alive with perseverative thought.

So, I'd decided to clean.

"I was looking for any party remnants from yesterday. Plus, I can catch up on my—" I paused, almost blurting out the title of my book, *American Thighs,* instead responding with, "medical journals."

Because obviously, listening to a medical journal while dusting a library at 12:30 a.m. was much less weird than listening to a bounty hunter romantic suspense audiobook.

Insert laugh track here.

Jace tilted his head, eyes playful as he walked slowly toward my side of the room, scanning the rows of bookshelves. "You listen to medical journals, huh?"

I turned back to the bookshelf, running the rag over its shelves. "It's what all the cool kids are doing," I replied, a sarcastic lilt to my voice.

I watched him out of the corner of my eye as he took his time inspecting the room. The library had wall-to-wall bookshelves except for the row I was currently dusting that had a fireplace centered in the middle of the wall. Across from the fireplace sat two leather couches facing each other. Large leather chairs were placed sporadically throughout the library, providing ample reading space. I often would curl up on my mother's lap on the chair by the window, wrapping my finger in her long, silky hair, listening to her as she narrated all the different characters from the stories we'd read together. Judy Blume was one of our favorites. I'd gotten the biggest kick out of Ramona and remembered getting a little mad at Beezus' attitude toward her sister. I'd always wanted a sister.

Now, thinking of Ryla's antics, I had to wonder what kind of karma was at play here. My sincerest apologies to Beezus.

Jace casually worked his way around the room until he was on the same side of the library as me, at the opposite end of the row.

"This whole place doesn't come with its own cleaning crew?" he asked, continuing to casually study the shelf's contents as he ambled closer to me.

"It did come with one," I grumbled, continuing to dust systematically down the rows of shelves, moving closer to him one book at a time. "But I cancelled them on Saturday."

In an effort to stick it to my father, I'd cancelled all cleaning services, house-keeping services, and grounds crew. In doing so, I'd merely stuck it to myself. But that email to Jeffrey felt so good, it was almost worth it.

"They not do a good job or something?"

"No, they were great." I dusted the next shelf a little harder. *Like goddamn cleaning angels*, I thought, finding Jace watching me. "My father likes to hold things over my head. Like if he does something for you, you owe him. I didn't want him to have another thing over me."

Jace's easy smile fell. "You can ask me and the kids to help you clean. You could put it on Brian, no, wait"—Jace snapped and pointed at me— "Barry."

I lifted my eyebrows at him. "You want to clean?"

"I wouldn't go that far," he replied. "But I'm a pretty decent cleaner. My sister moved out of the house when I was eight and my chores doubled. I can dust, mop, clean toilets, you name it."

I stood on my tiptoes to reach the topmost shelf. "If you're willing to clean with the kids, have at it. But I'm warning you, it's miserable. Ryla argues with me the entire time and gets mad if I redo anything after her. And Max "takes a break" after cleaning for ten minutes. They'll wear you down."

Jace held up his hands as he walked a few more steps toward me, the air compressing around me the closer he came. "No promises, but I have my ways." And then Jace had the audacity to wink at me, having no concept of what that did to the sixteen-year-old girl inside of me.

I shook my head, trying to shake some sense into that simpering teenager, telling her to have more self-respect and stop drawing hearts around our names. She, in true sixteen-year-old fashion, raked her eyes over my thread-bare college T-shirt and black leggings, finding them lacking.

"What are you doing in here?" I changed the subject, moving to the next shelf.

"I was getting some water and thought I heard something," Jace said absently, then whistled. He shook his head and hooked a thumb at the expanse of law volumes in front of him. "This is some collection. Do you think your daddy's read 'em all?"

"I wouldn't doubt it. He reads incredibly fast and has an almost eidetic memory. That entire side is history." I pointed to the wall opposite us. "One of his favorite things to do at the dinner table was quizzing me on Revolutionary War facts." It was one of my happy memories of childhood, before my mother died.

"Sounds like my childhood," Jace said, grinning. "Except with baseball facts. You're not a big history buff, I take it?"

"My mom was. And I actually liked it, even if it wasn't my thing."

"What was your thing?"

I grunted as I stood from crouching after dusting the bottommost shelf in front of me.

Reading about people falling in love. The more pining the better.

"Science, I guess; much to my father's disappointment."

Jace frowned. "What's wrong with science?"

My sigh was wistful. "He wanted me to be a lawyer. He was a defense attorney for years and would always brag about how I was going to follow in his foot-steps one day. He took on his first judgeship when I was ten."

I stood on my tiptoes to dust the tallest shelf on the bookshelf in front of me, only to have the rag plucked from my hands by Jace, who was now standing beside me. His body heat radiated into my side as his strong arm reached up to dust the top shelf.

"T-thank you," I stammered.

An amused smile played on Jace's lips. "You really underachieved there, being a doctor." He handed the rag back to me which I all but jerked out of his hands, his proximity felt intimate in a way I hadn't expected.

"Right?" I answered, my voice breathless. I cleared my throat, focusing on dusting the shelves methodically. "I guess it was a form of rebellion if I'm being honest."

"Is that why you're a doctor? Because he didn't want you to be one?" Jace asked, walking to one of the couches behind us and sitting down. As he leaned back, he rested his arms along the back of the couch causing his white T-shirt to stretch across his pecs.

Finding I'd been slowly rubbing the same spot on a shelf for way too long, I cleared my throat and sidestepped to my right to dust the fireplace mantle. "I actually wanted to be a doctor ever since my mom got sick."

I was met with silence. So much so, that I finally peeked over my shoulder at him.

He asked me the question with his eyes. *Well, what happened to her?*

I took a deep breath. "She died when I was twelve. An aggressive form of brain cancer."

Jace didn't tilt his head or frown with excessive sympathy. "That's a rough one, Polly. I'm sorry," he said softly.

Sometimes when people gave you sympathy, it didn't hit right. Exaggerated facial expressions and overly sympathetic words felt empty. Like they were only saying something to make themselves feel better. Jace merely sat quietly, watching me with thoughtful concern. He was different than the teasing, easy going Jace I'd come to know. I sensed he was giving me both the time and the choice to talk about it should I wish to. Usually, the thought of talking about my dead mother and dictatorial father seemed about as appealing as a case of shingles. But much to my surprise, I found I wanted to share that with Jace.

I let out a breath, walking over to sit on the couch opposite him. The cold from the leather seeped through my shirt and leggings as I leaned back.

"It *was* rough. It's still rough. I'm mad. And sad. I *miss* her. She was warmth and light and effervescence. And for some reason, she adored my father. She made him laugh. She appreciated his quirks. When she died," I took a deep breath in, the ache in my chest overwhelming for a moment before I started again. "When she died, my father changed. I was never allowed to grieve her. He became colder and domineering, caring more about his career than his own kid."

Jace leaned forward slowly and put his elbows on his knees, an implacable expression I'd never seen on him before etched in granite across his face.

"What did he do?"

His tone was low, rumbling in a way that made me squeeze my thighs together. Between his voice and the cold leather, I crossed my arms in an attempt to hide my peaked nipples, sending up my thanks to whoever invented the padded bra.

"Nothing like you're thinking. About a year after my mom died, when he thought I was being too rebellious, he moved me to a private school. Granted, my rebellion came in the form of me inviting Leah over for a sleepover and when he said no, I tried to sneak her in through that window." I pointed to said window in the corner. "Of course, he found out and Leah wasn't allowed to come over again for an entire year, and even after that, her visits were few and far between. Once my father won a Knoxville appointment for a judgeship, he was only home for a few hours, every couple of days. So, for the better part of the next five years, it was mostly just me, the housekeeper, and the grounds crew. My life was school, home, homework, repeat. I thought it'd be better after moving out right after high school, but he continued to be controlling over my life in little ways."

"How so?"

"He offered to pay for my college and med school. At first, I thought that would be great. I'd be out of the house to do as I pleased and still be debt free. Or so I thought. I started to get emails from his assistant, passive aggressive comments about how I was expected to act and what would happen should I be seen stepping out of line—like going to a party. Little threats that he'd take away what had been given, should I not do what he asked."

"Is that part of the reason why you call him father? At first, I thought it's because you'd lost your accent, but now I'm not so sure."

I opened my mouth in protest. Why, I didn't know. I had lost my accent.

"I've never called him Dad. It was always Sir or Father. I never really gave it a thought when I was little. It was a rule. And you don't say no to Judge Alberton."

"You seemed to say no to him just fine yesterday."

"And yesterday was the first time I've ever stood up to him like that. Trust me, I was scared shitless."

Jace leaned back against the couch, his relaxed posture returning. "You could've fooled me. I was standing right next to you, and you almost had me believing everything you were saying. You were so believable I thought you must have had some experience as an actress."

"Nope. No acting talents."

"I wouldn't be too sure about that." Jace leaned his head to the side and narrowed his eyes playfully. "Ryla has to get it from somewhere."

"Not from me," I protested as my gaze shifted left above the fireplace, eyeing the oil painting my father had commissioned after my mom died.

Following my gaze, Jace nodded to the portrait. "That must be your momma."

I nodded wistfully as I took in my mother, her features so like mine, the beautiful coloring of her eyes was spot-on. My father's eyes were serious, and laser focused; almost too hyper realistic. "That's a painting of a family photograph we had taken when I was nine years old. My father had it commissioned to be painted after she died."

Jace shifted, seemingly a little uncomfortable, at odds with his typical easygoing posture. Keeping his gaze on the painting, he asked out of the corner of his mouth, "You ever get the sensation of bein' . . . watched?"

Pausing a beat, he shifted his eyes to me and smirked, making me laugh.

"I know. Why are his eyes like that? No one told me that it had been commissioned, so one day, I was minding my own business, came in the library here, and bam!" I shuddered, recalling that day. "I was so scared, I rarely came in here again. And I'd loved sitting and reading in here for hours, even if it wasn't the same after my mom died."

Jace nodded thoughtfully. "I think I can fix that."

I didn't have any time to respond before Jace jumped up and pulled a leather chair over to the fireplace. After a quick test to make sure it could hold his weight, Jace hopped up, balancing nimbly on the arms of the chair, and reached for the painting.

I stood immediately. "What are you doing? Jace? Be careful!" My voice was anxious as I watched him balance precariously and jiggle the frame, then eventually pull it from the wall.

I sucked in a breath, speechless. I didn't actually think he'd be able to remove it. "I would have guessed it'd have been bolted to the wall."

Jace smirked down at me. "Mind giving me a hand? This weighs more than I thought."

"Then you shouldn't have pulled it off the wall!" I reached up and grabbed the corner closest to me.

"Too late now. Hold that left side." I gripped the frame's bottom left edge as he maneuvered the painting down to the ground, doing an impressive squat all while balancing on the arms of the chair. Once we got it on the floor, we propped it against the chair and stood back.

My father's eyes were still disturbing, but not as bad as when it wasn't hanging above you.

"Ryla looks so much like you," Jace murmured. "When you brought me in here on the tour this afternoon, I had to do a double take before I figured out that must have been you."

I looked forlornly at that little girl with a wide smile and hope in her heart. "Let's hope history doesn't repeat itself."

Suddenly, I felt pressure on my hand. Looking down, I saw that Jace was holding it. Our hands turned as if of their own accord, mine settling into his larger grip. I felt another squeeze and moved my attention to his face. His hazel eyes were warm and reassuring, a kind of radiance in their depth.

"It won't."

His grip felt different than it had this afternoon. Yes, it was still warm and strong, and yes, my core still throbbed, reminding me that I hadn't taken care of myself in a few weeks. But I also felt centered. Grounded. Like nothing was going to happen to me so long as I kept holding his hand.

"Well," Jace finally said, not letting go, "where to?"

I balked. "Jace, we can't move this."

"Sure, we can."

"But—"

"Does your father drop by a lot?" Jace interrupted me, dropping my hand and moving toward the portrait. He waggled his eyebrows. "Does he drop in unannounced to check the status of his creepy painting?"

"No," I huffed out, a smile playing at my lips. "Yesterday was the first I've seen him here since we moved in and I'm guessing it will be the last time he'll drop by unannounced."

Jace nodded, then bent at the knees and picked up the painting, walking it toward the door. "Perfect. Then there's no harm in moving it. Besides, I've always been a fan of asking for forgiveness rather than permission."

Anxiety gnawed in my gut as I watched him walk away, but then felt it shift to something different. Something that felt awfully like anticipation as I took in the bare wood paneling above the mantel. It looked so empty. Like the last day of school when your locker was all cleared out. It was an ending, but also a beginning. The closing of one chapter just before you started a new one.

"Jace?"

He turned his head back to me.

"Thank you."

Jace nodded. "No more cleaning at night. The kids and I got it."

I rolled my eyes. "You say that now . . ."

He winked. "They don't call me Jace Poppins for nothing."

"No one calls you that."

"Not yet," Jace replied blithely in a singsong, starting to move again.

I took one last look at the painting, then back to him. "If you accidentally drop that and scuff up my father's face, I won't tell anyone."

Jace's laughter rang down the hall as he walked out of the library.

I spent the next several minutes staring at the fresh start on the wall, an irrepressible smile on my lips.

CHAPTER
EIGHTEEN
JACE

"I find it interesting that women continue to fall for your antics."

"My antics are the best part about me. Without them I only have my chickens and they're much less charming."

Vamp Got Your Tongue by Lena Benjamin

I gulped. I knew this was going to be an issue.

I was standing in Polly's kitchen on Monday morning in front of Barry, a recipe for flaxseed almond pancakes staring at me. Mocking me.

Did I know what the hell a flaxseed was?

No.

I was in deep shit.

I didn't sleep well. The image of Polly in the library, tight black leggings and thin college T-shirt, was burned into my mind as much as the feel of her delicate hand, holding on to me, trusting me. She'd been pretty as ever this morning. I made coffee as we made small talk in the kitchen, keeping my hands busy so I didn't accidentally reach out to grip her waist and bury my face in her neck, breathing in all that she was. I held the coffee cup in my hands as Polly explained that Ryla and Max typically slept until half past seven or so, my eyes tracking her down the hallway when she left for the day.

I watched the rain fall outside as I drank my coffee, taking in the grand view of the Smokies in the distance. This property was easily twenty or thirty acres. I couldn't see a neighboring property from my vantage point here. Anger flared in my gut, recalling what Polly told me about her upbringing in this house. How isolated she must have been. After finishing my coffee, I pulled up Barry, bringing me to my current predicament.

Cooking was "not a gift I received," as Pop so delicately put it years ago. Scrambled eggs and toast were as gourmet as I got. So, when Polly asked if I could cook during our tour yesterday, hope in her eyes, I lied.

"What is flaxseed?" I asked my phone.

"It's in there."

I jumped and turned, staring at Polly's mini-me in heart pajamas, carrying a giant elephant under one arm and what looked like a small goat with horns under the other.

My eyes shifted to where she was pointing: the pantry. Made sense.

"Good mornin' to you, lil' miss. I was fixing to grab the almond flour and flaxseed so I can make us some pancakes, what do ya say?"

Unmoved by my enthusiastic Southern charm, Ryla, hair and face still a little sleep rumpled, walked over to me, tossed her stuffed animals on the counter, crawled up onto a stool, then looked to me like an owl and blinked.

Alrighty. Someone wasn't a morning person.

"Be right back."

I went into the pantry, but it was hopeless. I had no idea what a flaxseed was. It sounded more like a sneeze than a food.

"Can you make pancakes?" Ryla asked, suddenly appearing in the doorway of the pantry like a ninja, making me jump into action. I tried to make myself look busy by rummaging around the pantry shelves.

"What? Sure, I can."

In response, Ryla gave me a *sure you do* look that a girl her age should not know how to do. Maybe it was ingrained into every woman's DNA, because I'd seen exactly five people give me that look and they were all female: my mother, my sister, Rae, Sienna, and now, this six-year-old spitfire.

Ryla took a few steps into the pantry and muscled a large paper sack into her arms. I knelt down, taking it from her, reading the front of the package. *Almond Flour* read the label. I gave a resigned, breathless chuckle as Ryla moved on quietly, next plucking a small plastic canister from the same shelf and holding it up. *Ground flaxseed* it read. Grinning sheepishly, I ushered her out of the pantry and put the ingredients on the island next to Barry. I eyed the recipe again, then back down to Ryla.

She lifted her arms up.

I stared at her.

She stared at me.

"Pick me up," she ordered, making me jump to attention and pick her straight up, holding her by the armpits.

"Put me down," she ordered again, pointing to the island.

Once I placed her on the countertop, she sat cross legged, then spun Barry toward her.

"Flaxseed almond pancakes, strawberries, turkey bacon," she read aloud, then eyed me, seeing through my lie and directly into my soul.

I hedged my bets, squinting at her out of one eye. "When does your brother wake up?"

She shrugged. "Later."

"Does he eat breakfast?"

"Sometimes."

Helpful. Truly helpful. I pointed to the menu, taking a deep breath and trying again. "Does he eat this breakfast?"

"No. He has the honey Cheerios."

Interesting. More interesting because it wasn't written down.

"How committed are you to these pancakes?" Because strawberries and turkey bacon I could do. Flaxseed almond pancakes? Not so much.

She continued to look at me blankly.

I tried again. "Let me say it this way. If I make the strawberries and turkey bacon, will you eat the Cheerios instead of the pancakes and call it a deal?"

Ryla crossed her arms, looking ready to play hardball. "What will you give me?"

I crossed my arms right back. "I like your style. What are you thinking? A high five? A piggyback ride? What kind of currency are you expecting here?"

"Ten dollars."

"Ten bucks?" I shouted, lowering my voice when I remembered Max was sleeping. "Try again. You think I was born yesterday?"

She actually brought her index finger to her chin and tapped it, making me sweat. A mischievous smile spread over her face. "A dog."

I frowned. "I think you're getting colder here."

"One cup almond flour," she read aloud, looking down at the menu, then back at me.

This girl was a human lie detector.

The defeat in my voice was obvious as I dropped my arms to my sides. "What kind of dog?"

CHAPTER
NINETEEN

POLLY

American Thighs by Lady Jane
Narrated by Brittney Houston

My clinic day was back-to-back patients followed by a meeting at the high school with Leah's friend, Rose.

Rose Hammel was a warm hug of a person. She was just as cheerful as I'd pictured from her emails last week. I couldn't decide what I liked about her best: her thick Tennessee accent, her contagious enthusiasm for the school, or her office. I marveled at all the Disney princesses and Star Wars figurines along her shelves while we talked. I'd been a little nervous, wondering how we'd get along, but she was clearly a kindred spirit.

"Leah told me about the grant the school was awarded last spring, the one meant to expand disability and 504 plan accommodations. Congratulations."

Rose beamed, her tight curls bouncing as she nodded.

"I tell you what, I practically scared Reggie half to death in his office next door when I found out. I shrieked so loud he came runnin'—expectin' a spider, 'cause he knows I hate those little devils and he'll take 'em outside for me now

"

and again." Rose paused, seeing my confused expression. "Oh sorry, sugar, that's Mr. Sievers, the guidance counselor. His office is right next door." Rose pointed behind me, then continued on. "The grant is great news for the district. We've got more kids than ever needin' accommodation, which is wonderful, knowing that we're helpin' more students succeed, but that also means we need help. Reggie and I try to attend every meetin' so we can walk the families through the evaluation process, but we can't get to 'em all, there's just too many students needin' help. What I'd really like is to hire a special education advocate for each school in the district. That way, the advocate can work with every student and their family needin' an IEP or 504 plan."

I shook my head. "I'm not familiar with a special education advocate, what's that?"

"An advocate knows the federal and state school laws for disabilities. They work with a family to help coordinate with us at the school level, so the students get the services they need," Rose explained.

"That sounds amazing. What else is the grant money going toward?"

Rose flipped through her stack of papers and pulled out a packet.

"Here's the proposal I gave to the school board at their meetin' earlier this month. I proposed updates for special education technology aids, like tablets with those text-to-speech apps, and to expand the standard 504 plan templates to include each individual mental health disorder, like sensory processin' disorder and the like."

I flipped through the proposal as she talked. "Please excuse me if this question sounds ignorant, but how does the district determine if a student meets criteria to be eligible for service? Like, for ADHD as an example."

"Shoot, that's not ignorant, hun. If I had more folks askin' questions like you, there'd be a heck of a lot less judgment 'round these parts. Like how people still judge me when my accent slips now and again. Growin' up we were as poor as church mice. Even though I got myself an education and a 'highfalutin vocabulary,' per my meemaw, people still think I'm dull as a sack of nails."

I'd known Rose for all of ten minutes but the thought of anyone insulting her infuriated me, even if I was mildly curious what Rose considered to be her accent "slipping".

"Now what were you sayin', hun? Oh, that's right, determinin' who needs what. Well, if a student already has a diagnosis from an outside provider, like a counselor, we use their medical notes to help determine eligibility."

Being a pediatrician for years, this is something I already knew. "What if the student doesn't have an official diagnosis? How long does that take? Because it's been taking months to get my patients into a counselor, much less a neuropsychologist or psychiatrist."

Rose pointed to her nose. "You got that one right. That's exactly why the last part of my proposal aims to reduce wait times for a medical provider down to thirty days."

My eyebrows hit my hairline. Thirty days? It's been taking months for my patients to see any mental health provider, period. I shook my head slowly. "Is that even possible? Unless a family can afford to pay out of pocket for a private provider or has a favor called in, the wait times have been months."

Rose's mouth twisted grimly. "It's the same here, I'm afraid. We're tryin' to build up our referral pool and have the grant provide stipends for private providers to assess the student within thirty days, but it's been a tough row to hoe so far. First, we gotta get the board to approve the stipends. Then, we gotta get a confirmed list of providers willing to see these kids." Rose smiled and winked at me. "That's where you can help us."

I sat up straighter. "Me?"

Nodding, she slid a paper across her desk. "I need someone on the medical side who can help me recruit these providers."

I scanned the sheet, wincing as I took in the full, single-spaced list of provider names, and balked. I wanted to help, but I didn't want to overpromise. "Listen, Rose. I'm a single mother. My ten-year-old son, Max, is going to need his own 504 plan due to his anxiety. I'd love to help, but I don't know if I have the extra time to research and field all of these calls."

Rose held up her hand. "Oh, no, Dr. Alberton—"

"Polly, please," I interrupted.

"Polly," Rose corrected with a small grin. "I'm not expectin' you to make all those calls, I've already contacted them. There are few providers with a mark next to their name who've indicated a *preference* to speak with a doctor, rather than a *coordinator*." Rose pointed to herself, then let her drawl slip a little more. "I didn't tell 'em I was an ER nurse for a decade before this. Better to let 'em think I'm one of them backwoods folks who was raised on moonshine and mud."

My mouth gaped. "Did someone actually say that to you?"

Rose's eyes flashed. "Not in so many words, bless their hearts."

Looking at the list, I saw only a handful of names with a star next to their names, which seemed much more manageable, but I frowned just the same at the thought of talking to these providers. I didn't want to bring her into my family drama, but I could handle talking to elitist jerks. I'd spent over twenty years placating the biggest jerk of them all.

"When will you start hiring advocates?" I asked Rose.

Rose glanced at her shut office door, then leaned closer to me. "We haven't started the hirin' process, yet. The school board has to approve my proposal first and they were deadlocked at the last meeting: three said yes, three said no."

"Did they give a reason?"

"Not out loud. Brad Goldenstein, that's the school board president, found a loophole that the grant funds could be used for anythin' the state considers a disability, including orthopedic disabilities. He announced this last month, when lo and behold, a proposal of his own materialized out of thin air. It had some small upgrades to equipment for students with physical disabilities, but he proposed that the majority of the funds should go to resurfacing the high school and middle school basketball courts and football fields. Mind you, he's got four sons—all of whom play basketball and football. He tried to explain it away, saying it would reduce injury. And while I don't oppose anything like that, only three percent of the students in the district have orthopedic disabilities. But forty percent of our students, which is above the US average, have a plan for a mental health diagnosis."

"The rest of the board didn't see through him?" I asked Rose.

Rose's face took on a sour expression. "It's really only two of the members who are the holdouts besides Mr. Goldenstein, but he, is the stickiest of 'em. One school board member is for sure in Goldenstein's pocket, and the other member took the opinion of Dr. Dixon over any of us who work in special education. When Dr. Dixon spoke in favor of Mr. Goldenstein's proposal at the last school board meetin', the vote was split three to three."

I wanted to tell Rose that sticky wasn't the right word. Smarmy, slimy, and sleazy were what came to mind.

"Any idea why Dr. Dixon would be in favor of this Brad Goldenstein's proposal?"

Rose chuckled sadly. "Dr. Dixon plays golf with Mr. Goldenstein weekly and somehow managed to snag tickets to every Vols game this year." Rose leaned forward and patted my hand. "That's University of Tennessee football, hun. I forget you're practically a Yankee."

I actually knew that reference, but let it go. "With Dr. Dixon retiring, how do you see my role in this?"

Excitement danced in her eyes. "What we really need, is someone who can advocate for these program upgrades to the school board. We need someone who won't roll over to Goldenstein's demands. I 'reckon if we can even turn one vote in our favor at the next school board meetin', our proposal will get the green light."

What kind of political nightmare had I walked into? I suddenly felt caught. Rose didn't want someone who would roll over to any demand. I had a lot of practice placating smarmy, elitist pricks, but standing up to them was a new development.

"When's the next school board meeting?"

"It's the first Friday in August so about three more weeks."

It was an awful lot to take on. I know I needed the money, but was I really what the school district needed?

Then, I pictured Max crying in the backseat of my car, pleading with me to take him home every morning when I dropped him off for kindergarten. I recalled the frustration I felt when his school attributed his behavior as "normal" school adjustment for his age, telling me he was smart so there was no problem. How good it felt to finally meet with a doctor at Max's IOP program who understood what we were going through, who helped Max regain some control, only to be met with a brick wall at his school when he was discharged from his IOP. I wondered if things would have been different for us, if there were someone like Rose at his school.

.   .   .

I was nodding before I even realized it. "It sounds like we have a lot of work to do."

———

The next hour flew by; Rose and I made plans to meet again later this week. I was truly excited by something at work for the first time in years. It felt like I could make a difference not only for my son, but also for kids with similar struggles.

Pulling into the driveway, I saw Jace and Ryla sitting in one of the spare garage bays, door open. Ryla waved happily to me. As I got out of the car, I noticed Jace was sitting strangely: sitting on bent knees, his arms were straight, and his palms flat on the garage floor. I squinted as I walked closer. It looked like there was something . . . oh my God! There was something looped around his neck!

Hurrying closer, I saw that yes, there was indeed one of Ryla's jump ropes tied around Jace's neck and the other end was held by my daughter. Panic gripped me as I took in Jace's tongue, which was hanging out of his mouth, and his chest was moving up and down in short pants.

"Ryla! Did you tie that around Jace's neck? Jace, are you ok?"

Jace merely looked at me, calm as ever, despite being strangled by my daughter.

Ryla shook her head at me. "This isn't Jace, Mom. This is Kevin."

"Ruff!" Jace . . . *barked.*

I stopped short, looking between Jace and Ryla.

"Excuse me?"

"I'm puppy training him."

"Ryla." I pinched the bridge of my nose and softened my tone, lest she pull on that leash. "Please explain what's going on. Because from where I'm standing, it looks like you made a leash out of your jump rope, looped it around Jace's neck, and are making him act like a dog you named Kevin."

"I know what we're doing. We're almost done with training. He only has to earn his gold star for stay and then we're done."

Ryla pointed to a makeshift poster behind her, which I hadn't noticed until now.

Sit: ⭐

Fetch: ⭐

Speak: ⭐

Roll Over: ⭐

Stay

Well. Just . . . well. *This* was an interesting turn of events. Biting my bottom lip, I turned my head slowly to find Jace watching me. He was still panting but had raised his eyebrows in the strangest resigned puppy/human expression ever, as if to say, *Just go with it.*

"Ok," I squeaked out, fighting laughter. "I see you're fine here." I glanced at my watch without actually seeing the time. "Guess I should head inside for dinner. When you're . . . done here, why don't you come inside? Oh, and uh, Ryla? Is"—I coughed to cover my laugh—"Kevin, housebroken? Maybe he should stay outside and Jace can come in with you when you're finished."

"Wuf!" Jace/Kevin barked, eyes twinkling.

"Shh. Quiet, Kevin," Ryla admonished.

I had to bite the inside of my cheek to stop from laughing, practically running into the house before erupting into belly laughter. As I walked through the house, my worries from the day melted away with my laughter. A light sensation took root in my chest as I bounced up the stairs, one that I hadn't felt in a long time.

I found Max in the playroom after changing out of my work clothes. He was working on the red shoes of what looked like a one-foot-tall Lego statue of Boyfriend from Friday Night Funkin', complete with blue hair and a red baseball hat.

"Look at that! It's amazing!" I said, walking toward him, giving him a hug before I sat across from him.

Max flashed me a smile. "Thanks."

"I don't remember you getting this set."

"Jace found the instructions online from a mod and helped me find all the right pieces," Max said as he continued assembling his Lego creation.

Did I know what a mod was? Why, yes, I did. I gave myself a quick mental high five that I still understood some of Max's lingo thus far, knowing that in a few short years I'd probably have no idea what he was saying.

"I guess I'm not surprised we had all the pieces," I teased. Max loved collecting things, most of the time just to collect them, but sometimes he'd also play with them.

"Jace even played some Friday Night Funkin' and was sooo bad," Max giggled.

"It sounds like you had fun."

Max's eyes flitted up to me, then back down, his cheeks still upturned with a smile.

"How did your journal entry go today?" I asked, still admiring his Lego work.

A guilty expression crossed his face. "I didn't do it, yet."

A flash of panic went through me, thinking that he could relapse if we didn't follow his therapist's instructions perfectly. But the typical bone deep, heavy feeling I'd carried with me on the daily wasn't there to drag me further into panic mode, giving me the mental energy to pause and think before responding.

I placed my hand over Max's. "'Yet' is a great word. And feelings are hard to think about, right? It's tougher still to put your feelings into words. Tell you what. We can do the exercises together, tonight. I'm so glad you had a good day."

His answering smile filled my heart with joy and that feeling of lightness persisted on my way to the kitchen to make dinner.

I was almost done preparing an oven meal kit for dinner when Jace carried Ryla inside, piggyback style. Ryla was chattering and giggling in Jace's ear and that light feeling turned to a glowing, so much so that my chest practically ached. I'd never seen Ryla do that with anyone except Giselle. Certainly, never with her dad. David was more like a distant relative than a father. He was away from home more often than not since she was one year old. When he was home, he was a very hands-off father, particularly with anything that involved a traditionally female task. And of course, I wanted to make it so that I was the perfect mother, wife, and doctor, thinking that if I did that, everything would be okay. Instead, I enabled the passive relationship he had with the kids, until he acted more like an elderly great-grandfather than a father. Like he was someone you tell happy stories to but never make happy memories with.

"Polly! When did you get home?" Jace exclaimed as Ryla continued to giggle on his back.

"A few minutes ago," I answered, playing along. "Ryla was outside with her new dog, Kevin. It looked like training was going well."

"That Kevin is a menace! Don't let him fool you. We left him outside with a bone and some water. No inside sleeping for that rangy mutt!"

"How did everything go today?" I asked as Ryla climbed down.

"I think it went ok, what do you think?" Jace had his hands on his hips, smiling down at Ryla, who smiled impishly at him, shaking her head teasingly, her entire body vibrating as she giggled.

"Not good?" I teased, taking a knee in front of her. "Then what's with all this giggling, huh?" Peals of Ryla's laughter rang through the kitchen as I tickled her belly.

"I missed you," I whispered after her laughter quieted, giving her forehead a kiss. "I was just finishing up dinner. You want to head upstairs and wash your hands? I need to talk to Jace for a minute and then you can help me if you want. Or do you want some tablet time before dinner?"

"Tablet time!" Ryla shouted and ran out of the room.

Jace held out a hand to help me up, but I popped up on my own despite longing to take his outstretched hand. Would his grip feel as safe and strong as it did yesterday?

I plucked a dish towel off the island and folded it, playing off any hint of how I was feeling. "It sounds like the day went well. I was worried for a minute when I saw that rope around your neck. I thought I'd need to get a lawyer on the phone."

Jace leaned against the island counter on his hip, facing me. "I was worried for a minute, too," Jace teased, putting a finger in the collar of his shirt and turning his head from side to side. Picking up an apple to slice it, I quietly ignored how the movement of his neck made my mouth go dry.

"How was your day?" Jace asked.

I stopped mid-slice. "My day?"

Jace narrowed his eyes. "Yeah. Your day." He raised his eyebrows. "You alright?"

"Fine! My day was fine. I'm fine. Work was fine," I stammered, then rolled my lips over my teeth and pressed them together. I couldn't admit that it'd been so long since someone genuinely asked how my day was going, that I actually misunderstood the question.

He cocked his head to one side. "You sure? You can tell me. I know your job must be hard."

"Sometimes. But today was kind of great, actually."

"So more than fine?" Jace teased.

"Yes," I chuckled, peeling some of the apple slices. Max didn't like the texture of the skin. "I recently accepted the position to be the medical director of the school district. I met with the special education coordinator at the school today, and I'm kind of excited about it. Even if it's strangely more political than I expected."

"How so?" Jace asked, stealing an apple slice. He winked as he crunched it between his teeth. I had to tear my eyes away from his jaw as he chewed.

He is your employee. He is NOT a steak. He is your children's nanny.

"The school district received a grant this spring to support special education programs. Apparently, there are members of the board, including the school board president, that wants to use a large portion of the grant to resurface the school's basketball courts and football field. I guess the old medical director was always a sure supporter for him."

"It's that what you did back in Chicago? Work with school districts?"

"No, this is new. I was aware of what an IEP or 504 plan was, only becoming more familiar with it when I tried to get one for Max this past spring. They never taught us much about specialized education plans in medical school or my pediatrics residency. But I do see a lot of kids with mental health problems and the system is so backed up, it takes months for kids to get care. If we can have kids see the providers they need faster and work in concert with the school and their families, it could change a lot of lives, including my son's life."

"That sounds pretty incredible, Polly." Jace's voice was closer than I expected. I glanced up and startled, not having noticed that Jace was so close that I could feel the heat of him against my side.

I cleared my throat nervously and shifted away from Jace. "Uh ha! I don't know if I'd go that far. I'm not counting my chickens, as they say. How did things go here?" My tone was too bright.

"I'm afraid we didn't follow your schedule to the letter." Jace nodded and I followed his gaze to Barry, the tablet.

"What do you mean?" I wiped my hands on a towel and turned on the tablet.

Nothing on the kids' daily checklists had been checked off.

"We started off with breakfast, but then we just went where the day took us. Ryla showed me her dollhouse after breakfast, which turned into an impromptu Barbie fashion show. Then Max taught me how to play Friday Night Funkin', which, by the way, was incredibly hard and your son needs to take piano or drums or something, because that kid's rhythm skills are amazing." Jace ran his fingers through his hair as he continued, "Then after lunch, Kevin the dog showed up and the checklist kind of went out the window."

Jace was absently rubbing his hand through the tangle of curls at the back of his head, looking at me with raised eyebrows, as if waiting for me to be, what . . . mad? Mad that my kids were happy and laughing and clearly had a great day? I was confused how he could possibly think I'd be mad. Then, I looked back down to the schedule, realizing for a moment, how this must look to anyone else.

Controlling.

Like I was some sort of anti-fun momzilla, making a checklist for my kid's day. Max's therapist didn't see any problem with creating structure for the kids, in fact, he encouraged it. This past year was a constant juggling game of coordinating the kids' schedules, meals, laundry, housework, and counseling appointments—and that's not to mention all the other odds and ends. If the kids needed new shoes, who got them? If they needed haircuts, who scheduled them? It was all here on Barry, keeping me sane.

But somewhere along the way, I lost the fun stuff. A sinking feeling settled in my belly, weighing me down.

"I'm sorry. We'll do better tomorrow." Jace's quiet words came from my right, obviously mistaking my silence for censure.

I flashed a smile, shoving my feelings of embarrassment and horror and disappointment into a box deep within myself.

"It's totally fine. My kids are happy, healthy. We're all good."

"Polly—"

"Please, no need to apologize," I cut him off, the heavy feeling in my belly moving into my chest and turning into pressure—the intense need to be alone was suddenly overwhelming. "I'm sure you're eager to have some free time. Thank you for your help today. You're free! Go! Before Ryla makes you be a cat!"

My attempt at a joke fell flat as Jace stepped back, a troubled look in his eyes. "You sure? I can help with supper. I don't mind."

How could I explain that I wasn't mad at him, and it had everything to do with me? I waved him off, stepping backwards a few paces.

"Yes, really! Take your freedom and go. The kids will only take advantage of you if you stick around. Well, Ryla at least . . ." I trailed off with a humorless laugh.

I would love to say that I stopped talking right then, but that would be a dirty lie. No, instead I entered the portion of the evening I'd like to call, *Polly felt so awkward she blabbered in run-on sentences until she borderline insulted his Southern roots* portion of the evening.

Coming soon to a theater near you.

"You're young! You should be out drinking and living life at one of those, what do people call it?" I looked up at the ceiling and snapped my fingers. "A honky-tonk!" I practically shrieked. "Yes! A honky-tonk. You should go and dance and drink some moonshine at a honky-tonk until the wee hours of the morning!"

Jace, to his credit, was looking at me with confusion, not with pity or fear, which was most certainly deserved. Though, his kindness didn't stop me from wanting to dissolve into a puddle on the floor.

"Alright. If you need me, you know where to find me." Then, like a polite Southern gentleman, he gave me a head bob along with a dimpled smile I didn't deserve. "Y'all have a good night."

I held my breath as I watched him walk out of the kitchen, not letting it out until I heard the faint snick of his door close.

Bending at the waist, I fell forward onto the island countertop. I rocked my forehead back and forth against the cool granite in pure self-loathing until I heard one of my kid's footsteps on the stairs. I forced myself upright to act like everything was ok—I was well practiced at that.

Later that night, I found myself sitting at the table after dinner, my laptop in front of me. Usually after dinner, I tried to spend a little time with the kids. But tonight, like so many nights over the past few months, I had things to do: emails to return, new shoes to order for Ryla, etc. The conversation I'd had with Jace played on repeat in my head until I read the same email three times and finally closed my computer, utterly exhausted. Rubbing my face, I leaned back in my chair and looked over at my kids. They were both on their tablets, the house dreadfully quiet. The laughter and smiles from when I got home had been extinguished.

We'd reverted to our factory settings.

CHAPTER
TWENTY

JACE

I may not be allowed to love her, but that doesn't mean I'll let anyone hurt her.

Katja Millay, *The Sea of Tranquility*

I woke up agitated, having slept fitfully and waking well before sunrise. Something had spooked Polly last night. At first, I thought it was because we didn't get anything done on her checklist, but then she got all nervous and cute, babbling about honky-tonks and moonshine, making me confused. It was all I could do not to wrap my arms around her, reassuring her that whatever it was, it was going to be alright. I'd stayed in my room the entire night, eating a protein bar I'd found at the bottom of my gym bag for supper. I'd listened to the sounds of Polly and her kids until they went to bed, then the silence that followed.

I'd purposefully come down to the kitchen early the next morning, not wanting to miss Polly before she left for work. Pale morning sunlight was streaming through the windows so I didn't turn on the lights as I waited for my coffee to brew.

Polly rushed through the kitchen doorway as if on a mission, immediately walking to the table and to rifle through her purse, which must have been sitting there all night. Hair high up in a bun, her elegant neck was on full display. She was wearing earbuds, like in the library on Sunday night.

Curiosity had been playing like a song on repeat in my mind since that night, wondering what book she was listening to, because she sure as hell wasn't listening to a medical journal. Maybe it was another quirky comedy about a group of drag queens that compete in drag races after their show. Or maybe it was something a little more suspenseful, a little grittier, like the *American Tail* bounty hunter series, of which she'd read two books that I knew of so far. When I'd learned about Polly's upbringing, the sad story about her momma passing, the neglectful nature of her father, the undiluted anger I felt surprised me. It was no wonder Polly liked reading books about strong women. Because in the last two days, those little glimmers were there, peeking out of her. How dare her father take a woman as strong and bright as Polly and try to change her, forcing her to be anything else but herself.

If she were ever mine, I'd give her room to shine, hoping to bask in her light as long as she'd have me.

Polly was still rummaging through her purse, not having seen me standing near the back of the kitchen. I shifted my weight and took a slow step in her direction, holding up my hands so I didn't startle her.

Polly gasped and before I could blink an eye, she pivoted toward me, grabbed her purse like a WNBA pro, and chest pressed it directly at . . . *my* man purse.

"Why," I squeaked out, clutching my pocket-Jaces and sunk to my knees.

"Oh my God! I didn't see you!" Polly yelled, rushing to me.

"S'fine," I wheezed out.

"Are you sure?" Polly leaned over me, putting her hand on my shoulder.

I could only nod.

Polly sighed and looped her arm through mine. "Let me help you to the couch," she said, helping me stand despite the deep pulsating ache in my groin. "Do you need ice?"

"Ice?!" I hollered, hitting an octave I'd not reached since the sixth grade.

Polly jerked back, holding up her hands. "That's what you do for an injury! Would heat be better?"

My voice came out pained as I rasped, "I thought you were a doctor."

"I don't know! I don't have balls!" Polly yelled, sounding flustered.

Two seconds passed until I smirked, which was followed shortly by a soft chuckle from Polly and then we were both laughing quietly, the tension between us finally breaking.

I managed a slow step backward. "I didn't think it was possible to laugh after getting hit in the nuts," I said, stifling a little groan with each step back.

She walked over to grab her purse from the floor, smiling apologetically. "Probably haven't pictured being attacked with a purse while making coffee, either. Are you sure you're ok?"

I nodded, finally able to lean back against the counter where my coffee had finished brewing. "I'm fine. It's not the first time the Vargas jewels got hit."

"When was the first time?" Polly busied herself, grabbing a tall, handled thermos and filled it with tap water.

"I almost don't want to say."

Polly looked over her shoulder at me. "Now I want to know even more."

I groaned. "Fine. But don't laugh. Sam convinced me to help him shear a herd of sheep once."

Polly's eye twitched, and she turned back to the sink.

"Oh."

Her voice sounded strangled.

I sighed, acting disappointed, but I was secretly pleased we'd gone back to our easy banter. "Go ahead and laugh."

Polly's answering laughter filled the kitchen and my soul.

"Why on earth would you two shear a herd of sheep?" Polly grabbed a packet from a drawer in front of her, then held up a hand. "Wait, this is the same Sam who hired you as a clown when I wanted a magician, right?" She dumped the packet into her thermos and stirred it.

Ruefully, I shook my head. "One and the same. I did gain a healthy respect for sheep farmers that day. I try to appreciate their sacrifice every time I put on a wool hat." I ran my hand back and forth through my hair to emphasize it.

Polly's eyes moved to my hair and held there, my breath stalling as they remained fixed on my unruly curls for one beat, two beats . . . then, abruptly, wrenched her gaze back to mine.

My Vargas jewels gave a little throb. And not because they just got nailed with a purse. Maybe she wasn't as immune to me as I thought.

"Got a big day planned?" I asked, hoping she'd share more about her day, like she had yesterday after she got home, just before everything went to hell.

Shaking her head, she spun the cap on her thermos. "Nothing too big. The kids are still sleeping. I'll be home by three so I can take them to Max's therapy appointment this afternoon. You'll have plenty of time to get to Young Wills. I'm still not sure about Ryla trying another new thing. A few weeks ago she got kicked out of the YMCA swimming lessons. Maybe Ryla could go on Thursday, but I'm on call so I don't know. Or maybe it'd be better in the fall. I have to think about it. If you have any questions, it's all in the—" her eyes darted to Barry on the island next to her—"schedule."

Shoot. It *was* what I said about the schedule that spooked her last night. "I'll make sure the kids are all ready to go when you get home. And we'll get everything on the checklist done, don't you worry!"

With a thin smile, she turned to walk down the hall, her long legs eating up the floor until she was out of sight.

My Vargas jewels gave another little throb.

Yeah, you and me both.

———

When I pulled into the high school parking lot for Young Wills practice that night, I spotted a familiar forestry truck. The truck's tailgate was down and Jethro Winston, Sienna's husband, was attempting to unload a large tribal mask that looked similar to the mockup we'd designed for our set. The kids were putting on *The Lion King Jr.* for their end of summer performance and having a blast.

"Hey, Jethro," I called out as I walked up next to him.

"Jace." Jethro nodded.

"Whoa, get a look at these." I shook my head, studying the masks in the truck bed. At least three feet tall and two feet wide, the three masks appeared to be made from solid wood. Each was decorated with metal pieces soldered together in an intricate tribal pattern. These were clearly a work of art; being more fitting for a museum rather than a set piece for a kids' musical.

I glanced up at Jethro. "Is that real metal?"

"Yup. We got an artist in the family. Shelly said to tell y'all that she saw the design and made some improvements on it."

"It looks better than anything I could do. Seems heavy though. Want some help?"

"Nah, I got it." Jethro grunted when he tried to lift one of the masks, then set it down. "Actually, if you wouldn't mind picking up that side, Jace," he directed as we went about buddy lifting it. The mask had to weigh at least a hundred pounds. And there were two more in the truck.

We were breathing heavily, having just gotten the third and final mask through the entrance, when I heard a familiar voice from the hallway behind us.

"Well, if it isn't two of my favorite men." Sienna, lovely as usual, walked over to us. "Look at that thing. The picture did not do it justice. How many did Shelly make?"

"Three of 'em." Jethro pointed to the two masks we'd set in the corner already.

"Jace, thank you so much for helping." Sienna flashed her typical dimpled smile at me, then patted my cheek. As she bent to study the masks more closely, Jethro cleared his throat. Sienna turned her head to him, a wrinkle in her brow.

"Didn't carry it all by himself, did he?" Jethro grumbled, toeing the ground. Sienna laughed and went over to him, giving him a quick kiss, stroking his cheek. "Thank you, my love."

Looking appeased, Jethro rubbed his hands together gesturing to the masks. "So, where do you want 'em?"

Sienna, who'd gone back to studying the masks, waved her hand toward the auditorium. "On the stage. Wow, she really outdid herself."

I cleared my throat. "Has uh, this artist ever made a set design piece before?"

Sienna looked up at my question. "I'm not sure, why?"

"Well, this weighs, what would you say," I looked to Jethro who scratched the back of his head, "a buck? Maybe a buck ten?"

Jethro nodded in agreement.

Sienna narrowed her eyes, understanding the problem. "Oh."

Jethro looked between us. "What is it?"

"They're too heavy for the kids to move on and off stage between the scenes," Sienna answered, pointing at the masks.

"Can they stay onstage? Like permanent set pieces?" Jethro asked.

Sienna and I shook our heads. We all looked at the masks for another minute, then I snapped my fingers. "Wheels. You think we can put these things on a dolly?"

Sienna crouched down, inspecting the base of a mask. "Probably. It's flat enough. Good thinking, Jace."

Jethro clapped me on the shoulder, then addressed his wife. "Y'all sure about keeping the boys here with you? I can take 'em."

"We'll keep them. But do you mind stopping at home to pack some overnight things for them? I just talked to Rae, and she and Jackson offered to keep them at their house tonight for a little 'auntie and uncle' sleepover." Sienna slunk closer to Jethro, going on tiptoes to whisper in his ear, causing the tip of it to flush pink.

I pretended to look in the other direction until I heard Jethro cough and say in a very animated tone, "I'll head right home." He nodded to me. "Jace." Then he winked at Sienna, who blew him a kiss as he walked out the door.

Sienna and I started toward the auditorium when she asked, "So, what's this I hear about you being a nanny?"

My steps faltered for a beat. That answered the question I'd had since Sunday— if Rae had filled anyone in on my new job. I'd been so distracted these last few days that I was only now skeptical why neither Rae nor Sienna had dropped by Polly's house under the guise of being neighborly. And while I usually admired their generosity and tolerated their questions, I didn't want to get into it today.

I underplayed my response. "Just that, I suppose. I'm watching two kids, having some fun, making some money."

Sienna, not one to be deterred, eyed me with suspicion. "What brought this on? I've never known you to accept a babysitting job for anyone but me or Charlotte, and I know you've gotten a lot of offers."

"Why Miss Diaz, are you feelin' a little jealous?"

Sienna laughed. "Oh, don't try that tone on me. I have three boys and can smell evasion a mile away."

Switching tactics, I decided to go with a simplified truth. "There's no conspiracy. The woman I nanny for is a single mother. She and her two kids live in a house up near the Donner Lodge. Her daddy's a judge in Knoxville. She doesn't have much help. And with my parents planning on moving, I needed a place to stay. Simple as that."

I did not add, *unless you count that she's incredibly beautiful and the more I talk to her, the more I like her, even though it'd take ten lifetimes traveling at light speed for me to be in her same galaxy.*

A look of surprise came over Sienna's face. "Your parents are moving? Since when?"

I opened the auditorium doors, allowing her to pass. The sound of kids running and playing onstage before practice filled the cavernous space. "It's a new thing." I shrugged my shoulders as we walked down the aisle, past the rows of seats. "Pop's arthritis is getting worse and there's a condo in Florida for sale near my brother."

Sienna reached out and touched my arm. "I'm so sorry to hear about Nick's health. You let us know if they need anything. And you know you're welcome to stay with us anytime. I'm sure Rae and Jackson feel the same."

"That's kind of you. And I'm flattered y'all are worried about me, but really, I'm fine."

"I do worry about you, suddenly moving in with a family no one knows. And it's not just me. Rae's worried, too."

Speaking of the devil, we'd just reached the front of the stage when Rae materialized out of thin air. Standing shoulder to shoulder, Rae and Sienna fixed their gazes upon me.

"You get anything out of him?" Rae asked Sienna out of the corner of her mouth, even though her eyes remained on me.

"Single mom. Two kids. Doesn't want to talk about it. You didn't tell me she was a single mom." Sienna also spoke from the corner of her mouth, clearly talking to Rae, but looking at me the whole time.

I rolled my eyes.

"I thought I told you that?" Rae murmured to Sienna

"You did not," Sienna answered.

"I swear I did."

"I think I'd remember if I—"

I cleared my throat. "Ladies! As entertaining as y'all think this is, what do you say we start rehearsal?"

Rae turned to Sienna. "I remember coming to town, barely knowing anyone. It would have been lonely if I didn't have you."

"And with two kids? I can't imagine all the things she must have on her mind. She must be exhausted. What about bringing her a welcome basket? Jen would probably contribute a cake or two, Cletus is usually all too happy to share his sausage, and Charlotte—"

Rae nodded excitedly. "Oh! Charlotte could . . ."

Their voices dimmed as Sienna's words resonated. *All the things she must have on her mind.*

I thought of Polly's schedule. She was likely just trying to keep her head above water. I understood that families had important dates and times they needed to keep track of somewhere. As far as I was concerned, Polly was a super-hot, supermom of two, and it didn't matter what I or anyone else thought. But I could imagine how it felt, having someone like me come in and feel like I'd judged how she kept it all together.

I snapped back to attention when I heard Rae and Sienna discussing some sort of meal schedule. These two quasi older sisters/aunts of mine would not be showing up at Polly Alberton's house, meal schedule or otherwise.

"You two really don't need to do that. She's fine. She has a friend in town."

"Then why all the secrecy?" Rae crossed her arms, looking put out that I'd shot down their plan. "No one knows anything about her, and there's a big gate across the front of her driveway, which, is so tall you can barely see the house except for some big stone columns and the roof."

Sienna and I slowly turned our heads toward Rae.

Rae simply looked down to examine her nails. "I might have done a ride-along with Jackson when he checked out her place."

I sliced my hand through the air, causing both women to jump. I felt a little bad, but I was getting frustrated. "No more checking out her place. No welcome baskets. No meal schedules. She's a private person. And she's a doctor. Of course she doesn't want her personal information spread around town."

"What kind of doctor is she?" Naturally this is what Sienna picked up on out of everything I just said.

I blew out a breath, answering in a flat tone, "A pediatrician."

"That's great! We needed a good pediatrician in town!" Sienna exclaimed.

Rae looked side to side. "I thought you were going to bring kids along today?"

I sighed. "They were busy tonight. But they might come on Thursday."

Rae clapped her hands as Sienna burst out, "Tell her to come along, too!"

Resigned, I replied, "If she's on call, she won't be able to come. But I guess I could ask."

"Perfect!" Sienna beamed, then cupped her mouth and turned to the stage. "Ok everyone! Who's ready for some warmups?"

Rae patted my back, then leaned in to whisper in my ear. "See? That wasn't so hard."

I shook my head.

I'd been bamboozled. Again.

CHAPTER
TWENTY-ONE

POLLY

Mariana Zapata, *The Wall of Winnipeg and Me*

"Mommy? Can Jace read me a bedtime story?"

Ryla was all tucked into bed, two bedtime stories already in, lights almost out. I'd come home this afternoon to find Jace, Ryla, and Max giggling in a cushion fort in the basement. Really, I couldn't have been more surprised with how well this week had been going, with Jace and the kids at least. I'd come home to happy, smiling kids two days in a row.

If only this afternoon hadn't been followed by another awkward night with Jace. When Jace came back from Young Wills practice, he'd given me a cautious wave, then walked to his room, no doubt feeling banished by the controlling momzilla.

"You know that's not his job, sweetie."

"Giselle read to me at night."

"Only on the nights I wasn't home."

"Nu-uh, sometimes she read to me when you were here."

Stopping this merry-go-round, I said, "If I get called into the hospital this week, I'm sure Jace will read to you."

"When is that?"

I tickled her. "So anxious to be rid of me?"

She giggled and snuggled in next to me, charming her way into one more story. After another five minutes of reading, she was out. I went to Max's room next. We took turns reading to each other at night (tonight it was Max's turn). After working through his relaxation exercises, he was also asleep.

I noticed a light turn on downstairs when I was making my way across the hallway to my room. Instantly dropping to the floor, I held my breath and listened. Based on where the light was coming from, I realized Jace must be in the kitchen. So, I did the next most rational thing: I crawled on all fours to spy on him from the top of the stairs.

After a few minutes, I saw Jace walk from the kitchen to his room. He had a glass of milk in one hand and a sandwich in the other. Because of course, he was eating. He had to eat sometime.

What did you expect, Polly? You banished him to his room last night, then you nailed him in the balls with your purse like he was an intruder.

I was really winning at life, making it so my nanny of two days felt like he couldn't even leave his room for meals. And after he did everything so perfectly.

Perfectly.

A ghost of a memory skirted the edges of my mind. About perfection and mistakes. Once I heard Jace's bedroom door shut, I crawled to the edge of the stairs and sat on the top step, deep in thought. Wasn't the point of the schedule to make sure I did everything perfectly? Regardless of how much I'd sched-uled, regardless of how much I'd tried to control everything, my house of cards came tumbling down anyway. I was divorced, anyway. My father thought I was a failure despite bending to his demands, anyway. My kids were miserable, anyway.

Perfection wasn't doing anyone any good.

I shot up, starting down the stairs. After all, change starts with a single step— or wait, was it a journey that starts with . . . something? I couldn't remember the exact quote, or who said it for that matter—it could have been Jesus, Shakespeare, or some ancient Chinese philosopher for all I knew. I studied science, not literature. Regardless, the point was the same: If I didn't begin, I'd never get there.

Fortified by that thought, I strode into the kitchen and fired up Barry. For a moment I considered pitching him in the garbage, but I settled for deleting most of the mundane scheduled things except for basic appointments and chores. Then I sat there for a solid minute, watching the blinking cursor.

"What would you do, Mom?" I whispered aloud. I was thinking about my childhood, something I hadn't done often before moving back here. A wisp of laughter floated in the air, and I looked through the windows, seeing the glow of lights illuminating the patio and pool area beyond. I held my breath, not wanting to stir the air. But all that greeted me was the quiet hum of silence.

Looking at the cursor again, I wrote down two words. I smiled at the new checklist, thinking of the kids' reaction when they saw it tomorrow.

- **HAVE FUN**

Turning off Barry, I walked back to the stairs. But before I put my foot on that first step, I turned, facing the east wing.

A journey of a thousand miles didn't have to begin with a single step.

Maybe, it could start with two.

———

I knocked on Jace's door before I lost my nerve. Opening it swiftly, Jace looked surprised, then nervous as he put a shirt on over his head. He must have just gotten out of the shower. His hair was wet, turning the color a rich mahogany, his trademark curls straightening so they almost hit his chin. My brain stuttered as he pulled his shirt to his waist, covering his very toned chest and abdomen inch by glorious inch.

Noooooooooooooooooooooo! my body cried out as he pulled his shirt to his waist.

Fantastic. The teenager living inside me had aged. She was now eighteen and on the cusp of a sexual awakening.

Simmer down, sister.

Almost losing my courage, I focused back on Jace's face and took a deep breath in. "Look—"

Jace immediately laughed, ducking his head. Remembering our conversation about how nothing that proceeds "look" is good, I huffed out a small laugh as well.

"This isn't anything bad. I mean, I'm not offering you half a billion dollars or anything, but I swear, this isn't bad."

I took another quick breath in and out. "Look," I started by rote, then immediately covered my mouth, eyes going wide as Jace barked out another laugh.

"I don't know why I said that again," I mumbled from behind my hand as Jace's shoulders shook.

I put my hand down, pressing my lips together, trying not to laugh because I wanted—*needed*—to get this out. "I wanted to come and apologize. I don't know how to do this." I pointed between him and me. Then thinking I'd given the wrong impression, I quickly amended, "I mean, me and the kids and you in the house. I'm sorry about yesterday when I essentially exiled you here. I didn't want you to feel like because you live here, you have to help us 24/7.

Jace opened his mouth, but I held up a hand to signal I had more to say.

"Please, I need to get this out. I don't mean to be so strict about the schedule. We've had so many changes this past year, and it's only me. I've used the schedule as a way to keep track of things. But over time, it got out of hand."

Jace held up his hands, signaling his turn to speak. "First, make a thousand schedules. You have the right to parent the way you want. What I think doesn't matter. Second, I get it. Once you're home, I'm off the clock. But know that if I want to talk to you or play with the kids, that's my choice. I don't feel forced. I'll be honest with you. You'll never make me do something I don't want to do."

The tension in my shoulders had started to ease at his words, and I could feel my cheeks upturning in a smile.

"The same goes for you," he continued. "Be honest with me. If you want time alone with your kids, or I say something you don't agree with, you have every right to tell me to fuck off." Jace winced, then added, "Sorry."

"Did you just apologize for swearing?"

"I guess I did, yeah."

I stood up straighter and smirked. "Well, *fuck* that."

Jace and I were both laughing as I half turned, making a motion to leave, but finding that I didn't want to. "There's some leftover lasagna in the fridge if you'd like it. I don't want you to think you have to eat a PB&J every night."

"Spying on me, huh?" Jace leaned against the doorframe, dimples popping as his arms crossed over his chest, causing my insides to quiver.

"I don't want to be accused of a hostile workplace."

Jace opened his mouth to reply as I heard . . . barking?

I peered around Jace, looking into the dim room. "Umm, Jace? Ryla didn't actually talk you into getting a dog, did she?"

"That's a show I'm watching on my tablet. It's called *Treasure Dogs*. Twenty dogs and their owners compete in the world's largest scavenger hunt." He looked over his shoulder and back to me, eyes practically smoldering when he asked, "It would look better on a big screen. You up for watching an episode with me?"

————

"I can't believe Dennis missed that! Rosie had it!" I lamented, turning my head toward Jace, who'd just finished off his second helping of lasagna. We'd set up in the basement theater room, sitting side by side in overstuffed loungers. We'd just finished the third episode of season one of *Treasure Dogs*. Jace had argued that I needed to start with the first season, even though he'd been halfway through the second.

Jace nodded his head, grinning. "Rosie was definitely signaling to the park bench." Dennis was Rosie the German shepherd's owner, and he missed Rosie's cue when she was pawing at the park bench, so they only got second place in the challenge. Rosie was obviously the most talented dog of the group and already my choice for the winner.

"Please tell me Dennis doesn't lose the whole thing for her. Rosie needs to win! Dennis doesn't deserve her."

"I can't give it away. It'll ruin the surprise."

"Are all the episodes on Zoola?" I asked.

Jace muted the TV and turned in his seat to face me, using the arm of the lounge chair as his backrest. He stretched out, letting his long legs dangle over the other arm of the chair. His curls had dried all frizzy, making me think he must put some product in it normally.

"Yup. All available for your binging pleasure." Jace's damn twinkling eyes and dimples were out in full force; my lower belly flipping when he said the word *pleasure*.

"I need to know! Does Rosie at least make it to the final?"

Jace watched me intently, responding in that low, languid tone of his, the one that made me feel all melty on the inside. "You'll just have to keep watchin' it with me to find out."

I forced a rough swallow. I was reading into everything way too much tonight.

"Do you watch any other shows?" I asked.

"Not unless you count a Braves game every once in a while. Though I mostly watch those with my pop."

"That's baseball, right? Do the Braves play in Tennessee?"

Jace shook his head. "They're out of Atlanta. My pop grew up there. He loves to tell the story about how he and his friends won tickets to the first Braves home game in 1966. The ticket stub is still framed and hanging on my parents' wall."

I did the mental math twice, surprised at the number I came up with. "How old is your dad?"

"He turned seventy-five last week," Jace answered easily.

I stilled. That was older than my own father.

"How old is your mom?"

"Same age, she turns seventy-five later this year."

My mouth fell open. She had to have been at least fifty years old when she had him. Was he adopted? My eyes bounced between Jace and the ceiling, staying quiet, not wanting to ask him a rude question.

"Go ahead and ask, you won't offend me."

I turned in my lounger to face him, mirroring his pose. "Are you adopted? Or was your mom really fifty years old when she had you?"

He smiled lazily, not looking offended by the question in the least.

"She was actually fifty-one."

I shook my head slowly in amazement. "I don't know your mom, but I think she just became my own personal hero. Did she and your dad get married late? Or did she have a hard time getting pregnant?"

Jace shifted his position, folding one leg under his body. "I don't think so. I have an older brother and sister."

"How much older?"

"My brother was fourteen when I was born, and my sister was ten."

Smirking, I waggled my eyebrows. "Oh ho ho, you were an oops baby."

"I was an oops baby," Jace nodded. "Though my parents have never admitted that. I've never asked, either. Honestly, I try not to think about it." He shuddered.

"I always wanted siblings. I pushed for two kids with my ex-husband so they could have one another. He finally agreed, which led to the indomitable Ryla's existence here on earth. Looking back, having to convince my husband to have another child was a major red flag. You shouldn't have to push your spouse into wanting kids with you."

"May I ask what happened between . . . ."

"Me and their dad?" I asked softly. Besides Leah, I don't think I'd told anyone else the story, preferring to keep things to myself. To my surprise, it continued to feel like a relief to share things about myself with Jace, rather than hold everything in, keeping all my secrets pent up inside myself.

"We were married for twelve years. I met him during medical school. He was a few years older than me and worked from home in IT. Looking back at that time in my life, meeting David, well, when you spend the formative years of your life living under judgment and expectation, anything by comparison feels like freedom. I hadn't realized I'd moved from this cage," I gestured to the house, "to a bigger one. I didn't realize until after Ryla was born and he was gone most of the time running his yachting company that he'd been silently controlling me in the same way my father would. Not to the judge's scale, but still. It was there."

Jace's eyes narrowed. "What do you mean?"

"Little things. Furrows of his brow or the silent treatment if I didn't do things his way. If I'd say I was thinking of cutting my hair, he'd make a face. And I wanted to please him. He was the same with the kids. He had no idea how to handle Max's anxiety, which started as separation anxiety in preschool. When I dropped him off for school, I'd have to pry his little fingers from my coat." I paused, blinking against the moisture gathering in my eyes at the memory.

Gathering my composure, I shook my head and continued. "David was convinced it was a phase, arguing against evaluation as he felt it would label Max unfairly. When Max's anxiety improved in the first grade, I thought David might be right. Over time, other anxious traits emerged that I ignored, never wanting to rock the boat with David. Max's teachers never said anything about it because Max was smart and it didn't affect his grades. It's one of my biggest regrets to this day, not standing up for Max by pushing against David for an earlier evaluation. I mean, I know better! I'm a pediatrician, for Christ's sake. I should have stood up for Max when he couldn't stand up for himself. Maybe if I had, Max would have had the support in place that he needed during all the changes this past year."

"How did your ex get a ong with Ryla?"

I snapped my head to Jace at his question. I'd been lost in thought as I spoke, almost feeling like I'd been talking out loud to myself.

Blinking, I replayed Jace's question in my head and smirked. "Poorly. Ryla had a temper from birth and David had no idea how to handle her outbursts. He started the yachting company before she was two, in part, I think, because he wanted to get out of the house. In hindsight, it's not surprising that he didn't want to be a father anymore. I don't know if he ever wanted to be one. But I was still floored when I read the line item in the divorce agreement where he requested relinquishment of all custody of the kids."

Anger and bitterness bubbled up in me as the memory replayed in my head.

"I could never regret having Max and Ryla, but I'm angry with myself for choosing such a horrible father for them. And I'm angry at myself for being so deferent."

"I can't imagine you being deferent to anyone," Jace mused.

I laughed humorously. "I was a different person then."

"How does somebody give up custody of their kids? Is that even legal?" Jace asked.

"Yep. When we settled our custody agreement, David was out of the country and planned to remain so for the next year. So, the judge agreed with both my and David's attorney to award me with both legal and physical custody of the kids. David still has to pay child support and technically has some visitation rights, but it's a whopping two weeks out of every year. He's legally required to give me and my attorney two weeks' notice and has yet to get in contact to set up a visit with the kids. I doubt he ever will."

"May I ask another question?"

I gave a small nod. Jace was adorable when he asked permission like that. I don't know what that said about me, but it possibly explained why I liked books with a dominatrix tendency.

"Why aren't you sitting on a yacht sized pile of money? You both worked full-time, you have full custody—and you mentioned he still has to pay for child support. Why are you living here, in your father's house, instead of your own private island?"

I sighed, turning in the lounger, laying my head against the backrest. It was the million-dollar question. Literally.

"He used custody as a bargaining chip to get two-thirds of the proceeds from the sale of our house. Which was really the only asset we shared. Otherwise, I would've had to co-parent with his mother when David was on his yachting trips, which was all the time. David was smart enough to know I'd rather die than have my kids be around her in any capacity. She was a critical parent, just like my father."

A look of surprise and something a little bit darker than anger clouded Jace's face.

"David also claimed that he supported me financially while I was in medical school and residency. His weasel of a divorce attorney basically made it seem like David's business was in the red, even though I know they turned a profit. But I couldn't prove that. So, they cut a deal where I only had to pay five years of spousal support instead of the full twelve, as long as I didn't go after David's business."

"Wait. You mean to tell me you're paying him spousal support, he got two thirds of the sale from your house, has no physical or legal custody of your kids, and all he has to do is pay you child support?"

I winced. "Yes."

"How much is the spousal support?"

"About a third of my salary."

Jace gave a low whistle. "I don't see how this could happen. Can't you hire someone to find his money? My sister's a lawyer, she'd be losing her mind. What lawyer let him get away with that?"

His words were a soothing balm after a year of feeling repeatedly burned. "Honestly, I just wanted it to be done. At this point, I'm happy it's over. David was never going to be a good father. I want to help my kids move on rather than drag them through a painful legal battle for years."

Jace continued frowning. "I'm serious, Polly. My sister is in family law and practices in Chicago. All you have to do is ask, and I'll make the call."

My heart gave a little thump, or maybe it was my hormones trying to knock my scruples loose. Either way, I ignored them. "No. But thank you, truly."

Jace sighed and ran a hand from the back of his neck through his hair. "I never thought to ask this, but what's the kids' last name?"

I smirked. "They've always had my last name. My father strongly encouraged it as a condition of our marriage: that I'd keep my last name and so would our kids. David hated his last name, so he easily agreed."

Jace raised his eyebrows in silent question.

"His last name is Pensis."

A ghost of a smile passed over Jace's features before asking in a strangled voice, "Is that spelled . . ."

"Phonetically? Yes. It honestly looks a lot worse than it sounds."

Jace's shoulders shook as I pressed my lips together to keep from laughing.

"So, you were almost . . ." Jace's voice was breaking.

"Don't say it!" I whispered.

"Dr. Pensis?"

I barked out a laugh as Jace threw his head back, his hair bouncing as his shoulders shook. My eyes watered and my stomach cramped. Our laughter eventually quieted, but then one of us would look at the other and we'd start laughing all over again. After several minutes of this, I eventually closed my eyes, settling back into the lounge chair with a smile on my face, feeling relaxed and happy.

It was peacefully quiet for a minute before I turned to ask Jace a question.

"What about your name? If your parents are boomers, how'd you get the name Jace?"

Jace was also lying back in a reclined position with his legs outstretched and turned his head at my question.

"It's kind of a funny story, though not as funny as almost being named after a dick."

I bit my lip to keep from laughing again.

"I'm named after my Papa Vargas, my pop's dad. He and my yaya, that's my grandma, immigrated from Greece to Atlanta before Pop was born. My mother and Yaya didn't get along, from what my sister told me. Anyway, when my mother was pregnant with me, Yaya got sick, so they went to see her before she died. Apparently on her deathbed she grabbed Momma's hand and made her promise that she'd name the baby"—he pointed a finger at himself— "after my Papa Vargas, and then died one minute later. Making it literally, her dying wish."

I narrowed my eyebrows. "Jace? I don't see how that's funny. Like at all."

"Calm yer britches, I'm a gettin' to it," Jace teased, putting on a thick accent. Which, you know, *swoon*.

"My Papa Vargas's name was Antonios Jason. Momma shortened Jason to Jace, ignoring the name Antonios altogether as a way of spiting Yaya, but still keeping the peace with the family."

"Your mom sounds like she has a little temper in her. Does your dad speak any Greek?"

"Only some curse words."

"What are your siblings' names?"

"My sister's name is Sarah and my older brother's name . . ." Jace squinted one eye closed, "is Kent."

"Kent! As in the clown?"

Jace chuckled softly. "I know. I have no defense, except that you were standing there, staring at me like I was a pervert and Kent had pissed me off the night before, so his name popped out."

I wrinkled my nose. "You two don't have a great relationship I take it?"

Jace sighed, looking up to the ceiling. "We didn't really grow up together. My parents had high expectations for Sarah and Kent. They were both accountants with steady, stable jobs and wanted that for their kids. Kent is a CPA and does real estate in Florida."

"Your parents never pressured you into being an accountant?"

"Nah, they pressured me plenty, but by that time, Kent was off in Florida, living his own life. I dropped out after a year of college. I didn't want to waste money on a degree I wasn't going to use. I haven't found a career worth pursuing yet and have no interest sitting behind my desk. I'm happy with the jobs I have; I've always liked variety."

I gagged, bound, and sat on any disappointment I felt when he said he liked variety. "Maybe Kent's just jealous of you."

"Well, naturally. He didn't get the Vargas hair, after all," Jace joked, running his hand through his curls, making them flop haphazardly around his face.

"Have you always kept your hair long?"

"This is short for me. I cut it not too long ago because it was getting in the way at sparring. It was down to here for most of my life." Jace made a motion to the middle of his neck. "I liked it, but it didn't make me too popular in middle school, let me tell you."

I sucked in a breath, imagining Jace with long curly hair, down past his chin. I wondered if he ever wore it in a man bun. I was always a sucker for a man bun.

I was so lost in thought that I blurted, "How do you get your curls to be so pretty?"

Immediately, Jace closed his eyes and put his hand over his heart, acting like I'd wounded him.

"It's like middle school all over again," he groaned dramatically.

"That's not what I meant! I just meant they're usually so well defined that I want to know what products you use!" I protested, realizing I was digging my hole deeper, laughing as Jace covered his face with his hands and moaned in mock offense.

After another minute, I was able to get myself under control and let out a long audible exhale, a content feeling radiating through my bones.

"I didn't mean it like that, and you know it," I told Jace, who still had his hands over his face. "Your hair was one of the first things I noticed about you. It caught in the wind and looked sort of wild, yet, sort of beautiful at the same time."

My words came out unintentionally breathless. Jace stilled, then slowly dragged his hands from his face, his eyes instantly ensnaring mine. I tried to think of something else to say, but words left my brain when Jace's fervent, wanting stare dropped to my mouth. Flutters made their way through my chest as my palms broke out in a cold sweat. His tongue peeked out from between his lips, wetting them, triggering a reflexive pulse in my core. I felt pulled toward him, unable to bear the space between us. Jace swallowed as he inched slowly toward me.

Then, like the involuntary reflex it was, I yawned.

Jace blinked twice and sat back, the spell effectively broken. Picking up his phone, he nodded. "It's past my bedtime, too."

His shirt rode up as he got up and stretched, revealing another glimpse of lean, tanned skin. My heartbeat was still pulsing in my ears as I averted my gaze quickly, then hoisted myself up.

"Ready?" Jace asked, smiling like nothing was amiss. I nodded and adjusted my shirt over my black leggings, hoping he didn't notice the trembling in my hands.

We walked upstairs together, making small talk about *Treasure Dogs*, until we got to the staircase that led to my and the kid's bedroom. I turned around after going up one step, finding myself even with his height.

"I guess I'll see you in the morning!" I said too brightly, trying to cover the rapid thrumming in my chest, still not recovered from whatever had just happened downstairs.

"Sweet dreams, Polly." Jace's words were lighthearted, but his eyes were intense and vibrant.

I shivered as goosebumps spread across my skin, jumping up a stair and giving a lame wave. I ran up the rest of the way, forcing myself not to look back.

I shivered as I changed into pajamas. I shivered through brushing my teeth, trying not to picture that sliver of abs or how his head tipped back when he laughed.

I rolled my eyes. I needed to get a grip. If Jace were my younger, *female* employee and I was his older, *male* boss, I'd be considered a lecherous old creep.

I froze while putting moisturizer on my face. It was worse than that. I was like Mr. Freaking Rochester from *Jane Eyre,* leering at my attractive, young employee from the shadows. And instead of a wife locked in the attic, I had a creepy painting of my father, whose eyes followed you wherever you went.

Whatever interest I'd felt, whatever flirting I'd thought was happening, I had to ignore it. I laid awake in bed for a long while, not even opening my e-reader, sexual frustration my companion, until I finally drifted off to sleep.

CHAPTER
TWENTY-TWO

JACE

Samantha Young, *On Dublin Street*

"You about done there, little miss?" Ryla shook her head without looking at me, happily swinging her feet and watching her tablet at the table. Ryla had the habit of eating her Cheerios one at a time, the slowest I'd ever seen anyone eat cereal before. It was Wednesday and the kids had summer school, which meant we had to leave around nine. But I couldn't find Max anywhere.

"Max?" I called out as I walked upstairs, not getting an answer. I checked the kids' bedrooms and the playroom, but nothing. Maybe he'd gone to the basement. I knew he liked the quiet and comfort of the theater room; I'd found him there yesterday, midafternoon, curled up on a chair, until Ryla and I enticed him to build a fort with us.

I paused, seeing Polly's *open* bedroom door.

"Max?" I called in the direction of her room.

There was no reply. I hesitated. I shouldn't go into Polly's room.

From our conversation last night, to seeing '**Have Fun**' added to Barry this morning, Polly continued to surprise me. Talking to her felt effortless. I'd never had this much natural, instant chemistry with a woman. I'd found myself waking up before my alarm this morning, just like the previous two days this week, excited to see Polly before she left for work.

Was her room tidy, her bed made with crisp, hospital corners each morning? Or perhaps her room was the only place she could take a free breath, letting piles of chaos rule. My curiosity battled my integrity as I took a step toward the threshold of her door when a noise from downstairs halted my progress.

I jogged down the stairs, seeing that Ryla was still at the table, eating her Cheerios one by one. Then I heard that noise again, this time from the front entry area.

Max snapped his head up as I opened the study doors, holding what looked to be a Harry Potter wand.

"Are you doing magic?"

"Oh, yeah. I um, kind of," Max started to say. I pumped my fist, walking into the study.

"Yes! My man! That's what I'm talking about!"

Max's face did an impression of a deer in headlights, so I pulled back my excitement. Studying the magic kit in front of him, it looked to be a deck of cards, crayons, and some tape. Very makeshift.

"What are you working on?" I sat down in a chair opposite him.

I only received a shrugged response.

"I started to do magic when I was about your age. I could show you a few tricks if you want."

"Really?" Max shifted his eyes to me.

I leaned forward, smiling. "Yeah. I have my old magic kit at my parents' house. I could pick it up and show you some tricks later today if you'd like."

Max nodded and I stood, clapping him on the shoulder. "I'll get it after dropping you and your sister off. We can check it out this afternoon. What do you say, sound like a deal?

———

After dropping the kids off at summer school, I picked up my magic gear from my parents' house, needing to check on their place anyway as they'd left for Florida that week. The lawn needed a mow, but it was too wet on account of the rain we'd had all week. I texted them both an update, letting them know I'd mow it this weekend if it dried out.

Back at the Alberton house, the quiet sounds of the house felt strange. In the few short days I'd been here, I'd become accustomed to the noises of the house: Ryla's determined steps *anywhere*, Max's quieter movements, and Polly's quick pace. After working out and showering, I put my laundry in the washer. Seeing a basket of folded towels on top of the dryer, I made a split-second decision and grabbed it. I didn't know which bath towels went in each bathroom, but it's not like there were an infinite number of bathrooms in this house. I could figure it out.

The towels in the basement and first floor bathrooms were dark gray. When I opened the linen closet in the kids' Jack and Jill bathroom, I only saw white towels.

Which, put me in a pickle. The towels in the basket were purple.

And that's how I found myself at the threshold of Polly's bedroom door, again.

On the one hand, it was a major invasion of privacy. On the other hand, I could see the door to her ensuite bathroom from here. And I was hired to help her out. It'd be silly to leave the basket at her door; it'd only give her another thing to do.

Decision made, I entered her room.

A hint of her sweet perfume laced the air. A queen bed with rumpled, light purple sheets and a white duvet sat in the middle of the room. A few unfolded clothes lay across a chair in the corner and there was a long line of shoe boxes —at least three high and five across—under the far window. Otherwise, her room was neat and clean. Her floral perfume hung in the air. I took a masochistic inhale, and then, on her bedside table, I saw it.

A tablet.

It looked about the size of an e-reader. My hand twitched toward it, followed by one step. I'd finished all the books Polly had been listening to, and I was jonesing for another fix.

You're an adult—pick out your own romance novels. Like a man.

Decision made, I ignored the e-reader and marched into her bathroom.

Immediately, I knew it was a mistake.

There, hanging over the rail of her glass shower doors, were two lace bras. My mouth went dry, seeing the silky material, the delicate, lacy cups that looked like flower petals. I was instantly jealous of them, knowing what skin they touched, what secrets they held. I turned quickly toward the cabinet in the corner, coming face-to-face with a towel bar mounted to the wall.

Was there a purple towel hanging there?

Of course not, not with how this day was going. On that towel bar hung my wet dream come to life.

Lace fucking panties.

I stared at them, wondering how soft they were. My dick throbbed as I imagined Polly in them, laying out on her bed for me, gasping as I'd lean over her and bring my nose to that silky center, then inhale.

I glanced down at the basket of towels. Polly couldn't know I'd been in here, good intentions or not. I left quickly, making the decision to put the basket back in the laundry room. When I walked past her bed again, my eyes trailed to her e-reader on the bedside table. The devil on my shoulder, who had speedily recovered from a small stroke at seeing Polly's underwear, spoke up.

Whispering to me.

Taunting me.

Open it, Jace, open it. No one will know!

Technically, I'm only looking for a book recommendation. What's the harm in a book recommendation? She'd given me free reign of her library downstairs. And what was an e-reader if not a library of sorts?

I dropped the laundry basket at her bedroom door.

I walked to her bedside table and picked up her e-reader.

It turned on. No password needed.

After hitting a few buttons, there it was: her library.

My Roman Empire.

The devil on my shoulder was cheering while the angel was shaking his head.

Polly had been reading the *American Tail* series—but I saw she now had a total of four books in that collection. Polly's taste in books ranged from books that featured everything from vampires to drag queens, to ones whose covers would make my Gran, God rest her soul, do the sign of the cross. I'd never remember all these titles. Taking a few quick pictures of her library screen with my phone, I hightailed it out of there, racing down the stairs with my contraband.

I had some books to order.

It was raining all afternoon, so after picking up the kids from summer school, we spent the afternoon practicing magic. After all, having fun was now officially on the schedule, much to the kids' amazement, and what's more fun than magic?

My life had turned upside down in a week. Last week, I was driving strangers to and from the airport, contemplating where I was headed in life. Today, I was teaching a ten-year-old how to pull things out of a hat and giving a six-year-old a piggyback ride around a stone mansion, pretending I was a horse.

When Polly got home, it was impossible not to wonder what she wore under her work clothes. It got significantly worse when she went upstairs to change and came downstairs five minutes later, wearing a fitted dry fit T-shirt and compression leggings. Was this woman trying to murder me? I distracted myself by helping her make supper. Like it had the night before, our conversation flowed naturally, loving it when she'd throw her back in laughter. And yes, it was hard not to get distracted when she'd arch her back—hard being the operative word.

I couldn't remember a time I'd laughed as hard as I had with Polly and her kids these last few days. During dinner, Ryla put a jumbo meatball on a fork, turning it into a character that walked around her plate. When Mr. Beefcake got a little frisky and did a little kick for flare, the meatball flew right off the fork and hit the light fixture above the island. We were all silent as the meatball initially stuck to the glass, then slowly slid down and dropped to the island, where it began a roll and then eventually tumbled to the floor.

Both Ryla and Max looked at Polly with worry when to my delight, Polly snorted. The snort turned into a chuckle, which made Ryla and Max giggle, and before I knew it, we were all laughing our butts off. Our laughter echoed throughout the house until our stomachs ached.

It might have been the most fun day I'd had all year.

Later that night, I heard a soft knock at my door. It was earlier than I expected Polly to come to my door, she'd just gone up to bed with Ryla ten minutes ago after I spent no less than thirty minutes teaching both kids the song, "On Top of Spaghetti".

My heart rate picked up just the same. But when I opened the door, it was Max who stood there.

"Hiya, Max. You alright?" He nodded, leaning around me to peer into my room.

"Do you want to come in?" When he nodded again, I stepped back. He took a few timid steps into the room and looked around.

"Have you been in here before?"

Max's shoulders inched up his neck. "Only once. It was dark and sort of scary."

I couldn't argue with him there. This room was straight out of some sort of Victorian museum. After Polly told me about her momma, it made more sense why the room felt more like a mausoleum than a bedroom.

"Aww, well. New places can be like that. Feel free to look around."

"Is that a fireplace?" Max walked toward the far side of the room, then recoiled. Max whispered, "What's that doing in here?"

I knew what he was staring at. Leaning against the fireplace grate, was the painting of Polly and her parents that I'd moved from the library.

"Uh, it needed to be cleaned. So, I told your momma I'd store it in here for now."

Max still looked creeped as hell, wide eyes staring at the painting.

"You know what, I can fix this." I picked up a large blanket and put it over the painting. Then, I moved some clothes off one of the leather chairs next to the fireplace and gestured for Max to sit. I took the seat across from him.

Both of our gazes naturally fell back to the painting, which was now covered with the blanket.

I still felt watched. I glanced at Max and raised my eyebrows. "It's not any better, is it?"

"It's like I can still feel his eyes on me." Max's voice was full of quiet revulsion.

I jumped to my feet. "Agreed. I've got just the place. Be right back."

I stashed the painting in the study for now, then came back to my room a minute later. Max already looked twenty pounds lighter.

"That's better, huh?" I asked, sitting in the chair opposite him. "What'd you think of the magic tricks we practiced today?"

He shrugged. "They were good." The chair was so deep, his feet dangled a few inches off the floor.

"I started doing magic when I was a little older than you are now. I must have practiced every day in seventh grade."

"How'd you get so good?"

"With practice." I tried not to show how excited I was that he was finally starting to ask me questions. All week it'd been me gently asking him questions, but this was the first time he'd sought me out. "And I started with the easy stuff. Once I mastered one trick, I moved on to the next. They all added up over time."

"How'd you do that quarter one? Behind the ear?"

"That one? Easy. Let me just find a coin or two. . ."

CHAPTER
TWENTY-THREE

POLLY

Our hearts are made up of all different broken pieces that belong to others, and when we find the right one, they show us how they can all fit together again.

Vi Keeland, *Happily Letter After*

"Max?" I whispered down the hall, having found his room and bathroom empty. I'd just snuck out of Ryla's room after she'd fallen asleep while we were reading her first book.

When I walked upstairs with Ryla and Max to get them ready for bed, I felt alive and light, like the day was just beginning, rather than winding down. Last night, talking and watching TV with Jace, then tonight at dinner, laughing with him and the kids—it felt like second nature. Like I'd known him for years rather than weeks.

Max wasn't in the library or basement. Picking up my pace, I walked quickly down to Jace's room to see if he'd seen Max anywhere, stopping when I heard voices coming from the partially open door.

"Like this?" I heard Max's voice.

"Yes! That's it, Max! You are now the master of that trick. You can pull a quarter out of anyone's ears now, I 'reckon."

That was Jace. I crept closer to the door.

"Who taught *you* this trick?" Max asked.

"You're lookin' at him. My family wasn't much into magic, even though my parents would watch my tricks whenever I asked. I mostly practiced alone in my room. I didn't have a lot of friends when I was your age."

"You?" Max's tone was full of amazement, making me smile. I turned, resting against the wall beside the door, shamelessly eavesdropping.

"Yup. That's sometimes how it is in middle school. In high school we all chilled out a bit, and I met my friend Sam. He's been my best friend ever since. Eventually everyone wised up to how great I was. I have a lot of friends now."

"Did you ever, like, worry that you wouldn't make any friends?" Max's questions caused my heart to ache. I pressed my fisted hands to my chest; the urge to hug Max was strong.

"Let me tell you something about friends, Max. Up until high school, everyone's just figuring themselves out. They're trying to make themselves look cool, doing things that they don't want to do, changing themselves to fit in with everyone else. Then, after high school, you learn that it's our differences that make us cool. And your real friends, those who like you for being yourself? They're the ones that have your back and stick with you."

There were tears in my eyes once Jace was done, his words hitting home in more ways than one. Jace just gave Max more fatherly advice in one night, than David ever had.

"What if I never find one?"

Max's tiny voice broke my heart.

"If you're lucky, you'll find that person before high school. If not, you'll find them eventually. You gotta keep trying and see who sticks. But you won't find them, if you don't try. And you certainly won't find one, if you're not being yourself."

Jace's words put it back together.

CHAPTER
TWENTY-FOUR
POLLY

To be yourself in a world that is constantly trying to make you something else is the greatest accomplishment.

Jessica Park, *Flat-Out Celeste*

"Mom, do I have to go?"

"Max, we just pulled into the parking lot. We're already here. We talked about this last night after you and Jace did some magic tricks for me, remember? I'm on call tonight, so I have to bring you to Young Wills practice along with Ryla, in case I get called in. Ryla sits and waits through your counseling sessions, something she doesn't like to do, so it's all fair. You can sit next to me the whole time. Besides coming inside and sitting with me, you don't have to do anything you don't want to do."

I could see his eyes were getting wet, which usually tugged on my heartstrings so much I would give in, taking him home, not making him go anywhere. But he needed to practice doing new things. He wasn't going to get anywhere staying in our house. Frank, his therapist, confirmed the same thing today.

Ryla, who'd been chattering away in the backseat the entire way here, had been silent during our exchange. I braced for a blow up, but then, she took my breath away as she reached over and held Max's hand.

Max looked up at her with a feeble smile, then rolled his shoulders back, dropped her hand, and got out of the car.

I glanced at Ryla, but she was already getting out of the car, completely unphased, like her actions didn't just mean the world to me. She wasn't aware of this, but if Ryla were to ask me for anything right now, I'd give it to her. A new Barbie. Ten flushable mini-toilets. Hell, even a dog named Kevin.

Ryla took a hold of my hand and Max grabbed the other one as we made our way to the auditorium. Max's hand tightened around mine and I squeezed it twice as we entered the large space. On the stage, a group of kids were congregating around two women with long, dark hair. Ryla wriggled her hand out of my grip as soon as she saw Jace on the stage and shouted his name. I saw him squint, searching for us, then light up when he spotted us.

Jace backed up a few paces, then made a running start and leapt off the stage like Johnny Castle on his way to save Baby from the corner. He tucked his legs into a tight cannonball, then straightened them out and landed in a crouch, practically giving me heart palpitations as he unwittingly made a teenage fantasy of mine come to life. Because if any girl tells you that she didn't want to be Baby at the end of the movie, when Johnny jumped off that stage, then looked back at her all sexy and adorable, they're a dirty liar.

Whoops and claps erupted from the kids when Jace landed. He did a half turn and bow complete with a flourish, shouting, "Don't try that at home, kids!"

Ryla had picked up speed and was running full throttle down the aisle toward Jace. I don't think she'd ever seen *Dirty Dancing*, nor would I allow her to at her age, but she did what I could only describe as a trust leap when she was within a few feet of Jace. I opened my mouth to shout a warning just as Jace turned and caught her swiftly, lifting her straight up into the air and spun her around—thankfully not in *Dirty Dancing* style but still, Ryla's face beamed.

Grabbing her hand, Jace walked up the aisle toward Max and me. "Welcome!" His face was full of elation, free and happy.

"Thanks!" I ignored the butterflies in my stomach and gestured to the seats on either side of us. "Where should we sit?"

"Anywhere you'd like." He looked down at Ryla. "What do you say, Ryla. Ready to go?"

Anyone could see Ryla was ready to go. She was practically bursting out of her skin with excitement, like the Energizer Bunny on methamphetamines.

"Sounds good." I took a step forward only to be met with resistance as Max pulled at my hand, silently letting me know he didn't want to sit any closer.

"We'll hang out right here. I'll be watching, Ryla. Have fun!"

Jace glanced between Max and I, an understanding passing over his face. He crouched down in front of Max. "I'll be right up there, Max. If you ever want to join in, come straight up and find me. If you want to hang out back here, that's ok, too. Thanks for coming."

And Max, my brave boy, whispered, "You're welcome."

Five months ago, we'd have still been in the car as tears streamed down his face, trying to work through breathing exercises to help him calm down. I squeezed Max's hand, silently communicating how proud I was of him, as we took a seat.

"Jace, watch me!" I heard a kid yell before he did a running jump and summersault off the stage.

"Benjamin Winston! I better not see you do that again!" the taller of the two women onstage yelled down to the little acrobat.

"Sorry, Momma!" the little cutie drawled as he scampered up the stage's side stairs.

Jace and Ryla were now onstage and approaching the two women, both of whom had noticed them. I was a good twenty rows up from where they were standing, but I could tell both women were incredibly pretty. After Jace gestured to Ryla a few times, Ryla turned, her little face squinting out to the audience. Finally spotting me, she waved enthusiastically, which had both of the women's heads snapping in my direction. The taller woman, who had hourglass curves, shaded her eyes like she was trying to see me better.

I gave a sly wave back to Ryla, watching as the voluptuous, dark-haired beauty got down on one knee in front of her. After talking for a minute, she gave Ryla a high five, who then took off like a shot to join the group of kids onstage. Jace and the woman continued a conversation. At one point, he must have said something funny because she tipped her head back and laughed, her long pretty hair cascading down her back, her olive skin beautiful and luminous even from where I sat.

I narrowed my eyes. What did I expect? He'd said he liked variety, right? I was so focused on their interaction I didn't realize that someone had come up beside Max and I, until I heard them speak.

"You must be Polly and Max?"

Giving a tiny start, which also caused Max to jump, I whipped my head to my left. The shorter of the two dark-haired women was now standing next to us. She was one of the most breathtaking women I'd ever seen up close.

I blinked twice, still seeing her in front of me.

Nope, not a mirage.

"I'm sorry for startling you. I thought you'd have seen me walk up the aisle."

Taking a quick glance at the aisle in front of me, I couldn't disagree. I really should have seen her. I was too busy fending off exasperating jealously that I missed her completely.

I stood and held out my hand. "Don't apologize, we were just . . . taking it all in. I'm Polly, Polly Alberton."

"It's nice to meet you. I'm Rae James. I help run the program along with Sienna and Jace."

"Thank you for including my daughter, Ryla," I said, then winced. "And I sincerely apologize for anything she does in advance. This is my son, Max." I turned to point out Max, whose was staring at Rae a little dazedly.

"Hi, Max." Rae flashed a megawatt smile at him. Twin circles of pink appeared on his cheeks.

My thoughts exactly, bud. Because this woman was sincerely gorgeous. Her face was flawless and . . . familiar. Did I go to school with her? Surely, not. I would have remembered her—*everyone* would remember someone like her.

"I'm so glad you could come. I must admit, we've been excited to meet you since we found out Jace was working for you."

"We?"

"Sienna and I. She's up onstage. Her son, Ben, was the one who somersaulted off the stage just now." Rae grinned and gave a little head shake.

"Kids," I said absently, still studying Rae to piece together why she looked so familiar.

Focusing her attention back on me, she asked, "I hear you're a doctor. What brings you to Green Valley?"

"I grew up here. And we needed a change of pace," I answered noncommittally.

Rae narrowed her eyes a bit at my words, but I was still drawing a blank where I'd seen her before.

"Do we . . . know each other?" I asked hesitantly. "I'm so sorry if we did. I moved away right after high school and haven't been back much at all since."

Rae shook her head. "I'm not from here, either. I grew up in Ohio and moved here after I got married. Do you know Jackson James? He's the county sheriff and my husband."

Married. The tension in my shoulders immediately eased for a reason I did not want to fully examine.

"Wait, the county sheriff? I think I spoke with you and your husband on the phone recently, when I was checking references for Jace. Your husband was nice . . . ."

Kind of.

The phone call with Sheriff Jackson James and his wife started off as a call to make sure Jace wasn't a serial killer, and I ended up sweating halfway through the call feeling like I was the one getting interrogated.

"And he seemed . . . protective," I continued.

"He's the best." A small smile played on Rae's lips as she looked down for a beat, then back to me, smile gone and eyes sharp. "And we're both protective."

Huh. Unless I was reading the room wrong, I think I was just threatened. Because that's what you do for the people you love. You protect them.

I smiled at Rae. I liked her already.

"How long have you been doing the Young Wills program?" I asked.

"A little more than a year now. There wasn't a local drama program for this age group. We try to keep it a fun, equal playing field, on a first come, first serve basis for the kids who live in the school district. The first few months we had to work out the kinks. There were a few people who signed their kids up thinking this would be a professional acting school and then when we weren't Julliard, got all miffed."

I frowned. "Why would someone ever think you were running a professional acting school?"

Rae blinked, looking surprised by my question for a moment before her face settled into a soft, genuine smile. "I have no idea." Shifting her feet, she nodded at me. "It was very nice to meet you, Polly. I'm glad you came back to town."

Thoroughly confused, but flattered that I kind of made a friend, I nodded back. "Me too."

"You make sure to come back next week and bring your cuties along, too." Rae's eyes flashed as she gave a sweet finger wave to Max before walking back toward the stage.

I sat down, a little breathless, watching her leave. I looked over to Max, his cheeks still in a furious stage of blush.

"She was nice, huh?" I teased and bumped his shoulder.

"Monkey!"

I turned my attention to the stage. The kids were standing in a circle with Jace front and center. They were all jumping around the stage, acting like monkeys. Ryla was right in front hopping from one foot to the other, arms curled, her little mouth pursed. Choruses of "Ooo, ooo, ooo! Ah, ah, ah!" filled the air as kids pounded their chests. Jace was hysterical, jumping around in front of the kids, making them erupt into laughter at his antics.

"Horse!" came a shout from the side of the stage, from the woman that Rae called Sienna. Everyone immediately started to gallop, stretching out their necks and prancing around the stage.

"Sloth!"

The kids immediately stilled, moving in slow motion. Jace, not to be outdone, started an impossibly slow arm stretch. Opening his mouth wide, he let out a long, sliding groan, imitating a slow-motion yawn. I couldn't help my wide smile as the kids immediately copied him, filling the auditorium with elongated yawn-groans of their own.

"Chicken!"

Conflicting emotions suffused me as I continued to watch Jace. He looked utterly free. Had I ever been that free? Had I ever experienced that kind of aimless joy? That complete inhibition where I was truly myself, open and honest, not caring what I looked like or what others thought of me?

The answer was no. I'd never endeavored to be that brave, to be that fearless.

I had all these strings weighing me down. Grief from my mother's death, the weight of my father's expectations, the feelings of failure from my broken marriage, the pressure to provide for my children so they could thrive and flourish. How light would it feel if I could merely snip, snip, snip those strings, letting myself float up and fly free, dancing like no one was watching, or better yet, dancing as if everyone was watching, but not caring what anyone thought?

And then a wall of guilt slammed into me, that I'd even include my children in that thought, that I'd ever think of these two little loves of my life, as strings. I'd always felt a sort of pity toward my ex, who seemed to view our kids as inconveniences. But was I any better? Sometimes I treated spending time with them like a task I had to check off each day.

And though I did feel a certain type of envy watching Jace onstage, it wasn't true jealousy. I didn't have any desire to be up there, clucking like some bizarre, carefree poultry. It was the contrast between us. The untroubled appearance of Jace, of every child on that stage in comparison to me. How I'd made myself so very stuck in this life: stuck beholden to my father, stuck being the parent and person I was—versus the person I wanted to be.

But really, what would I do, if I could do anything—*be* anyone? The weight of this question knocked the wind out of me for a moment, making it difficult to breathe.

I tapped Max on the shoulder, praying to the Lord, herself, that Max would let me go to the bathroom by myself. Luckily, he'd begun reading his book and nodded his head, allowing me to go to the bathroom in peace.

Harsh automatic lights blinked on when I walked into the bathroom. Leaning on the sink, heart pounding, I tried to slow my breathing.

If I were braver, stronger, what would I do? Who would I be? What was I waiting for?

I'd never dared to ask myself those questions before, I was too afraid of the answers and the inevitable disappointment that would follow.

Footsteps in the hallway prompted me to immediately start washing my hands, lest anyone come in and see me leaning on the sink. Albertons always act appropriately in public. Albertons always do and say the right thing, even if they don't mean it. Albertons do not have goddamned epiphanies in the high school girl's bathroom.

Before I left, I dared a glance in the mirror. Staring into the green eyes of my mother, feeling like she was here with me, really here with me, guiding me, for the first time since her death.

When are you going to start figuring it out, Polly?

CHAPTER
TWENTY-FIVE

JACE

And I've never wanted to be someone's someone. But damn do I want to be her everything.

Ginger Scott, *How We Deal with Gravity*

"Listen up team. I've got some exciting news for this Friday morning. I just found a brand-new box of Honey Nut Cheerios that wasn't expired in the back of the pantry, so we're all set for the next week. And, the forecast has spoken: there is no rain for the next three glorious days, so we can finally use that pool out back and go swimming. Who's excited?!"

"Me, me, me!" Ryla jumped up and down in front of a line of ten stuffed animals, all of whom she'd been instructing in a rousing game of school in the living room.

"That's the kind of enthusiasm I like to see!" I pointed at her, then glanced at Max, who didn't respond. He was playing a video game.

"Max?" I lowered my voice, wondering if he'd heard me. He glanced at me out of the corner of his eye, then went back to his game.

He definitely heard me. Ryla had gone back to teaching, so I sat next to Max.

. . .

"Nice move." I nudged his shoulder after he won a race using a Corvette. "That's a sweet ride."

Another quick side eye was the only acknowledgement of my presence. There was definitely something bugging him. He'd been giving me some multi-word answers in the last few days and now, almost nothing.

"I drove one like that once," I dropped casually.

Max's head whipped to me immediately. "For real?"

I nodded. "A guy at the country club owns one and only trusts me to drive it."

"He gives you his car to drive? Like for fun?"

I sat back, leaning on my hands. "Not exactly. I valet on Sundays. People drop their cars off at the front of the country club, and I drive them back and forth to the parking lot."

The disappointed look on Max's face was almost comical. I nudged his shoulder again.

"So, what do you say about swimming later?"

He continued to stay silent.

"Do you know how to swim?" I tried again.

He still didn't answer me.

"He swims. He's scared of the bees," Ryla chirped from behind us, selling her brother out. Hard.

"Ryla!" Max turned and glared at her.

Ryla scowled at Max defensively, then started talking sassy and self-righteous, which I'd noticed she did when she was angry. "You are too! You got all scared when one landed on your arm in the pool and then you showed me that video where that kid got stinged and his face was all puffy and now you won't go outside!"

Max's eyes were glassy, his breathing getting faster as the siblings stared each other down.

"Alright, alright." I held up my hands. "Ryla, you know how you're not supposed to jump on the bed? My bed is all clear. Have at it, short stack."

She stood up straight, her posture practically regal as she slowly made her way out of the living room. She gave me one last glare as if to say, *I know what you did there, peasant, but I accept your offer,* then skipped off down the hallway.

Max had picked up his controller again but was sitting motionless, staring at the floor.

I sat down next to him. "Y'alright?"

He shrugged.

"You know, without bees, nothing would grow."

Judging by Max's silence, I could see that wasn't the angle I should go with. I decided to sit quietly next to him and wait it out. A few minutes later, it worked.

"I'm scared a bee will sting me and then I won't be able to breathe," Max whispered.

I wondered if Polly knew about his fear of bees. She hadn't mentioned it, and I hadn't seen anything about it on Barry.

"I'd be scared, too, if I thought that was going to happen. You know that can only happen if you're allergic to bees? Have you talked to your momma or maybe your counselor about this?"

He shook his head reluctantly.

"Don't you think your momma should know? I could help you tell her later today—"

"No!" Max suddenly looked up at me, his expression laced with panic.

I held up my hands, remaining calm. "Why's that?"

He put down his controller and turned to look out the living room window. "She's really busy," he mumbled, "and there's probably nothing anyone can do about it anyway."

I didn't think that was the whole truth, but I kept those thoughts to myself. "Tell you what. Let me worry about telling your momma. If I can figure out a way to help, how about you agree to talk about it with your counselor?"

Max turned back to glance at me, then looked down, appearing to be working things out in his head. "I guess so," he finally answered.

I smiled. "Deal."

———

The rest of the morning was filled with researching bee phobias, bee repellants, and bee allergy treatments. Once I discovered that certain plants and smells repel bees, I thought about growing those plants in Polly's back yard. I wasn't a gardening expert, so I knew I'd need some help.

Jace: Do you remember what kind of sun momma needed to grow her onions in the garden?

Sarah: Who is this?

Jace: Do you know or not?

Sarah: How should I know? Ask momma.

In hindsight, I shouldn't have asked my sister. And asking Momma was not an option. Deciding to go with buying full-grown plants and putting them in above ground planter boxes, I was able to do a lot of things myself. I made calls to the local hardware stores in town, placing the orders for the plants and supplies I needed. But what with having the kids and my car not being big enough to carry even a quarter of the supplies at a time, getting things here would be tricky.

That's where Sam came in. He owed me no less than ten favors by now, and it was time to cash in.

Jace: I need shovels, potting soil, and a big truck

Sam: You know better than to text me this shit

Jace: I also need you to pick up 20 marigold plants, onion plants, basil and mint. And six above ground planters

Jace: I'll send you a copy of the pickup order from Bills and Eager Beavers

Jace: You owe me

. . .

A few minutes of silence passed. It wasn't until I sent him a picture of my face with the red rash after Ryla's birthday party that I finally got a response.

Sam: What's the address?

I hesitated. If I gave him Polly's address, which he definitely knew from the party, I'd have to tell him that I was nannying Polly's kids. And sure, he'd probably assume, (correctly), that I get inappropriately hard around her, not realizing that it was so much more. No knowing that I had this feeling that this woman could be *it* for me. Figuring out I had no other option, I sent him her address.

Sam: Why do I know this address?

Sam: Why are you at Polly Alberton's house?

Sam: Are you really not going to answer my texts?

Sam: Fine. I'll be there no later than 2. But this is the last favor I owe you

A few hours later, Sam messaged me that he was at the gate, and I buzzed him through. After parking, Sam hopped out of the truck with a confused look on his face. "Why are we at Polly Alberton's house? Did she hire you to do some landscaping or something?"

I put my hands on my hips. "No. She hired me to watch her two kids. I've been living here since Sunday. One of her kids, Max, has a bee phobia, so we need to remove all the flowers and pots from the back and put in plants and herbs that repel bees. That's why I needed all this stuff."

As I spoke, Sam's expression turned from surprised to supremely self-satisfied.

"Bruh." Sam shook his head, a smug grin in place. "Only you would get a job out of that clown gig. And after you made me feel bad about it? You hittin' that? I mean, don't get me wrong, she is one high-class MILF—"

Even though I thought I'd prepared myself, and even though this was my best friend, who'd shown up with a truck, shovels, and dirt, thinking that we were burying a body, I still lost it.

I grabbed Sam by the shirt and slammed him against the side of the garage, putting my forearm to his throat.

"That's the first and last time you talk about her that way, you got it?"

Sam's eyes practically bugged out of their sockets—with surprise, I wasn't holding him *that* hard. Sam held up his hands and I released him.

He cursed as he stumbled forward to catch himself. "Fuck! Have you completely lost it?"

A giggle from behind us had me closing my eyes.

"Watch your language," I murmured to Sam under my breath. Turning, I spotted Ryla standing directly behind me, watching us with rapt attention.

"Hey there, Ryla. This is my friend Sam. We were just playin' around, but I promise not to do it again. It was wrong of me, and I am very sorry."

Ryla's eyes were full of mischief. "He said a bad word."

I got down to the balls of my feet in front of her. "I know. And he's also very sorry. *Right, Sam?*"

Sam stepped forward, nodding down at Ryla. "Uh, yup, very sorry. You shouldn't say those words until you're older. Like uh, fifty."

"Are you fifty?"

"Fuck no!" Sam retorted.

"Sam!" I barked as he shouted, "Sorry!" again and Ryla launched into a fit of giggles.

I scrubbed my hands down my face. This was not going at all how I'd planned.

Trying again, I stood and gentled my voice. "This is my best friend, Sam. Sam, this is Ryla. One of Polly's kids."

Ryla studied Sam as I spoke, then as if he'd passed some sort of internal test, she started hopping between the cracks in the driveway. "I have a best friend. His name's Eric. He's seven. I'm six." After a few feet, she turned and looked at Sam. "Wanna see my room?"

"No!" I barked, then held my breath and counted to three. "Ryla. You can't invite strangers into your room, alright? Especially not male strangers."

Sam shot me a look like I was completely off my rocker.

I wasn't normally a nervous person. The opposite, in fact. But I hadn't asked Polly about any of this, she didn't know about Max's bee phobia, and when she came home tonight and saw that I completely changed her entire backyard without permission, she'd be fully within her rights to fire me on the spot.

"Don't you worry about Jace, Ryla. He's just having a hard day." Sam eyed me one more time, then crouched down to her level. "I brought some things over 'cause it sounds like we're doing some plantin'."

Ryla pumped her fist in the air. "No more bees!"

"You know it. Wanna help me carry this stuff to the backyard while Jace takes a breather? I think he might need it."

CHAPTER
TWENTY-SIX

POLLY

Sometimes an understanding silence was better than a bunch of meaningless words.

Mia Sheridan, *Archer's Voice*

All day I'd been restless, the questions I hadn't yet answered were turning over in my mind. It didn't help that I received an email requesting a meeting between me and the school board president Brad Goldenstein—just him and I. Why would we want to meet with me alone? Considering what Rose told me about him, I had a feeling he was up to no good.

I finished up the last of my work after a full day of clinic, my restlessness turning into giddy anticipation as I walked to my car, thinking about the night ahead. I had a few books on my TBR that I wanted to read. Maybe the kids would be so tired, they'd crash early, and I could get a jump start on them. Or maybe Jace would want to watch a few episodes of *Treasure Dogs* with me.

It was most definitely the thought of diving into my TBR that had butterflies fluttering in my stomach. Or the thought of watching my new favorite TV show.

Definitely.

A text came in from Leah right after I started my car.

Leah: Don't forget about book club tomorrow.

I'd briefly texted with Leah this week about how Jace was fairing with the kids and yes, she reminded me about book club. What I hadn't done yet, was come up with a plausible excuse to miss it. Maybe if I didn't answer her texts for the next twenty-four hours, I could feign an illness.

Leah: Stop thinking of ways to get out of this. Meet me at my house at noon. We can drive to Rose's together.

Polly: I haven't read the book yet.

Leah: Liar. And even if you hadn't, no one would care.

Polly: Are you sure your friends are ok with me coming along? I don't want to intrude.

Leah: Yes, I already told them you were coming.

Leah: Bring wine.

Seeing no way out of this, I sent a resigned text in response.

Polly: Fine. Have a good night.

I was able to detach from my worries about tomorrow as I listened to my audiobook on the way home. I loved books with quirky side characters. This one had a quirky grandmother who made dick flower pictures out of diamond art. Picturing my father coming home and finding a large gemstone dick flower canvas in the library made me laugh aloud, the smile staying on my face for the rest of my drive home.

An unfamiliar truck in my driveway had me gripping the wheel in panic, then relaxing as I recalled Jace sending me a text asking if his friend Sam could come over today.

"Mommy!" Ryla yelled, running through the open garage door, looking to have spent the entire day outside. Specks of dirt were in her hair and dark, muddy streaks were painted across her clothes and cheeks.

"You're home!" Ryla cried, slamming into me and wrapping her arms around my waist, muddy clothes and all.

"Come see what we did! We're in the backyard and it's a secret!" I tried to keep up with Ryla, but my heels kept sinking into the grass. After finally taking them off, I walked around the house to the backyard and immediately came to a halt.

Heat prickled my skin. Jace wore a white, dirt-streaked muscle tee. His biceps bulged as he lifted something; I had no idea what. I was too distracted by the topknot holding half of Jace's curly hair back, the bottom half of his hair clinging to his neck.

My mouth opened and closed like a fish. I had no idea I had a thing for muddy, sweaty men with long hair. But between the sweat and dirt and popping muscles I somehow made a mental note to ask Leah if she was aware of any books with a hot farmer trope.

"Zap!" A loud noise sounded from behind me, making me spin. A large square wire box that I hadn't ever seen before hung from a pole. Slowly, I turned around in a full circle to survey the rest of the backyard.

It'd been completely transformed.

Gone were the flowering plants and baskets. Instead, I saw a half dozen raised garden beds containing what looked like marigolds and herbs, plus some other plants I couldn't identify. Tiki torches were lit and scattered along the perimeter of the yard, citronella candles were burning and scattered every five feet, and there was another large wire box hanging up on the far side of the pool.

Looking up and seeing me, Jace halted, his expression immediately shuttering.

"What's going on?" I called out to him. He seemed to take a steadying breath, then walk slowly toward me. Movement drew my attention as his friend Sam appeared from behind a group of trees in the far back corner of the yard, in the direction where an old shed sat on the property.

"Polly, you've met my friend Sam, right?" Jace gestured to Sam once we all met near the bottom of the stone patio stairs.

"Yes. We've met. Hello, again," I said flatly to Sam, remembering being out here with those absurd baby goats.

"It's so nice to see you again, Pol—" Sam glanced at Jace, who for some reason, was giving him a hard glare—"Ms. Alberton. I'm so sorry, again, for the mix-up about the clown and the petting zoo. I sincerely apologize and will be refunding you back your money as we discussed," Sam said, reiterating the promise he'd made over an email earlier this week.

"Thank you." I turned my attention to Jace, who continued to look more nervous than I'd ever seen him. "What's going on?"

"We're killing bees!" Ryla whooped from beside me, jumping up and down.

"What?" I asked, whipping my head to Jace.

"Ryla!" Sam yelled, backing up a few steps. "I have a few more trays that need to be loaded into the back of the truck and some buckets that need hosing down. Want to help me?"

"Yessssss!" Ryla grinned wickedly and ran around the side of the house.

"But you're not going to spray me with the hose again, right? Ryla. . . ." Sam's voice got fainter as he followed her to his doom.

Once they were out of sight, I placed my shoes on the ground and crossed my arms, waiting for an explanation from Jace.

I was not expecting what came out of his mouth.

"Max is afraid of bees and that's why he won't go outside."

I played his words over in my head. "What? Max won't go outside? Since when?"

Jace put his hands on his hips. "Apparently, he saw a video about a kid who got stung and almost died around the same time a bee landed on him in the pool a few weeks ago."

My gaze fell to the pool. Max had been in the pool a few weeks ago with Leah and Ryla when I went to Sunday brunch. I gasped and covered my mouth. Jace was right. Ever since then, Max had avoided going outside. Now his panic attack outside the school last week made more sense. It happened as soon as we got outside. Shame filled me that I hadn't noticed this about my own son.

"He told you this?"

"Not exactly. Ryla told me, then Max filled me in on the rest, eventually."

Ryla knew, too? I surveyed the yard, at all the work they'd done, speechless.

"I researched bees today. The flowers that were planted in your backyard attracted a lot of bees. I took them out and brought in marigolds, mint, basil, anything with a strong smell. Sam had some spare tiki torches we put around the yard. None of it will kill bees, but a strong smell repels 'em. This way, at least the bees won't be near the house. I have these zappers, too"—he pointed to the large metal contraptions hanging up— "to cut down on some of the mosquitos. I figured Max might be freaked out by any bug that could bite him, so that way we can cover our bases. Ryla had a blast. And I haven't seen a bee in two hours." Jace smiled and looked around the yard proudly. "I think Max might actually come outside now."

I was silent as I listened to Jace's explanation, watching him point out all the different things as he was talking. Even though I was grateful, because this might be the kindest gesture I'd ever received, shame was heavy in my chest. And defeat. I tried so hard to keep it all together. Why would Max tell Jace about his fear, and not me?

"And uh, I made this." Jace ran over to the patio table and back, opening a little zippered pouch. Leaning in, my heart gave a little wayward thump as I took in the liquid Benadryl, hydrocortisone cream, an ice pack, and insect repellent.

"I thought Max could keep this close to him when he goes outside. The bug spray would be for anytime he goes outside and the Benadryl and ice pack are just in case he gets stung. He could use it right away. We could call it a 'bee pack', or something." Jace shrugged. "I thought it might make him feel better."

Jace bent at the knees to meet me at eye level, his worried eyes flitting between mine. "Polly?"

Emotion clogged my throat. I shook my head, not wanting to speak. Knowing if I spoke aloud, I'd cry.

He nodded. "You're mad. I figured. I told Max I'd talk to you about it only on the condition that he'd talk to his counselor. And none of the yard was his fault. It was all my idea. I can take it all back. All I need to do is—"

I launched forward, cutting off his words as I wrapped my arms around his neck, holding tight. Jace's arms wound around me immediately, anchoring me, holding me up, keeping me together.

"It's perfect," I whispered, hanging on to him.

"Oh." Jace breathed out more than said the word as we held tight together, his strong arms the only thing keeping me from absolutely breaking.

When I felt steadier, I gave myself one more moment before pulling back reluctantly. Jace's hands trailed down my arms and loosely circled my wrists, like he didn't want to let me go either. The loss of him made me feel heavy, weighed down by life and all of the stressors that came with it.

I gave Jace a small smile, picked up my shoes, and asked about my priority in that moment. "Do you know where Max is? I need to go talk to him."

Jace glanced up. "He's in his room."

I was at the top of the patio stairs when I looked back, finding Jace was in the same spot, watching me go.

"Jace?"

His eyebrows raised, face hopeful.

"Thank you."

———

I found Max in his bedroom, sitting on the ledge of the bay window that overlooked the backyard.

"It's looking pretty good out there," I called out, causing him to glance toward me. "Can I come in?"

At his shy nod, I went to sit next to him. My heart broke as I took in his demeanor, eyes downcast and sad, shoulders slumped.

"Is there a reason you didn't tell me about the bees?"

Max shrugged and shook his head meekly.

Instantly, guilt filled me. My question was about me. About how it made me feel not knowing about Max's fear. I realized that I'd been doing this a lot. I was so busy that I forgot to take the time to just sit beside him. To give him room to talk. I'd gotten so obsessed with therapy schedules and journal entries, so worried that Max could relapse, that I was talking *at* him rather than taking the time to sit and *listen*. So, I didn't say anything. I simply looked out the window and waited, observing Jace work around the yard at first, then watch a soaking wet Sam return to the backyard beside a skipping Ryla.

It was a few minutes before Max spoke, but he didn't talk about what I thought he was going to talk about.

"Mom?"

"Yes?"

"You know that picture in the library? The painting? The one that Jace moved?"

I nodded.

"Why don't you ever talk about her?"

For a wild second I thought he was being existential and talking about me, like the me I was before my mother died, the me that I should have been. But then, like a punch to the stomach, I realized he was talking about my mom.

"Was she mean?" Max asked in a small voice, sounding younger than his ten years.

"No. Not at all. She was kind. Funny. Smiled a lot. Loved to dance and have fun. She would have loved you so much."

Max appeared thoughtful as he continued looking out the window.

"I'm sorry I haven't told you stories about her. I think it hurt too much. I missed her. I still miss her. It makes talking about her hard."

Tears pricked my eyes, making my vision blur as I felt Max's not so little hand grasp mine, which I hadn't realized was pressed to my chest, right over my heart. I released a breath, somehow keeping my tears at bay. Bringing our hands down between us, I threaded my fingers through his and held tight.

Max squeezed my hand once, twice, then sent me a reassuring smile—something I always did when I walked him into school to provide reassurance. A gentle reminder that things were going to be ok.

With that simple gesture, Max showed me what he couldn't put into words. That talking was hard. Putting your emotions and feelings into words was hard. And just like it was hard for me to talk about my mom, it was hard for Max to explain how he was feeling out loud. I knew this. It was part of the reason why his therapist and I agreed it was a good idea to have him re-evaluated by a neuropsychologist. But you don't always need words to communicate. You can be there for someone with your words *and* deeds. It could be something as basic as a hug or elaborate as removing all flowering plants from your backyard and installing giant bug zappers.

Sometimes being there for someone simply meant showing up, sitting beside them, and listening.

I squeezed Max's hand once, then twice. "I love you, Max. So much. I promise from now on, I'll take more time to just listen."

We sat quietly then, giggling as we watched Jace and Ryla sneak up on Sam with the hose, spraying him from behind, then giggling more as Sam chased them around the yard. As the minutes passed, I no longer felt disappointed that Max might not share anything with me today, because I understood that he eventually would, as long as I kept giving him the space and time to do it.

"There was a video," Max began suddenly, "and a kid got stung on his face. His throat swelled up. He couldn't breathe. He almost died." Max paused, then whispered, "I don't want to die."

I wanted to scoop him up and never let him go. I wanted to wrap him up in Bubble Wrap and tell him that I'd fight off any bee that came his way. I wanted to confiscate all electronics and never let him watch anything again. But whether it's bees, or a bear, or a human being, I couldn't fight off all his demons for him. I was his mother. It was my job to protect him when he was too young to do it himself. Now that he was older, it was my job to equip him with the tools he needed to protect himself.

"Jace said I should talk to Frank about it," Max added, referring to his counselor.

"What do you think?"

Max shrugged. "I think I probably should."

I nodded in return, trying to blink back tears, the lump in my throat making it hard to swallow.

Max leaned forward, wrapping his arms around me in a hug. A tight hug. A hug that told me all I needed to know. That he loved me. That he didn't know how to tell me.

And thank you for listening.

CHAPTER
TWENTY-SEVEN

JACE

When someone comes along and makes you feel butterflies, you need to chase them.

Vi Keeland, *Happily Letter After*

Sam and I worked the rest of the afternoon and into the evening. Not a bee in sight, we all ate a late supper together on the back patio, Max included. I saw Sam off when Polly took the kids up for bedtime.

The sun had set by the time I finished showering that night. Walking through the darkened house, I grabbed a beer from the fridge as I craned my ears, listening for any noise upstairs. It was way past the kids' bedtime, and I was sure Ryla crashed hard. I wanted to go up and check on Max, but if he and Polly were together, I didn't want to intrude.

Taking a long pull, I looked outside, straightening as I took in a familiar dark figure sitting outside on the patio steps. At the sound of the door, Polly jerked her head toward me. My heart sunk as moonlight illuminated the reflection of tears on her cheeks. I strode over, sitting next to her on the step. She'd turned her head, hiding her eyes from me. Her shoulders shook with quiet, muffled sobs and she sniffled, refusing to look at me as she wiped her cheeks with the back of her hand. Slowly, I reached out with two fingers, placing them under her chin and gently turned her face to me. Her swollen eyes and tracks of her tears were a one-two punch to my chest. I brushed my thumbs under her eyes, brushing her tears away, not having any other thoughts than wanting to take this sadness away from her.

"What is it, darlin'?"

"Nothing. Just thinking about something someone said—"

In that instant, I was resolved, clarity giving my mind a peace I hadn't felt in days. Because it was simple: Polly should never be sad. She should always be happy. And whoever said something to make Polly sad, was a dead man.

It's a good thing I had shovels, topsoil, and a willing best friend.

I dropped my hands to my knees. "Tell me who made you cry. I know the maze of roads by Bandit Lake like the back of my hand after driving for Lyft all these years, so I know all the best places to hide a body."

Polly's sniffles instantly quieted. She cocked her head to the side, her eyes less hazy than a few moments ago.

"What?" Her voice was still thick with tears. "It's not like that. And while I'm . . . flattered?" She squinted one eye. "Maybe that's not the right word, but no one did this to me except myself. I'll be fine. You don't have to stay." She turned to look into the distance.

When I didn't move for a good minute, she turned back to me with furrowed eyebrows.

I crossed my arms. "I'm staying here. What's goin' on?"

She huffed. "You're a little bossier than I thought you'd be."

Not rising to the bait, I waited. And waited some more. Finally, she sighed and looked down, speaking hesitantly as she kept her eyes trained on the steps in front of her.

"Max asked me about that family picture. You know, the painting you moved from the library?"

"I can put it back. If I'd known how much that cree—*ative* picture meant to you, I'd never have moved it."

"It *is* creepy. That's not what I meant." Polly patted my knee, letting her hand rest there as she gave the night sky a searching look. The first stars were probably starting to make an appearance, but I wouldn't know. All of my focus rested with her hand on my knee.

"Max hadn't asked me about it before. And then tonight he asked—" Her voice broke and I instinctively put my hand over hers, stroking the soft skin there with my thumb.

"He asked why I never talk about my mom. My first thought was that I must talk about her sometimes. But looking back, I don't. I don't talk about her. Ever. I don't even know if the kids know her name. And she had a lovely name. It was Gloria. Don't you think that's lovely?"

I nodded, feeling helpless as I watched a tear escape down her cheek.

"She was the best mom," Polly continued, wiping her tear away. "She was funny. She'd played with me and tickled me until I couldn't breathe. She filled this house with music and fun and joy." Moonlight reflected in her eyes, making them light up as she talked about her momma.

"She'd play hide 'n' seek and loved to cook. She tempered my father. He wasn't always this horrible person. At least, I don't think so."

She sucked in a shuddering breath. I could feel the tremble of her body next to mine.

"And then she died . . ." her voice trailed off and she whispered the next part. "And I didn't realize a part of me died with her."

Polly shuddered again, and I couldn't *not* put my arm around her any longer.

"I kept thinking about how disappointed she must be that I didn't keep her memory alive. I was so used to putting little pieces of her away, tied up and forgotten somewhere deep inside myself, that I'd stopped thinking about her. It was easier than being sad all the time. But I didn't realize how keeping it all inside was weighing me down. Since I've been back here, all the puzzle pieces of my memory have been set loose, bringing her back to me in bits and pieces. Then tonight, as I sat out here, another little piece of her came back."

A sad smile curved her mouth, making me pull her tighter to my side.

"She told me right over there," Polly pointed to the edge of the yard, "that I didn't have to be perfect. That mistakes can make you feel the most alive. And I forgot all about it. I've hidden so many pieces of myself away to forget her, that I'm afraid I won't know how to put them together again so I can find who

I'm supposed to be. And then I feel guilty, because how can I be a good mom, if I can't even do that? How can I teach my kids to be strong and unafraid to be themselves, if I can't do the same thing?"

"Are you actually saying you don't think you're a good mom?"

She scoffed. "I'm a mother, that's about it."

"You're jokin', right?" She rolled her eyes at my response. I removed my arm from around her, taking a hold of her shoulders, turning her to fully face me. "Polly." My voice was soft, yet serious. "You're an amazing mom."

She shook herself free from my grasp. "I'm not looking for fake praise."

"It's not fake praise. Your kids love you. You've sacrificed everything for them. You're trying to be a mother and a father to them, thanks to your asshole ex, and now you're back home in a place that has painful memories for you so that you can put them in a good school, in a stable home, with good people around you. They feel loved. Can you explain to me how this makes you a bad mom?"

Polly was shaking her head before I finished talking. "I don't listen to them. I don't let them have fun. Max didn't tell me about his bee phobia and worse, I didn't even notice."

"Do you know how much I kept from my momma growing up? This won't be the first time your kids keep the truth from you."

Polly tipped her head back, giving a little groan. "I know. But they need someone who's fun. I never do anything fun. I had so much fun with my mom. I'm not making those memories with my kids. How can I if I'm not even a fun person? Someone who's unafraid to make mistakes? They don't need a mom who's essentially turned herself into this perfectionist robot. My name might as well be Barry."

I chuckled at that and shifted, sitting shoulder to shoulder with her, an idea taking shape like the black silhouettes of the mountains drawn against the starry sky.

"You should make a list."

I could almost feel Polly side-eyeing me. "I think a list is going backward."

"Hear me out. It could be a *fun* list. The list can only have fun things you want to do or like to do. Or better yet, have never done. But they can only be fun, that's the rule. No sneaking 'doing the dishes' on the list."

"What if I find doing dishes to be fun?"

"Then I guess I'll start calling you Barry."

Polly blew out a shaky laugh at my joke. "I don't even know what to put on the list. Giselle did all the fun stuff with them. I don't even swim with my kids. I sit on the side of the pool watching them. What kind of mother doesn't get in the pool?"

"They're six and ten. I think there's some time left."

Poly sighed. "I guess I could put going swimming with my kids on the list."

"There you go. You're off to a great start. Now how about something just for you? What about the get together your friend, Leah, asked you to go to tomorrow? I already told you I can watch the kids, that's no problem."

Polly sighed, then practically grumbled, "Fine. I guess I could go meet Leah's friends with her tomorrow."

"See? Progress already." I smiled, easing myself back on my hands as Polly turned and asked, "What would you put on the list?"

I tilted my head back and forth, weighing the options. "You could go with the classics, like a hike and a picnic, or planning a vacation." I saw a flash from deep back in the yard, giving me an idea. "Or you can start small. Wait right here."

Hurrying inside, I went to the pantry, finding two empty mason type jars with lids. After pounding some quick air holes in the lids with a screwdriver and hammer from the garage that I'd used this afternoon, I pocketed a small flashlight and went to grab Polly. A few minutes later, we were walking toward the back of the yard, a jar in each of our hands.

"Where are we going?" Polly asked, a little breathless as I led her quickly past a set of trees.

"You'll see." I grabbed my flashlight and aimed it low at the ground. I put my jar under my arm and slowed a step, placing my hand on the small of her back to lead her to our destination: an old shed at the back of the property.

Once we got there, Polly burst out laughing.

"Oh my God. It looks like a black-market flower sale."

Behind the shed were all of the flowers, planters, and hanging plants that Sam and I had removed from her yard this afternoon.

Switching the flashlight off, I placed it on the ground and grabbed a small handful of grass. "Alright, now. Take the lid off one of those jars," I instructed.

"Now what do we do?" Polly asked after I stuffed a bit of grass into her jar.

"We wait."

I could hear her breathing beside me as my eyes slowly adjusted to the dark.

"All I hear are mosquitos," Polly whispered, swatting the air.

"Patience."

I could practically hear her roll her eyes, just like her daughter. And then, I saw it. A flash in the dark.

"There! Did you see it?" I pointed in front of us.

"Where?"

"Over by that tree, to our right," I whispered.

"Jace, it's dark and there are about ten different trees to our right."

Putting my jar on the ground, I stepped back and came up behind her, my left hand lightly holding her waist. I breathed in the sweet smell of her neck as I moved closer to her, feeling her stiffen.

"Is this ok?" I asked, my breath stirring the small hairs that escaped her bun, tickling my nose.

"It's fine," she rasped, then shivered.

"Are you cold?"

"Me? No! I'm fine!" she said loudly.

I chuckled, stirring up her hair again. "Shh. You don't want to scare them away."

"I don't even know what we're looking for!" She whisper hissed back.

"There it was again." I reached down with my right hand, grasping her hand in mine and bringing them up to point at the tree in front of us. "Right there."

Polly was quiet as I saw another flash and she jumped. "Jace! I saw it! Are those . . . fireflies?"

"I grew up calling them lightning bugs. But yes, that's what they are. And yes, we're gonna catch 'em."

"I've never done that before." Her tone went from wistful to playful in a moment. "But there's a saying in medicine. See one, do one, teach one. You do it first and then I'll go."

Laughing, I shook my head and dropped her hand. "You'll be fine. This isn't brain surgery. Take the lid off your jar. Yep, like that. Now, when you see the flash, walk toward it slowly. Then when it's in front of you, scoop it from the air, like you're catching a fish with a net, then slap the lid on top of your jar."

I felt her nodding as I talked. "Ok. Ok, I can do that." She rolled her shoulders back and moved to take a step forward, then balked. Her head turned back to me, the faint moonlight turning her skin opalescent. Her lips were within a few inches of my own.

"I can't see where I'm going. I feel like I'm going to fall."

I moved my hands to her waist to steady her, the warmth from her body, the swell of her hips beneath my hands causing a stirring within my chest. My lips were just below her ear. More whisps of her hair tickled my face, but I didn't dare move as I spoke softly, "Go ahead and walk, darlin'. I'll go where you lead."

Another shiver went through her body before Polly took a step forward, then another. I followed behind her, lightly guiding her steps, making it so she didn't fall. She was quickly getting a hang of it, waiting for a flash, then walking, then waiting and walking again, until finally—

"Jace! I got one! I got it!" She turned around and held the jar between us, securing the lid to the top of the jar. We peered inside and then—*flash!* The lightning bug lit up the inside.

Polly's smile stretched wide on her face, her joy evident, the mere fact that I'd made her happy, lighting me up on the inside.

"Can we name him Ed?"

I wouldn't be surprised if my answering laughter could be heard miles away.

———

Ed and Thomas, the two lightning bugs we caught, were living happily in their jars on the back patio. I'd had a shower earlier that night, but when I got back to the room, I needed another one.

Hot water pounded on my back. I could still feel the curves of Polly's body under my hands. My dick had finally calmed down, but at the first thought of Polly, Jace Junior sprang back to life. Which wasn't too hard to believe. Since meeting Polly, Jace Junior was in a *semi*-permanent state of being, so to speak.

I grasped my length, giving it firm strokes. Last night, I'd started on the third book of the American Tail series that started off with a shower scene that was fire. I imagined Polly here in the shower with me, doing everything that was laid out in the book, my fantasies running wild. I pictured her fisting my cock, biting my shoulder, licking my neck, and whispering dirty things in my ear. I imagined water running down her body, her nipples hard, her core hot and ready for me as I turned her against the shower wall and thrust deep into her from behind.

I exhaled deeply, stifling my groan as I came hard, leaning back against the shower wall to catch my breath. I'd never been so confused about a woman before now. It was somehow simpler in the weeks I'd only been valeting her car. Then, she was this unattainable mystery of a woman, but she'd become real to me, and every new thing I learned about her made me want her more. She was strong and passionate with wit for days, yet at the same time humble and vulnerable. I genuinely cared for her. And I genuinely cared about her kids. I felt protective over her, in a way I didn't realize until today, when I had my best friend pinned against the garage.

Then tonight, pressing up against her, feeling her shiver . . . it sure felt like interest. And even though she was out of my league in a hundred ways, even though I knew it was impossible, if I ever got the confirmation that this attraction wasn't one sided . . . I was fucking going for it.

CHAPTER
TWENTY-EIGHT
POLLY

Friendship is like peeing your pants; everyone can see it but only you can feel it.

Penny Reid, *Neanderthal Seeks Human*

I was strangling the neck of a wine bottle with my sweaty hand as Leah and I walked up to Rose's front door. I lied to myself, blaming the sweat on the summer heat, but I knew better. Nerves wracked my body. I couldn't remember the last time I'd hung out with a group of girlfriends. Oh, wait. Never. Because you'd have to *have* girlfriends in order to hang out with them.

I turned to Leah just before she grabbed the door handle. "Wait! Isn't forcing me to go to book club going against this "best friend" code?"

Leah put her arm around me, giving me a half hug. "Nice try. But no. This is in the glossary of the best friend code."

"There's no glossary in the best friend code."

"Maybe it's in the appendix. Whatever. A true best friend can call someone on their crap and push them out of their comfort zone because they know and understand their friend's true boundaries. They're gonna love you. Let's go."

Without waiting for my reply, Leah opened the door and shouted, "We're here! I hope y'all are eatin' because I didn't have time for lunch!"

Rose's home smelled like cinnamon and baked bread. As I toed off my shoes, I spotted a fully decorated, artificial Christmas tree with seashell ornaments and aquamarine garland; a large sand dollar sat at the top of the tree. Darting my eyes to Leah, she didn't seem to give the tree any mind, so I assumed this was maybe just an eccentric entry way decoration.

As we made our way through the living room to a hallway, I huffed out a laugh when I spotted another artificial Christmas tree near the other end of the living room. This one was massive, easily eight feet tall, and decked out with all different Disney ornaments. And if I wasn't mistaken, it was rotating.

"Polly?"

I whipped my head to see Leah standing in the hallway, presumably waiting for me to follow. I merely pointed to the tree and raised my eyebrows.

"Isn't it great? That's the Disney tree. I'm so jealous. It would never last in our house. Bernie would knock it right over. Some of those ornaments are vintage." Leah gave a longing look at the tree, then turned, done with that conversation. I followed her, the mystery of the summertime Christmas trees distracting me from my nerves.

A cozy kitchen had a rectangular island where four women were gathered. Two women were seated on one end of the island, drinking wine. They both had ash-blonde hair and glasses, and had to be identical twins because they looked, well, identical. Rose and a woman with dark hair were organizing a tray of cookies at the opposite end of the island.

As I debated how to say hello, Leah announced our arrival as subtle as a herd of elephants. "Y'all, this is Polly, my best friend, the one I told you about. She's agreed to come hang out with us, and if we're not nice she won't come back. So . . ." Leah took a deep breath in for dramatic effect, "Best behavior! Smiles! Be welcoming!" She pointed to one of the identical-looking women drinking wine. "That means, you, Tiffany."

"What the hell, Leah?" The woman—Tiffany presumably—shouted, narrowing her eyes behind her black-rimmed glasses.

"I said what I said," Leah deadpanned as Tiffany shrugged and took another sip of her wine.

"Honestly, Leah, if she's doesn't come back, it'll be because of you, not us," the identical-looking woman sitting next to Tiffany quipped.

"Me?" Leah's tone was incredulous as she reached for a chip, scooping up a generous helping of taco dip. "No way. We're ride or die." She then shoved it all into her mouth.

"Polly! It's so good to see ya again. Welcome!" Rose came around the island and went right in for a hug, then linked her arm through mine and turned me to face the group. "Y'all, this is Dr. Polly Alberton, the new medical director for the school, and the savior of my hair color. I was going gray, wouldn't you believe, with all the stress I'd been under."

She pointed to the identical twins at the end of the island.

"That's Tiffany," Rose said, pointing to the women with the black framed glasses who raised her wine glass in greeting. "And this is her sister, Margo. They're identical twins, if you can't already tell."

Margo, who wore funky multicolored retro glasses, gave a short wave.

I held up the hand holding the malbec in an awkward hello gesture. "Hi, I'm Polly—Leah's former friend."

Rose and the twins cackled while Leah could only let out a disgruntled noise as her mouth was full of taco dip.

"It's alright. We're used to Leah at this point, we won't hold her against you," Tiffany joked.

Rose pointed toward the woman with dark hair carrying over the cookie tray. "This is Eliza. She works at the superintendent's office, so you might see her from time to time."

Eliza nodded hello and said, "I was happy to hear that the district was getting a new medical director. It's nice to meet you. And Rose isn't joking about her hair. I helped her dye it last month."

"And then she gave me a ride to the salon the next day to fix it!" Rose exclaimed.

"Thank you all for having me," I said softly once the laughter quieted, looking between Tiffany, Margo, Rose, and Eliza. I slid my eyes to Leah. "Though it doesn't seem like you had much of a choice."

Leah, who'd been pouring herself a healthy serving of white wine, rolled her eyes at my comment.

I held up the malbec I brought. "I brought wine!"

"Sold!" Tiffany toasted her wineglass.

Rose took the wine bottle from me and set to open it as Tiffany said, "I've been looking forward to this all week. I slowly lose my sanity every day watching my three boys. It's nice to have some real adult time."

"And you think you get that here?" Margo raised an eyebrow at her sister.

"As long as none of y'all barge into the bathroom when I'm in there, it counts as adult time. And adult time talking about books? Yes please!"

"How old are your kids?" I asked.

"Five, three, and my youngest just turned one."

"I have two boys, four and eight." Margo bumped Tiffany's arm. "Guess we don't know how to make anything else."

"So, what you're saying is, you both have a lot of free time?"

Margo chuckled. "Spoken like a fellow mom. You must have kids, too?"

"A ten-year-old son, and my daughter just turned six."

Margo sighed wistfully. "I think it'd be nice to have a girl. Though I don't know if I'd have enough energy to try for one more. We might have another boy and then I'd be in real trouble."

"Don't do it!" Tiffany coughed into her fist.

Eliza took a seat next to Margo. "You recently moved back here, right? Leah told us you live near the Donner Lodge. It must be gorgeous out there in the fall."

It was, from what I could remember. I glanced at Leah, who was eyeing up the cookie tray. "You really did tell them everything, huh?"

"I don't know why you ask questions you already know the answer to," Leah mumbled.

"Oh, sugar beets!"

We all looked to Rose, seeing that the handle of the wine opener had snapped off, leaving the metal corkscrew stuck in the cork of the bottle.

Tiffany blew a raspberry, Leah made a sound of distress, and Eliza and Margo asked if Rose was alright.

"I'm fine, though I 'reckon we'll be sticking to sweet tea for the rest of the day."

"Sweet tea, my ass! Does anyone have a knife?" Tiffany asked, standing up.

"Wait!" I exclaimed, foreseeing suturing in my future. I turned to Rose. "Do you have a hair straightener?"

Puzzled expression in place, Rose hesitated. "I do, but . . ." she eyed my already straightened hair, "Why?"

"I'm going to use it to open the bottle."

———

"Nothing's happening."

"You gotta give it time to warm up, Leah."

"That's what she said."

Snickering sounded from behind me as I rotated Rose's straightener around the neck of the wine bottle. Something I'd been doing for the last thirty seconds. We were all crammed into Rose's half bath: Rose and Leah beside me, Tiffany, Margo, and Eliza craning their heads around from behind us, all of our eyes glued to the cork. As the straightener's plates slowly heated the glass, the gas from the bottle should expand and push the cork up and out of the bottle.

At least, that's the theory.

Forty-five seconds in and still nothing. I was just a weirdo holding a straightener to a wine bottle.

Maybe this wasn't a great idea. They were going to kick me out of this club before I was even a member.

"I think I see something! Oh, wait. No, nothing yet," someone murmured from behind me.

"Do ya know how long it's supposed to take, sugar?" Rose whispered as I continued patiently holding the straightener to the bottle.

I shrugged. "I think only a minute."

"Maybe you need to rub it."

"It's not a genie, Tiffany," a different voice mumbled, followed by a cackle that I think was Margo's.

"Or a dick." *That* was said loudly in my ear by my best friend.

"Y'all are assholes," Tiffany grumbled.

I bit back a laugh, loving the banter of these women.

"Look!" Rose's shout quieted all of us as the cork suddenly jerked. Then after a few more seconds the cork wiggled up and out of the bottle followed by shouts and claps and whoops and I think even a "Well I'll be!".

Putting the straightener down, I grinned from ear to ear and held up the now cork-less bottle victoriously, which only made them cheer louder.

Maybe I was going to fit in here after all.

———

Two hours and three bottles of wine later, we were spread out in Rose's living room, a large rotating Disney tree beside us, discussing something I never thought I'd discuss with other people before: romance novels. For the first half hour, we talked about the book we read which was hands down, the best slow burn I'd ever read.

"I wasn't expecting to like it so much," I admitted. "I never thought I'd like a slow burn that much."

"Mariana Zapata is the queen of the slow burn. Read *Wait for It* next. I'll do a buddy read with you," Eliza offered.

Rose, who was sitting next to me, grabbed my hand. *"Wait for It* is one of my favorites! Can I read it with y'all? It's high time for a re-read."

It was after this that Margo asked the question if you could take three book boyfriends to an island with you, who would you take and why? Everything kind of went off the rails from there, wherein we talked about anything and everything books in the most enthusiastic, tangential, talk over one another without anyone getting angry kind of way.

"Have any of you read anything by Lady Jane?" Tiffany asked. She was on the floor across from me, sitting in front of Margo who was braiding her hair.

"I have!" I replied. "I started with *American Tail* and the series keeps getting better. I started the fourth book this week and I'm loving it."

"Do they end on a cliffhanger? I don't start a series if the books end on a cliffhanger. Someone did me dirty once, recommending a book like that without warning me first." Tiffany pressed her lips together in a line and turned her head to glare at Eliza.

"It was one time!" lamented Eliza from her spot on the loveseat next to Margo.

"People don't forget," Tiffany deadpanned as Margo turned her head so she could finish braiding her hair.

"Is *American Cream* the fourth book in the series you're talking about, Polly?" Rose asked me, looking down at her phone.

"Yes. I'm actually reading it right now. And to answer your question, Tiffany, they don't end on a cliffhanger. Each book is a standalone with a sort of romantic suspense femme fatale vibe. This last one has a female MC who's a bounty hunter undercover as a dominatrix and it's *very* spicy. I've listened to all of them and the narration is spot on."

"Who's the narrator? I can be picky about my narrators," Margo asked, finishing up Tiffany's braid.

"Brittney Houston."

"She's great!" Eliza said. "The narrator for Ann Richter's books is fabulous, too."

"Did Ann Richter write the *Brag Queen* series?" Margo asked, picking up a small notepad she'd been studiously taking notes in all afternoon.

"I've read those! *Drags to Riches* was my favorite. They were as illuminating as they were hysterical," Tiffany snorted.

"Would y'all quit talking so fast? I can only add so many books to my Kindle at a time and I'm trying to write these all down for my TBR. Ann Richter wrote what now?"

Margo hopped up, showing Rose the list of books she'd written down.

Eliza sighed. "The last thing I need is to add more books to my TBR. It's already a mile long and that's before I took a detour into monster romance books this past month. The last book I read was a doozy."

"Are you talking about the book where the sunscreen is the MC with the micropeen?" Leah suddenly asked, startling me. She'd been sitting on my other side the whole time, but hadn't moved or spoken for the last twenty minutes. I honestly thought she'd fallen asleep from the sheer volume of food and wine she'd consumed upon our arrival.

"Did you just say micropeen and sunscreen? Like the sunscreen has the . . ." I made a gesture that made everyone laugh. "How would that even work?"

"I feel like the length of the micropeen would be SPF dependent somehow," Margo pondered aloud, causing Tiffany to snort.

Rose winked at me. "Eliza reads the most wackadoodle books."

"Which I freely admit!" Eliza held up her hand. "But they make me laugh. But at least you're calling them books and not smut. I'm so sick of people who tell me I'm not reading real books because it's a romance. Like adding sex to a book makes it fake literature in some way."

Rose scoffed. "If folks think I read romance for the sex they can go right ahead. I know the truth."

"I've read books for the sex," Margo shrugged and Leah snickered under her breath, "Haven't we all?"

Rose gave them each a hard look. When she was satisfied that no one was going to speak, she continued, "I read romance on account of the happily ever afters. I have no desire to read hundreds of pages about folks who don't end up together. I've lived sad endings, I have no interest readin' about 'em. And I could care less if the heroine comes a hundred times or if the hero has a dick the size of a baseball bat. I read to escape, smut or no smut."

Tiffany quirked her mouth and tilted her head to the side. "But, like, maybe a little smut."

Rose ignored her. "I want a book that'll take me on a million journeys with laughs and suspense and tears and still leave me happy at the end. Think about Disney! Can y'all think of one that has a sad ending?"

"*Old Yeller*!" Leah called out followed by Eliza shouting, "*The Fox and the Hound*!"

"My point is, I pity the folks who judge romance readers. As if the books we read are fluff. Like just because the books I read have some sex in a few chapters makes them somehow less worthy. Those folks are like the adults in *Peter Pan*, who no longer believe in magic. I, for one, am glad we find joy in readin' romance."

Rose paused briefly and looked around the room, finding that for once, we were all quiet, hanging on her every word.

"It means the child that loves to dance and sing, the one that dreams with their eyes open, is inside us all, alive and well."

CHAPTER
TWENTY-NINE

POLLY

We are all looking for a place in life, somewhere we fit. It's not a place that changes who we are or what we do – perhaps it shapes us, makes us better, makes us more – but mostly it shelters us with a sense of peace, a sense that whatever we do, wherever we are, we're not alone in it.

Samantha Young, *Into the Deep*

Girlfriends, I decided, were great. Fantastic, even. Besides Leah, my experience with female friendships consisted of two faced, catty wenches. These women were the opposite. They were accepting, genuinely wanting my opinion. I enjoyed myself so much, I was a little disappointed they only got together once a month.

"It was a real treat to have you here with us, Polly," Rose said at her door. Leah and I were the last ones to leave.

"I had the best time. I can hardly wait for the next book club," I answered honestly.

Leah was standing behind Rose and flashed me a smirk that was so smug, I could practically hear it aloud.

"Say! We're getting' together for Eliza's fourteenth anniversary of her twenty-fifth birthday next Saturday. You should come! The more the merrier!"

I glanced between Rose and Leah. "I can check to see if Jace can watch the kids. What book are you reading?"

"No book. We're taking a class at a fitness studio in town." Leah's voice sounded guarded.

Rose reached out and clasped my hands. "You'll *love* Stripped. Suzie's the best. We're gonna go to the Donner Bakery after for breakfast."

"What's Stripped?"

"It's a fitness studio downtown that teaches everything from senior aerobics to pole dancin'! Eliza signed us all up for the Intro to Chair Dancin' class. I'll bet it's a snap to have you join us." Rose snapped to emphasize her point, beaming at me. "Please say you'll come! It's gonna be a scream and a holler!"

Rose was looking at me like an endearing rainbow on steroids, which made it impossible to refuse her.

"Of course, I'll come," I said, side-eying Leah, who looked to be biting back a smile.

As I drove home from Leah's later that afternoon, instead of listening to an audiobook, I settled for peace and quiet. The lush greens of the trees against the bright blue sky were saturated with color this late in July. For so long, it felt as if I'd been in a haze, like a fog had settled over my life and I was following the path of least resistance that had been laid out for me.

Now, for the first time, I was forging my own path. I was making real friends. I had something exciting I was working on in my career. And I was getting to know Jace. A gentle heat stirred low in my belly as I thought of him the night before, his breath on my neck, his hand in mine as he pointed out fireflies in the yard. A tangible ache spread through me as I thought of the hug we shared. How good it felt to be pressed up against his firm body. How even when he was sitting on the stairs, wiping my tears, yes, I felt embarrassed, but it was strangely freeing. Having someone with me when I was at a low point, offering me comfort and a helping hand without conditions or judgment. It was strange to think of how much my life had changed in a week. Like the wind shifted and the fog lifted when Jace waltzed into our lives, fitting in seamlessly, like he was the new and improved Mr. Mary Poppins.

Maybe that was why, this morning, when I got an email from a childcare company asking me if I was still interested in finding after school care for my kids this fall . . . I promptly ignored it.

———

The kids and Jace were swimming when I got home from book club.

Jace was standing thigh deep in the shallow end, snorkel mask and arm floaties on, and for all intents and purposes, looking completely ridiculous. I couldn't keep my eyes from tracking the water droplets that rolled down his olive toned skin. A situation was brewing inside my body that I could only describe as a cat in heat: my pulse started to race, I was sweating, and I'm pretty sure I breathed out in a manner that was both a sigh and a groan.

His arms were spread wide, palms facing out. His snorkel bobbled when he whipped his head back and forth between his two attackers: Ryla, lifejacket and goggles on, stood on the pool stairs, her Nerf water blaster trained on Jace, and Max, standing waist high in the shallow end, also carrying a water blaster, had Jace directly in his sights.

Jace's plea was muffled by his snorkel. "Now, now, you two wouldn't gang up on poor, old Jace like this, would you?"

"Don't listen to him, Max! That's how they get you!" my daughter shouted, ostensibly the four-star general of this operation.

"Ryla? Maybe we shouldn't . . ." my sweet pacifist son protested, causing Jace to swing his head toward him.

But that was Jace's mistake. You don't turn your back on an assassin.

As Jace's head swung to Max, Ryla yelled, "Fire!" unleashing her full payload. Water hit Jace full-on in his face, chest, and back as he flopped in the water.

"What is going on out here?" I shouted in mock consternation, walking down the patio stairs.

"Mom! You're home!" Ryla shouted. "We're protecting the crystal! He's trying to get it from us!" She pointed to the presumed crystal, a.k.a. an aqua-blue pool noodle sitting by her feet on the edge of the pool stairs. "We can't let the evil sorcerer get it, he's gonna use it to steal all the chocolate in the whole world!"

Her head whipped to Jace, who'd taken advantage of Ryla's distraction to launch himself up and out of the water in exaggerated play-acting movements. Jace was only a few feet away from the "crystal" now, but Ryla was closer. Grabbing it, she looked to me and shouted, "Mommy! Catch!"

And then she launched it like a freaking javelin right over the middle of the pool.

As impressive as the throw was, I was focused on something else.

In order for me to catch it, I'd have to jump into the pool.

If I jumped . . . I'd be swimming. In my clothes.

In that instance, a lifetime of, *That's not appropriate, Polly,* or *What would people think, Polly?* went out the window.

Because who was I before my father told me who I should be?

I spared one millisecond to look at Jace. His eyes were focused on mine. A flash of excitement in them.

"Help is on the way!" I started running, then leapt out over the water, caught the noodle midair, and sunk into the pool.

———

"I think they're asleep," Jace whispered, muting the movie. I looked down at Ryla, spread-eagle on a big quilt, and Max, curled up in a ball under his weighted blanket. I wasn't surprised they'd totally zonked out. The kids were delighted that I'd jumped in the pool and swam with them. I'd changed into my swimsuit shortly after my epic save and continued to swim until we were pruny and exhausted. After swimming, we'd all dried off and changed into jammies and had a movie night, ordering pizza and eating it on the floor of the living room.

It was the nicest night I'd had in a long time.

Jace and I were sitting on opposite ends of the couch in the living room. His hair was adorably frizzy again, after air-drying. My eyes must have flicked up to his hair one too many times because he finally caught me, grinning sheepishly.

"How bad does it look?" he drawled, running his hand through the frizzy locks.

"It's fine."

He narrowed his eyes at me.

"What? It's just a shame you're not pursuing a clown career. It'd be economical. No wig needed."

Jace groaned and covered his heart with his hand, a gesture of his I'd come to recognize. "Imagine you're a thirteen-year-old with a delayed growth spurt, dressed in a black cape, holding a white-tipped wand, with this mop top under a black top hat, begging his family to watch his magic shows."

"I bet it was adorable," I blurted, then mashed my lips together.

"I was certain that I was going to be the next famous magician."

"What made you leave magic behind?"

"When I realized I wasn't willing to put my body through high-grade torture."

"What?" I asked.

"Have you ever seen David Blaine's stuff?" I shook my head prompting Jace to bring out his phone and lean toward me. I scooted over, folding my legs under me until I was sitting right next to Jace. I had to force myself to focus on his phone, rather than the mint on his breath from the peppermint patties we'd shared after pizza. I held my breath as the clip played.

Revulsion filled me as I saw the magician put metal through his hand. "There's something wrong with that guy. Is that what it takes to be a successful magician? No wonder you stopped."

I'd turned my head to Jace as I spoke, scooting back when I realized my lips were only a few inches from his.

Jace's eyes had dipped to my mouth, then back to my eyes as I inched further back on the couch. Shaking his head, he turned toward me and sat cross-legged on the couch.

"It was just as well. The next summer, I hit my growth spurt, gained ten pounds of muscle, and joined the baseball team."

On their own accord, my eyes drifted to his arms when he said the word, *muscle*. My gaze snapped back to his face, only to see him eye me curiously. I reached for a question—fast.

"Did you do any theater in school?"

"Junior year. About the time that a sixteen-year-old guy just wants to get laid. All the hot girls were in drama club, and they needed guys for the play they were doing."

"What was the play?"

"*Romeo and Juliet.*"

"What role were you?"

Jace rolled his eyes, resigned. "Sam still calls me Romeo occasionally."

Of course, he was Romeo. He'd be perfect. I wondered who the teenage Juliet was who played opposite him.

"So, you never did magic again?" I asked after unclenching my jaw.

"Not until after high school. I've done a few magic shows here and there for kids I babysat, and then during the summer program at the school a few times. I was too busy driving for Lyft, helping Sam with odd jobs, and a few other things to do it any more than that."

"I've never had that many jobs at once. Is there anything you can't do? Besides cook, that is."

Jace's face fell. "Who told you?

I waved him off, trying to keep my face neutral. "No one. I figured it out on my own."

His voice was flat. "It was Ryla, wasn't it?

"Oh yeah, she sold you out the first day," I said, smiling wide.

Jace snapped his fingers. "Damn it. I knew I shouldn't have been a dog."

"Was that what you did to buy her silence?"

"It wasn't just for fun!"

I laughed quietly, mindful of the kids, then tilted my head back and forth, eyes teasing. "Oh, it was fun."

Well, that came out more rough and ready than I expected.

Seemingly unfazed, Jace dragged the tip of his index finger across his neck. "So, says you. I still have rope burns."

Watching his lips form the words *rope burns*, his finger dragging over his skin . . . it did something to my gut. A flash of something filthy went through my mind. Heat sizzled in the air between us. I swallowed and Jace's eyes dipped to my throat. I imagined what his finger would feel like, tracing across my collarbone. Maybe he'd follow it with his lips, skimming their way up my neck as his hands caressed their way down my body.

A sudden snore from Ryla made us both jump and I immediately moved back, deciding I was out of my mind from chlorine, adrenaline, and lust poisoning.

I attempted to stand up, but the cushions were deep and soft, making me fall backward on my first attempt. Jace stood up gracefully on his first try (of course) and held out a hand to me, pulling me to my feet. I stumbled forward a step, my hand pressing into the firm planes of his abdomen, which felt hot and smooth and *hard* beneath the black jersey of his shirt. Jace's smile fell almost imperceptibly, and I stared at his lips, knowing that if I raised myself on my tip toes, our lips would touch. A shudder ran through me at the thought.

"Y'all good?" he whispered.

I gulped. "I'm fine. We should probably get to bed—*THEM* to bed. The kids. To bed."

I stepped to the side, trying to act unfazed. Because I was very much fazed. In fact, I wanted to get fazed by Jace over and over *and over* again.

I looked down at my sleeping children in front of us and mentally berated myself. I was a pathetic cougar flirting with a guy half my age when my kids were sleeping ten feet away.

Get it together, Mrs. Rochester.

I moved toward Ryla, but Jace got there first.

"I got her. You get Max." Before I could protest, he slipped his arms under my sleeping six-year-old and lifted easily.

Ryla roused enough to wrap herself around Jace like a spider monkey, then instantly fell back asleep. As I watched Jace carry her up the stairs, I had to force my heart to slow down and my brain not to jump to conclusions—even though there she was, on the edge of the high dive, ready to jump.

He is your kids' nanny and fourteen years your junior.

But I knew that was unfair. He was more than that. He was my friend.

A friend that you imagined fazing on your couch twelve point seven seconds ago.

I woke a sleepy Max, carrying his weighted blanket over my shoulder as he stumbled up the stairs to his room. He fell asleep again as soon as his head hit his pillow. I crept out of his room and shut the door, my heart taking off in another galloping rhythm when I saw Jace sitting at the top of the stairs.

"Hey," I whispered, "Thanks for carrying Ryla to bed."

Standing up, he nodded and took one backward step down the stairs, our heights becoming even. His rich hazel eyes were watching me with a fervent intensity that made my core throb.

"Everything ok?" I asked, mouth dry.

The silence between us held until my palms twitched forward at the same time he took another step down.

"I leave around five-thirty for the club tomorrow morning. I have a few things to do tomorrow so I won't be home, back here, until the late afternoon."

"That's fine," I said despite feeling disappointment that he wasn't going to be here. He started to turn when I called out, "Wait!" halting him on the stairs.

I didn't have anything I wanted to say. I just wasn't ready to have him leave yet.

He quirked an eyebrow as he waited for me to say something, the heavy silence continuing to stretch between us as my mind drew a blank.

Actually . . . that's a lie. My mind had a lot of thoughts—only none of them were appropriate.

Kiss him! –Sixteen-year-old Polly.

Tear that shirt off his body and wear it like a cape as you run your hands over his slabs of abs! –Twenty-four-year-old Polly

Tackle him to the ground and mount him! –She-cougar Polly in heat.

"Don't expect another forty-dollar tip," I blurted.

A wide smile stretched over his lips. "I thought I'd at least earned a fifty considering how many extra hours I've been putting in."

I shook my head, smirking. "You'll be lucky to get a quarter if you keep that attitude up."

Jace grinned, shuffling down a few more steps, then turned back to me once more, eyes serious. "You give him hell tomorrow—I'll be right outside if you need me."

I watched as Jace jogged down the stairs, then down the hall, longing and disappointment growing with each step he took away from me.

I laid awake for a long time that night. Glancing at the clock, I saw it'd been two minutes since I last checked the time. Which meant it'd been four minutes since I'd pulled out my earbuds in frustration, after I imagined the male character in my book with curly brown hair instead of blond, with an easy grin and dimples instead of a stiff upper lip, and bright hazel eyes instead of blue ones.

My clit ached as I rolled to my stomach. I laid there for another few minutes before sitting up and turning on my bedside light. I glared at my earbuds. I was aware I was being ridiculous. So what if I imagined Jace as the male character in my books? Whatever I did in the privacy of my own bedroom was my own business.

Resolutely, I grabbed the damn ear buds and turned off the light. Laying on my back, I turned on *American Cream.*

"Don't come," Helena whispered in his ear as she squeezed her cunt around his rock-hard cock."

I slid my hand under my panties, finding myself slick and hot, then slid my fingers up to circle my clit.

· · ·

"She cupped her breasts, bringing them to his mouth. He obliged, greedily sucking a taut nipple into his mouth, earning a hiss of pleasure from Helena."

I reached up with my other hand and grasped my nipple, teasing it, imagining how good it would feel to have Jace over me—or better yet, below me, totally at my mercy.

"She rewarded him, rocking her hips up and down, moaning at the sensation of her clit dragging against his studded cock. He popped off her breast, letting out a frustrated grunt as his wrists pulled against the hand-cuffs behind the chair."

I increased my pace, rubbing and circling my clit, pinching my nipple, my breaths coming in pants. I'd never had that during sex. That feeling of control. Sex had always been in a bed, missionary, and brief. The thought of being in control, taking what I wanted and having my partner love it just as much, spurred my climax on.

"Helena smiled, knowing she had him right where she wanted him. "Don't you dare even think about coming. I want to fuck you until you're begging me for release. Until you're so deep inside of me, you don't know where you end, and I begin. Until you're so mad with lust, you can only remember my name."

My orgasm ripped through me as I pictured coming around Jace's cock, his arms pulling against the restraints as he tipped his head back and found his release, the only thing louder than the mutual pounding of our hearts being the sound of him crying out my name.

CHAPTER
THIRTY

POLLY

"I'll be the one doing the riding and putting you away wet, thank you very much."

American Cream by Lady Jane
Narrated by Brittney Houston

"**D**ean Manford hasn't heard from you."

I paused, the Belgian waffle I'd ordered was halfway to my mouth. *Nooo,* I thought, *don't ruin this waffle for me.* I reluctantly put my fork down. The brunch hadn't been going horribly. Sure, it started out with my father's disdainful eye rake of my outfit, but as I finally decided to wear what I wanted, rather than what I was expected to wear, I'd anticipated that. I tried to pepper him with questions about his job so he couldn't start in on me. But then the waffle came, dusted with powdered sugar, and I kind of got distracted.

"Yes. That's because the kids won't be going there. They'll be attending school in Green Valley."

I'd already set up a meeting next month with Mr. Sievers and Rose to discuss Max's school accommodations.

Based on my thirty-eight years of experience and the way his eyes hardened, my father didn't like that answer.

"I didn't expect you of all people to ignore your children's education."

"Are you implying there is something inferior with the local school district? They're among the top twenty school districts in the state. I should know, I work for them."

The only sign of his alarm was the vein bulging in my father's forehead, otherwise he looked stoically calm.

"I might as well tell you now, I accepted a position as the medical director of the Green Valley School District. They received a grant to support kids with mental health disabilities, and they need a medical director to help advocate for how they use the grant money."

My father looked around, no doubt because my voice was slightly raised. He was worried about who might overhear.

"I can send Jeffrey the details to save him the trouble of looking into it," I finished.

"May I remind you about the deal we had when you moved here," he began.

"The deal was to have brunch, once per week. No, I haven't forgotten. Nowhere in there did it say you had the right to dictate where I work, where my kids go to school, nor for that matter, did it give you any other control over my life. Now, unless you'd like to explain to your constituency here why your daughter left in the middle of brunch, let's move on to safer topics, like the weather."

I picked up my fork with a trembling hand and took a large bite of waffle.

It was fucking delicious.

He wanted to make her laugh. He wanted to sit and listen to her talk about books until his ears fell off. But all these were things he could not want, because they were things he could not have, and wanting what you could not have led to misery and madness.

Cassandra Clare, *Clockwork Prince*

"You're hitting like my great-aunt Shirley."

I dodged Sam's punch and backpedaled, making a signal for time. I'd felt off since Polly left the club after her brunch this morning.

When Polly arrived for brunch, surprise kept me rooted in place as I opened her car door. Her pink and white dress fell in soft layers to just below her knee. I bit back a laugh when she handed me her keys with a smirk and a quarter. Her wavy blonde hair cascaded in loose waves to her mid back, swaying as she walked into the club. She looked different, lighter. Like someone had turned a light on inside of her.

My face instantly fell when I turned to see my pubescent coworkers watching her with interest. Something deep inside my chest had growled at their looks. They thought she was beautiful now, but they didn't get to see my Polly the way I got to see her, sitting on the couch in a thread bare T-shirt over leggings that molded to her shape, hair up in a bun and laughing at something I'd said. She wasn't perfect, not like the mask she wore here, but she was perfectly real.

I cleared my throat, causing their heads to snap in my direction. Nodding sharply to them, I said, "Boys." My eyes, on the other hand, told a different story: *Hands off, kids. This one's mine.*

Forty minutes later, Polly's father left, barking at one of the guys to collect his car. Worry had filled me. I'd wanted to run into the club and check on Polly, but I couldn't. I bounced up and down on the balls of my feet until she emerged a few minutes later, eyes bright and cheeks red. I tried to talk to her, but she only gave me a brief smile and a nod when I asked how her brunch went. Her behavior wasn't dismissive, nor was it sad really, or even angry.

She seemed distracted. What had her father said during their brunch? What if she was so distracted on the ride home that she got into an accident, or like, hit a deer?

Fuck. She could be on the side of the road right now, unconscious.

"What's wrong with you, Romeo?"

I snapped my head up from where I'd been standing with my hands on me knees in the boxing ring. "Fuck you, too."

Sam shook his head in exasperation as he punched his gloves together.

"That was me asking how you're doin', asshole. Relax."

Breathing out, I tilted my head back and forth, trying to keep my shoulders loose. I'd been on edge since Polly left the club, and now I was snapping at my best friend.

"Sorry." I bounced on my feet and hit my gloves together. "Let's go."

Sam got in three more punches—three more than he should have—before he stopped and put his gloved hands on his hips. "Jesus, Jace. You sick or something?"

While some friends may take advantage of their best friend on their off days, Sam wasn't one of them.

"My head's not right today. I think I'm gonna take off." I started toward the ropes, Sam falling into step with me.

"Anything I can help with?"

I glanced at him out of the corner of my eye. "If I tell you something, can you keep it to yourself?

Sam grinned around his mouth guard. "I knew it. You're hitting that, aren't you?"

I growled and started stalking toward him as he backed up. "Joking, joking."

"Forget it," I mumbled, taking off my gloves. "I gotta bail. I have to mow my parent's lawn and then get back to home."

I blinked, realizing it was the second time I'd called Polly's home, my home.

Luckily, Sam didn't pick up on my slip up. "I'm sorry, ok? Come on. Tell Uncle Sammy."

"Don't call yourself that again." I hopped down from the ring and Sam quickly caught up to me in stride, wisely saying silent, for once.

As we walked to the locker room, I reluctantly admitted, "I quit my job at the club this morning."

Sam stayed quiet.

"And I'm thinking of applying to college again. I've been turning over the idea of teaching for long enough. Working with kids every day, making a difference in their lives. Sometimes all it takes to change a life is having one person in your corner. I think I'd like to be that person."

Ever since I'd worked with Max on magic, seeing his face light up with every trick he learned, I could feel it: this is what teaching would feel like.

Sam scratched his neck. "You've never told me your decisions ahead of time before. Usually, when you want to do something, you do it."

"Your point?"

"I don't think it's quitting your valet job, or even college that's bothering you. You haven't been acting like yourself for over a month now."

Sam had a point. He also wasn't an idiot.

"It's the girl." Sam stopped short, just before the locker room, crossing his arms.

I narrowed my eyes. "She's not just a girl."

Wry smile in place, Sam rolled his eyes. "Yeah, yeah, I know. I figured that out when I was moving a ton of flowers behind a shed in the middle of nowhere." I was silent as he continued. "And I also figured out that you're not just in it for the puss—" his words cut off at the sharp look I sent him.

"My point is," Sam started again, "Is that I figured out she's not just some chick 'cause I've never seen you this way. And I'm a little relieved, just saying," Sam held up his hands. "But can you do us all a favor and stop being a chickenshit and get on that already?"

My best friend turned toward the locker room and pushed the door open, murmuring under his breath, "Before you drive us all insane."

———

After giving my parents' lawn a mow, I sent them a text and made my way back to Polly's. I'd been checking my phone obsessively, wondering if she'd text me, worrying if she'd made it home safe. Glancing in the rearview mirror, I noticed a black SUV. It'd been behind me since leaving my parents' place. But it was too far away for me to make out the license plate. I stepped on the gas, putting more space between me and the SUV, and on the next turn, it kept going past me. I shook my head. I was being paranoid.

About ten minutes later, I was walking into Polly's house.

I froze in place when I stepped into the kitchen. Music blared from a speaker on the table, which was completely covered in boxes, plastic bowls, and towels. Ryla was sitting on the table, swinging her legs and singing her heart out. Tinfoil pieces wrapped around random strands of her hair. The tips of Polly's hair were similarly wrapped in foil. She stood behind Max with a bowl of what looked like blue paint in one hand and a small brush in the other. Max's hair had a blue spiked strip down the center. And they all were wearing plastic sheets draped like capes around their shoulders.

"What're y'all doing?" I grinned, walking toward them.

"Jace! We're dyeing our hair!" Ryla shouted.

"You don't say?" I rubbed my chin. "I thought you were making tinfoil hats." Ryla giggled and Polly's eyes flicked to me then back to Max, a small smile on her face as she continued to dye Max's hair.

I leaned back against the island. "When did y'all decide to do this?"

"Momma came home with all of this stuff and said she's dyeing her hair and then shouted about who was with her and then Auntie Leah called her nuts."

"Ryla!" Polly scoffed, laughing lightly.

"Anything special bring this on?" I asked Polly, whose small smile hadn't left her lips since I walked in.

"Belgian Waffles," she said quietly, almost to herself.

"I love this one!" Ryla exclaimed and hopped off the table. Max giggled and Polly's eyes flashed with delight as Ryla started to sing.

Watching Polly and her kids, seeing her elbow deep in hair dye as Max giggled happily at his sister's antics, who was using a paintbrush as a microphone, it was like something finally snapped into place.

I didn't feel aimless, anymore. I felt found.

Who knew it'd be with this little family?

As much as it pained me to admit it, Sam was right. I was on edge because I knew what I wanted. I wanted Polly, but I wasn't sure if she felt the same way about me. There'd been a few little looks between us the last few days, and then a palpable moment last night when I swore, she was looking at my lips, just like I was looking at hers. After I put a sleeping Ryla in her bed, I waited on the stairs for Polly, resolved that as soon as she came out of Max's bedroom, I was going to kiss her and to hell with the consequences. And then, I lost my nerve. I didn't want to be another person that demanded something of her, forcing her into a situation she didn't need or want.

Looking at her now, seeing how happy she was, I was glad I didn't attempt anything last night. At best, she thought of me as a friend. So, if she needed a friend, I could be a friend. Even if it meant my balls were going to be blue for the next decade.

An hour later, after washing the kids' hair in the sink, Max had blue hair sticking up every which way and was using the extra hair dye to paint at the table while Ryla sat on a stool as I attempted to brush her hair.

Polly was taking a shower. I was trying not to picture it.

"Ouch!"

"Sorry, lil' miss." I sprayed more detangler in her hair. I'd always thought my hair was thick, but Ryla's was next level: thick and strong, snarly, extra sensitive, and not to be messed with. Kind of like Ryla herself.

"You have to start from the ends," Ryla explained.

I gingerly started at the ends and sure enough, that did work.

"The pink looks really pretty," I told her as I was finishing up.

"I'm gonna show Eric tomorrow and he's gonna be like whoa and I'm gonna say, yeah, my mom did it."

"Is that right?" I asked her softly.

"Uh-huh. Max wanted blue like Boyfriend, of course, and I wanted pink because that's the best one, and Mom chose purple. We have red, too."

I waited, figuratively hearing her gears turning. Four dyes. Three heads. One person left.

"We could dye your hair!" Ryla shouted as I placed the brush down.

"Have you seen this hair?" I pointed at my curls even though she couldn't see me.

As if sensing my unease, Ryla turned. Her eyes were brimming with mischief as she sensed the weaker prey in front of her.

"It'd be so fun! We could be twinsies!"

I looked at the pink streaks in her hair. That's what I was afraid of.

But then she pressed her hands together, stuck out her bottom lip and begged, "Pleeeeease?"

And like the weaker pretty I was, I asked, "Is red the only color left?"

Ten minutes later, I was sitting on a chair with a plastic sheet draped around my shoulder. Max grinned from his spot in front of me as he clipped the drape together and nodded to Ryla, who was standing on a step stool behind me.

"This is washable, right?" I eyed the red hair dye on the table with trepidation.

"I have no idea," Ryla answered honestly.

I was picturing myself looking like Ronald McDonald, when Polly burst into the kitchen in shorts and a white tank, the lavender tips on the ends of her blonde locks fell to just above her breasts.

There are kids here. You will not get excited. You won't even twitch.

"Ryla! What in the world? What are you doing?" Polly asked, every dip and curve of her lithe body on display in her outfit as she walked toward us.

Fuck.

"Jace said he wanted to dye his hair red!"

Polly crossed her arms. "Oh, he did, did he? It was all his idea?"

"Uh-huh," Ryla lied.

Polly raised her eyebrows at me. "Are you sure about this?"

I could only nod in response. All of my blood rushed directly south of my equator when she crossed her arms, causing her tits to push up higher.

Polly's lips upturned on one side.

"Ok then, Ryla. Scoot over. We'll do this together."

THIRTY-TWO

POLLY

Was it love or cardiac arrest? Fucking hell, did people actually like this feeling? It was horrible!

Melanie Harlow, *Some Sort of Crazy*

Ryla and Max lasted all of five minutes dyeing Jace's hair before they wanted a snack break. The front of Jace's hair was already saturated with red dye, so I quickly took off my gloves and gave the big bag of Cheetos to Max and two snack bowls to Ryla. I didn't have enough time to make them something healthy.

That's the story and I'm sticking to it. But between you and me, I finally had my hands in Jace's hair. Was I really going to take the time to wash and cut up an apple?

"Are you sure you want me to keep going?" I asked, moving back to my spot behind Jace as the kids scampered to the living room with their loot.

"I'm pot committed at this point." I could hear the smile in his voice. "You might as well finish, I wouldn't want to look silly."

I bit down on my lip to stifle a laugh. "Of course. Dip your head forward for me." My voice coming out more husky than intended.

My mind flashed to last night, imagining me riding him, restraining him, commanding him. I was grateful he was facing away from me, so he couldn't see my cheeks heating. As he tipped his chin to his chest, I moved my hands through his thick hair, finger combing it before I dyed it. But I couldn't help reveling in its lush softness. I instinctively spread my fingers out underneath his mess of curls, rubbing and stroking his scalp. It's like my hands had suddenly gone rogue—I wasn't even aware of what I was doing until Jace let out a breath, just this side of a groan. He tipped his head back, his hazel eyes bright and luminous, staring at me.

I wanted to grab his face and kiss him. Upside down. Then right-side up. Backwards, forwards, it didn't matter. It was like Dr. Seuss' *Green Eggs and Ham*: I wanted his mouth in a chair, I wanted his mouth here and there, I wanted his mouth *everywhere.*

Swallowing tightly, I jerked my hands out of his hair.

"So, how was your day today?" I chirped, shifting to put on a new pair of gloves, then picked up the brush and plastic bowl, giving the red dye a stir. I was not going to read into his rough swallow or how reluctantly he moved his head forward again, like it took effort to dip his chin to his chest.

"I sparred with Sam after work and stopped at my parents' place to mow their lawn. I didn't want them to come back to an overgrown yard when they get home from Florida next week."

"That's nice of you." I started to paint the remaining sections of Jace's hair. "Is that something you've always done for them, or is it because they're out of town?"

Jace hesitated and scratched his forehead with the back of his thumb. "I actually live with them. My pop has rheumatoid arthritis. He's got it mostly under control with medicine now, but it still flares once and awhile, especially if he overdoes it. I've slowly taken over the outside house maintenance these past few years and help out my mom when he has a flare. I wasn't living with them because I'm some freeloader, despite what my brother, Kent, may imply. I actually have a fair amount of savings compared to others my age."

Jace shifted in his chair, uncharacteristic tension radiating from him. The muscles in his shoulders and neck went rigid, like he was bracing himself for judgment.

I could imagine what people might think of Jace, not knowing anything about him, this blithe, twenty-something, guy, no career, living with his parents. But from what I've seen this week, Jace couldn't be further from that stereotype. Carefree without immaturity, he seemed older than his years in a hundred ways, approaching life with a whimsical optimism that I'd come to admire.

I was very suddenly, very angry at his brother. I had to gentle my touch to stop from aggressively layering the dye on Jace's hair.

"Can I just say, I have no interest in meeting your brother, ever. From the little you've told me, he sounds like an asshat."

Jace barked out a laugh as he brought his fingers up to his face again, scratching at his temple. "My sister will be thrilled to hear you think that. But my momma still has a soft spot for him. It's got to be a firstborn child thing." Jace's tone flattened. "It can't be his winning personality, that's for sure. Still, my parents put an offer in on a condo in Florida recently, so they're gonna be living close by him from now on, for better or for worse."

I vaguely recalled Jace mentioning that he'd needed a place to stay on the day of Ryla's party, but so much was said that day, I didn't recall it until now. Had that really only been a week ago? "Is that why you needed a place to stay? Because they're moving?"

"Partly. Sam's been trying to get me to live with him for a while now, so I'll probably move in with him come fall."

I nodded absently, the thought of Jace leaving felt like adopting a puppy and bringing it home, only to find out it belonged to another family.

"All done," I announced as I shucked off my gloves. "You need to leave that in for another twenty minutes. Then your transformation to Kent the Clown will be complete."

THIRTY-THREE

JACE

Because I'm holding on to my last shred of humanity, and if you stand here in those goddamn shorts for another ten seconds, it's going to snap.

Catherine Cowles, *Fragile Sanctuary*

"Knock, knock."

I glanced in the direction of my door at Polly's voice, not that I could really see her.

I'd been laying on my bed with my eyes closed for the last ten minutes because they burned too badly to keep them open. The skin on my forehead was prickling and itchy. I thought I'd washed all the dye out of my hair, but my eyes were tearing so badly, it was hard to tell.

"I wanted to check on—Oh no." I heard her footsteps approach the bed.

"It's fine," I said, eyes still shut. "Just a little reaction to the dye. I only need to rest my eyes a minute and then I'm sure it'll pass."

I felt the bed dip, followed by the sensation of Polly's fingers ghosting over my face. "Jace, your eyelids are swollen and there's a rash along your hairline. Do your eyes hurt?" Her voice was filled with alarm.

I forced them open, wincing at the sting. "It burns a bit," I admitted.

"OK. Stay here and keep your eyes closed. Do you have any allergies? Or do you take any medications?"

"No to both." I closed my eyes and sighed, feeling instant relief.

"OK. I'll be right back. Stay here." She left the room swiftly. The previous alarm in Polly's voice had been replaced with steady authority. A professional reflex, no doubt, but it also had the unfortunate side effect of making me imagine Polly returning to the room in a white lab coat with nothing underneath.

A couple of minutes later, I heard the urgent cadence of her footfalls coming down the hallway, then smelled her floral perfume floating over me before the bed dipped as she came to sit next to me again.

"Max's bee pack came in handy. I brought Benadryl and the steroid cream. I had some allergy eye drops on hand, too, and a cold cloth. Do you think you can sit up?"

Her guiding touch was light on my shoulder as I sat. I tried opening my eyes, but the burning still made it too painful.

"Here. This is the liquid Benadryl. It'll make you sleepy, but it'll help." Polly's touch was gentle, but deliberate as she opened my hand, placing a little cup into it.

"Jace?" she asked after I took the medicine. "This is the second time I've seen you with a rash on your face. Does this happen frequently?"

"Only rarely now." I groaned in relief as I laid back down.

"How rarely?"

"I used to get rashes like this when I was younger and used whatever shampoo was already in the shower. Now that I stick to the same shampoo and stuff to style my hair, it hasn't happened in years."

I scratched my forehead only for Polly to grab my hand, stopping me.

"Jace! That's what an allergy is! That's not normal." Her tone was two parts exasperation and one part amusement.

"Really?"

She laughed and I could hear the sympathy in her voice. "Yes. Now let me put in some eye drops, it will help."

That's all the preamble I got before she pried my eyelids open and efficiently put one drop in each eye. I flinched and blinked rapidly; they burned like a mother fucker.

"Big baby," she teased, low and raspy.

I heard the pop of a cap opening and then Polly was smoothing lotion over my forehead and around my eyes. Her soft breaths came out like pants. I had to picture sitting next to my Gran in church to keep from reacting as Polly continued torturing me in the best way possible.

A sigh escaped me when she put the cold cloth over my eyes, feeling the swell of her breasts press against my chest as she leaned over me.

It felt like heaven.

The cool cloth felt good, too.

"You rest. I'll come check on you later."

I reached out blindly and caught her hand. And maybe it was my imagination, but as I brushed my thumb along the back of her hand, I swear I heard a soft exhale.

"Thank you," I said, keeping our hands entwined for a few more moments.

Polly eventually placed my hand beside me on the bed, letting it go, but then, very deliberately, Polly stroked her fingertips across the top of my hand before stepping away.

I would've given anything to see her face right then, to know what she was thinking.

"Rest now."

Polly's voice was liquid metal: smooth, scalding hot, and dangerous.

Because the way that Polly was acting today, her coy smiles, the lingering touches, the definitely-not-imagined massage to my scalp this afternoon, it all gave me hope.

And while my brain knew it's the hope that kills you, someone would have to explain that to my heart.

And the idiot in my pants.

CHAPTER
THIRTY-FOUR

POLLY

My body was panting, "He's hot. Can we have him?" while my mind was screaming, "Oh, dear God, what the hell are you thinking?"

Samantha Young, *Down London Road*

Ryla and Max were all smiles when I put them to bed. They loved their new hair colors, and frankly, so did I. Sure, it would wash out in a week, but every time I saw the lavender tips of my hair, a flush of giddiness filled me. It was convenient that the kids were distracted by the excitement of the day because I couldn't focus on a god damn thing. I repeated the same sentence twice while reading a book to Ryla at bedtime, then trailed off in the middle of a relaxation exercise with Max.

My heart was pounding as I walked to Jace's room later that night. I knocked lightly on the door, receiving no answer.

He was probably asleep. I should let him rest. But what if his rash was worse?

Maybe you can nurse him back to health, purred the cheeky twenty-four-year-old inside of me.

After a quick debate, I opened the door. The curtains on the far side of the room were pulled back and the full moon cast a soft light around the room, tempering the shadows.

Jace was asleep, in the same position I'd left him two hours ago. My lips quirked as Jace quietly snored, even and deep. The cloth over his eyes felt warm, so I removed it and checked his forehead. The rash had faded significantly and there was less swelling around his eyes. After rinsing the cloth with cold water in the bathroom, I laid it back over his eyes causing Jace to stir.

"Shh. It's me," I whispered, sitting beside him. "How are you feeling?"

"Looadss better." Jace's sexy Tennessee drawl was more pronounced than normal due to the sleep or Benadryl, I wasn't sure which. He lifted the cloth and squinted toward me. "What timess it?"

"Just after eight, the kids are sleeping. I wanted to come check on you."

"Thanksss," he slurred again as I smothered a laugh.

"Benadryl hits you hard, huh?" I asked, a strange shaky feeling building in my chest.

"Dunno. First times I tried it."

"It's a good thing I have off tomorrow. Who knew that you could be felled by a first-generation antihistamine?" I teased, making a move to stand. He reached for my hand, like he'd done that afternoon and I reached back, letting him.

"You leavin' me alone?"

"You needin' company?" I returned boldly.

Stupidly.

He smirked, letting my hand go and placing the cloth back over his eyes, letting me know he had more awareness than his slurring suggested.

"Least you could do. Wasn't *my* hair dye." He blindly patted the bed next to him in . . . invitation?

I swallowed nervously as I walked around the bed. My hands were shaking. "Bringing out the big guns, huh? Guilt! You sure you're not a parent?"

Incredibly conscious of every dip of the bed as I crawled next to him, I finally settled on my back beside him.

I was sure the pounding of my heart was audible, but Jace's peaceful, even breathing set a rhythm that finally calmed my racing heart. Over time, small things came into focus: the downy softness of the coverlet beneath us, the heat from Jace's body radiating into my side, the texture of the linen canopy above the bed.

Jace was so quiet, I thought he'd fallen asleep until he asked, "Was the deal with belshin waffles?"

His question surprised me. I found myself searching for an appropriate answer when I realized there was no need to search. With Jace, there was no need to tailor my response; I merely needed to tell the truth.

"I ordered them today."

"Good choiss."

"It's the first time I ordered something I actually wanted in front of my father. Maybe, ever. Over the years I'd learned what my father expected of me in public. With clothes it was nothing revealing, demure colors and high neck-lines only. I bought the dress I wore today on a whim months ago, never thinking I'd get the opportunity to wear it. Turns out, the world didn't end with my father's derision."

Jace was still, but I knew he was listening.

"On the way home I was preoccupied, thinking about all the things I wanted to do but was never allowed. Like dyeing my hair. Before I knew it, my car was in the drugstore parking lot."

I absently fingered my hair. "I thought about all the other things I missed as I drove the rest of the way home. Dances, football games, birthday parties. Friendships." I was suddenly hoarse, angry tears building behind my eyes.

I cleared my throat. "It's like I'm finally feeling angry at the loss, at missing that part of life I didn't get. Hoping that it's not too late."

"Too late for what?" Jace had taken the cloth off his eyes and rolled toward me, looking more awake than a moment ago, the reflection of the moon illumi-nating a rim of gold in his hazel eyes.

I swallowed roughly, gathering the courage to say it.

"For my own happy ending."

The moonlight bathed our skin in white light, making Jace's face look like it was carved out of marble. Emboldened, like we were in a bubble of safety, I cupped his cheek. His skin was warm and supple beneath my hand. Touching him and finding him real felt impossible. Like I couldn't believe there was finally someone in this house for me again; the first time I'd felt that way since my mother was alive. Somebody that understood me. Somebody who gave without expectation.

Finally.

His intoxicating scent made me want to drink him in. I inclined my head, and he did the same; our lips were millimeters apart, my body yearning, aching to know what his lips felt like.

Powerless to the inescapable pull, our lips touched. I relished the relief of finally knowing what his lips felt like, the subtle pressure, the soft brushes. They fit together perfectly, like Jace's lips were meant to kiss mine, and mine alone.

I leaned into him more fully, greedily, my hand gripping his cheek, his stubble rough against the palm of my hand as I held us together. His hand came to rest on my waist as our lips brushed and sucked and pressed, drinking each other in, savoring like we both knew this moment wasn't meant to last. Moving closer I felt something wet on my arm and pulled back from Jace with a gasp, only to realize it was the cold cloth laying between us.

I swallowed a laugh as I took in Jace's heated stare. His lips were full and red, the moonlight reflected his wide, dilated pupils . . .

Shit.

I slammed my eyes shut and rocked back. "I'm sorry! First I made you all blissed out on Benadryl and then I forced myself on you. I'm so sorr—"

"Shhh." Jace covered my lips with two fingers, silencing me immediately. "You weren't taking advantage of me. I wanted to kiss you. I've dreamed of kissing you, of taking my time, savoring the way you taste . . ." Jace's eyes swept down, then up my body lazily, a fire igniting everywhere his gaze lingered, "until the only kiss you remember is mine."

Can a human body liquefy from mere words? Because those were the hottest words anyone's ever said to me, and they were uttered by a delectable man inches away whom I wanted more than air in this moment.

I longed to lean into him again, but there was a glaze over his eyes. With a sigh, I moved off the bed and made my way to the door slowly and opened it, fighting the urge to return to him with every step.

As I turned to the pull the door shut, Jace croaked my name, as if the distance between us was just as painful for him as it was for me. Lifting my gaze, I saw he was half sitting up, watching me intently.

I took a slow breath in. There are certain decisions in your life that change the course of it irrevocably.

"I can't go there tonight, Jace. Not when I essentially drugged you. So, sleep. I'm dropping the kids off at summer school in the morning and then I'm coming back home."

Jace's eyes were completely focused on me, glistening in the dark.

Right here and now, I was singularly aware that what I said next could change my life forever.

That my words could keep me locked in a cage.

My voice was barely a whisper, but I knew he could hear it.

"If you still want me tomorrow, tell me again."

Or, they could set me free.

CHAPTER
THIRTY-FIVE

POLLY

"A real man doesn't fuck you for your money. He fucks you because you're gorgeous. Because you come like a rocket. Because you have eyes that show him everything you're feeling. He fucks you because nothing has ever felt better."

"Oh."

"Yeah, oh."

Devney Perry, *Tinsel*

"**G**ood morning. I sincerely apologize if I crossed a line last night. I understand you are my employee, and I am your employer, so please accept my sincerest apologies for my actions. It will not happen again."

I scowled at my reflection.

"Don't be such a weirdo, Polly! You can't say that!" I hissed at the weirdo in the rearview mirror talking to herself.

I'd just dropped the kids off at summer school and made a pit stop at Daisy's for donuts.

I'd woken up as Morning Polly who was now replaying Nighttime Polly's actions over in her head. Morning Polly was rational—Morning Polly, was mature. Nighttime Polly was clearly smoking a joint in one hand and flipping her father off with the other while singing "Free Bird" at the top of her lungs.

Was I the one drunk on antihistamines last night? What other possible explanation could there be for me attacking Jace's mouth with my own and then essentially telling him to come get me in the morning?

I palmed my forehead. He's friends with the county sheriff! What if they're waiting at the house to arrest me?

I leaned forward and blasted cold AC in my face. I had to calm down. The kiss was not illegal. More morally frowned upon, maybe—but at least it was mutual.

I relived the memory of Jace's lips on mine. How his scent invaded my senses, sweet and something addictively Jace. Maybe I needed to pair that memory with something bad. Like the smell of dead fish. Perfect! When I caught myself thinking about Jace that way again, I'd think of a dead, rotting fish. That should cure me in no time. Feeling marginally better at my negative association plan, I pulled out on the road home.

Jace's car was still in the driveway and, to my sincere relief, a police cruiser was nowhere in sight. Grabbing the donuts, which I'd thought would be a sweet peace offering but now felt like a pitiful bribe, I went inside, pausing just inside the door.

"Jace?" I called out down the hallway.

I didn't hear anything. Walking toward the kitchen, I sighed. Maybe he was still sleeping. Maybe I could sneak upstairs and—

"Ahh!" I crushed the bag of donuts to my chest. Jace was standing at his normal morning spot by the coffee maker, arms crossed. Haphazard red curls notwithstanding, he looked good. Soft gray T-shirt, worn jeans, and bare feet good.

His lips were pressed in a firm line.

You've kissed those lips. You know what they taste like.

"Jace! You startled me. How is your hair—I mean, lips—EYES! Your eyes, how are they?"

"Fine." He uncrossed his arms, leaning back against the counter, face still unreadable.

FINE? *That* was his reply?

"Marvelous! I got donuts!" I chirped, wincing at my tone. I strode to the island, avoiding eye contact with him. I set two plates on the counter and opened the bag to—

"Polly."

"Jesus!"

A low voice *directly behind me* had me spinning to see that Jace had moved. He was now directly behind me, less than half a foot.

Jace pointed to himself, an amused smile on his face. "It's Jace, actually."

Was he *enjoying* my embarrassment?

He slowly advanced and I backed up a step, the hard granite countertop pressing into my back. He rested his hands on either side of me, boxing me in.

"Do you want to pick your own donut?" My tenor was unintentionally breathless.

He leaned in close, his sweet scent making me woozy with want. "As good as those donuts are, I'd rather have something else."

His voice was honey dipped in whiskey dipped in sin.

I gulped.

His multifaceted hazel eyes fixed on me. No, not just on me.

On my lips.

"What?"

"You."

And then Jace brought his hands to my cheeks, cupping them with gentle urgency, and pressed his lips to mine.

Jace's kiss was warm and strong and urgent and all the things necessary for life.

I never wanted to stop kissing him. His lips were somehow both gentle and insistent, brushing against my own, then surging with the most perfect pressure that I flat out *moaned*. I met his fervor with my own, desperately seeking purchase. My hands instantly threaded through his hair to grip the curly strands and hold on for dear life because I'd never, in my entire life, been kissed like this.

His lips opened and sucked on my bottom lip, a flash of his tongue teasing me, making me desperate. So yes, it was my tongue that licked at his bottom lip in response, eliciting a deep, exhaled moan from Jace.

His left hand slid from my cheek and through my hair, sending tingles through my scalp. His right arm dropped and wound around my back, pulling me in, pressing my body flush against his. My nipples went hard as our tongues caressed each other, licking and sucking, savoring each other, frenetic with want. A deep groan rumbled through Jace's chest, my peaked nipples practically vibrating as they were pressed deliciously against the firm expanse of his muscular chest. A throb of pleasure pulsed in my clit. Out of breath, I tore my mouth away from his, dropping my hands to the solid countertop behind me.

His red hair was wildly mused from my grip, his lips swollen and pink.

"I'm too old for you," I panted, chest heaving.

Jace's response was to slide his hand further into my hair and cup the back of my head, pulling me so close our lips were millimeters apart.

"I think you have me confused with someone who gives a damn."

And then he devoured my mouth again.

Full-on goosebumps erupted down my arms as his tongue stroked mine. I lost all deliberate thought, acting on pure need alone, throwing my arms around his neck, pressing my body against his. He closed his lips around my tongue and sucked, hard, causing my knees to buckle in pleasure. Jace hooked his arms underneath my butt and lifted, swiftly depositing me onto the island countertop in front of him.

We were both gasping for breath as Jace gripped my hips and leaned his forehead against mine.

"I've been dreaming of this since I first saw you," he panted. "But I've been desperate, aching for you, the more I got to know you. Learning about you, laughing with you. Being with you like this . . ."

He trailed off, inching back so he could look into my hungry eyes.

What?! I wanted to shout.

He grabbed a stray lock of my hair that had fallen across my face, flashing a coy smile as he rubbed it between his fingers, then tucked it behind my ear.

"You're all I want, Polly." His words were genuine and true, his expression guileless. "The only question is, do you want me too?"

Yes.

The unspoken word hung in the air between us as I searched his face, my desire and longing a battle cry in my body. The typical internal battle, the one that warred between what had been drilled into me as right and appropriate versus what I wanted was no longer there. Jace's words affirmed that he was here, in this moment, wanting me just as much as I wanted him, essentially melted away my reservations. And without them, I found that the bar of expectation that had been set for me had been broken down, whittled away until it offered no resistance. The war within myself was over before it began.

Maybe what I wanted wasn't bad. Maybe what I wanted, was actually the right choice.

"Yes," I whispered. A momentary look of shock passed over his features, followed by heat. Desire sparked in my belly, spreading throughout my body, soaking my center.

"Finally," was what I thought I heard on an exhale when Jace captured my mouth in a fierce kiss. One of his hands braced on the counter behind me as the other cupped my cheek. I snaked my arms around his body, caressing the firm planes of his back.

He licked the seam of my mouth, and I instantly opened for him. I groaned on an exhale as we stroked and licked and sucked at each other's mouths. I loved it. Each stroke of his tongue caused a small shiver of pleasure in my core.

I hadn't French-kissed many people in my life, and to be honest, it wasn't my favorite. This kiss with Jace obliterated any memory of any kiss I'd had in my entire life. If this was what kissing was like in France, I needed to go there. Immediately. Hats off to France, you know what the fuck you're doing.

Jace's lips trailed kisses across my cheek. When he moved to the skin below my ear, giving it a small, playful suck, a bolt of lust shot to my core causing me to arch my neck and gasp in bliss.

It took me thirty-eight years to discover I had an erogenous zone below my ear.

And Jace, the overachiever, figured it out in less than five minutes.

I grasped the bottom of his shirt in my hands, lifting it in earnest, desperately wanting to feel his skin beneath my palms. I made a noise of frustration when his shirt caught on the button of his jeans. Chuckling low and sexy, Jace backed up a step and reached behind his back, pulling the shirt over his head with one hand. The motion caused his biceps to pop and his red hair to go every which way, making me giggle.

My laughter abruptly stopped as my eyes trailed down his chest to the rippled glory of his abs. He took a step closer to me. Mouth dry, I placed my hands on his upper arms, sliding them gently up to curve around his shoulders, luxuriating in the feel of firm muscles beneath warm skin. I traced his collarbone, then moved lower, my fingers smoothing down to the solid muscles of his pecs; they were so firm, the skin covering them so taut, that for a moment I wondered if he was real.

Without thinking, I flicked his chest lightly with my fingers, then realizing what I just did, covered my mouth with my hand and giggled.

Jace chuckled as he leaned into me, and I felt a puff of air against my forehead before he placed a soft kiss there. The notes of his cologne were fresh and warm and comforting, coming off his skin in waves, drugging my senses. Leaning forward, I nuzzled and pressed an open-mouthed kiss on his chest, making him shudder. My fingers continued tracing down the individual ridges of his abdominal muscles and all humor faded as my fingertips fell below the waistband of his jeans, finding a very prominent bulge.

My mouth watered.

I tilted my head back to look into his eyes.

I gulped, finding them focused on me, serious and wanting. His hands dropped to the hem of my shirt. He raised his eyebrows in question, and I lifted my arms in response. My T-shirt was removed quickly, revealing my bra—which I'd forgotten was beige. Granted, it had some lace and a few petal designs, but I instantly tensed.

A plain beige bra for the middle-aged mom.

Jace, however, wasn't looking at me like I was plain *or* middle-aged.

His eyes carved their way down my body, looking at me like he was a starving man in front of a five-course meal.

"I have an IUD."

Oops. I hadn't meant to say that out loud.

But with Jace's starving expression, why shouldn't I let him know that my restaurant was open for business?

At my revelation, his eyes flashed, and he leaned toward me, putting both of his hands on the granite countertop, effectively boxing me in again.

I took a deep breath in. "I haven't had sex in a long time. I've been tested, and I'm clean. You?"

Jace's face softened. "I test after every partner. There's been no one for months. You're safe with me, darlin'."

You're safe with me.

His words pierced my heart, straight through to my soul. Because I did feel safe with Jace. If I was being honest, I felt safer with him than almost anyone else I knew. It didn't matter that I'd only known him a short time. I felt safe to be myself. Safe to be imperfect. Safe to try something for the first time.

"I know. You're safe with me, too." My words were strong. Resolute.

And then we exploded.

Jace practically tackled me, our hands wildly stroking up and down each other as if we couldn't pick where we wanted to touch first. His mouth trailed kisses down my neck, his hands cupping me over my bra. A curious smirk came over his face as he traced the petal designs on my bra. Then quick as a flash, he pulled a cup to one side and enveloped my nipple with his mouth.

"Jace!" I gasped and threw my head back. Bolts of lust surged directly to my clit. As his tongue continued to lavish attention to my nipple, his other hand reached up to stroke my other breast. I was panting hard, making soft keening noises as Jace continued to shower my sensitive peaks with lapping strokes and sucks. His hands went behind me and with a practiced hand that I didn't want to even think about, unhooked my bra. Fully bared to him, he growled and cupped my breasts together. I cried out as he swiped his thumbs over each peak. Unable to take anymore, I grabbed his face and pulled him to me, finding his lips swollen and wet.

Licking into his mouth, I experienced the wettest, filthiest, greediest kiss I'd ever had. As much as I didn't want it to end, I finally let his face go and wantonly leaned back on my hands, breasts on full display.

"Upstairs?" I asked, quirking an eyebrow.

Jace's expression turned feral. "I'm nowhere near finished yet."

He gripped my hips, sliding me off the counter and onto shaky legs. He deftly undid the button at my waist, bringing my jeans and panties down to my ankles. Stepping out of them, I kicked them across the kitchen, kind of sure, but not totally sure, what he was going to do next.

Fully naked before him, he gently pushed me back against the island. My skin protested at the cold from the granite as Jace lowered himself to his knees. His eyes trained on mine as he slid his hand up my left calf to my thigh, picking my leg up and draping it over his shoulder. He raised his eyebrows and smirked.

Wait, was he really going to do that while I was stand—

Jace dove straight for my aching, drenched center.

If French kissing wasn't something I'd done very often, a man going down on me was practically nonexistent. Sex was missionary and brief in the latter half of my marriage. I came, sometimes. He came, every time. Quick. Efficient. Check it off the list.

I braced my hands on the counter behind me as my right leg threatened to buckle as Jace licked my clit rapidly back and forth with sure strokes. I sucked in a breath, closing my eyes from the pressure building inside of me. But it was when he started to massage my clit with his tongue that I shouted his name, then clutched and held onto the back of his head, keeping him there.

"Keep going, a little harder," I begged, desperate for release.

He proved to be a good fucking listener as the force of his tongue intensified. I was shamelessly seeking friction, gripping the back of his head, canting my hips in time with his sure strokes.

"Ahh!" I was close but not quite there. Jace brought his fingers to my core and parted me, pushing in with two fingers, giving me the exact amount of pressure, exactly when and where I needed it.

I cried out, arching and gasping as waves of release pulsed through me. Thighs shaking, the only thing holding me up was Jace's hand which slid to grip my ass, my right leg, and an elbow I'd pressed onto the countertop.

As my orgasm faded, he gently pulled his fingers from me and helped ease my thigh off his shoulder. He never broke eye contact with me as he stood, the intimacy of the moment thick between us. I was still catching my breath, the internal pulses of release still throbbing in my core.

Once he could tell I was steady on my feet, he towed off his shoes, then yanked his pants to the ground. He pounced on me so quickly, grabbing the back of my head and pulling me to his mouth, I didn't have any time to process a fully naked Jace.

Our lips parted as we shared the taste of myself on his tongue. Feeling the press of his hard length against my lower belly, I pulled back. Pressing my forehead to his, I looked down between us to see what rested there, straining up to me. He was thicker than my previous partner, all one of them, and I could see the deep, pink tip already leaking clear fluid. I reached down to trace that bead of moisture, transfixed as I painted it around the head of his cock. Then I wrapped my hand around his impressive girth, stroking him, luxuriating in the velvety softness. It was Jace's turn to groan and exhale, his eyes closing in bliss as his head fell back.

I felt powerful and sure as I stroked him up and down, already in a frenzy by the idea of where I wanted him most. I moved in to taste his arched neck, giving a slow lap of my tongue along the muscle there, as if I was licking where I was stroking, tasting salt and sweetness of my tongue. Jace's moan filled the room as I sucked just below his ear.

"Do you want me to get something from my room? We can keep going or stop here, the choice is yours," Jace rasped. I tilted my head back to see if he was really asking permission to keep going—like I hadn't just ridden his tongue in the middle of my kitchen and wasn't palming his dick like I was claiming it as my new territory. I looked between Jace's eyes, wondering how he could go from damn fucking sexy to earnestly sweet in less than a second, but the fact that he didn't assume anything, the fact that he was giving me an out, was all the answer I needed.

"I want you. I want to feel all of you, no room stops needed."

An almost giddy grin came across his face before he kissed me again. It started sweet, but then my hand, which had gone still, squeezed and stroked up, prompting a low growl from his throat.

Jace picked me up, my legs wrapped around him, my clit pressing against his perfect washboard stomach, igniting an urgency within me again. I kissed and sucked on his neck, rocking against him as he walked us through the kitchen and unceremoniously sat on the couch, me mounted on his lap.

I gripped the back of the couch and rode him, chasing the friction I found against him with each tilt of my hips.

Jace's hands cupped my breasts as he licked and sucked my nipples. "Yes, yes, yes," I chanted, moving lower on his lap, rubbing my slick folds up and down his hard length, my wetness coating him, my clit pulsing with each push against the head of his dick.

Jace moved his right hand down my body, thumbing my clit, then fisted his cock and lined himself up to my entrance. Slowly, I lowered myself onto his impressive length, my mouth opening from the unexpected fullness. I winced a little bit as I started to slowly move, if I'm being honest. I moved up and down on his cock slowly until the discomfort gave way to pleasure.

Considering pelvic floor physical therapy was the most action I'd gotten after Ryla was born, it was a wonder my vagina hadn't atrophied into nothing. With that errant thought, I gave a tentative squeeze with my pelvic muscles.

Jace's eyes shot open as he shouted, "*Fuuuuck!*"

Huh. Guess pelvic floor PT worked.

My body hummed as I thrust myself up and down his cock in a steady rhythm. Jace fought for control, his head falling back on the couch, eyes half lidded as I alternated thrusting and squeezing his length, enjoying this power.

"Look at me," I demanded, not recognizing myself at all.

Jace's eyes sprang open, brilliant rings of hazel around their dilated centers.

"Don't come yet," I commanded, uninhibited and free, taking what I wanted, something that Jace was more than willing to give me.

"I'm trying," Jace's voice was strained. He groaned as I bottomed out on his dick. "Fuck, you're amazing."

Slowing my pace, I slid all the way up and down again, feeling another throb of his dick as he fought back his release, and I was right there with him. Sweat broke out against his forehead.

"Fight it, Jace. Don't you dare come." I changed the cadence of my hips, eliciting another curse. Our breaths came out in shaky gasps. Jace thumbed my clit alternating between soft, sure circles and downward pressure. His left hand, which had been gripping my hip, slide to palm my ass. I cried out when his long fingers skirted the edge of an area I'd never explored with anyone else before.

"Yes, yes, yes," I chanted in rhythm as I rode Jace hard, coming apart under his perfect touches. My body spasmed, my muscles clenching around his cock, intense pleasure pouring through me as I gave into the most intense orgasm of my life.

Jace finally let himself go, grabbing my ass with both hands, jerking me further onto him as he found his release, muttering a wickedly filthy, *"Fuck"*, with each surge of himself inside of me.

As we both came down, I completely collapsed on top of him in a boneless, blissful heap. Jace whispered words like, *so good, so beautiful,* as his fingers traced soft circles on my back. My forehead rested on his shoulder, and I tenderly nuzzled it with my nose, loving the feel of his skin, so firm yet so soft at the same time. I'd never felt so fully worshipped, so fully sated. It was like I was in my own little haven of happiness.

"Polly?" Jace's voice rumbled next to my ear.

"Mmhmm?" I was still floating on a cloud; my ears hadn't yet stopped ringing.

"Do you have things to do today?"

I slowly pulled back. His red curls wild, lips swollen, eyes adoring.

What did he ask me? Oh, did I have things to do today? Of course I did. I was a single mother. I had a never-ending to-do list a thousand tasks long.

He rolled his eyes. "That was a dumb question. It's just you're naked and finally in my arms. I selfishly want to keep you here as long as I can."

I tapped my lips with my finger. He had a point. I had a naked Jace Vargas beneath me and six hours before I had to pick up my kids. "I might be persuaded to put off my to-do list until tomorrow."

Jace barked a laugh, and I tipped forward. Our kiss was breathless and fun as we laughed against each other's mouths. Jace leaned his forehead against mine, a gesture that I already was thinking about as ours.

"How about a shower?"

CHAPTER
THIRTY-SIX

JACE

I always thought you looked like mine, but you sure do fucking feel like you're mine, too.

Mariana Zapata, *Wait for It*

The steam from the shower was hot, but Polly's tongue on my cock as she blew my ever-loving mind in the shower was the hottest experience of my life.

She ran her tongue up the underside of my dick, fisting the rest in her sexy as fuck grip, then sucked the tip, making me curse again.

I'd been cursing a lot.

I had to brace myself with one hand on the shower wall as I held onto the shower door handle. This was going to be over far sooner than I wanted it to be.

Her wet lashes clung together, making her green eyes pop as she looked up at me. Her look was teasing, as she gripped me, killing me inch by damn inch, as she slowly stroked me up and down.

"Does it feel good when I squeeze your cock like this?" she purred, squeezing me with perfect firmness.

I groaned. Because, yes, it felt really fucking good.

"Is this how you like it?" It was a simple enough question. But her voice was sultry, like smoke and desire and everything I learned to fear in church.

I cursed. Because, yes, I really fucking liked it.

We'd made out in Polly's bathroom as we waited for the shower to warm up. Her sitting on the counter as I explored the feel of her soft curves under my hands, her heels digging into my ass. Sex with Polly was on a whole different level. I can't lie and say the lessons I learned from those romance books didn't help me, because I used every trick in my arsenal.

We laughed as I slipped stepping into the shower. We held on to each other as we took turns washing one another, taking our time, paying attention to every new sensitive spot we discovered. When I got to my knees to pay special attention to that bundle of nerves between her legs, she came on my tongue, again.

After that, I stood as she, eyes playful, slowly sunk to her knees and gripped my cock, asking "Is this what you want?" I'd only blinked, not sure she was real. Because fuck if her dirty talk didn't turn me on. The fact that she even *did* dirty talk was mind-blowing enough. She then went about tormenting me in the best possible way, alternating between little sucks and licks, steady strokes, and dirty words.

I loved that she took charge. And she seemed to like it just as much.

"Do you want my tongue again?"

I nodded yes to her question—so eagerly I was surprised my teeth didn't rattle. And then, a memory flickered in my mind, of a shower scene kind of like this. Could she be acting out a scene from a book? Was I really this lucky?

She sucked me further into her warm, wet mouth as she held on to my hips. Her vibrant green eyes flashed, looking up at me as she took all of me, not stopping until her nose made contact with the skin at the base of my dick. She shocked me as her clever little hand slid from my hip to where she gently, perfectly, held the Vargas jewels. An intense surge of pressure shot to the base of my spine; my groan was so loud, the shower's glass doors shook.

I gave her the signal to stop and she popped off immediately. Wild with desire and a filthy idea, I pulled her to her feet and spun her around. Her hands hit the shower wall in front of her as I grabbed her hips and sunk into her wet heat from behind.

Our mutual cries of pleasure echoed off the shower walls.

"Jace!" she cried as I leaned forward, panting into her neck, thrusting again and again.

Her hands stayed braced on the wall as I brought one of my hands down to stroke her clit. My other arm slid up her belly to where my fist lined up just below her breast, hugging her to me.

"I'm not letting you out of here until you come on my cock, one, more, time," I grunted, accentuating my words with each thrust of my hips.

Polly was panting. "I don't know . . . if I can . . . again."

Opening my palm, I slid up to cup her breast, lightly pinching her nipple as my other hand continued the firm strokes at her center.

"Come for me, darlin'," I breathed into her ear, "I'm waiting for you."

It wasn't until I felt her clamping around my cock that I finally gave into my own pleasure, shuddering and shaking, barely able to hold Polly upright as I followed her release with my own.

Eventually, Polly turned in my arms, our fingers threading together at our sides. Our lips met in a soft, breathless kiss. But this was Polly, and I couldn't help myself from licking at the seam of her lips, begging entry. She pushed against my hands, moving back.

"Hold on, cowboy. I know you're twenty-four and can probably go for days, but I need a minute to rest."

Laughing, I pulled her into my arms, my hands smoothing down her body to stroke her butt, squeezing both globes in my palms.

"That sounds like a fun challenge."

Lazing her palms down my back, she chuckled. "We have a few more hours. Let's dry off, eat a donut, then do it again."

I barked a laugh. "I like where your head's at."

———

"Why are all these donuts squished?" Polly asked, looking sexy as hell in a tank top and shorts, hair all wavy from air-drying, as she rummaged in the Daisy's bag in her kitchen.

"You crushed them against your chest when you came in, remember?" I murmured into her neck, my lips brushing against the top of her shoulder. Now that I was finally allowed to touch her, I couldn't keep my hands off her. I nipped at the base of her ear, then licked the skin there. Her head fell back against my shoulder, and I grinned, loving how crazy that spot made her.

Polly turned in my arms, bringing her arms around my neck. "I can't be blamed for my actions when I find someone lurking silently in my kitchen."

"Honestly I'm just glad you didn't throw the bag at my balls again."

Polly playfully swatted me on the shoulder then turned to rummage through the bag again. I stepped to the side and leaned against the island countertop on my hip, my hand automatically coming to rest on the small of her back.

"You want to pick your own donut? I have chocolate, vanilla, and jelly filled."

It was hard to focus on anything but Polly's swollen lips, remembering what they were wrapped aroundago not a half hour ago. "You pick," I said, voice strained. "Though I'm not too keen on the jelly ones."

Polly looked like she was hiding a smile as she put one chocolate and one vanilla donut onto the plates in front of her.

"What's that look for?"

She shrugged as she picked up the plates and headed to the table. "Your word choices surprise me sometimes. What twenty-four-year-old uses the word keen?"

"The best ones."

Polly chuckled in response, and I pulled out her chair for her.

"Nah," I said, sitting beside her. "It's probably because I have older parents. I was raised differently than my friends. I didn't have a cell phone until I was sixteen and wasn't allowed to have social media until high school, not that I used it much anyway."

"Were your parents' strict?" Polly asked, picking up her chocolate donut and taking a large bite, but not before putting a paper napkin on her lap.

"Nothing like yours. They had high expectations for how we all did in school, always telling us that we needed to do our best. They haven't always been happy with the path I've chosen since high school, probably wishing I'd chosen one that ended with a college degree and full-time job with benefits, but I still feel loved by them."

Polly swallowed and wiped her mouth on her napkin. "If you're making good money, what's the problem? Is it just the stability that a college degree can give you? A college degree isn't always synonymous with making a lot of money."

"Where were you when I needed you all these years?" I shook my head. "It's the stability, I think. My momma's a worrier. I think me having a degree would help her worry less."

"So, if you were, say, a teacher. Would they be happy with that even if you didn't make a lot of money?"

"Are you a mind reader, Miss Polly Alberton?"

Polly picked up her donut. "No. Why? Is teaching something you've thought about?"

I looked down at the table, wiping at an imaginary smudge. "Yes, actually. I've always liked working with kids. They're mindful. Optimistic. The way they see the world is simpler, somehow. I like the idea of working with middle schoolers, which is a time when they're just starting to lose that. I'd like to help them hold onto that a little longer. I'd like to help them see their potential, believing in them even if no one else does. I'd probably make less money than I do now, but that's not why I'd be going into teaching in the first place. And now with my parents moving to Florida, I wouldn't have to stay close to help out as much."

The last thing I said put a cute little furrow in her brow. I brushed my lips against it to smooth it out.

"Is money the reason you never pursued teaching? Or because you wanted to help your parents?"

"I've never been *keen,*" I laid into the word playfully, making Polly roll her eyes, "on wasting money on a degree until I was sure about what I wanted to do with my life. As for my folks, while I don't look at them as a burden, I guess I was hesitating, not wanting to commit to a college program, wondering what might happen if I wasn't around to help take care of them. I don't think they'll get the same support with Kent down in Florida. But, they're looking at a condo, so maybe it'll be alright. No need for a live-in maintenance man." I pointed at myself.

Eyes soft, Polly stroked my cheek. "You're a good son, you know that?"

I leaned into her touch. Her fingers were a little rough, providing a kind of friction against my skin that felt unreal.

I turned slowly in my chair and leaned into her space. "I think we've had enough conversation for a while, don't you?"

Polly's eyes dropped to my groin, then back up to me, eyebrows lifting in silent question. I let a slow grin spread over my face, grabbing her hand and bringing it to Big Sir, who was making a valiant comeback. Her eyes went wide and I chuckled, letting a little of the devil into my voice as I rasped, "Darlin', you ain't seen nothin' yet."

CHAPTER
THIRTY-SEVEN

POLLY

Christina Lauren, *Josh and Hazel's Guide to Not Dating*

Floating on a cloud of blissed-out contentment, snuggling next to a very naked Jace Vargas, I could only imagine my face could be described in one way: dreamy.

Sex with Jace was indescribable. That time in the shower . . . I shivered. I'd done something I never thought I'd have the guts to do—acting out something from a book during sex. It made me feel strong and powerful. David never even knew I liked to read books, and I never had any intention of telling him; he would have only written it off as frivolous smut.

"What's going through that head of yours?" Jace asked, trailing his fingers up and down my arm.

"Certainly not that time in the shower," I teased, deciding to keep my reading hobby to myself for another day . . . or forever.

Jace's chest vibrated beneath my cheek. "Believe me, that will live on repeat in my brain for years to come."

I turned my head, brushing my lips over his chest, still marveling that I was even allowed to do that.

"What did you have planned for today?"

"A million and one things. I do need to reach out to some providers for the school this afternoon." I gave him a little squeeze. "But I don't regret taking this time with you."

Hugging me to his side, I felt him brush a kiss to the top of my head. "I hope not. I'll keep the kids occupied this afternoon so you can get some work done."

I knew it was a nice offer, but something was bothering me—something we needed to talk about.

Scooting back, I propped my hand on my hand to face him. "We need to talk about something. Two somethings, actually."

"Would that be a girl who's six going on sixteen and a boy that keeps beating me at Friday Night Funkin' even though I'm trying my best?"

"Yes. Don't get me wrong, I want this," I toggled a finger between him and I. "And I want this again." Jace puffed out his chest and I rolled my eyes. "But you work for me. Ryla and Max are my children."

"And here I thought you rented those kids," Jace teased, his face turning serious as he took in my unamused expression. Propping himself on his hand to face me, he said, "Sorry. It's a reflex. Go ahead."

"I want to be careful. I don't know what the future holds for any of us right now. And with Max and Ryla, they have to be my first priority. I can't bring anyone into their lives they can't bear to lose. It'd break them . . ." I trailed off, knowing that losing Jace wouldn't just break them—it was my heart I was risking as well. "It's not a good time to tell them, or anyone else, that something is going on between us. I'd like to keep this private, just between us, for now. Also, it has to be outside of your regular time with the kids. I don't want to feel like I'm paying you for sex."

Jace flashed a grin. "That's a relief. I don't want to feel like you're paying me for sex either."

Groaning, I rolled onto my back, my voice muffled as I lamented, "You know what I mean."

Jace chuckled as he gently pulled my hands from my face. "I know what you meant. I can keep it separate. Nothing has to change between us while the kids are around. But if I want to do something nice for you, or spend time with the kids out of my regular hours, know it's because I want to. I'm not expecting sex in exchange."

I lifted a single eyebrow in challenge. Jace smiled coyly. "Well, not exchange per se—but we get to keep doing this, right?"

Laughter burst from my lips as Jace rolled over me, planting his hands on either side of my head. He looked infuriatingly cute as his red curls hung down and I reached up, rubbing the locks between my fingers as he spoke.

"We were friends first. And I'll keep being your friend. Which means I get to do nice things for you. And I like spending time with the kids. No strings attached. Granted, it might be harder now that I know what your lips taste like." He leaned down, brushing a kiss over my lips. Instantly, I parted for him, my fingers moving into his hair, pulling him closer.

Polly! Focus!

I tore my mouth from his and pushed him back.

"See! This is why we needed to have this conversation, otherwise I'll want to do that all the time!"

Settling back on his side, wearing nothing but a bemused smile, Jace winked at me. "If we're being honest, I've had some practice at that already. Because I've wanted to do that long before today."

Despite wearing matching birthday suits and spending the better part of the day exploring every inch of his gloriously naked body with my lips, I felt suddenly, inexplicably, shy. I looked down at my hands, rolling one thumb over the other. How long did he mean? I didn't want to ask. But why would he say that if he didn't want me to know? I glanced at him out of the corner of my eye, then quickly looked down again. What if it was only this past week? That's the most likely answer. And who cares? He clearly liked me now . . . but I would have been aware of him a lot longer than he would have been of me.

I felt a tug on my hand as Jace threaded our fingers together, and I reluctantly turned to face him, a knowing smile on his face.

"What?" My question was high pitched, feeling like my insecurity was written all over my face like words on a page.

"Ask me."

I smoothed a wrinkle in the sheet covering me, stalling. "Ask what?"

He reached out to caress my cheek. "You were wearing a black dress, with these pearl buttons down the back. Your hair was down, but your eyes were hidden by your sunglasses. And you had these red high heels on."

I bit my lip.

"And then you bent over to reach into your car."

I sucked in a breath. "That was the first time I met you."

Nodding, he placed two fingers below my chin, inclining my head toward his. "I've wanted you since the moment I first laid my eyes on you. I couldn't remember ever seeing anyone as stunning." He waggled his eyebrows. "Except if I'm looking in the mirror of course."

This earned him a laugh and playful shove.

"We can keep this between us for now, if that's better for you. I can be patient." His sincere words were paired with a heated look, igniting my craving for him once again. Sitting up, I let the covers fall, baring myself from the waist up. Jace's expression turned eager—no— *desirous.* I felt wanton and powerful, insecurity stripped away as his gaze licked its way up my body. I shivered, my nipples pebbling under his perusal. A low, throaty moan left my lips as I embraced my inner she-cougar, pushing him to his back, moving to sit astride him.

"Patience isn't really my virtue," I crooned, then glanced at the clock, knowing we had to leave to pick up the kids in less than an hour. "We'll have to be quick."

"Good thing for you, speed is *my* virtue." He grinned and rolled us over, pinning me underneath him.

Luckily for me, Jace was a gifted liar.

———

After picking up the kids that afternoon, Jace and the kids hung out while I did some work in the study for a few hours. Rose had looked livid on Saturday when I pulled her aside to tell her that I had received an email from Mr. Goldenstein, requesting a personal meeting with me. Despite being furious, she patted my arm and told me not to worry, she'd handle it. When I checked my email this afternoon, I'd received an email from Mr. Sievers, the school guidance counselor, saying that he and Rose would be joining my meeting with Brad next week.

My eyes were starting to glaze over when Jace peeked his head in, asking if I had more to do or if I wanted a break.

"A break." I pushed my laptop closed. "Preferably with food."

"Yay! We made dinner!" Ryla burst in, clearly having been waiting right outside the door. Grabbing my hand, she pulled me to my feet and past a smiling Jace, then into the kitchen, chattering happily the entire way.

Dinner was filled with Ryla's animated stories, Max's shy smiles, and sexual tension. Were Jace's T-shirts always so tight? Did he dry them on high heat or something? I was sitting across from him, and honestly, the white baseball tee with navy sleeves on its own, shouldn't be *that* appealing.

Someone needed to inform my libido of that, however, because she was looking at Jace's shirt like white was the new red and she was a bull preparing for a charge. I couldn't stop my eyes from slowly easing down his body, or the movement of his jaw as he chewed. Of course, I'd always noticed he was handsome. But considering I'd traced the line of his jaw with my tongue this very day . . .

Jace, apparently, was completely unaffected by my presence. He split his focus between Ryla and Max, taking the time to listen and smile encouragingly. I mean, I know I wasn't wearing anything as sexy as a baseball tee (I was wearing my signature leggings and a black sleeveless shirt, thank you very much), but it'd still be nice to be appreciated.

As Ryla continued to talk about *something*, I caught Jace's attention and smiled. Then, and I'm not proud of this, I brought a bite of chicken to my mouth and chewed . . . very, very slowly.

Nothing.

Cordial smile in place, Jace picked up his water glass as if nothing was amiss and took a sip. He then returned his attention to Ryla, asking her questions without missing a beat.

I had no right to feel disappointed. He was only doing what we agreed upon earlier this afternoon.

Later that night, after putting the kids to bed, I couldn't sleep. To my extreme disappointment, I'd been hyperaware of Jace all evening. And much to Jace's credit, he'd acted like normal. Right before I took the kids up to bed, Jace had the audacity to tell me he was watching an episode of *Treasure Dogs* tonight, *if* I wanted to join him in the living room.

He *whistled* on his way back to his room.

We were only a few episodes from the first season finale so yes, I did want to watch *Treasure Dogs*. But what if I went down there and he was still wearing that infernal baseball tee? I might spontaneously combust. And what if he kept acting like he hadn't made me come on his tongue, *twice,* this very day? Again, spontaneous combustion seemed like the most likely outcome.

Basically, all evidence pointed to my inevitable incineration, so it felt safer to stay in my room.

I still couldn't sleep. After an hour of tossing and turning in bed, I finally went downstairs for water. At the bottom of the stairs, I looked down the hallway to Jace's bedroom.

All was dark.

I knew I was being ridiculous. As I stood at the kitchen sink, feeling unsexy and matronly, a sudden noise made me turn.

Jace was standing in the doorway. He was still wearing that damn baseball tee, but his jeans were gone. He was wearing tight, black boxer briefs.

As expected, my body went hot.

"What are you doing up?" I whispered.

Jace's eyes were molten. He strode to me without hesitation and buried his face in my neck, breathing me in, our arms encircling each other reflexively.

"Is this what you always wear to bed?" His words were muffled as he kissed then sucked at the point just beneath my ear.

I was still wearing a plain black top, but I'd changed into linen sleep shorts with grey stripes.

"You've been driving me crazy." Jace continued to kiss along my neck. He pulled back, regret in his eyes, shaking his head. "I'm sorry, Polly. I know we agreed to the rules for Max and Ryla, but you're just too damn sexy for me to resist."

Huffing out a small laugh, my she-bull was raring to go as our lips and tongues tangled, my hand immediately fisting in his shirt as his hands slipped beneath the waistband of my shorts to cup my ass.

Eventually we broke apart, gasping for air. "I know what I said," I whispered. "But I'd like to add a rider. Nothing in front of the kids. But when they're sleeping . . ." I trailed off, letting the implication float in the air.

"Are you sure?" Jace looked over his shoulder. "I don't want to do anything to hurt them." He turned back to me, tender affection in his eyes. "Or you."

I let go of his shirt, folding my hands over his exceptional heart. "I know. I'm sure. Once they're asleep, they rarely wake up." I stood on my tiptoes, putting my lips directly beside his ear. "And there's a lock on my bedroom door."

Grabbing my hand, Jace wasted no time leading me up the stairs. He didn't return to his own room until the sun peaked over the horizon.

CHAPTER
THIRTY-EIGHT

JACE

She told me once there is a clock in the hearts of parents. Most of the time it is silent, but you can hear it ticking when your child is not with you and you do not know where they are, or when they are awake in the night and wanting you. It will tick until you are with them again.

Cassandra Clare, *Queen of Air and Darkness*

"Will they like me?"

"Absolutely. In fact, I think they'll love you."

Ryla was sitting in her booster seat in the backseat of my car, legs swinging. She'd paused while belting out all the lyrics to "I Just Can't Wait to Be King" to ask this question. I'd gotten a call from my momma this morning. Pop was having a flare of his rheumatoid arthritis. They'd come back early from Florida because of it, but hadn't had time to go to the pharmacy yet. Momma had sounded frazzled over the phone, so I offered to pick up his steroids and pain medication that had been called in for him.

So here we were, on our way to my parents' house, even though they had no idea I was a nanny.

"Max?"

"Yeah?" He pulled back one of his headphones.

"They're going to love you too. Stick close to me if you like. If you need a break, just grab my hand and give it two squeezes."

Nodding, Max put his headphones back on and returned to looking out the window.

When I'd gotten my parents' message this morning and called Polly, she'd only seemed concerned about their welfare, having no problem with me bringing the kids to their house. Her reaction surprised me some, but it shouldn't have. Her kind heart was one of the best things about her. Despite being exhausted, I'd lain awake the previous night for a fair while. More than I was used to. Partly because I was holding a sleeping Polly in my arms, but partly from worry. I'd wondered what the future held. What happened at the end of August, when Polly didn't need me as a nanny anymore?

We'd gotten to my parents' house just after lunch. Max was looking at the house furtively whereas Ryla was already out of her seat and reaching for the door handle.

"Not so fast, little miss. A few ground rules. Take off your shoes by the front door. My momma doesn't exactly know I'm working by y'all, so she might ask a lot of questions. Max, you already know to stick close to me. And Ryla?" I took in the outfit she selected for herself: leopard shorts, a pink tutu, black T-shirt, and unicorn headband. I winked at her. "Just be yourself."

Going up the front walk—I knew Momma would be appalled if I let "company" in through the garage—Ryla grabbed the pharmacy bag from my hand, replacing it with her hand. Max was holding onto my other hand, so Ryla rang the doorbell for me.

"It's Jace!" I yelled when I heard movement from the other side of the door.

Momma opened the door, eyes narrowed in question. "Jace? Why are you—" She stopped speaking once she saw the kids standing next to me, confusion heavy on her face. She glanced back at me, eyes widening as she clocked my red hair.

"Surprise!" I cried, holding up our still joined hands. "Momma, this is Max," I inclined my head as I introduced them, "and Ryla. I've been working as their nanny for the last few weeks. Their momma is a new pediatrician in town."

I didn't add that I was also falling in love with her. That'd have to wait for another day.

Momma's eyes blinked twice. "Nanny?"

"Jace is our new Giselle!" Ryla exclaimed high and sweet, smiling wide . . . but she continued holding my hand, letting me know she still felt a bit shy.

I stifled a chuckle as Momma openly gaped at Ryla, probably wondering what she just said.

"Alright if we come in?"

At my teasing tone, she narrowed her eyes slightly, then put on a polite smile. Her manners were deeply ingrained.

"Yes. Please, come in. I was right about to put a batch of cookies in the oven."

Apparently, that was enough for Ryla. Trust, granted. Dropping my hand, Ryla walked through the door like she owned the place, stepping right up to Momma. I gave Max's hand a squeeze as we followed her inside.

"Your daddy's in his recliner, resting." Momma looked down to Ryla, eyeing the pharmacy bag. "Here, why don't you give that to me—What'd you say your name was again?"

"Ryla."

"Ryan?"

"Ryyyy-llaaaaa."

"Ryla?" Momma finally said to which Ryla nodded happily. Momma smiled warmly down to her. "Well, Ryla. I'm Jace's momma. You can call me Susan."

Cuckoo! Cuckoo!

"What was that?" Ryla startled. Max took a step closer to me.

"It's our cuckoo clock," Momma explained.

"A what?"

"You've never heard of a cuckoo clock before?"

"No."

"Let me tell you, you're in for a treat. They don't make ones like this anymore."

I shook my head. That damn thing went off on the hour, every hour, for as long as I could remember. It drove my sister insane.

As Momma took Ryla over to show her that absurd clock, I took Max in search of Pop, finding him in his typical spot in front of the TV watching the Braves. He was in obvious pain, had an ice pack on his hand, and he wasn't keeping score—which was a dead giveaway that he was hurting.

"Jace." Pop's voice was strained, giving me a weak smile when he first saw me in the doorway and a double take when his his eyes lifted to my hair.

"Who's this?" he asked, spotting Max behind me.

"This is Max. I've been nannying for him and his sister this last week."

"Hiya, Max. Have a seat over here. I'm Nick." I studied Pop dubiously. He'd barely blinked an eye when he saw Max. Pop wasn't dramatic, don't get me wrong, but he had the worst poker face. *Someone* had spilled the beans.

Pop muted the TV. "I'm just watching the Braves' game. You like baseball?" he asked Max, who shrugged.

I glanced from Max, then to Pop and offered, "He might be more of a video game guy, though we've been gettin' into some magic lately."

"Well, you got a great teacher, Max. This one was pullin' the wool over my eyes since he was your age."

"He'll be doing the same to me, I expect, he's a natural." I winked at Max. After a couple minutes of small talk, Max glanced between his tablet and me in question, to which I nodded, letting him know it was alright to use.

Pop watched our exchange intently.

"I heard you were watching some kids," he said softly, once Max was absorbed in his tablet.

I quirked an eyebrow.

"Sherriff James mentioned it before we left for Florida. I didn't bother tellin' your momma. She'd do nothin' but worry. I knew you'd come around to tell us in your own time sooner or later."

Wincing, he shifted the icepack over his hand.

"How's the hand, Pop?"

"Ack, it'll be alright. Just a little swollen. Darn knees are the real problem." I looked down and sure enough, he had two more bags of ice on his knees under the TV tray. "Probably doin' too much in Florida."

"And here I thought Florida was supposed to be good for your joints."

He snorted. "Ain't that the truth. Nah, but your momma was so happy. All that sunshine. And it was good to see your aunt and uncle, I suppose. Kent's got a brand new boat and wanted to show us all around."

That was news to me. I was surprised Kent didn't rub that in my face when he was here.

"When do you think you'll put this place on the market?"

"Your momma was talking about being down there by early fall, but with me outta commission now, that'll put us back a few weeks. Maybe by the end of September. I'm in no rush. I've lived here all my life, raised my kids here. I don't want to feel run out of my own home."

Somewhere Sarah was pumping her fist in satisfaction.

"I'm happy to help. Really, whatever you need."

"I know you are, son." He paused, looking ready to say something else, but the ice pack slipped off his hand and he went to make a grab for it, then flinched.

"I got that, Pop. Don't worry." I adjusted the icepack back onto his hand. "I picked up your medicine, let me go get it.

I motioned to Max to take off one of his headphones. "I'll be right back. You want to come with me?"

"You can feel free to stay here with me, Max." Pop piped up. "I'd love some company. I can't keep score today 'cause of my arthritis, if you'd like to do it for me."

"I'm not sure how," Max replied.

"Here," Pop held out the score sheet and pencil to Max, who eventually took it.

"You go on and take a look at that, Max," Pop said, "and we'll just see how things go."

Pop was just starting in on how baseball was a blend of strategy, skill and teamwork when I made my way to the kitchen, wondering what kind of standoff I'd see between Ryla and Momma. I hadn't heard any explosions so it must be going ok. I found them at the kitchen counter, their backs to me. Ryla was standing on a chair next to Momma, a too-big apron tied around her waist.

"It's all squishy!" Ryla's little hands were mixing something together in a bowl.

"It starts off that way, then you gotta mix and knead it with your fingers so it'll turn all soft. Then once the soup's boilin', you drop it into the pot. A few minutes later, you have a nice, soft dumplin'."

Ryla continued to chatter and my momma gave gentle encouragement as she taught Ryla how to make one of her staples, chicken and dumpling soup, which she made whenever we were sick.

"Smells good," I said, walking into the kitchen, making my presence known. Then, the strangest thing happened. They both stopped talking and looked over their shoulders at me.

In unison.

And they gave me the exact same look: *May we help you?*

I held up my hands, then grabbed the pharmacy bag from the table. "Just bringing Pop his medicine. As you were."

They turned around as if I hadn't spoken, continuing their conversation without missing a beat. I doubled back down the hall, slowing when I heard Max's voice.

"And that's called a ball?"

"Yep. If it's outside that little square there, that's called the strike zone, that's a ball. And if you get four of 'em before you get three strikes, the guy at bat gets to go to first base without hitting the ball first. It's called a walk."

"Because they like, don't have to run there?"

"Exactly right! You got it. Now what you need to know about the strike zone is . . ."

I stayed outside the living room, leaning against the wall, feeling a strange contentedness listening to Pop teach Max about baseball, just like he'd taught me when I was young.

———

"No!"

"Did they call that strike?"

"What a load of horse manure!"

That's what me, Max, and Pop, respectively, yelled at the TV when the ump called a strike on an obvious ball at the bottom of the ninth. The Braves were tied with the Twins at three a piece, and we had a runner on first and second.

"Yeah, they called that a strike." Pop looked over to Max and winked. "But we got one out left." He leaned over and patted Max on the leg, which meant that the pain meds must be working a bit. He hadn't been wincing as much since he took his first dose of medication over an hour ago.

"Though that ump should get his eyes checked if you ask me," Pop grumbled under his breath. Max and I looked at each other in silence, stifling our laughter.

"Nah, we got this. Tanner's up next," I reassured, nodding at the TV.

"Tanner?" Max looked down at his score sheet. "Oh yeah, he's the fourth batter in the order. So that means he's good, right?"

"The best. Made the all-star team this year." Pop nodded, eyes glued to the TV, an empty soup bowl next to him. Ryla had brought him his second helping half an hour ago, informing us that she and Momma were now making homemade moon pies.

I hadn't seen either of them since.

Tanner knocked the first pitch high into right field.

"That's goin'!" Pop yelled, and I stood, prompting Max to get to his feet as well. We watched and cheered as the ball sailed over the right field fence.

"Home run! Let's go!" I cheered, hands up, smiling wide at Max as we high fived and watched the all-star third baseman round the bases on his walk-off home run.

A few minutes later, after watching the celebration on TV, we sat down. My daddy was all smiles as usual after a Braves win.

"It doesn't get better than that. A walk-off home run on a perfect July day. The only thing that'd be better is doing a catch outside. You bring your glove, Max? Jace yours is still in the garage, I 'reckon, and we've got plenty of baseballs laying around."

Max looked down, suddenly quiet.

I glanced to Max, not entirely sure if he's ever thrown a baseball in his life. "Nah, we didn't bring it along. Maybe next time, though."

Frowning, my daddy studied Max, then nodded. "Well, no harm there. We got plenty in the garage. Why don't you boys go out and toss a few around? It'd do my heart good to see someone gettin' use of 'em."

Max's cheeks flushed red so I took a knee in front of him. "Hiya, Max. We don't need to do anything you don't want to do, alright?"

His red-rimmed eyes moved between me and his lap.

"Have you ever thrown a baseball before, Max?" I asked softly.

Shaking his head slowly, Max continued looking down.

"You know, I learned when I was about your age," I lied. I was barely four when Pop was tying my right arm behind my back until Momma stopped him. I looked over my shoulder and gave Pop a wide-eyed stare, teeth slightly clenched. "Right, Pop?"

Pop shifted in his chair. "Absolutely. Was terrible at first, too, could barely throw five feet in front of him."

I frowned at him. He didn't need to lay it on *that* thick.

I looked back to Max. "Tell you what. Let's go out and try on some gloves. That's it. We can bring them back home, and if you ever want to learn how to throw, you ask me. Anytime. I got you."

I waited quietly for his response, watching his face carefully to gauge if we were going to have to leave, when Max surprised me.

"I'd like to. But what if . . ." there was a little tremor in his voice. "What if I'm no good?"

"You won't be at first." I smiled. "And you won't be good on your second or third try either. I was plain awful, just like Pop said—"

"Yup," my daddy chimed in happily from behind me. I barely held back a roll of my eyes.

"—but I didn't give up. I made plenty of mistakes. Making mistakes is part of life, Max. That's the only way you learn. Don't let the fear of failing keep you from trying. I kept at it and made the team in high school. Played all four years. Some of the most fun I've ever had."

As the words left my lips, I really and truly heard them. Was that what I was doing in my own life? Was that the reason I hadn't pursued teaching, because I'd been afraid of failure?

I stood and held my hand out. "I'll only play catch with you on one condition. Let's go out there and play the worst, most horrible round of catch ever, deal?"

Max wiped his eyes; some of the wariness had left his expression. "I guess I can try it out."

Pop chimed in, "Attaboy! I'll be watching through the window. And I don't wanna see you make a single catch—or throw, you hear? Only misses!"

Max looked warily at Pop on his way out of the room. After Max left, I turned back to my old man, throwing my arms out to my sides, throwing him a *what the hell was that?* expression.

Pop just sat there, an ear-to-ear grin on his face. And then he did the strangest thing. He winked at me.

As if he was proud of me, too.

As if I'd just scored my own home run.

———

"She a spirited little thing, isn't she?" Momma said, taking a seat next to me on the concrete stairs in the backyard. Ryla had joined Max and me after he'd gotten the hang of catch. He could actually have a good arm if he stuck with it.

Now, they were playing hide and seek with the baseball; Ryla reassured me twice she wouldn't throw the ball at Max.

I grinned. "That's one word for it."

"She asked me if I was alive when the dinosaurs were living."

I barked out a laugh. "Welcome to Ryla. What you see is what you get."

She chuckled. "Oh, but that's girls for you. Sweet as sugar one minute, sassy as all get out the next. And Max—so polite! I barely got any time with him. You'll have to bring them over again soon."

"Just wait. I give it five minutes before someone is hurt or crying."

"Well, that's parenting."

"So I'm coming to find out." We were quiet for a few minutes. It was Ryla's turn to hide, and after trying to scale a too-tall tree, she was squatting behind a bush.

My mother broke the silence. "Ryla implied you've been living with them, too. Is there a reason you didn't tell us about your job?"

I let out a long breath, shifting toward her. She appeared surprisingly calm, almost resigned. Like being around Ryla and Max, even in this short amount of time, had softened her.

"Not really. It happened fast, I guess. And if I'm being honest, I didn't want to feel like I was holding you back."

"Holding us back?" she asked with wide eyes.

"If you want to move to Florida, move to Florida. If y'all want to sell the house, sell the house! I'm not reliant on you. I pay rent, I help you and Pop around here plenty. And you know what? I'm happy to do it. But I'm not a child. And to be treated like I'm one just 'cause I don't have a career like Kent or Sarah, I guess . . ." I took a deep breath in and let it out. "Well, I guess I just didn't want to hear it anymore."

I hadn't realized how much keeping something from them was weighing on me, until I felt it leave my chest. It wasn't like me to keep something from them. Secrets poison everything, good intentions or not. And glancing at Momma, seeing sorrow in her features, I knew she felt that too.

"I'm sorry, Momma." I put my arm around her shoulders, giving her a squeeze.

Her face turned wistful. "No, don't apologize. I'm the one who's sorry. I know I need to stop bothering you about college. I've already heard an earful from Sarah and your daddy the other week. It was somehow easier when you were young. My role was more defined. And I worry. I worry about your daddy. I worry about you. I worry about Sarah and Kent plenty, too."

"You don't have to worry about me, I'm doing fine."

She chucked my chin. "A parent will always worry about their child. No matter how old they are."

I brought my arm out from behind her, leaning my elbows on my knees, watching Ryla giggle as Max pretended not to see her. He was such a good kid. I guess I understood where she was coming from. Over this past week, I'd been filled with more worry than I'd ever recalled. Max had such an uphill battle to climb. Middle school. High school.

Would I still be with them when he was that age? What if I wasn't there, would he be alright?

And then, a worse thought. What if *someone else* was there, taking my place?

Instant jealousy filled me at the thought of another man in my place. I thought about Max graduating from eighth grade, then getting his driver's license. How it'd feel to see another man in his life, hugging him, teaching him the rules of the road. What if he wasn't patient? Or kind? My stomach started to cramp. And Ryla, she's had the same wiggly tooth all summer. What if I wasn't there when she finally lost it? When she was the lead in the school play, I wanted to be in the front row. I didn't want to sit next to the man who got to spend the rest of his life with Polly and the kids.

I wanted to be the man that spent the rest of his life with them.

It suddenly felt like time was speeding up; it'd already been both the longest and shortest week and a half of my life. I already considered them, Polly and the kids, my home. It was way too soon to tell Polly any of this, especially based on our conversation yesterday. But . . . what if I kept waiting for her to feel the same, but she never did?

"You're wonderful with them," my momma said, interrupting my thoughts. "You should bring their momma around the next time. We'd love to meet her. Ryla couldn't stop talking about her, she just kept saying 'my mom this' and 'my mom that'. What was her name again?"

"Polly."

"Polly! What a pretty name." Momma turned to me with an innocent smile on her face. "Don't you think?"

I narrowed my eyes, she and Sarah looking more alike in that moment than ever before.

I didn't have the time to deflect Momma's question because Ryla came tearing out of the bushes just then, screaming her head off, hands moving frantically above her head.

"Spider!! SPIDER!! Jace! Max! RUN FOR YOUR LIIIIIIIIIIIVES!!!

I jumped up. Saved by the Ryla.

CHAPTER
THIRTY-NINE

POLLY

Lauren Oliver, Delirium

Ryla?" I asked, glancing at her in the rearview mirror, seeing a face full of chocolate. I knew she'd been too quiet on the ride. It was no surprise that Ryla, the little deviant who squirreled away Hershey's Kisses in her backpack, had been eating them without me knowing. I'd been more preoccupied than usual on our way to Young Will's practice. Ryla and Max had also been busy filling me in on stories about Jace's parents, baseball, and cuckoo clocks after Max's counseling session this afternoon. I'd stopped quickly at a red light and was almost rear-ended by an idiot driving a black SUV who'd been following us way too close but luckily, we made it to the high school for Young Wills practice in one piece.

I turned around, facing the backseat. "Did you, by any chance, eat chocolate on the way here?"

"No."

I raised my eyebrows. "No?"

"Nope."

I looked to Max, but he was absorbed in his graphic novel. I turned my gaze back to Ryla.

"How'd that chocolate get on your face then?"

She covered her face with both her hands, her voice coming out all muffled. "Eet mufft haf bem dere sins yunch."

"I see."

I searched the car for something I could use to wipe off her face, finding a wad of extra take-out napkins stuffed in the center console. Wetting them with a water bottle, I turned back to Ryla.

"Look—" I stopped short, almost laughing when I realized what I just said. I tried again, my tone a bit softer this time.

"If you want to walk into Young Wills with chocolate on your face, confidence blaring, I'm all for it. Honestly, no one should judge you for what you look like. If you like chocolate on your face, I like chocolate on your face. You can either choose to wipe it off with this"—I held up the napkin—"or leave it on your face. It's your decision. You go, girl!"

I followed up my vintage saying with the ancient rock-on hand symbol, despite the fact that she probably had no idea what it meant. I was probably only five years away from her calling me "cringe" and asking me to drop her off around the block.

Plucking the napkins from my grasp, she started to wipe her face without a word.

A minute later, we'd disentangled ourselves from the car and were walking through the parking lot to the high school auditorium entrance. A little thrill went through me at the thought of seeing Jace. Except for seeing him briefly this afternoon when he'd dropped the kids off at Max's therapist's office, I hadn't seen him all day. It seemed almost silly to miss him already when we'd spent the entire night together; and yet, here I was, an extra spring in my step and butterflies in my stomach.

Max grabbed my hand on our way inside. I squeezed it twice and he squeezed it back. "The three amigos are coming!" Ryla shouted as she grabbed my other hand. Ryla had picked up the habit of calling us the three amigos since Giselle left. She'd seen a TV show with the reference and asked me what it meant. I told her it was a group of three friends, who protected and loved each other. The reference to the actual movie went completely over her head, but still, she liked it so much that she'd yell it out on occasion whenever the three of us walked hand in hand.

It had felt as if it was us against the world, this year, keeping our heads above water one day at a time.

Jace had been waiting for us; he came outside when we were only halfway across the lot, jogging over to meet us.

"You made it! I was just checking to see if y'all were here." Jace fell into step beside Ryla, who held out her hand to him.

"Hi," I responded, a little breathless. A slow smile took over Jace's face and he opened his mouth to say something when Ryla made a noise and held out her hand more insistently. Settling for winking at me, Jace took her hand and started to swing it as we all took off once again.

"Look, Mom! Now we're the four amigos!"

And like a magnet, my head swung over to Jace, a bemused expression on his face at Ryla's words, not knowing how dangerous they were to my heart.

Because as we neared the doors, I could see the reflection of us in the doorway. The four of us, hand in hand, smiling and happy. Like a family.

"You know what feels better than anything physical?" Esben looks at me for a long time. "How it feels to be falling for someone the way that I'm falling for you."

Jessica Park, *180 Seconds*

There really is no other smell like that of a prop room. The air was thick with dust, old sweat, and rubber as I searched the high school prop room after Young Wills practice that night. It'd been a long day, made longer still by the half hour of digging amongst the prop bins for the hyena masks the drama teacher thought were hidden somewhere in here.

"Jace? You still in there?" I heard Sienna's voice as the door opened. "Dios mío, it smells like a dirty gym sock in here."

"You kind of get used to it after a while." I grunted as I picked up the last and largest of the bins from the back of the room, stopping right in front of Sienna to put it down. "This is the last bin. If the masks aren't in here, we're out of luck."

We were quiet as we dug through the bin. I was nervous—I'd been stalling all rehearsal. Finally, resolved that I just needed to grow a damn pair, I went for it.

"Hey, Sienna. You told me about a professor friend you have at that liberal arts college a while back. I've been thinking about applying to the performing arts education program they offer. Thought maybe I could teach drama in a middle school, kind of like what I'm doing now, but like, get paid for it."

Sienna's mouth and eyes went wide. She lunged forward, over the plastic bin and all, hugging me around the neck.

"I'd be happy to!" Sienna pulled back, a happy grin still in place. "Rae and I were just talking about you the other day. We both think you'd be a wonderful teacher. What brought this on?"

"Something my pop said today," I answered. "And working with Polly's kids and y'all here at Young Wills. I think I realized that helpin' kids achieve their dreams, might just be mine."

Sienna put her hand over her heart and fanned her face with the other. "Sir, you need to warn a woman before you say all that, it hit me right in the feels. Please say you'll stay in Green Valley. Our boys would be so lucky to have you as their teacher."

"Thank you. I truly appreciate that. But let's see how things settle out first."

We spent the next few minutes searching until we reached the bottom of the bin with no luck. "Well," Sienna said, repacking the bin with me, "we could always try the middle school."

Rae came in then, carrying Sienna's youngest son, Pedro, in her arms. "This one's been looking for you, I think." Pedro squirmed out of her arms and ran toward Sienna, wrapping around his momma like an octopus.

"Whew, what's that smell?" Rae wrinkled her nose.

"Thirty years of adolescent body odor and rubber," I joked, making Sienna cackle.

"No, that's not it." Rae sniffed the air again. "Do you smell it, Sienna?"

Sienna nodded and Pedro looked at her with serious eyes. "I don't smell, Momma." She nuzzled his nose with hers. "Of course you don't, my angel."

I sniffed the air as Rae continued to walk slowly around the room. What the heck was she talking about? I'd say Sienna's earlier assertion was right: all I could smell was a sweaty gym sock.

Then, Rae came right up to me, put her nose up to my neck, and inhaled deeply.

"Hey!" I hollered. Rae took a step back, putting her hands on her hips. "It's just as I thought," she said dramatically, her head shaking slowly from side to side.

I gestured around me defensively. "You try searching a prop room for a half hour and see how you smell."

Rae laughed as Sienna added, "I thought the same thing. He smells just like Ben did when he wanted to impress that girl and got into Jethro's cologne."

Rae snapped and pointed at her. "Axe body spray."

I reared my head back. "I do *not* wear Axe body spray!"

I may have been using some extra cologne these past few days, but I hadn't heard any complaints.

Sienna laughed as she set a squirrely Pedro on his feet.

Rae squatted next to me, helping me put the rest of the props in the bin. "Polly's really nice, Jace. I'm happy for you. And you smelled fine before, no need to overcompensate." Rae's eyes lifted and she pointed to my red hair, which they both teased me mercilessly about at the beginning of practice. "But that situation might take some professional help. I know a good colorist in Knoxville. I got you covered."

After putting the large prop bin back, ignoring the two know-it-all-bamboozlers, I gave a small wave without looking behind me. "I'm outta here for the night. Y'all are the two meddlesome older sisters I never wanted!"

"See you next week!" Sienna shouted.

"And use protection!" Rae added.

Their ringing laughter was so loud it carried down the hall until I reached the exit.

———

It was after ten by the time I got back to Polly's. I'd texted her earlier, letting her know I'd be late. To which she texted back, *I'll be waiting,* with a winking smiley face. I'd never known intimacy like this with a woman. Sex with her was scorching hot, but also fun at the same time, the teasing and laughter between us making her all the more addictive. She knew what she liked and wasn't afraid to take it—adventurous in a way I loved. I loved talking to her just as much.

There were a lot of things I loved about her.

A text came in from my sister as I got out of my car, reminding me that I'd been dragging my feet on calling her back. Since I'd asked her about the plants last week, she'd been texting me more often. I had no doubt Momma had already called Sarah today, telling her all about my and the kids' visit. Sarah knew me well, there was no lying to her. Just like Rae and Sienna possessed sorcery of some kind to figure out that something was happening between Polly and me, my sister had the same intuition. If I wanted to respect Polly's wishes and keep it between her and I for now, avoiding my sister seemed the best tactic.

All was quiet in the house when I came in through the garage. Was Polly upstairs in her room? Maybe she'd started without me, her hand pressing her sweet, wet center, her lips parted and panting. Would she be wearing those petal bra and panties again? My dick throbbed, straining in my jeans just thinking about it. I couldn't wait to peel them off her again.

I heard a noise and turned, noticing light from beneath the basement door. Opening it, I heard the din of a TV, so I walked down the stairs only to find Polly wrapped up in a blanket and sitting in one of the overstuffed lounge chairs. She was watching *Treasure Dogs,* her hair was piled high on her head, and she had a tissue in her hand. I heard a sniffle.

"Everything ok?"

Polly looked at me with big, tear-filled eyes, then scrambled to get the remote and pause the episode.

"Shoot!" She checked her watch. Biting her lip, her eyes darted between me and the screen. "I'm so sorry—I've just watched three of them. I'm almost to the end of the finale. I know I said I'd wait for you to watch the finale together —" She couldn't finish because her face crumpled and she began to cry.

Ditching my bag, I strode over to her, dropping to my knees in front of her. I wrapped her in my arms, rubbing her back. Having her in my arms again after a long day felt like a relief.

"Was it the season finale that has you this upset?" I was pretty certain that Rosie, the dog she liked, won it all, but maybe I'd been mistaken. Polly pulled back and nodded, abandoning her tissue to wipe her weepy eyes on the sleeve of her sweatshirt.

"It was just so . . ."

"Sad?"

"No!" Polly looked almost miffed. I bit back a laugh. "Rosie won and you should have seen her. She was running around, barking and leaping, and I'm just so *happy!*" Her voice was high and creaky, breaking on the word happy as she began to tear up in earnest again.

Trying not to laugh, I brought all her sweet softness into my arms and picked her up from the chair, eventually cuddling her onto my lap as I sat on the carpeted floor in front of the lounge chair. I gently stroked her hair until her cries quieted. Polly sighed and tucked her head under my chin. Her topknot tickled my face, but there was no way I'd ever move. Not until she decided she was ready to get up again.

"I'm sorry. This probably isn't what you had in mind when I said I'd wait for you, huh?" Polly pulled back, gazing into my face.

I stared into her teary eyes, her make-up less face. I'd never seen anything prettier. I leaned in, not being able to resist kissing her. "It's exactly what I wanted."

She gave me a playful one-eyed squint and snuggled back down into my chest. "How was the rest of practice?"

"It was good." I hesitated, wondering how Polly would react, but wanting to share what I'd decided. "I asked Sienna for the contact info for the professor who heads up a performing arts education program at a liberal arts college near Knoxville."

Polly sat up and turned, smiling brightly. "You'd be perfect for that, Jace. Watching you at Young Wills—it's like watching magic happen. Those kids follow you with their eyes. They look up to you. It's a gift you have, encouraging each and every one of them to perform without fear. It's just, *wow.*" Polly gave a short laugh, then rolled her eyes. "For lack of a better term."

"Thank you, darlin'. But I'd have to apply first. At lot of their courses are online, and I was thinking if I apply now, maybe I could start in spring, or who knows, maybe even this fall."

Her eyes dimmed for a moment, then a polite expression came over her face. I could feel tension in her body as she spoke. "Well, you'll have to let us know how that's all going when you find out. Good luck."

The formality in her tone startled me—reminding me so much of the Polly I'd met that first day, who now seemed like a stranger to me.

"How's your dad?" Polly asked abruptly, changing the subject.

I sat back and patted my chest. Polly hesitated, but then relaxed against me again even if I could still feel the rigidity in her spine. "Better. Got his meds, seemed to be in less pain by the time we left. He got on with Max real well. Taught him how to keep score of a baseball game. I figure Max will be ready to live in the 1960's if time machines are ever invented."

I felt the puff of air from Polly's laugh on my neck and her muscles begin to relax.

"How'd your momma react to meeting the kids?"

"Once she could say Ryla's name, they got on great. I've already gotten two texts from Momma asking to bring them back this week."

I felt Polly nod. "That's ok with me, if it's ok with you."

I trailed my hand slowly down her arm. "They want to meet you too."

I felt the tension in her back return. "Oh, umm, me? I'll be pretty busy with the school stuff, so maybe in a few weeks."

"Ryla talked you up a storm, I'm afraid. We don't have to tell them about us, but even if we did, they'd love you." I squeezed her close to me. "It'd be impossible for them not to."

Polly scoffed and sat forward, her back to me. "I don't know about that. I'm a thirty-eight-year-old woman taking advantage of their young son who has his whole future ahead of him. They may like me as your employer, but once they find out I've deflowered their precious baby boy, I don't think it'll go so well."

I held back a laugh as I sat up, cuddling close to her so that my nose brushed the nape of her neck. "I hate to break it to you, but I think the jig is up on my deflowering situation."

As Polly muttered something unintelligible, I slid my hands up her arms and settled my fingertips at the base of her neck, trying to massage out some of the tension still sitting there.

"Do you want me to meet your parents?" I could hear the hesitation in her voice, the insecurity there.

"I do. But this is new. And like we agreed, we can go at your pace. I'm not in a rush."

She muttered something like *tricks* and *magic fingers* as I kept finding new spots of tension. She let out a breathy moan as I hit a spot in her neck that made her entire posture melt. I scooted forward until my front was flush with her back, my legs bracketing hers. She tilted her head to the side as I changed my massage technique to include slow, opened mouth kisses on her neck. My groin tightened with each little moan or gasp from her lips.

"Jace?" Polly panted. "Can I ask you an honest question?"

"Mmmhmm," I hummed, feeling goosebumps break out on her arms. I gently sucked at the juncture of her neck and shoulder, canting my hips, my hard length aching with each brush against her backside.

"Is there a reason you smell like rubber and a boys' locker room?"

CHAPTER
FORTY-ONE

POLLY

Lady and the Vamp by Lena Benjamin

Jace, the kids, and I fell into an easy rhythm for the rest of the week. He'd see me off in the morning before the kids were awake, usually crowding me into the counter, stealing kisses until I had to force myself to leave the house. It'd been ridiculously hard to focus on work this entire week as half of my brain was concentrating on truly important things. Like how much I liked Jace's smile. And his kisses. And the way he said *darlin'* all low and sexy.

After work, Jace and I would make dinner, and we'd all eat together. On Wednesday, Jace took us bowling. Max had been invited to Belle's birthday party next week, which was going to be at a bowling alley. So Jace and his friend Sam taught us how to bowl. They were hilarious together, constantly one upping each other, then pretending to fall in new ways on the slippery bowling lane, seeing who could make the kids laugh the hardest. At night, Jace joined me for the kid's bedtime routines, reading to Ryla and learning Max's relaxation exercises. Then, once the kids were asleep, well . . . let's just say today's chair dancing class was going to be painful. I really hoped there'd be a lot of stretching before the class. I was in desperate need of some stretching.

"What are you listening to?"

Gasping, I turned from the mirror over my dresser to see Jace leaning casually against the doorframe. My heart took off like a hummingbird.

I wondered if that would ever stop.

I removed my earbuds. "Good morning."

Jace let his eyes trail lazily down my body. It was just before nine on Saturday morning, and I was getting ready to go to my first chair dancing lesson. I was in compression leggings, a tight purple cropped tank, and a hoodie. Uncrossing his legs, Jace prowled toward me.

"I don't know if I can let you go to this class," he purred, reaching out and lightly grasping my hips. "You look good enough to eat."

"Don't start, Romeo."

He narrowed his eyes. "I should have never told you that."

"Too late. Besides, the kids are awake and downstairs, they could come up here any minute. And if I don't leave in five minutes, *I'll* be late. I should be back in a few hours at most."

I turned back to the mirror, slipping my ear buds in my pocket.

"So what were you listening to?" Jace moved to sit on my bed behind me. I glanced at him in the mirror, then went back to gathering my hair into a ponytail. I still hadn't told Jace that I read romance, even though I'd seen him eyeing my e-reader on my nightstand a few times. I didn't know what was holding me back. I felt comfortable with Jace. I knew logically, from past experience, that Jace wouldn't judge me—or at least I didn't think he would. But there was still this part of me, maybe it was my pesky, bruised heart, that made it hard to trust anyone. So, I'd kept this last little secret hidden away, safeguarding it deep within myself.

"More medical journals?" he drawled as I looped the hair tie around my hair.

"Just a memoir that Leah recommended," I lied.

"Oh yeah? What's it about?"

Shit. I didn't think this through. I was currently reading *Lady and the Vamp* which was a vampire marriage of convenience rom com. "Umm, it's about a scientist . . . who's working on a cure for, um, an incurable disease."

Technically not a lie. Vampirism *was* traditionally thought to be incurable.

Jace smiled sweetly. "I like a good book. Maybe we could read one together sometime?"

"Umm, yeah. Maybe," I said noncommittally and looked at my watch. "Geez, is that the time? I still need to get my water so I can meet the girls on time." I grabbed my workout bag and turned toward the door.

Jace walked after me. "I made your water for you, it's on the island."

I hoisted my bag over my shoulder. "What?"

"You don't drink coffee," Jace said simply, shrugging his shoulders. "At least not in the morning, only in the afternoon and even then, it's on ice."

I shifted my weight. "Hot coffee makes me feel nauseated."

"Best to avoid it then. I noticed you hadn't made one yet today, so I filled your thermos and put in one of those collagen packets you like."

The simplicity of this gesture threatened this fragile new life I was building. I was feeling *feelings* for Jace that were way too fast and way too soon. And if Jace kept doing and saying these things, I was liable to do something truly ridiculous, like tackle him to the bed and make him promise to never leave me, ever. I took a slightly different approach.

"Thank you," I whispered, stepping up and cupping his cheeks. I searched his face, wishing I could read his mind, wondering if he was feeling the same unfathomable feelings as me. That in this short period of time, I was falling for this man, but I didn't know if he was falling with me.

"You're welcome." Jace's smile reached his eyes, but then I jumped back as I saw them darken and turn hungry. I giggled as I dodged his playful lunge, fast walking my way to the door with my bag slung over my shoulder.

Later, after saying goodbye to the kids and getting on the road, I took a sip of my water and smiled. I recalled a time early in my marriage to David, when we were at a restaurant for breakfast and the server asked if I wanted coffee.

"Yes," David had said, turning both of our mugs over, implying we'd both wanted coffee. And what's worse, I didn't dispute it. I didn't drink it, but still —I didn't say *anything*. We'd been married for a few years at that point and David didn't even know that hot coffee made me feel sick. What did that say about David? More importantly, what did that say about me? Cleary, I didn't feel comfortable telling him anything about me.

Wasn't I falling into old patterns, then, keeping things from Jace?

———

Stripped was not what I'd had in mind for a fitness studio that taught chair and pole dancing classes; though, to be fair, I hadn't really known what to expect. I'm sure, as the name implied, that people thought this was a strip club. Yes, there were poles. Yes, women were dancing on them. But that is where the comparison to a strip club started and ended. The studio was bright with hardwood flooring, a ballet barre, and splashes of color throughout. Hands down, it beat any of the industrial style gyms I'd belonged to in the past that housed rows of treadmills and ellipticals, everyone staring ahead monotonously like sweaty, workout robots.

"Alright ladies! Now for the cross-knee hold!" yelled the instructor, a beautiful woman with shiny black hair pulled into a sleek ponytail. A dozen women of all shapes and sizes did an impressive move where they crossed their legs around their pole and dipped backward, arms stretched back and down over their heads, reaching for the floor.

"And slide!"

Fascinated and ten shades of impressed, I watched as the women slid down the pole. Some did a sit-up-like maneuver, grabbing the bar with their hands before sliding down. The instructor and a few others, however, slid down the pole upside down, landed with their hands on the floor, then did a back walkover off the pole.

I almost clapped.

"I strained something just watching them. What kind of class did you bring us to, Eliza?" I heard Tiffany murmur.

Eliza, Tiffany, Margo, Rose, Leah and I all were standing in a single-file line in the back of the studio wearing matching expressions of shock and awe, except for Eliza, who looked delighted.

"That's an intermediate class. Come on y'all, we can drop our bags and stretch here." Eliza waved us over to a small area with cubbies and—please and thank you—bright yoga mats so we could stretch.

I groaned as I sat down on a mat, which had Leah quirking her eyebrow. "You alright there?"

"Just a little sore." Pasting an innocent expression on my face did nothing to quell the suspicion that had narrowed my bloodhound best friend's eyes.

Eliza plunked herself down on my other side, settling into a butterfly stretch. "I always wanted to take a class here. The hubs turns forty-five next month. I hope to use some of the moves I learn from class today for his birthday present." Eliza waggled her eyebrows as she spoke.

"Has he had his check-up recently? You might wanna check on his heart. Y'all wouldn't believe how many heart attacks came in that started during sex back when I worked in the ER," a worried Rose piped up from behind us.

"His heart's in fine working order." Eliza gave a sly grin. "Plus, we started *American Tail* last week and that strip scene halfway through the book? Let me tell you, he was up for it."

Tiffany high fived Eliza as Margo groaned. "There are some things you can feel free to keep private, Eliza."

"So, do you all, like, talk about what books you read with your significant others?" I asked the circle of women.

Tiffany replied, "I tell everyone what I'm reading, what the hell do I care?"

"Kyle doesn't care what I read. Sure he may tease me about reading smut sometimes, but I just caught him watching *The Holiday* on his tablet the other night, so it's not like he has a leg to stand on," Leah said flatly.

"I think I'm the minority here, but my husband and I read books together. Most romance books only have a few chapters with sex on the page anyway." Eliza winked. "And those few chapters benefit my husband as much as they benefit me."

I nodded absently, leaning forward to stretch out my hamstrings. It'd been incredibly hot when I actually acted a few things out from books I'd read. The thought of actually acting them out with him, of him being an *active* participant was never something I'd seriously considered as a possibility. I had yet to jump the hurdle of even telling him I read romance novels regularly . . . but what if he met me with curiosity rather than judgment? Instead of embarrassing maybe it would be, sort of, thrilling.

A blush crept up my cheeks, and I forced myself to think about something else. As I switched to a different stretch, I caught Leah's suspicious gaze.

"Yoohoo! Charlotte!" Rose called out. "I thought I spotted you out there. Y'all were doing moves that'd make me sore for ages!"

A tall, pretty blonde standing next to the cubbies smiled. "Rose! What brings you in?" she asked, then looked around to all of us. "I see y'all brought the whole gang. What's the occasion?"

"It's Eliza's birthday and she signed us up to try chair dancin', if you can believe it." Rose said as both she and Leah stood.

"Suzie's the best! These are the best workout classes I've ever done," Charlotte said, dabbing her face with a towel.

"Anything that lets me stay in my jeans without doing lunges for five minutes straight will be a win for me," Leah said, gesturing for me to stand. "Charlotte, I'd like you to meet my best friend, Polly Alberton. She moved back to town last month. She's a pediatrician and has two kids close to Kimmy and Josh in age. Polly, this is Charlotte Mitchell. She's worked as a teacher's aide for the school district."

Charlotte's eyes widened when Leah introduced me. I extended my hand so I could introduce myself properly, when Rose spoke up from my other side.

"Polly is also the brand-new medical director of the school district and has been helpin' me with the grant proposal, you know, the one you told me about last school year. She's a gift. I couldn't have handpicked anyone better!"

I gave Rose a patient smile then opened my mouth to introduce myself when I was cut off again.

"She also has the best taste in books!" Eliza added as Tiffany yelled, "And she can open up a bottle of wine using only a hair straightener!"

Slightly embarrassed by everyone's enthusiasm, I held out my hand again and was finally able to speak. "Hi. I'm Polly. I promise I don't usually travel with a fan club."

Charlotte's handshake was eager and warm. "It's nice to finally meet you. I'm Charlotte Mitchell. And this isn't the first time I've heard people sing your praises. I'm friends with Rae and Sienna. A few of my kids are in Young Wills, too. Jace Vargas has babysat for my kids dozens of times. We adore him. He's watching your kids, right?"

"Yes." I confirmed, my voice a little stiff. My supposed fan club already knew Jace worked for me, so my unease wasn't from that. It was definitely due to the woman in front of me, who was my height with honey-blonde hair and similar green eyes, whose kids loved Jace whom he's watched *dozens of times*. My eyes, of their own volition, clocked her left ring finger. At the sight of a sizeable diamond, my chest relaxed, making me feel both lighter and pathetic simultaneously.

I felt more than saw the women of my fan club watching our exchange with rapt interest. I hope no one picked up on the fact that I checked out Charlotte's ring finger to see if she was married.

"My *husband* picked up the kids from Young Wills these past few weeks." Charlotte said, putting an emphasis on husband and twisting her diamond ring as she spoke. Well, that's even worse. No one else perhaps saw it, but Charlotte definitely saw me eyeing her ring finger. I quickly debated explaining myself, but resolved the best-case scenario at this point was to stay silent and hope Charlotte thought I was gay and checking her marital status for my own interest.

Charlotte continued, "Are you going to be there with your kids next week? I'd love to talk about your work with the school a little more and your kids, seeing as they're so close in age to mine."

"Umm, maybe. I mean, I should be there. My schedule can be a little unpredictable."

"Oh honey, don't I know it." Charlotte waved her hand at me. "Having kids is pure chaos. Here, give me your number. I'll text you if I'm going to be at Young Wills."

"It's 555-1027." Leah volunteered from beside me using her phone number superpower.

"Got it." Charlotte nodded, looking down at her phone. "There. I just texted you, so you should have mine, too. It was so nice to meet you, Polly. You ladies have a great workout!" Charlotte waved as she walked out of the studio.

A text appeared on my phone from Charlotte, and I looked between Rose, Leah, and the ladies on the floor stretching. "What just happened here?"

Leah merely shrugged. "Charlotte's good people. She's a great friend to have in your corner."

"You're gonna love her." Rose nodded vigorously before returning to the floor to stretch.

I surveyed the group of women in various stages of stretching around me. "Is this what having real friends is like?"

Leah smirked. "Welcome to the other side."

Charlotte was right about one thing; the class was one of the best workouts I'd ever had. It took me out of my comfort zone, but once I got the hang of it, I felt empowered and strong. I was definitely going back. I'd also resolved to tell Jace about my reading hobby tonight, before I lost my nerve. If I wanted whatever this was between Jace and I to be different than my marriage, I had to start out with honesty.

As I drove down the road toward home, I decided to roll my window down to let the breeze in. After all, the sun was shining, my audiobook was blaring, and I was going home to two kids I adored and a man that had the stamina of a twenty-four-year-old. After one deep lungful of air, however, I realized it was humid AF and Tennessee had bugs close to the size of my eyeballs, so I shut the window and turned the AC back on.

Aaaahh, sixty-degree, max-cold bliss.

Walking into the house, I could instantly tell that something was wrong. The lights were off, there was a low din from the TV, a bucket and mop sat next to the sink, and the smell was off.

In the living room, Jace held up a finger to his mouth. Ryla was asleep under a fleece blanket on the couch, her head on Jace's lap. There was a large bowl on the floor beside her.

"She threw up an hour ago." Jace whispered. "She was able to take a small sip of water and keep it down. She fell asleep about ten minutes ago." He saw me glance toward the stairs and added, "Max is fine. A sympathetic puker, so I'm told, so he's been staying upstairs."

I knelt down next to Ryla, holding the back of my hand to her warm forehead. "Poor thing. I'm glad to hear Max feels ok." I pulled out my phone. "I didn't get any texts."

Jace shook his head. "I didn't text you. I didn't want to bother you. I knew you'd be home soon, and we had it under control. She'll be happy you're here when she wakes up. She's been asking when you were coming home about every other minute until she fell asleep. 'When's Mom coming home? Mom makes everything feel better,' she was saying."

"Really?" I asked, tears unexpectantly pricking behind my eyes as I brushed her hair back from her pale forehead.

"Yep. Hasn't mentioned Giselle once. Only you."

I nodded, the lump in my throat making it hard to talk.

"Mom?" Our attention snapped to Max, who was behind us on the stairs, incredibly pale. "I think I might—"

And then he threw up all over the stairs.

CHAPTER
FORTY-TWO

POLLY

You tell me that magic is just desire made real. Maybe spells are nothing more than words that you believe with all of your heart.

Deborah Harkness, *Shadow of Night: All Souls Trilogy Book 2*

The next several days were filled with sleepless nights as my kids took turns vomiting and having diarrhea. Thank God for Jace, who stayed up with me when the kids got sick at least once per hour that first night . He ran to the store for Gatorade and saltines without question and at one point called Sam who dropped off an industrial strength carpet cleaner. Thankfully, neither Jace nor I got sick. Plus, I got to miss Sunday brunch with my father, so it was a 'you win some, you lose some' kind of situation.

On Tuesday night, Jace came home to see us all snuggled under blankets in the theater room. He carried a large basket from Sienna and Rae, packed to the brim with cookies, wrapped loaves of bread, and a cryptic note tied to a bundle of sausages.

By Wednesday morning, the kids seemed back to normal. I was exhausted but felt marginally better after a full night's sleep—even though I was a little disappointed I was in my bed all alone.

I was a lot disappointed I was alone.

I was pretty sure that whatever GI bug felled my kids, also killed whatever romantic feelings Jace had for me. Besides last night, when he tilted my chin up to assess the dark circles under my eyes, Saturday morning was the last time he'd touched me. Ryla was bouncing around the house with energy, up at the crack of dawn, so I couldn't even talk to Jace like normal when I left for work that morning.

Later that afternoon, I took a late lunch to meet Leah at Daisy's Nut House for donut-burgers. She'd been raving about them, and I understood why. Donut? Yes. Burger? Yes. Donut-burger? Hell yes.

"Before I forget," Leah said after taking a fortifying sip of her iced coffee, "we told Eric he can bring a friend along bowling to Belle's birthday party next Friday and he wants to ask Ryla. I thought I'd ask you first."

"Would I have a problem with Eric inviting Ryla to the party?" I repeated, lifting my eyebrows. "Leah. I wouldn't mind if Eric wanted to *marry* Ryla. I'd start saving for her dowry tonight. Though, I'd watch her with a bowling ball if I were you. You sure you don't want me to come?"

"Nope, kids only. Belle made that very clear. We're only invited because 'we're the money.' I'll plan on bringing Max and Ryla home with us from summer school on Friday so we can take them to the party. The party should last about four hours or so. Take the free time and run!"

We were laughing when our food was delivered. The donut-burger looked amazing. I'd lost my appetite the last few days, but it was back with vengeance. After taking a bite, I looked at Leah with wide eyes. She nodded as if silently saying, S*ee? I told you.* She then proceeded to take the largest bite of a burger I'd ever seen in real life. At least one third of her donut-burger was gone.

"How is this so good?"

"Grease and sugar," Leah mumbled, her mouth full. After swallowing, she asked. "So, purple tips," I rolled my eyes, "how's it going with your *nanny*?"

She said nanny so suggestively I was tempted to roll my eyes again. Not that I hadn't been expecting the question. Leah had been texting me nonstop since Saturday.

"It's going great. The kids love him."

Leah gave me a flat look. "Not good enough. You've ignored my text messages enough. Spill." She took another gigantic bite with relish.

Craning my head around us, seeing no one within earshot, I turned back to Leah and lowered my voice. "You can't tell anyone. But Jace and I . . ." I didn't finish, not really knowing how to. Because really, what were we?

Thankfully, Leah didn't need clarification. A very pleased and very smug expression overtook her face.

"I knew it! Thatta girl. Way to get back on the horse. Soooo." Leah's eyes flashed as she took a sip of her iced coffee and smacked her lips. "How was he? Are we talking bases? Home runs?"

It was impossible to hide the giddy smile that came over my face when I thought about Jace. "I don't even know how to put what's happening into words. Amazing? Surreal?"

"I told you he was a unicorn."

"You did. And he's better than anyone I've ever seen with the kids, possibly even Giselle. He completely gets Ryla, and Max has opened up so much. I know he's younger than me but being with him feels easy. I laugh more than I ever have. And Jace is so *himself*. Unapologetically. It makes me want to be that brave. To try new things. It's freeing and all the things I want."

"But . . ." Leah dragged out the word.

"But then my kids got the plague, and he hasn't touched me for four days so I've pretty much convinced myself that it's over. If it's not, it's only a matter of time before he figures out this wasn't what he signed up for and leaves. I *can't* let the kids lose yet another person in their lives. It'd break them. And what about what's best for Jace? He wants to go back to college to study teaching. Is being here, with us, with me, really what he wants? And that's not to mention the fear that my father is going to find out about all this."

Leah was frowning and shaking her head before I finished.

"First," she held up three fingers and started ticking them off, "vomit takes any sexual desire from your body and kills it dead. I wouldn't take that one personally. Second, it's up to Jace to decide what he wants, not you. And third, your father is a Grade A Pensis who deserve a nice vacation in my butthole."

I snorted, almost choking on my iced coffee as Leah calmly picked up and took another bite of her donut-burger.

"How long have you been waiting to say that?"

Leah put her hand over her mouth while chewing. "A long time."

I slumped back in my seat. "I haven't talked to Jace about any of this, except that we're keeping things private for now."

"That's your first step. Ask him those questions. The worst he can do is leave, right? And from what you've just said, it'd be better if he leaves now, rather than when the kids get too attached. If he does leave, then it wasn't meant to be, and you don't have to waste any more time finding someone worthy of your heart."

"While that's very kind, my fear is that maybe he *could* be the one. What if it's too soon to have these serious conversations and I scare him off?"

Leah seemed to ponder this for a moment. "Ok. Answer this question. If you had no father to please, no world to judge you, what would you want?"

"I'd want my kids to be happy. I'd want to live in a house that I own free and clear. I'd want a job that I loved and felt passionate about, and . . ."

I looked at Leah helplessly, the plain truth suddenly causing my heart to ache.

"And I'd want Jace to be there with me, for all of it."

In my mind, I'd pictured Jace beside me in each of those scenarios. I wanted a future with Jace. Or at least a chance at one.

I inhaled a shaky breath. "What if I do that, ask him for that, and he doesn't want me—want us? I'm so tired of being hurt, Leah."

In response, Leah, best friend of mine, didn't tilt her head with sympathy. She didn't come around the booth to give me a hug. She merely frowned and put down her burger, which was how I knew she really meant business. "Life is a risk. Weren't you just telling me that you want to be brave? To be free and try new things? If there's a future out there that you want, fight for it."

"It's not that simple—" I started, but Leah cut me off, eyes imploring and voice wholly serious.

"It is. *It is* that simple, Polly. You've always had these flashes of your true self come out here and there throughout the years. But now, it's like someone turned on this light inside of you. Like you're finally yourself. And you're just as fucking great as I always knew you'd be."

She reached across the table and gripped my hand fiercely, an intense look in her eyes even though they'd become glassy.

"It's time to fight *for you.* Don't let your head overrule your heart. Don't give anyone up who makes you look and feel this alive, just because you think you'll lose them. And certainly not because of what others may think. Think about you and your kids and what's best for all of you." She let go of my hand and picked up her burger, shoving the rest of it in her mouth. "To hell with everyone else."

I brushed away a tear and smiled at Leah, suddenly remembering one of my first memories of her.

"You know that day in second grade when Steven Barns shoved his pet snake in my face during show-and-tell and you stomped on his foot?"

She nodded, then swallowed. "Little creep deserved it."

"I won the lottery that day and didn't even know it." I reached across the table, placing my hand over hers.

"Damn, straight." Her words were soft as she turned her hand over and gripped mine, squeezing twice.

After a few moments of making big spectacles of ourselves, Leah suddenly made a chopping motion. "Alright. Enough of this emotional crap. It's time for a serious talk. I still require the answer to my question. And you know what that is." Leah quirked her eyebrow and I groaned.

"Leah, we're almost forty. We have children. Can't I just call it sex and not a home run? I don't even watch baseball."

Leah's look was flat as she shook her head.

"Fine," I intoned, giving in. "But I don't think I can use bases. Or home runs."

Leah widened her eyes. "Are we talking grand slams?"

I nodded, not able to keep the grin off my face. "And Jace has a Louisville Slugger."

After work that night, I walked into a quiet house. Any mother will tell you that when your house is quiet, start worrying.

"Jace? Max? Anyone home?" I was walking into the living room, wondering if someone was sick again before stopping short. Jace was standing at the bottom of the stairs, dimples popping.

I bit my lip, trying not to laugh nor tackle him to the ground like a cougar in heat. Because Jace was standing there, looking so ridiculously, goddamn cute in a tuxedo T-shirt and jeans, that my ovaries quivered.

"Jace. What in the world are you wearing?"

"Ho ho ho! 'Tis not Jace, this evening, madam," Jace said in a horrible faux-French accent. "Tonight, you may only call me Jacques!" He paired this with a flourish of his hand. I heroically smothered my laughter.

"Ze magic show es all ready for you and ze performers do not want to be kept vaiting." Jace tsked and pointed to his watch. "And you are already late! Hurry, madam, I do not vant you to miss ze best seat in the house."

Jace extended his arm for me to take. I swallowed hard as my fingers trailed along his biceps, the smooth touch reminding me how, after peeling off my leggings, he would lightly trail his fingers up my leg, making me shiver in delight.

Jace led me up the stairs to the playroom door, where a bedazzled **Stage Door** sign hung. He opened the door to the playroom and ushered me inside.

"Right zees way, ma chérie. Ve have a reserved seat for you. Ze best seat in the house!"

I gasped. The playroom had been transformed into a theater of sorts. The room was dark. The red rose curtains from my parents' bedroom hung over some sort of wire to give the impression of stage curtains. Flashlights were propped up by pillows and placed at regular intervals along the floor, illuminating the curtains to make them seem like old fashioned stage lights.

I felt the sting of tears as I took in my mom's curtains. I wasn't mad, not at all. She'd have been so happy that someone was using them, especially if it was for something fun. Blinking away the tears, I saw two chairs facing the stage. Jace held out his hand, directing me to my seats. Totes Baa-goats sat on one seat while the other seat was empty except for a glittery paper complete with ribbon curls and stickers. In the center, bubble letters spelled: *Welcome to the First Annual Alberton Magic Show. Tipping encouraged.*

I laughed, taking a seat and Jace leaned down, whispering low and silky in my ear, "Ve have a very special show planned zis evening. Oh yes, only ze best for you."

My inner thighs trembled. Was he trying to kill me?

Jace suddenly jogged to the middle of the makeshift stage and faced me, stretching his arms out wide.

"Madam and Totes *Baaa*-goats! Velcome to our show! It is my esteemed privilege to announce our first act. Ze great, and Ze powerful, Master Magician, Max-a-million!"

With that, Jace flung both arms toward the playroom door. It opened to reveal Max dressed in a black top hat, red bowtie, with a black T-shirt and pants. Max grinned shyly as he spotted me, and Jace and I hooted and clapped as he walked onto the stage.

"For ze first trick of the night, I present to you, Max-a-million, with"—Jace paused with dramatic effect, looking at my son, with nothing but sheer determination in his eyes— "ze Mad Hatter."

Pride filled me as I watched Max pick up a hat from the table in front of him, take a deep breath, begin.

"Good evening. My first trick is the Mad Hatter. This may look like an ordinary top hat." Max waved the top hat around, showing it to me and then glanced over to Jace, who was standing off to the side. Jace held up his thumbs in encouragement, mouthing some words, and Max immediately stood up straighter, throwing his shoulder's back.

"But it's not a normal top hat. It's a *magic* top hat." Steadily, Max placed the hat upside down on the table and waved his wand over it. "You can see that this hat is now filled with . . ." Max reached inside and started to pull out a green ribbon. "Ribbons!" He continued pulling, the ribbon turned first red, then blue, then yellow. He held the ribbons up when it was done, triumphant smile on his face as I clapped along with Jace. For the next five minutes, I sat stunned as Max continued to pull things out of the hat: a paper airplane, a yo-yo, and then, a bouquet of silk flowers which he presented to me.

At the end of Max's act, Jace and I gave him a standing ovation. Jace walked back to center stage and clapped Max on the back. "Sank you, Max-a-million, for zose phenomenal tricks!"

Max waved as he walked out of the playroom. I clapped and whooped until he was gone.

Riveted, I turned my eyes back to Jace, who was now preparing the stage by placing a glass cup upside down over a quarter on the table.

Jace rubbed his hands together. "Next up, ve have another special act. Here, ees Lady Ryla—"

"*Enraged Bacon*!" came a whispered shout from the darkness beyond the door.

Jace paused briefly, taking a moment to absorb what Ryla had just whispered. But being the consummate professional he was, went right on with the show.

"Excusez-moi, ve have another special act. Here es, *Enraged Bacon*," Jace said this with gusto in his French accent, making me press my lips together, trying not to laugh, "with Show Me Zee Money!" Jace again held his hand out with a flourish toward the door.

Ryla burst in wearing a Batman mask, a feather boa, and her dress-up Elsa gown. Walking toward the stage as if to a sold-out crowd in a major arena, she waved and blew kisses to everyone and no one.

"Thank you, thank you!" Ryla announced, continuing to wave at her "audience", making me laugh and clap all the harder until she held up her hands in a stop gesture. "Stop, geez. You're embarrassing yourselves."

I heard a squeak from Jace but kept my eyes on my daughter who was gesturing to the table in front of her.

"You will be amazed to see I can make this quarter disappear!" Ryla waved her hand over the quarter, her face alight with joy. Cupping her hands around the glass she slowly slid it to the side. Sure enough, the quarter vanished. I'd just been completely fooled, having no idea how she just did that.

"Ta-da!" Ryla cried to my and Jace's wild applause.

"And if I do this," Ryla cupped her hands around the glass again, "you will be amazed to see that I can make the quarter come back!" Ryla slid the glass back to its original spot and the quarter reappeared.

For the next twenty minutes, the kids took turns doing a few more tricks. Max came back to do a dollar folding trick, then Ryla with a disappearing crayon trick. Jace and I cheered wildly for each trick. I ate up their performances, my mother's curtains flowing around the stage as if her spirit was alive and watching with us. My heart was dancing. The only time I'd felt more joy were the days my children came into this world.

As Max and Ryla took their final bows, I stood, giving them one last standing ovation, shouting, "Bravo!" over and over. Jace was also grinning and clapping over his head, pride shining out of each pore.

Once the bows were over, I rushed up to my kids, getting to my knees and gathering them up into hugs.

"Max-a-million! You were wonderful!" Max's face was joyful, a big goofy grin on his face. I'd become so used to seeing him weighed down, that seeing him so light and happy took my breath away.

"Ahem," I heard from beside me and turned to see the indomitable Enraged Bacon herself.

"And you!" I gathered up Ryla into a hug. "How did you do that quarter trick? You had me so fooled!"

Looking pleased as punch, Ryla peered up at Jace who had come up beside us. "A magician doesn't reveal secrets, right Jace?"

Jace, who was standing there, dimples popping, merely nodded to her. Looking at my tiny Enraged Bacon like she was a sweet cherub instead of hell on wheels.

I'd never seen anyone champion my children as much as he just did. During our applause, he caught my gaze and put his hand over his heart. *Look at what they did,* he seemed to say. I suddenly felt hot and tight, my own heart pounding in my chest. Jace had turned the light on for my entire family, not just me.

Nervous anticipation filled my gut and lodged in my throat. Did we do the same for him?

CHAPTER
FORTY-THREE

POLLY

"I don't fit in your world."

"Neither do I," he said, his expression tender yet resolute. "So let's make our own. We've done it before."

Tracey Garvis-Graves, *On the Island*

After the magic show was cleaned up, the after-dinner dishes were done, and the kids were in bed, Jace grabbed my hand and tilted his head toward the patio.

"Come sit with me."

So that's what I did. With the night sky providing our backdrop, Jace and I sat at the outside patio table side by side, holding hands, listening to the nighttime soundtrack of katydids and crickets, and of course, an occasional giant ZAP from our bug zappers.

"You're quiet tonight," Jace whispered.

I whipped my head toward him. I'd been lost in thought. Wondering how many nights I'd get with Jace like this. Even though I was the one to put the qualifier on us, wanting to go slow and keep things private, I still felt this insecurity. This fear of getting hurt.

"Am I?"

I knew I was. I was trying to think back to Leah's words today and bolster my confidence, but it wasn't working.

Jace picked up one of my hands and brought the back of it to his mouth for a soft kiss.

"Everything alright, darlin'?"

I had to hold back a shiver. His dimpled grin, his husky drawl, his kindness and his patience . . . Jesus take the wheel, the keys, and the whole damn car, I was tempted to pinch myself because how on earth could a man like this be real?

I pulled my hand to my lap, huffing an exasperated breath. "I'm having a hard time believing you're real. How'd you get to be this romantic?"

Jace brought his beer to his lips, taking a pull, his throat working as he swallowed. "It's a skill."

I pointed to him. "That! Stop doing that! Your sexy unicorn ways are breaking my brain, and I have things to say!"

"Did you just call me a sexy unicorn?" Jace's face crinkled adorably in confusion.

I focused on the ground, not wanting to be distracted. Leah was right. I had to fight for what I wanted.

And I wanted Jace.

"At the magic show tonight, I saw a side to Max I hadn't seen for a long time. When he was young, he was curious and silly, loving to giggle. And then after the divorce, I was trying so hard to keep everything together, that I failed at being his mom. You helped me see that. You helped bring that silly part of Max back."

Taking a deep breath, I turned my watery gaze on Jace.

"And Ryla is no longer a feral badger that I fear bringing into public. I'm still saving up bail money, don't get me wrong," I added as Jace laughed. "My point is, thank you. For everything."

A frown took over Jace's easygoing expression. "Why does this sound like you're saying goodbye?"

"You've done so much for us, for me." I looked down in my lap, a ball of nerves in my chest making it tight. "It wouldn't be fair to make you stay here, if you didn't want to. To hold you back. You have a gift, Jace. And a dream. It wouldn't be right to keep you from that."

Jace took a long pull from his beer, then set it on the table. Picking up his chair, he turned it toward me fully, then reached out and grabbed my chair, turning it so I was facing him as well. He leaned forward, resting his elbows on his knees, the intensity in his hazel eyes holding mine.

"Who said I don't want to stay here? I thought I'd be here at least through August. Do you not want me here anymore?"

I shook my head vehemently, my nerves taking over. "No! That's not what I want. If it was up to me and you wanted to stay forever, I'd say yes in a heartbeat. But you haven't tried to touch me in days, and the kids are a lot. Between your future in teaching and my father, I don't see how this, you and I, could work."

Jace's jaw tensed. "Polly, it took every shred of willpower I had not to crawl into bed with you last night. But you looked like you were about to fall over from exhaustion, and I knew if I was there, there'd be no sleep for either of us."

"Oh," I said on a whispered exhale.

"I wasn't going to tell you this yet, but I applied to an online university this week. I also talked to the professor that Sienna knows on Tuesday, and I'm going to apply to their program as well. If I'm accepted, I thought we could look at the time requirements together, working out my class schedule with what works best for me to stay here and watch the kids this fall and then, well," Jace smirked, "for however long I can get with y'all after that."

I hesitated. It was like someone was offering me a cookie, but I felt like the moment I reached for it, a giant hand would swoop in and snatch it away.

"Is that what you want?" I hedged.

"Have I ever given you the impression that I do anything I don't want to do?"

"No," I answered quickly, searching his face, my stupid hopeful heart beating wildly in my chest.

"You're right. I don't. Once I'm in, I'm all in."

My pulse pounded in my ears. I wasn't yet able to trust that I could really have what he was offering me, free and clear.

"What about my father? If we tell people about us, he could find out and then he'll kick us out of here. Max and Ryla are just getting settled. I don't want to uproot them again."

Jace nodded his head thoughtfully. "There are a few important people in my life that I trust not to say anything. For everyone else, we could keep up the appearance that I'm your nanny and that we're just friends until you have another place to go."

"Could that work? We'd have to pretend for I don't know how long."

Jace's eyes were dancing in the moonlight as he leaned toward me. "I don't know if you're aware, but you have the lead from the Green Valley High School's illustrious *Romeo and Juliet* production sitting across from you." He flashed his dimples. "And I'm a fabulous actor."

I ran his plan over in my head, looking for any weaknesses. Yes, my father could find out. And if he did, yes, he could kick us out of the house.

But sitting here with Jace in the starlight, *this* was the future I wanted. This was the future I wanted to fight for.

And that was worth all the risk.

"How in the hell are you single?" I blurted out. "You could have a dozen girl-friends or, like, your own personal Jace harem."

Jace didn't laugh or roll his eyes, he merely tilted his head. "I thought I already had one."

"Am I your girlfriend?"

"I guess if you're askin'," he teased.

"But I'm like . . . old." I made a face.

"Alright, this needs some discussin'. I could care less about our age difference. You're hot as hell, love with your whole heart, and as a bonus come with two great kids. If anything, I should be the one worrying about what you see in me. I'm a homeless, twenty-four-year-old kid without a college degree. I promise if you give us a chance, Polly, I'll work hard to be the kind of man you deserve."

Unable to stand it anymore, I grasped Jace's face, pouring everything I felt into the kiss. His lips instantly opened, his tongue finding mine as we savored each other, showing our love with our actions, until we finally broke apart.

I looked down. How I ended up in Jace's lap, I have no idea.

I traced the outline of his cheekbones with my thumbs, trying to memorize this moment, still feeling like somehow, something would take him away from me, but willing to fight for this. For us.

"I better not catch you saying anything bad about my boyfriend again. I know how to kill someone and make it look like an accident."

Jace's hands trailed up my arms until they encircled my wrists. "Darlin', you say the sweetest things."

"Y'all must be rubbin' off on me," I teased in my best drawl.

Jace's expression was practically predatory. "I'm here for all rubbin' activities."

CHAPTER
FORTY-FOUR

POLLY

"Her name was Aelin Ashryver Whitethorn Galathynius. And she would not be afraid.

Sarah J. Maas, *Kingdom of Ash*

Even though it was ninety degrees outside, it was freezing in the high school's main conference room that Friday. The room looked sleek and modern with a SMART Board at the front. I rubbed my hands together for warmth. Brad Goldenstein would be here any minute. I'd met with Rose yesterday and practiced what I wanted to say with Jace last night. I felt ready. I could do this. I'd spent a lifetime talking to intimidating men who wanted to use me as a pawn.

I was practically a professional.

Though, I regretted my outfit choice. Not because it wasn't fabulous—I'd worn a lavender blouse that matched the fading tips of my hair, linen pants, and peep toe wedges that I had bought but never yet worn. I felt fresh and light and . . . freezing. My only regret is that I didn't pair my outfit with a jacket. I inched closer to Rose to huddle for warmth. We'd tried to change the thermostat but apparently it was programmed to a certain temperature.

"Guess this is what they mean by hell freezin' over," Rose whispered, making me chortle just before the door opened and two men walked in.

The taller of the two men with deep-set eyes and a kind smile wore a green polo shirt with the school logo on it. He must be Mr. Sievers, the guidance counselor I'd talked to and heard so much about from Rose.

The other man was shorter and a little older, I'd place him around mid-fifties, with unnaturally black hair. He wore a white golf shirt and black slacks. This had to be Brad Goldenstein.

Rose gestured between us. "Reggie, Mr. Goldenstein, welcome. This here's Dr. Polly Alberton, the new school district medical director."

The man in the white polo tsked as Rose. "Future medical director, you mean. It still has to be approved by the school board."

"Indeed. How do you do?" I abruptly held out my hand to the man, wanting to shield Rose as much as possible. His stare was assessing as he grasped my hand. I tried not to shudder; his hand was cold and clammy.

"Brad Goldenstein. President of the school board. I own a manufacturing company called Goldensteel. Perhaps you've heard of it?"

"Unfortunately, not."

"Wait, did you say your last name was Alberton?" He looked dubious, like he was just learning my last name right now even though he'd sent me an email which had my last name as part of the address.

I nodded and tried to extricate my hand from his sweaty grip.

"Any relationship to Judge Alberton?"

I sighed inwardly. "Yes, he's my father."

Instantly brightening, Mr. Goldenstein smiled disingenuously, then covered our shaking hands with his other one. It was equally cold and clammy.

"In that case, please call me Brad. And if you ever want a tour of the Goldensteel, I'd be happy to oblige. Your father has been there before. I'm surprised you haven't heard of it."

I suppressed another shudder. I'd met these kinds of people before. The ones that liked to suckle at the power teat.

There would be no suckling at *this* power teat for Mr. Goldensweatyhands.

Happily, Brad dropped my hand when the man in the green polo next to him extended his own toward me. "It's nice to finally meet you, Dr. Alberton. I'm Mr. Sievers, but please call me Reggie. Everybody here does. If someone yelled out Mr. Sievers, I'd probably start looking for my grandaddy." I smiled, instantly liking him, his soft twang and smile putting me at ease.

I glanced at Rose as Reggie spoke and did a double take. Her cheeks were pink as she stared with heart eyes at "Call me Reggie" Sievers.

"Thank you, Reggie. I look forward to working with you."

"Should we sit?" Rose asked, gesturing to the conference table.

I took my place next to Rose, thankful when Reggie sat across from me. I wanted to stay as far away from Brad as possible.

"Mr. Sievers and I wanted to be here for this meetin' because, as y'all know, our school district received the Mill Grant last year. With Dr. Dixon retirin', I've been workin' with Dr. Alberton here, and I can already tell that with her experience as a pediatrician, she'll be able to help us so we can use the grant money to its best advantage. You were so proactive, Mr. Goldenstein, to want to meet with Dr. Alberton here, and I couldn't agree more. I thought it'd be a great opportunity so we could all go through the new grant proposal together."

Reggie was nodding encouragingly to Rose and Brad continued to look smarmily suspicious. That's the direct opposite of magically delicious, in case you were wondering.

"Thank you, Rose," I said, then faced Reggie and Brad. "First, let me say, I'm very excited about this opportunity. I reviewed the grant proposal as well as how many students currently have an IEP or 504 plan. Hiring special education advocates would be of great assistance to the students, as the special education staff are not currently able to manage the volume of students effectively. I've also been working on expanding the referral pool of specialty providers so the district can help accommodate and expedite medical evaluation times."

Rose held out a folder to Brad. "We have an updated proposal here. If you'd like, we can email it to the members of the school board before the meetin' next week."

Brad sighed loudly as he flipped through the pages. I glanced to Rose who gave me a discrete thumbs up so I continued on.

"A few of the issues we wanted to address today, were some things the district can do better to identify the needs of the students within the district. First, we have examples of surveys we could send to every family to evaluate how many students will be requesting accommodation. That way, we can better estimate the volume of need to determine how many advocates should be hired."

"What kind of survey questions are you proposing?" Reggie asked.

"Well," Rose answered eagerly, "the survey questions would help get a rough percentage of students that may need accommodations for the next school year, who are already gettin' services outside of school, or help figure out if they just want more information about the programs."

Brad scoffed. "You think parents are willing to give this information to the school? I can't imagine they want this publicized."

My irritation spiked at his derisive tone—particularly because it was aimed at Rose, who was sunshine in human form. Still, I plastered a neutral expression on my face. "It's an anonymous survey. In addition, we wanted to send out an informational email to lay out, step by step, how an IEP and 504 plan are created. One of the biggest barriers to receiving accommodations is from a fundamental misunderstanding about how the process works. Ultimately, I'm hoping to expand it to a monthly email that could include information about mental health screening, learning disability diagnosis and prevalence, the difference between an IEP and 504 plan, et cetera."

As I spoke, Brad's passive expression deepened into a frown. "You'd have to get those contents approved by the school board," he said, eyes sharpening on me.

"Absolutely." I nodded, staring right back at him. "The last thing we're proposing is partnering with local health clinics. Access to care is a big problem, and with the grant funding, we propose partnering with area providers. Not only will that help connect families to reputable providers, but we could also offer a stipend to help pay for the provider fees."

Brad cleared his throat loudly. "This sounds like a wasteful use of the grant dollars to me. Why would we pay outside doctors, lining their already rich pockets?"

I glanced at Rose, who was likely thinking the same thing.

Bless. His. Heart.

"And how many kids are we really talking about here?" Brad continued. "We only have a couple thousand students."

Rose jumped in then. "Over the last decade, we've seen a significant rise in the number of students requestin' accommodations for mental health concerns like anxiety, ADHD, autism, and depression—just to name a few of 'em. Why, in our district alone about forty percent of the plans last year were for kids with mental health conditions, which was—" Rose flipped through the pages in front of her, looking for the number.

"Seventy-five students," Reggie added softly, smiling at Rose encouragingly.

Rose flushed scarlet and stammered, "Right, seventy-five kids. And that number's only gettin' bigger."

Brad rolled his eyes. "Seventy-five kids? The entire football and basketball teams are at least twice that size. You're wanting to spend the entire grant on seventy-five kids instead of all the other normal ones?"

I physically rocked back into my seat. Did he just classify kids into normal and abnormal?

"Excuse me?" I asked.

"We are much better off using my own proposal. Bettering our sports fields prevent injury, and better yet, expanding the sports programs to include every-one, the normal kids and the kids who have physical disabilities. Heck, it could help the depressed kids, too. They're free to join a sport. After all, exercise makes those things that make you feel happy . . . what are they called?" Brad made a rolling hand gesture, appearing to be searching for the word.

"Endorphins?" I ventured.

"Yeah, that's right. If you ask me what those kids need, it's playing a sport. That'll help them more than any school program or doctor ever could."

Enraged, I wanted to stand up and shout, "*Please define those kids*!" Instead, I dug deep and forced an amiable expression on my face.

"Mr. Goldenstein, may I ask you a personal question?"

Brad crossed his arms and nodded.

"Do you have any health conditions?"

He scoffed. "I'm the picture of health."

I'm sure.

"Nothing? No asthma, allergies, high blood pressure?" I kept my face neutral.

"I take a pill for blood pressure," Brad said loftily.

"Ok. So, when you were in your doctor's office and they diagnosed you with said high blood pressure, instead of offering you a medication or talking about lifestyle changes, like exercise and diet, did the doctor look at you and tell you to just, get over it?"

Brad jerked back. "That's not what I'm saying."

"Oh, I'm sorry. That's right, that's not what you're proposing. So, then, your doctor must have told you to join a sports team?"

Brad's face turned a very satisfying color of pink as I held my hands together under the tablet to keep them from trembling.

"Look, if you want to make me the bad guy, go ahead. But there's a big difference between something you have no control over versus something that's all in your head."

It's like the years I'd had with my father were mere practice to face this blowhole. I metaphorically pushed my sleeves up: it was time for school.

"Certainly, you are aware that learning disabilities, ADHD, depression, anxiety, and autism spectrum disorder are all recognized diagnosable disorders, much like high blood pressure. Wouldn't you agree?"

Brad rose from his seat, trying to exert the authority he thought he had over me by standing. "You can talk down to me all you want. But high blood pressure is a lot different than some kid who's sad their girlfriend broke up with them."

And now, I had him.

"You're right. But I'm not talking about the emotion of "sadness". I'm talking about quantifiable, diagnosable, well-accepted mental health diagnoses, that happen to be protected disabilities under the state law of Tennessee. Did you know that a major depressive episode afflicts fifteen percent of teenagers across the country? It's not something a child can just wake up and 'get over' by joining a sports team. Mental health conditions are not character flaws. You can't will them away, that's not within the student's control."

I'd like to say I sounded calm. But that'd be a lie.

"What *is* within their control, is getting help through counseling, medication, and lifestyle management like exercise and a regular sleep routine and school accommodations. Those are evidence-based therapies that kids don't get either because they have parents like you who write off their medical problems like they're a character flaw or because they have no financial means of obtaining such treatment."

Brad sneered, "I don't know who you think you are—"

With trembling legs, I stood. The she-dragon inside of me had awoken in a fury from a long hibernation—likely from having smelled the scent of frailty from the smallest man who ever lived from the other side of the table—and she was ready for breakfast. She wasn't going to take this from him.

And neither was I.

"I'm Dr. Polly Alberton, we met a few minutes ago, in case you're having memory concerns. Low testosterone can do that to a man."

I said that last part aloud; I literally couldn't help myself.

"And if you continue to attach labels like abnormal to students with mental health problems, you are perpetuating the stigmatization of these disorders, exacerbating the problems these children face. I am sorry that this meeting happened this way, but I am afraid if this is your position, there is nothing left to say here, except that I will see you at the school board meeting next week."

After giving me another glare, Brad stormed out of the conference room.

Liberation twisted with nausea in my gut as I wiped my palms up and down my trembling thighs. I'd never felt better standing up to that sniveling turd of a man. I felt like climbing to the top of the school and belting out "We are the Champions" at the top of my voice.

Beside me, Rose looked awestruck. Reggie, thankfully, was smiling wide.

A Cheshire grin spread over my face. "I think I made a friend."

CHAPTER
FORTY-FIVE

JACE

"Because if it's possible to have a partner who gives all of themselves without reservation, who looks forward to working and sacrificing for me just as I look forward to doing the same for her, who can't help but love ferociously, brutally, and unconditionally—and even perhaps without reason or sound judgment—that's what I want. Because that's how I plan to love in return."

Penny Reid, *Ninja At First Sight*

After dropping off the kids at summer school on Friday morning, I sparred with Sam, dropped by my parents for a time, and was now setting up a romantic backyard candlelit dinner for my girlfriend for our first official date.

Because Polly Alberton was my girlfriend now. I still couldn't believe it.

I was carrying the candles out to the patio when my text alert sounded.

Sarah: Does your phone not work anymore?

Sarah: I talked to Momma. I know you're alive and well and nannying for two kids with a single mom.

Jace: Then you know I've been busy working

After placing the candles on the table, I frowned at where I'd put the spoons next to the plates. Did they belong next to the knife? Or was it the fork? Grabbing a spoon, I switched it with a fork, then switched them back immediately because that didn't look right, either. Scowling, I backed away from the table.

I couldn't stop thinking about Polly, about how she lied to me about what she was listening to last week. Watching her lie poorly was admittedly a little cute, which was interesting because I saw her lie to her father not too long ago without so much as a flutter. This week, I'd seen her reading or listening to her earbuds on occasion, but she'd abruptly change the subject as soon as I came into the room. If Polly couldn't trust me enough to tell me the truth about what she liked to read, could we really last?

Worse, the guilt that accompanied snooping through her e-reader like the world's weirdest cat burglar, was heavy in my mind.

Another text alert sounded.

Sarah: He lives! Two weeks now and it's been crickets.

Jace: Was there a question in there?

Sarah: Who are these kids? Who is this single mom you're working for? Why were you keeping it a secret?

I typed out three different responses to my sister before deleting them one by one. I was driving myself stupid. I should really ask Sarah what to do even though she'd be insufferable about it. My sister had the irritating habit of always being right.

Jace: I need some advice

My phone rang almost instantly.

"What happened?" Sarah whispered urgently, her breath coming out in little huffs like she was walking.

I sat down in a kitchen chair, leaning my elbows on my knees. "I'm seeing someone—"

"Yes, Mr. Gardner." Sarah's assertive voice sounded far away. "I'll have a copy of those court documents faxed over to you right away." Another ten seconds passed before she came back on. "If anyone asks, your name is Jeremy, and you work for the public works department in Evanston. You have five minutes. Go."

· · ·

"I'm seeing a woman, and I need to tell her something that I've done. It's nothing illegal, but I broke her trust. But if I tell her, I could lose her. Should I tell her? I don't want any lies between us."

"What did you do?" Sarah whispered.

I swallowed thickly. "I, uh, don't want to say."

"I can't give you advice if you don't tell me."

"I've been reading her books."

"Ok . . ." Sarah sounded confused.

I pushed off my elbows and sat back against the chair, running a hand through my hair. "I've been snooping through her e-reader without her knowing so I can read the same books she's reading."

"Why wouldn't you just ask what's she reading?" Sarah asked, incredulity thick in her voice.

"I get the feeling she wants to keep it private."

"What kind of books are they, like pirate romance or something?" Sarah chuckled.

I remained quiet.

"Wait. *Are* they pirate romances?"

Knowing I was going to regret this, I took a deep breath in, closing my eyes and said, "Not exactly. At least there haven't been any pirates in the books I've read."

A strangled sound morphed into wheezing which eventually turned into low chuckling. "Hold on," Sarah laughed, "I need to go somewhere else."

Sarah's voice was still on the edge of hilarity when she came on the line. "Soooo, let's see if I have this all straight. You have a girlfriend who reads erotica or romance or something like that, but she doesn't want to tell anyone, and you've been snooping around her e-reader so that you can read the same books she's been reading and you want to know if you should tell her."

Sarah was way too pleased with herself. I let out a sigh before answering. "Yes."

"Uh-huh. And why do you want to tell her?"

"I don't want any secrets between us."

"Uh-huh. While that's noble, it sounds like you'd be doing it more for your benefit. Let me guess, you're hurt she doesn't trust you enough to talk about it, and you feel guilty for lying to her?"

I didn't answer. Not only because she was annoyingly right, but also because Sarah's lawyer brain wasn't done.

"Telling her now would only serve to absolve you of your guilt and prove that she has a reason to distrust you. It wouldn't do anything but hurt her. She's probably embarrassed enough."

I stood up and started pacing back and forth in front of the kitchen table. "But I'm not judging her, she has no reason to feel embarrassed."

"Oh, little brother, I didn't mean embarrassed by *you*. I mean by society. By the Kents of the world. You have no idea the stigma women who read romance contend with. They're marginalized even within the book world. They're either lust-filled women who read smut for kicks, to which I say, what the hell is the problem with that?"

That was a hypothetical question. I was sitting down by this point, patiently waiting for her to finish. Sarah was on a roll and there was no getting off this train until we got to the station.

"The problem is that women are held to a higher moral standard. Thus, women who enjoy sex are regarded as shallow or bad compared to her male counterparts, which is not only hypocritical, but old fashioned. Or, women who read romance over other types of literature are deemed unintelligent; like a book can't be written well just because it has sex scenes. It's one of the most natural things in human nature, to fall in love. To have sex. As long as no one gets hurt, what's the problem with reading and writing about it? I should know, I've been reading romance for years. Remember when I used to hide them under my bed?"

"I remember Gran doing the sign of the cross at your door a lot."

"Exactly. And that further illustrates my point. We're judged by men and women alike. I wasn't reading porn, even if Gran thought I was."

I winced, because that's exactly what I'd thought Polly was listening to at first.

"So, you're saying I should wait for Polly to tell me in her own time?"

My question was met with extended radio silence. I moved the phone from my ear to confirm the timer was still running.

"Sarah?"

"Isn't Polly the name of the woman you're nannying for?"

"Uhhh," I replied, brilliantly.

"I knew it! I knew there was something going on with this single mother! Momma was all suspicious, and you were being cagey not answering my texts."

"As helpful as this is, Sarah . . ."

"Right. You obviously need to stop spying on her e-reader, immediately. Next, just start reading in front of her. Then, when and if she talks to you about it, listen without Judgment. You want her to share with you? Prove to her that you're someone worth trusting."

I resumed pacing around the kitchen slowly, processing my sister's words.

"She will you know," Sarah added in a gentler tone. "Trust you, that is. You're one of the good ones."

"You really are a good big sister. A little preachy, but good."

"I'm the fucking best!" Sarah snapped. "Oh, and Jace? This was the cliff notes version. I expect a call by next week to get the whole story about you and this Polly. I'll have the popcorn ready."

CHAPTER
FORTY-SIX

POLLY

"It was books that made me feel that perhaps I was not completely alone. They could be honest with me, and I with them. Reading your words, what you wrote, how you were lonely sometimes and afraid, but always brave; the way you saw the world, its colors and textures and sounds, I felt--I felt the way you thought, hoped, felt, dreamt. I felt I was dreaming and thinking and feeling with you. I dreamed what you dreamed, wanted what you wanted--and then I realized that truly I just wanted you."

Cassandra Clare, *Clockwork Prince*

"**A**nd?" Jace asked me, raising his eyebrows as I bit into my piece of toast.

"Not too bad. Only slightly burnt. It's edible, definitely edible."

"Damn it. I knew I should have gone with the classic PB and J."

"It's perfect." I squeezed Jace's hand, glancing at the votive candles, the marigolds scattered along the table, and the small Reserved card. "And the most romantic thing anyone has ever done for me at 3:25 p.m. on a Friday afternoon."

Jace smiled and held up his mug, which was filled with hot cocoa with whipped cream and chocolate sauce. 'Fancy' hot chocolate, toast, and eggs were the only things he could make, I'd been informed.

"I gotta work with the time we got." Jace looked at his watch. "We only have three hours before we pick up the kids."

I placed my hand on Jace's knee and proceeded to slide it up his thigh slowly. "Then we better make the most of the time we have." I darted my eyes to his mug. "You have any chocolate sauce left?"

I've never seen someone spring up from a chair as fast as Jace did in that moment. "Let me check the fridge real quick once," he called out on his way through the door.

Chuckling, I took a sip of my hot chocolate, even though it was ninety degrees outside. I felt energized since my encounter with Brad Goldendick this morning. What better way to spend that energy than with my twenty-four-year-old boyfriend?

The music on Jace's tablet stopped playing so I grabbed it, then swiped to open his music app. I was just about to press the Play button at the bottom, when my eyes snagged on a familiar picture.

It was an icon of the cover for *American Cream.* Clicking the icon, I saw that the audiobook had been downloaded and there was four hours and thirty-seven minutes left to listen.

I immediately checked the account information to confirm that yes, this was Jace's tablet. Was some strange home-sharing thing happening here? Was his music app picking up my audiobook library titles? Completely confused, I clicked on the audiobook tab in the app and gasped.

Every audiobook I'd listened to since the beginning of summer was listed. A sinking feeling settled in my gut as I tried to think of an explanation. This was either the world's biggest coincidence and Jace happened to be a closet fan of romance novels . . . or, what, he was looking at my e-reader and then downloading them on his own tablet?

At the thought, I realized that must be exactly what he had done. I clapped a hand over my mouth as anger and shock ran through my body. I kept my computer and phone with me all day, but my e-reader stayed on my bedside table.

Jace sauntered through the patio doors just then, holding up the chocolate sauce. He stilled immediately as he took in my thunderous expression. Jace's gaze flicked between me and the tablet I held in my hands. "What's going on?"

I couldn't put together coherent thoughts, so I did the next best thing.

I pressed play.

"Goosebumps broke out across the skin where I pressed my finger into each dip of the contoured muscles of his abdomen, barely able to keep a breathy moan from escaping my lips."

Eyes flying wide, Jace dashed toward me, but I sprang out of the chair and held the tablet behind me. It continued to play aloud, my glare communicating a thousand words.

"I was here on assignment, and he was a possible thief, fifteen years my junior."

"It's not what you think, Polly," Jace pleaded, holding up his hands, like he was trying to tame a wild animal. I scoffed inwardly. I didn't need taming. I needed answers.

Raising my eyebrows almost like a taunt, I held the tablet up higher, letting the words ring out.

"But oh my fucking delight, I wanted to trail my tongue up and down his chest like it was my own life-sized, personal popsicle."

Finally having had enough, I paused it, blanketing us in silence. Then with restraint worthy of a gold medal, I placed the tablet back on the table instead of hurling it directly into the pool.

We stared at each other. The only sounds were the blood rushing in my ears and Jace's heavy panting as he looked at me, panic-stricken.

"How long?" My eyes were hard, but my voice was soft, raw.

"Polly—" Jace started.

"How long?" I barked.

A sorrowful look passed over him, but I didn't give a damn.

"Since the first day I valeted for you. I turned on your car radio and it came on."

Heat crawled up my neck. I tried to remember what I was listening to the first Sunday we met, but I couldn't remember. Not that it would matter anyway. No wonder he was so curious about me, giving me those flirty looks.

A blistering wave of mortification swept through me. "Is that why you took the job here?"

"What? No—"

"Because you thought I was some sad, lonely mom, ripe for the picking?"

"No! That's not it at all if you'd let me explain—" Jace took a step toward me, and I instantly took a step back, which halted his forward progress.

"Explain that you've been invading my privacy by going through my books? What do you do, sneak into my room and look at my e-reader while I'm at work?"

Renewed humiliation filled me at the thought of him opening up my e-reader, looking and laughing at all of the titles and the covers. I suddenly felt exposed despite being fully clothed, wishing I had a coat to cover up with. "So last weekend, you already knew what I was listening to when you asked me about it, didn't you?"

Jace's eyes looked panicked, a pleading note entering his tone. "It's not what you think, it only made me want to know you more—"

"Yeah, I'm sure it did. What a good laugh you and your buddy Sam must have had after you told him how easy it was to bag the pathetic, single mother."

Jace immediately started shaking his head. "I *never* thought that. You don't understand—"

"Stop telling me what I do or do not understand!" I cried, my upper lip wobbling. "You took advantage of me. Of my privacy. I trusted you. You took this beautiful thing I thought we had, something special and real, and turned it into a lie." My voice was breaking, but I held my tears in. I didn't want to let him see me cry. He'd seen enough of me.

"Polly," Jace croaked.

"I'm going to my room. *Don't* follow me."

———

"And then what happened?"

Five pairs of eyes were watching me from my phone's screen. Once I'd gotten to my room and finished crying, I'd texted Leah.

She, of course, video called me and added Rose, who then added Margo, Tiffany, and Eliza.

"Then he told me he'd been listening to my audiobooks since he valeted for me that first week, which was in the beginning of June! He said it only made him want to know more. I mean, how mortifying! Here I thought we were actually together, for real, and it turns out he thought of me as nothing more than an easy lay."

They'd actually taken the news of my cougar status quite well.

Leah frowned as I spoke. "I don't think that's necessarily what Jace meant by that."

Rose was nodding encouragingly. "Leah's right, sugar. I don't want to sound indelicate here, but if Jace was lookin' for easy, he wouldn't have to look that hard. Single gals at the school flock to him."

And damn it all to hell if the green-eyed bitch herself didn't peek her head out of the depths of my soul right then and look around. Didn't she know which side she was supposed to be on? *Ahem, we're mad at Jace! Not jealous of the other single woman!*

"And it's true I haven't seen him around you," Rose added, "but most men, in general, wouldn't go through all that fuss, nannying two kids, just to get laid."

Despite the sea of anger in my body, her words resonated. My kids were hard nuts to crack. And I'd put up dozens of barriers. It's not like he gave me one wink and I dropped my pants, so to speak.

"Can I ask a question?" Margo interjected. "What's your real problem here? I mean, of course, besides the trust issues, which I'm not ignoring in any way. But like, so what? He's listening to the same books you read. It's not like he's stealing from you or publicizing your reading history online."

Margo had a point. Yes, he had invaded my privacy, but I trusted that he wasn't doing anything malicious with it.

"Have you had a guy steal from you?" I peripherally heard one of the women ask Margo, then more murmuring back and forth as I became more internally preoccupied.

I did trust Jace. I was mad about what he did, sure, but it's mostly because of my fear of Judgment, not the invasion of privacy. Just then, I heard a low knock. Tensing, I watched as a small piece of paper slid under my bedroom door.

Getting up while keeping the phone in my hand, I read the slip of paper: Look outside your door.

"What's happening?" I heard Leah ask.

"I just got a note that said to look outside my door." I put my ear against the door, hearing nothing.

Nervous anticipating roiled in my gut, unsure what I should do. I glanced down at my phone and gave a wan smile. "Thank you all, truly, but I think I'm going to hang up." I moved to end the call when a chorus erupted:

"No!"

"Wait!"

"I want to know what happens!"

I hesitated, looking at Leah and her friends, no wait, that's not right, looking at *my friends*. My friends who didn't judge me when I told them I read romance. My friends who didn't judge me when I told them I was in a relationship with a twenty-four-year-old guy. My friends who dropped what they were doing on a Friday afternoon to talk to me about a fight I'd had with my boyfriend.

I quickly glanced at the door, wondering if Jace was right outside, and quieted my voice. "Ok, but I reserve the right to hang up on your faces depending on what I find."

Taking a deep breath in and out, I opened the door to find an empty hallway. Peeking around the corner, I saw the stairs were also empty. Inexplicable disappointment filled me. I looked down then, only to discover a pile of books at my feet.

Squatting to take a closer look, I gasped and covered my mouth.

It was many of the books I'd read over the past six weeks; bits of scratch paper were sticking out randomly within some of the book's pages. At the bottom of the pile was an envelope with my name written in capital letters.

"What is it?" Leah whispered.

"I'm not sure yet, hold on."

I quickly maneuvered picking up the stack of books without dropping my phone, closing the door, then placing everything on my bed. With a trembling hand, I pulled two notes out of the envelope.

Polly,

"Read it out loud!"

I cleared my throat, reading aloud this time.

> Polly,
> I know you probably don't want to hear from me yet. I only have two things to say.
> First, I'm sorry. I shouldn't have broken your trust. You are this gift that came into my life when I wasn't expecting it, not knowing you'd be exactly what I needed. If you give me another chance, I promise I'll be more careful with your heart.
> Second, how would you like the kids to be picked up? I'm happy to pick them up and bring them back here. I enclosed a reply note for your convenience.
> Love, Jace

I pulled out the second note as I listened to the suddenly very loud women on the other side of my phone screen.

"He's a keeper!"

"I've never gotten a note like that."

"Marry him and have his babies!"

I read the second note to myself, sniffling and laughing by the time I finished.

"What's so funny?"

"Show us!"

Unable to suppress my goofy smile, I turned the note over to show them.

> ☐ Jace picks up the kids and brings me a donut

☐ *Jace picks up the kids and brings me a donut and an iced coffee*

☐ *Jace picks up the kids and promises to be my sex unicorn for all eternity*

"That's an easy choice, gotta go with number three," Tiffany chimed in. I laughed, warning them that I was putting the phone down as the women continued to chatter amongst themselves.

Reverently, I picked up the first book off the pile, *Barbarian Lover* by Ruby Dixon. Ignoring my throb of embarrassment, I flipped the book open to the first marked page. Jace marked one of the passages with a note, saying *Never give a girl a wooden mold of your junk.*

I burst out laughing, which prompted more chatter from the phone beside me. But I wasn't listening, I was too focused on the second book in the pile, one that was particularly steamy. But Jace's notes weren't lewd, nor were they mocking or thoughtless. Instead, Jace wrote a note during a sex scene that said, *Try this with Polly,* causing a flush of heat in my cheeks.

I kept moving through the books, giggling at Jace's notes which were funny and genuine. Just like Jace, himself. At the bottom of the pile was a book I'd read just before Jace started here. A novella that I'd binged until two in the morning. It was about how a smart, young woman, who was also a closet ninja, met her very sarcastic, and very British future husband in college. A few lines of text were marked.

"Because if it's possible to have a partner who gives all of themselves without reservation, who looks forward to working and sacrificing for me just as I look forward to doing the same for her, who can't help but love ferociously, brutally, and unconditionally—and even perhaps without reason or sound judgment— that's what I want. Because that's how I plan to love in return."

The words were swimming in front of me by the time I was done reading. The line of text was heartfelt and beautiful, yes, but that's not what brought tears to my eyes. It was the word written next to it.

Yes

I was wiping my cheeks as I finally brought the phone back up to my face to find five women, noses practically pressed to their screens. Quickly, I went through the last book and quote, along with Jace's note.

"I take it you've forgiven him?" Leah's question had a smile in it as I shrugged, a sob escaping my lips.

"You fight for this one, Polly," Leah continued. "I don't care how old he is, or if your father doesn't like him, or if he's horrible in bed." She gave me a knowing wink. "But this is why I read romance. I want to read about how a man loves their woman." She paused. "Or man."

"Or how a woman loves their woman!" Margo piped up and Rose nodded in agreement.

"Don't leave out the why-choose tropes!" Tiffany added as Eliza chimed in, "Or the sunscreen and monster tropes!"

Leah raised her eyebrows at me. "See? It's a person's devotion to their partner, their unconditional love, their imperfectly perfect words. Morally gray, reverse harem, closed-door, it doesn't matter. When one person puts another's needs first and shows us what true partnership is, isn't that what we all want?"

CHAPTER
FORTY-SEVEN

POLLY

I've been getting an awful feeling that you don't love me back, but that doesn't change what I feel about you or make it any less real. Even if you throw me out of your life forever, I want you to know that you'll always be the best part of me.

Susan Elizabeth Phillips, *First Lady*

I found Jace standing outside, hands in his pockets, looking out at the mountains when I came downstairs. I knocked on the glass of the patio door and he turned quickly, revealing solemn, weary eyes, his hair frizzy like he'd been running his fingers through it continuously.

I watched him visibly steel himself before coming inside. After closing the door softly behind him, he returned his hands to his pockets and watched me warily.

"Hi," I rasped, voice still raw with emotion.

"Hiya, darlin'," he drawled, tone unbearably sad.

When I'd walked down the stairs, I was resolved that I would talk to him calmly, getting the reassurance I wanted before deciding if I truly forgave him. And while that's what my brain told me, my heart was beating out a different story. Jace had already shown me little by little who he was. His strength of character. His patience. His kindness. When I saw him, I found that I'd already forgiven him. Yes, he made a mistake, but I trusted him. I trusted his apology. My chest ached, feeling full and true and happier than I could remember feeling, maybe ever.

"I'm sorry I overreacted," I said, which had Jace immediately shaking his head.

"No, *I'm* the one who should be sorry. The last thing I'd ever want to do is hurt you. I knew it was wrong when I did it. I have nothing left to say now except I'm sorry and it won't happen again."

I nodded, giving him a little smile. "I know."

Jace reared back. "You know?"

"Yes." I walked forward until I was right in front of him, my head tipping back to look into his eyes. "There are a lot of things to talk about, but the most important thing is this, I forgive you and I trust you."

A flash of relief passed over his features before he lunged for me, wrapping his arms around me, burying his head in my neck. I brought my arms around his shoulders and held tight, feeling the slight trembling of Jace's body. I soothed my hand up and down his back in slow, calming circles, gradually feeling his body relax as he clung to me.

"I didn't know if I'd ever get to hold you again," Jace murmured into my neck. "I told myself, just one more time, one more time and it'd be enough. And now I'm here, holding you." Jace pulled back, his face inches from mine, gazing at me like he was memorizing my features. "Now I know it for the lie it was. I could hold you every day like this, and it still wouldn't be enough."

His lip fused to my own, hot and demanding, my mouth opening immediately. His right hand clutched the side of my face, his thumb stroking along my jaw as his fingers extended back through my hair, cupping my head, holding me to him.

"It drove me insane, knowing you were listening to these books, wondering what you were doing to yourself, who you were picturing."

As he spoke, he trailed his fingers up my right arm to where my hand was holding tight to the back of his neck. Gently, he grasped my right hand, moving it from around his neck and pulled it to his mouth.

"I've never been more jealous of a hand in my entire life."

Without breaking eye contact, he sucked my index and middle fingers into his mouth, moaning and closing his eyes. I gasped at the erotic imagery, at the liquid fire that burned deep in my core as Jace's tongue swirled around my fingers, then freed them with a pop.

With a roguish smile, Jace bent at the knees and swept me up into a full-on princess carry. I'd love to say I was totally calm, and my arms folded naturally about his neck . . . but I think I actually let out a shriek and clutched to him like a skittish baby kitten.

"The more I got to know you, the better and worse it got."

I was hypnotized by his words as he carried me up the stairs.

"You were sass and sweetness all rolled into one. I've never looked forward to anything in the morning as much as when you'd come downstairs, your sweet perfume around you, having no idea just how beautiful you were."

Jace carried me into my bedroom, letting me down near the end of my bed. His fingers went to the sides of my lavender blouse and pulled it over my head, revealing the pink push-up bra underneath. His eyes were practically on fire as he brought his hands up to cup my breasts, bending to bring his face even with them, tracing his nose over the swells as his clever fingers teased and pinched and drove me insane. My clit throbbed with each pinch and roll of my nipples.

I was breathing hard as I went to unhook my bra, but Jace pulled back and gave a gentle shake of his head, moving to unhook it himself.

It fell to the floor.

Jace let out a soft breath before feasting on my bare flesh, caressing me, making me cry out, first in pleasure, then in distress when he removed his hands and dropped to his knees before me. His hands untied the belt of my linen pants quickly as he leaned in to kiss just above my navel, making me giggle. My pants fell to the ground in a rush, revealing my matching pink lace panties.

His chest rumbled in appreciation, then grabbed my ass with both hands and squeezed, making me grip his shoulders and gasp with desire.

"Your goddamn leggings were the death of me. They showed off every curve of these phenomenal legs," he said as his hands caressed slowly down my thighs to my calves, then moved back up to grasp my ass again.

His words were driving me to distraction as he slowly peeled my panties off. Once I'd kicked them away, I stood fully naked in front of him, panting, vibrating with anticipation. To my extreme disappointment, Jace didn't move to stroke me where I was wet and longing for him. No, he slowly got to his feet, removed his shirt and pants with impressive speed, then walked me backward, easing me down onto the bed.

Jace slowly prowled over me as I lay on my back. I was aching with need, desperate for his touch. Glancing down between us my eyes tripped over his proud erection, straining toward me.

A soft touch on my cheek brought my gaze back to his. "The night with the lightning bugs," he whispered, "being close enough to touch you, watching your eyes fill with delight when you caught one," Jace paused, searching my face with reverent eyes, drinking me in. "It was everything I could do not to kiss you, to hold you. Because there you were, the most beautiful creature on earth, and you didn't even know it."

I exhaled a watery sigh, his words doing nothing but stoking the fire within me. Finally, Jace's hand left my face, tracing down my flesh, until he finally skimmed the seam of my body. It was all I could do not to thrust my hips forward, to put pressure where it was needed most.

"I came so hard in the shower that night. Thinking of you. Thinking of doing just this." I gasped as he parted me, thrusting two fingers inside. I tipped my head back and cried out as Jace placed an open kiss to my neck, continuing to stroke his two fingers in and out of me until I was practically riding his hand.

Suddenly, Jace removed his fingers—I cried out in frustration and the bastard winked. He must know he was driving me insane with want.

"I thought I knew what it'd be like between us, but once I had a taste . . ." Jace brought his two wet fingers to his mouth and sucked, just like he'd done in the kitchen, groaning and closing his eyes. He released them in a soft pop, eyes opening at the same time, looking at me like he wanted to consume me.

His voice went molten, the heat burning me to my core. "I knew I'd never get enough."

Jace abruptly slid both of his hands between my thighs, spreading me wide. He gripped his cock, his eyes zeroing in on my pink center.

Jace's features were wicked and sinful and delicious as he stroked his cock up and down with his hand, looking his fill at my naked body. My mouth watered, wanting to do that, to feel the soft skin that covered his steel erection, to trace my thumb up and around the firm tip, watching his eyes half close in ecstasy as I pumped him, hard.

"When you look at me like that, it drives me wild."

I couldn't take my eyes off of what he was doing as he pressed the head of his cock against my swollen center, not sliding in, but *up*. I whimpered, yes fucking *whimpered*, when the head of his cock stroked my clit; I tried not to beg when Jace continued to make soft little passes over and over and *over* my secret spot, but I was mindless with desire and not in control of my actions.

"Jace," my words came in short gasps. "Come inside me, please, I need you."

"Not as much as I need you."

He pushed home, my core rejoicing in riotous relief. We cried out together as he pumped and rocked into me, our mutual rhythm sending little zings of pleasure through me with each thrust. I sighed and panted and shouted his name, desperate for release, but never wanting it to stop.

His hips accelerated, the sound of our skin slapping together a filthy soundtrack to our lovemaking.

"Tell me I can have all of you. Tell me you're mine." Jace panted out.

"I'm yours," I gasped, matching his thrusts, climbing toward the peak. "Always."

I pushed hard as Jace thrust in, intensifying the pressure, making me fly apart. I cried out, my orgasm pulsating through me, my muscles milking his cock as Jace gritted his teeth and almost roared with the force of his climax, pushing into the hilt and causing me to cry out again.

As we came down, our breathing eventually slowing, we melted into each other, luxuriating in the feel of one another. I closed my eyes, safely cocooned against Jace's chest.

My heart was just returning to its normal pace when Jace propped himself up on his arm.

"Did you really mean that before, when you said, that you were mine, always?"

There was wonder and awe in his question, but there was doubt, too. Like the words we'd uttered to each other were just that: pretty words spoken in the heat of the moment. He looked uncertain, as if bracing for what I'd say once reality set in.

Sometime during the last two weeks, I'd completely fallen in love with this man. This funny, charming, genuine man.

I answered with the simple truth. Because I was his. And he was mine. We'd work on the rest as it came.

"Yes."

He cupped my cheek, kissing me softly. When our kiss ended, he pulled back and looked thoughtful.

"I'd like to tell the kids about us."

My eyes widened. "Today?"

Smiling all cute and adorable, he shook his head. "No. But it's supposed to be nice weather all weekend. I was thinking we could all go for a hike tomorrow. I know some trails the kids would love, and it'd be an opportunity to add to your fun list. Besides, if we tell 'em on a trail, it'd be sort of special. Like we're making a new memory, just the four of us."

Just the four of us.

Telling the kids about us could be a mistake. One—or all of us could get hurt if something went wrong. But I was sick of playing it safe, of being afraid of making a mistake. I was ready to take a risk that made life worth living. I was ready to feel alive.

"Ok." I nodded, smiling at the surprise in his features at my quick agreement.

"And I want to introduce you to my parents on Sunday. As my girlfriend."

"Wow, when you go for it, you really go for it"

Jace gave me a cocky grin as he raked his eyes over my naked body.

"That wasn't how I meant it."

"Not in my head," Jace teased

I smiled, loving how easy this felt. "I know one thing for sure. I want you in my life. Yes, it's fast, but at this point, I can't see a future for me without you in it."

Jace lifted my hand and kissed my palm. "So, that's a yes for meetin' my parents as my girlfriend?"

I nodded. I didn't know what our future held, but as long as I was with Jace, I found I was startlingly okay with that.

Completely and totally relaxed, I closed my eyes, nestling back into his side, hoping we would not get out of this bed until it was time to pick up the kids.

"There's something else I want to do with you." His voice was playful.

"I hope it involves staying in this bed," I murmured, keeping my eyes closed.

"Nope!" His voice was chipper.

I cracked an eye open. "I know we agreed not to quibble about our ages, but I have a complaint."

Jace laughed, sliding down and off the bed, looking at the floor for what I presumed to be his clothes.

"Does it involve food?" I ventured.

Jace tilted his head back and forth as he pulled on his boxers. I whined in protest. Chuckling, Jace crawled back up the bed, kissing up my shoulder until he reached my ear.

"How do you feel about chocolate sauce?" His breath tickled my ear, and I shivered.

"I'm in."

CHAPTER
FORTY-EIGHT

JACE

A man who read actual books, and then read them again. It was almost as sexy as … well, nothing, because nothing was sexier than a man who read. *Except a man who read naked. Out loud. With chocolate.*

April White, *Code of Honor*

"So, about your books . . ." I started after swallowing a bite of my hot chicken pizza. We had about a half hour before we had to leave to get the kids. Polly and I were currently lazing about on a quilt on the living room floor.

"Any chance we can talk about this tomorrow?" Polly's lips were curved in a small smile, eyes closed as she relaxed.

Chuckling, I put down my slice, laying on my side next to her. Today was turning out to be one of the best days of my life, after it was almost one of the worst. After some of the most amazing sex I'd ever had, followed by licking chocolate sauce off my girlfriend's naked body, we took a lazy shower and ordered hot chicken pizza.

"Did you always read?" I asked.

"My mom and I read together. *The Boxcar Children*, Judy Blume, *The Baby-Sitter's Club*. When she died, reading fell to the wayside, like everything else. And then my father had that portrait made. I always liked to think he put it in the library *for me*, so that I could see her whenever I wanted. But now, I know it was for him. He didn't know me well enough to do anything like that for me."

My face was calm, but on the inside, that familiar desire to beat the tar out of her father churned.

"I started reading again when I was pregnant with Ryla. I couldn't sleep and a *Twilight* marathon was on TV. The movies were alright, but they had such a cult book following, I decided to download the books onto an old e-reader to see what the fuss was all about."

"What's *Twilight*?" I deadpanned. Polly's horrified expression made me drop my head back and laugh. "I know what *Twilight* is. No, I don't care that you've read it. Almost every girl I know has read those books."

Polly blew out a breath and shifted on her side. "Thank God. I thought that meant you were too young to know what *Twilight* was."

I decided not to share that those movies were all the rage during my fifth-grade year.

"I brought it up to David once, asking if he knew anyone who read them. He scoffed, telling me they were frivolous books for tweens. I never talked to him about it again. My e-reader became a place I could curl up and imagine life in a different place. Ryla's name actually came from this badass assassin queen from a book I read when I was nine months pregnant." Polly looked down, tracing the pattern of the quilt. "When I saw the audiobooks on your tablet, I was scared that you'd look at the safe place I'd made for myself and judge me for it."

I pressed a kiss on her forehead. This time, I was suppressing the familiar desire to beat the living shit out of her ex-husband.

"I've never judged you for it. I think I've established how turned-on it makes me."

Polly rolled her eyes. "When you told me you'd been listening to my books since you met me, I felt silly. Like, here was the real reason you were interested in someone like me. A sad, middle-aged mom who would give it up to anyone."

I opened my mouth to refute her words, but Polly shook her head, indicating she wasn't done.

"Then I called Leah, who called a few friends, and I realized I was being unfair. Nothing you'd ever done made me think you'd do that. It was all me."

"It wasn't all you. What I did was an invasion of your privacy. It started as a curiosity. I'm not gonna lie, when that came out of your car stereo, I was surprised."

She furrowed her brow. "What book was it?"

I closed one eye, answering hesitantly. "*American Tail* by Lady Jane."

Polly groaned, rolling to her back and covering her face with her hands. Gently, I pulled her hands away and made her look at me.

"All it did was make me want to get to know you more. Each week brought something new and different. Each week, it was like a new splash of color. What shoes you wore, what books you listened to, what you ordered. The more I learned about you, the more I liked you. But my favorite things about you, the ones you seemingly keep to yourself, the ones that you think are imperfect, have the most vivid colors."

Her eyes were filling with tears as I spoke, so I cupped her cheek so I could wipe them away.

"This time I've spent with you have been the best weeks of my life. I know growing up you were expected to be perfect. But perfect is boring. It's fake. Give me the real deal, any day of the week. I want to tell you, that everything you are and everything you want to be, all of your different colors, each one is beautiful."

CHAPTER
FORTY-NINE

POLLY

Love: a single word, a wispy thing, a word no bigger or longer than an edge. That's what it is: an edge; a razor. It draws up through the center of your life, cutting everything in two. Before and after. The rest of the world falls away on either side.

Lauren Oliver, *Delirium*

On the way home from the birthday party, Jace and I asked the kids if they wanted to go on an adventure hike in the mountains the next day. Ryla was all for it, no surprise there, and Max agreed with only a few conditions: he didn't have to try any new foods and if there were a lot of bees, we could go home.

The next morning, we spent an hour driving to the hiking trail Jace knew well, singing funny songs and taking time to stop and appreciate the beautiful mountain views along the way. Once we'd arrived, Max started to balk. Then, Jace produced two bug jackets, one for Max, and one for Jace. I knew that Jace had never worn, nor needed, a bug jacket. He'd only brought it along to make Max feel less alone.

My two children were glued to Jace's side during the first half of the hike, which meant I followed behind them, marveling at how lucky I was to have found a man that fit so seamlessly into our family. As we walked, Jace told us stories about how he'd come hiking here with his friend who was now a park ranger and how eventually he'd come to hike here by himself when he got older. We spread out a blanket at a picnic area for lunch, eating from a basket that Jace's mom had sent home with him this week.

It was there that I placed my hand in Jace's, and we told the kids we were dating.

Ryla had no less than one hundred questions whereas Max only asked a few. I stressed that it was to be kept private, just between the four of us, as Grandfather Alberton couldn't know. It was a risk, especially with Miss Ryla, but as she'd never liked her grandfather, I actually felt decently safe that she'd relish the opportunity to keep a secret from him. Max, my sweet boy, smiled and nodded when Jace explained that this didn't change anything between them, and they could both talk to him about anything. Ryla's last question, bless her heart, was if she could have a baby sister. After side-stepping that last question, the rest of lunch went on without any catastrophes. All in all, I dare say it'd been a pretty perfect morning.

It was after lunch that things started to go a little . . . less perfectly.

When Jace and I were packing up after lunch, Max and Ryla went to throw stones in a stream. Not five minutes later, Ryla ran back screaming bloody murder from a mosquito bite on her leg and proceeded to spend the next five minutes limping around, howling at us to cut off her leg. Jace finally convinced Ryla to let him carry her on his shoulders, or at least until her leg stopped "burning with mosquito death fire."

Ten minutes into the hike back, Max had to go to the bathroom. Max was uninterested when Jace told him he'd teach him to pee against a tree. Ryla, on the other hand, was very interested and aggrieved when I wouldn't let her try. Our debate on that did seem to cure her from the pain of her mortal mosquito wound, however. We spent the next twenty minutes hightailing it back to the trailhead, where the only flushable toilets were located.

When Max and I returned from the bathroom (in all honesty, I didn't want to pop a squat either. I'd seen too much poison ivy in my practice) we found Ryla and Jace at a picnic table, huddled over a map.

"Momma!" Ryla shouted when she spotted us. My heart stirred; my throat tight with emotion. Having grown up in Chicago, Ryla always called me mom —or mama when she was a toddler—but never *momma*. It brought a picture into focus: our future life here. Over time, I expected the kid's accents would get progressively more dipped. Jace and I would sit hand in hand as we watched Ryla's theatrical performances or quietly root for Max with each big step he took along his own path. Looking at Jace, seeing the love and affection in his eyes, I could tell he was thinking the same thing.

Ryla tugged at my shirt and pointed at the map. "We found a new trail! There's a lake at the end of it with fish and a waterfall!"

"Hold on there, Ryla," Jace said. "I said if there's a lake, there's *probably* fish, and even though that symbol means there's a waterfall, it might not be the right season to see it. Your momma and brother have to agree to walk with us, too. It looks easy enough, but it's about a mile just to get there which is a lot of walking for everyone."

"I can do it! Please? Please! I wanna see the waterfall!"

I looked at Max who just shrugged, then shifted my gaze to the sky, which had gray clouds in the distance. "Jace? I know you said the weather forecast was clear all day, but do you see those clouds?"

"There are always little showers here and there, but I 'reckon those clouds are a good twenty miles from here. My only concern is the length of the trail. It's two miles round trip. It should take about twenty minutes to hike one way, so if any one of us gets tired, speak up and remember, it's the same distance coming back as it is to walk there."

Twenty minutes and two unmarked forks in the trail later, there was no lake and no waterfall in sight. At the first fork, Jace gave a confident smile, telling us he knew exactly where we were. It was at the second fork that Jace started to look uncertain. He was looking down furtively at the map, then off into the distance more and more.

"Do you know where you're going?" Ryla shouted, pausing from drawing in the dirt with a stick.

I fought a laugh. Leave it to Ryla to ask what we were all thinking.

"Of course I know where I'm going. I just need to find a landmark." Jace continued looking between the map and the distance. I walked over to him and glanced down at the map, but it might as well have been in hieroglyphics; cartography was never my strong suit.

"You know exactly where you are, huh, Ranger Vargas?" I teased Jace out of the earshot of the kids. He pursed his lips, unamused. Hiding my smile, I went over to check on Max, who had been glancing nervously at the clouds, which admittedly were getting a deeper gray.

I held out my hand, which he took. "Ok Max. Give me one squeeze if you want to keep going and two squeezes if you want to head home."

I didn't have to wait long until I felt two squeezes on my hand.

"Jace?" I called out. "I think I might be done. My heels are hurting, and I don't think I should walk any further in these shoes."

Jace glanced up, looking from me to Max, understanding dawning. Immediately, Jace folded up the map. "Absolutely. Deal's a deal." Ryla started to protest, but Jace got to the balls of his feet in front of her, speaking so low I couldn't hear them. After a minute, he'd performed a Smokey Mountain miracle when, without a fuss, she climbed up onto his back for a piggyback ride. Max and I walked behind them.

I was just starting to enjoy the serenity of the landscape again when I heard Ryla exclaim, "Ahhh! A bird just pooped on my head!" She immediately let go of Jace's neck to claw at her face, and Jace, to his credit, quickly lowered her safely to the ground.

Speaking soothing words, I peeled back the hand from her forehead to reveal: *nothing.*

"Ryla, sweetie, there's nothing there. Maybe it was a bug," I tried to explain. However, this was equally as traumatic as she gasped, "A bug peed on me?"

She was an adorable little drama queen sometimes.

"*Nothing* pooped or peed on—Aaaah!" I shouted, my hand practically slapping my face as something wet landed on my cheek. I was relieved to see a drop of water on my fingers.

Jace held out his hand and looked at the sky. "I just felt a drop too. But not to worry, it's only a few drops. Those clouds still look a ways off. It might sprinkle a bit, but trust me, it's not gonna rain."

Drip. Drip.

Drip, drip, drip.

The sound of rain hitting the soft vegetation filled the air as a steady rain began not one minute later.

"Run for your lives!" Ryla screamed and took off. Jace ran after her as Max, who actually looked more resigned than anxious, hurried along with me as we followed them.

Five minutes later, we were soaked and huddled underneath the small awning of an information sign, looking out at the steady rainfall.

"It's gonna let up any second, and we're less than a quarter mile from the parking lot. We'll be in the car in no time. The mountains are known for little showers like this," Jace was saying, smiling, trying to reassure the kids.

And as if it were a movie, Jace's words hadn't even dissolved into the ether before the steady rain became a downpour.

"Oh, come on!" Jace yelled, shaking his fist to the sky.

I held out my hand and shivered, delighting in the sensation of the cool rain on my palm. I hadn't seen any lightning or heard any thunder; the darkest clouds had already passed. I took a few tentative steps forward, then spread my arms wide, becoming instantly soaked. Facing the sky, I let the cool rain run down my face as I turned in slow circles, laughing in delight. Ryla was looking at me like I was nuts and Max's eyebrows were high on his forehead as they watched me hold my arms up as if I had an imaginary dance partner and begin to waltz. Because if there was ever a time that called for dancing in the rain, it was now.

I was so absorbed in what I was doing that I didn't hear Ryla's question to Jace out of the side of her mouth.

"What's Momma doing?"

I also missed the proud smile on Jace's face as he watched me, and the twinkle in his eye as he looked down at both of my children and replied, "She's dancin' in the rain."

Hair plastered to my face, clothes utterly drenched, a warm hand grasped my outstretched one as a real person replaced the imaginary. And then, Jace began to dance with me.

We danced around the narrow trail in the rain, laughing as Jace tried to spin me, looking for all intents and purposes, like we were smoking something illegal. Ryla ran to my side, hugging me, then took Jace and my hands to start dancing in a circle. Eventually the dancing turned into spinning; we started to spin so fast that Ryla's head fell back, letting out a little whoop as she went airborne, her beaming face looking free and alive. We stopped, dizzy and giggling, and I glanced at Max. I held my breath, taking a beat to look right into his eyes as if to say, *I got you. Whatever you decide, I got you.* Suddenly, Max made a break for us, and instantly, Jace and I let go of our joined hands to grab Max's outstretched ones.

And then, we were just four imperfect people, soaking up all the imperfect moments, spinning in a circle and laughing in the rain, our conjoined whoops and ringing laughter floating up and mixing with the cool mountain rain.

———

On the ride home, huddled under jackets and the heater on full blast, Jace regaled Max and Ryla about camping stories filled with tents, bonfires, spooky stories and s'mores. Of course, this led to a dinner of microwaved s'mores once we got home and got all dried off. We capped off the night under a makeshift camping tent in the basement, made with two large king-sized sheets, chairs and pillows, using a flashlight to tell funny, not scary, stories.

Ryla's eyes had closed half an hour ago, and Max fell asleep not long after. Jace and I were sitting diagonally across from each other, cross-legged, our knees almost touching.

"I think you may have scared them off hiking forever," I whispered to Jace.

Jace groaned quietly. "I shouldn't have let Ryla talk me into that last trail. I need to redeem myself. That's never happened to me before. In good weather, on a trail I know, I'd never get lost. We can take them again, they'll love it. And camping! I bet they're gonna love camping with a real bonfire when they try it."

I tilted my head. "Have you met my son?"

Jace glanced down at them. "Ok, we can start small." He glanced back up at me with excited eyes. "Like camping in the backyard."

"I never went camping as a kid." I held up a hand when Jace's mouth went slack. "Which I'm totally fine with, incidentally. I never minded missing some of the regular things kids did. Really, I think the thing I would have liked the most was a basic sleepover with a group of friends."

"You've never done a sleepover at a friend's house? Not even Leah?"

I shook my head.

"It's a good thing I'm willing to do as many sleepovers as you want," he smirked. "I mean, I'm willin' to put in the extra effort here. We could play two truths and a lie, then spin the bottle, then progress to seven minutes in heaven. All with yours truly, of course."

I playfully pushed him on the shoulder. "What's two truths and a lie?"

"It's a game where you say three facts about yourself, one's a lie and two are true. Everyone has to guess which one's the lie."

"And that's . . . fun?"

Jace tilted his head back and forth. "I mean, it's usually played in middle school, but we can play for funsies." He rubbed his hands together. "Here's an example. My name is Jace Vargas, I played Romeo in high school, and I perm my hair." Jace pointed to his frizzed-out hair, which had dried all haphazard after the rainstorm today.

I couldn't help but laugh at the obvious lie.

"See? It's fun. You try!" Jace's whispered enthusiasm was infectious.

I looked down at my kids, then back to Jace. "I have two awesome kids. I love wearing pretty shoes, and I drink coffee every morning."

Jace nodded encouragingly. "See! You're getting it."

I grimaced, shaking my head. "There's a reason this is for middle schoolers."

He grabbed my hand. "We're just warming up. I'll try again."

He cleared his throat lightly. "I once dressed up as a clown for a six-year old's birthday party."

I smirked at the memory as he squeezed my hand.

"I'm great at predicting the weather by looking at the sky." He lifted his eyebrows at me, making me chuckle.

Jace then looked up in thought, his thumb stroking absently over my knuckles. When he faced me again, his smile had tempered, expression suddenly serious.

"And I love you."

My heart immediately began to hammer in my chest. I replayed his statements over in my head.

I once dressed up as a clown for a six-year-old's birthday party. True.

I'm great at predicting the weather by looking at the sky. Lie.

Which meant, by process of elimination, what Jace said last, had to be true.

And I love you.

I swallowed roughly.

I thought I'd been in love once. But then after years of being with David, I realized it wasn't love. You don't treat someone you love that way. With silent disapprovals in your facial expression and cold shoulders year in and year out.

Jace was like finding the sun. He'd filled my world with so much light that at first, I was blinded by it. Scared that when he got closer, he might not like what he found. But day by day, through his actions and words, he showed me that the sun was a good thing; it scared away all the shadows. The people that love you, stick around, even if you're not perfect in the harsh light of day.

He demonstrated what unconditional love was supposed to feel like.

"My name is Polly Anna Alberton."

He brought laughter back to me and my kids.

"I hate romance novels."

He taught me that magic, just might be real.

"And I love you, too."

CHAPTER
FIFTY

POLLY

The day when love is stronger than fear is the day we'll begin to discover our true power.

April White, *Marking Time, The Immortal Descendants*

I fell asleep holding Jace's hand in our makeshift tent next to my children.

We didn't sneak upstairs and make passionate love after saying we loved each other for the first time. We didn't post about it on social media. We simply kissed, my heart and body trembling, my soul light.

In the middle of the night, Ryla tapped me awake to use the bathroom, which woke up Max, so Jace and I, giving each other contented, happy looks, helped the kids up to bed. Ryla was wired, requiring back rubs and singing to fall back asleep.

The hallway was empty when I left her room a half hour later, but saw there was a small light on in my room. Going to the doorway, I saw that Jace was sleeping on top of the covers on my bed, a small lamp on.

There was a note on my e-reader.

I didn't open this.

I thought we could open it together, tomorrow.

Turning off the light, I grabbed a fleece blanket to put over us and burrowed into Jace's side, not waking until morning.

———

When I opened my eyes the next morning and registered that it was Sunday, I wasn't immediately filled with the normal dread of seeing my father. I was high on love, and I wasn't going to let anything bring me down today, which included, my father.

I wore a flowery midi dress with spaghetti straps and yellow wedges. I knew my father wouldn't approve of the colorful pattern or neckline. But I felt beautiful in it. That was enough.

"I'll call you after brunch when I'm on my way to your parents' house. What time are you getting there?" I asked Jace as I walked into the kitchen. He was coloring with the kids at the kitchen table. While driving to our hiking spot yesterday, Jace's parents had called to invite us all over for brunch this morning. At that point, since we had already discussed telling them about us anyway, we thought we'd take them up on their offer.

"Around eleven-thirty. And you're sure?" Jace asked, pausing his crayon masterpiece of a rainbow-colored kraken.

"Anything is better than having brunch with my father. Besides, you already told them I'm coming. No backing out now."

I kissed my two little loves, then paused next to Jace. Deciding to hell with it, I leaned in close and brushed a very quick kiss over his lips prompting kissing noises from Ryla behind us.

"I'll see you soon," Jace whispered, eyes soft and adoring. It'd be nauseating if I didn't find it so goddamn sexy.

When I arrived at the club a half hour later, my father predictably frowned as he half stood when he saw me approaching the table.

"Polly." He nodded, sitting back down.

"Sir," I responded, then picked up my menu. I was thinking about ordering the twice-baked French toast again, but this time with a side of bacon, when I heard my father clear his throat.

"Polly, we need to speak about a serious matter."

"Ok," I answered plainly, though I was wary. This wasn't his typical pattern. He'd usually attempt small talk then spring things on me when I was swallowing. Perhaps this was preferable as it carried a significantly smaller risk of choking to death.

"A member of the community has come forward to describe some unprofessional behavior you've displayed as well as some indelicate comments you've made, in public, about the school system. I have been advised, in no uncertain terms, that should your behavior continue, any funding to my campaign from this source will immediately cease. I have assured this person, with absolute certainty, that your behavior and opinions will be nothing but appropriate and professional from now on. After all, that is how you were raised."

My father must be referencing the meeting I had with that sniveling, conniving, evil leprechaun Brad Goldenstein. Brad failed to mention that he'd donated to my father's campaign when I'd met him. But to essentially *tell* on me to my father? For what? Being a responsible purveyor of evidence-based medicine and social policy? Is this the third grade?

That sweaty, smarmy tattletale.

I was trying to piece together a logical, calm reply when he continued to speak.

"It has also come to my attention, that you are involved in," he shifted in his chair, "an inappropriate relationship with the young man in your employ. Furthermore, that you have conducted yourself in unprofessional and vulgar behavior with this young man. If you continue this relationship, I will have no choice but to publicly disassociate from you, which would expose what you've been doing to the public. I cannot be associated with that type of behavior. Now, I don't want to do this, but you will have forced my hand. Certainly, no one will want a doctor, much less a doctor for their children, who engages in such improper behavior."

I laid my menu on the table in front of me with deliberate gentleness. I couldn't be trusted to have anything in my hands when I was thinking such murderous, enraged thoughts. Because my father had to be talking about my relationship with Jace, yet nothing else about what he said made sense. *Vulgar* behavior? How in the hell did he even know about us? We'd never done anything outside of the privacy of the house. The house had a security system and camera surveillance at the front door, but that was it, wasn't it? Horror snaked its way down my spine as the creepy portrait from the library, with my father's unsettling eyes, popped into my mind. As terrifying as the thought was, spying on Jace and I in private was the only thing that made sense.

"Have you—" I paused to swallow; bile was rising in my throat. "Are you spying on us?"

My father busied himself arranging his water glass and silverware. "I did what was necessary. I learned what I needed to know and will only continue to do so to ensure my rules are followed."

"That doesn't include recording people in the privacy of their own home without their consent! You of all people should know that's illegal!" I whisper-hissed.

Jerking back in his seat, my father scoffed with indignance. "I can assure you I did nothing of the sort."

Heart hammering in my chest, breathing fast, I tried to calm down, but rage made it hard to think rationally. Forcing myself to take slow, even breaths, I tried to think of other ways my father could be spying on us. Could he have stopped by the house unannounced and seen us through a window? That seemed unlikely. He'd never resort to lurking outside his own home. That wasn't his style.

My eyes narrowed on my father as I realized just what his style would be, the judge wouldn't do the dirty work himself.

"Jeffrey," I said flatly, thinking about the black SUV that almost rear-ended me. The same black SUV that I'd seen pulling out of the high school parking lot this Thursday as Jace, Max, Ryla and I walked out of Young Wills rehearsal.

A stiff nod from my father confirmed that it was indeed Jeffrey that had been following me, spying on us. How he knew what Jace and I were doing behind closed doors, I had no idea. I didn't have time to appropriately process the sickening invasion of privacy because apparently, my father wasn't quite finished.

"Your mother would be ashamed of you."

I closed my eyes, jerking back as if I'd been slapped. Instead of hurting me, his words finally woke me up. I opened my eyes and blinked, seeing a stranger in front of me. His skin was sallow and sagging. He looked angry, but underneath that, I could see the sadness. He looked hollow. Empty. Like someone living with a broken heart. By saving the worst for last, my father had just dealt me the blow that made everything worse and, yet, easier at the same time.

This, his supposed authority over me, ended now.

"No," I whispered. "She'd be ashamed of you."

It was his turn to flinch.

"You know, I was thinking about Momma—" My voice broke, and for a second, I didn't think I'd have the strength to say this, but then I thought of Leah. My kick-ass best friend who loved me no matter what, and I began again.

"I was thinking of Momma the other day—"

I thought of Max. My brave boy. And Ryla. How she doesn't have any fear of being unapologetically herself.

"—and how much she loved me. And I'd forgotten something. I'd forgotten how she'd told me to feel bad for people who are perfect. That if you're always perfect, never making a mistake, you can't really have fun."

I thought of Jace. My love and my friend. Who would bury my father in the hills of East Tennessee if I asked him.

"She said that it's the mistakes we make, the fun we have, that make us feel the most alive."

But most of all, I thought of twelve-year-old Polly, struggling to breathe, struggling to survive, who thought the only way to love herself, was through this man's approval.

"That's what happened, wasn't it? When she died, all that light, all that laughter, went with her. I look at my kids, and I see that light. I see her spirit living on in them."

My father's face was pale, like he'd seen a ghost. I took a deep breath, in and out, continuing to gather this newfound courage.

"I'm sorry that happened to you—that you had a love like hers and lost it. And I'm sad that I never got to meet that version of you. The version of you that Momma saw. I wonder if I would have liked him. I wonder if he would have liked me."

He looked so bereft, I almost reached across the table to lay my hand atop his.

. . .

"You had no right to treat me as you did. To make me feel as though I had to win your approval, to win your love, by being perfect. That's not love. That's control. And frankly, I'm ashamed it's taken me this long to realize that I was letting you do it. Jace and I have done nothing improper in public *or* private between two consenting adults. I am done giving you this power over me. Like my kids and I are merely pawns for you to move around however you want. So, I will make this incredibly easy for you. As of now, our deal is off. I ask that you give us one week to move out of the house. After that, we'll be gone, and all of your problems will be solved."

He looked to be trembling with anger, the vein in his forehead prominent and bulging.

I, on the other hand, felt a calm settle over my shoulders like a reassuring hug. Like I could feel my momma's spirit around me, smiling.

I'd love to say I left then, never to see him again. But that's not actually how life works.

The judge *had* been saving the worst for last; he just hadn't gotten there yet.

"I don't think you'll do that considering what I'm about to tell you," my father sneered. "I've been informed that Jace Vargas has recently applied to college so that he may work in education. Well, I have a family willing to vouch that he conducted himself improperly, in a criminally negligent fashion, in the presence of a minor on school property."

A brief sense of depersonalization came over me and I shook my head back and forth slowly, as if the picture in front of me was some sort of trippy Etch A Sketch, wishing I could shake it and it'd be gone. But no amount of shaking could make this go away.

"Should you continue this relationship with him, move out of my house, or act in any way that I deem inappropriate, I will have no choice but to have this family come forward. While it may not be legally substantiated without physical evidence, the damage to his reputation will be done. He will never be allowed to work with minors, your ability to work with minors will be threatened due to your association with him, and you and your children will live in ruin." He paused, lip curling maliciously. "Think very carefully, Polly."

CHAPTER
FIFTY-ONE

JACE

You are not the last dream of my soul.

You are the first dream, the only dream I ever was unable to stop myself from dreaming. You are the first dream of my soul, and from that dream I hope will come all other dreams, a lifetime's worth.

Cassandra Clare, *Clockwork Prince*

I checked my watch again, making it only four minutes after I'd checked it the last time. The kids and I had just gotten to my parents' house, and I was anxiously awaiting Polly's text letting me know she was on her way over to meet my parents . . . as my girlfriend.

We found Pop in the garage, music playing in the background as he inspected a very old set of golf clubs. He was never much of a golfer.

"You thinkin' about picking up a club again?" I called out.

Pop smiled briefly, then held up a finger. He glanced toward his workbench. "Alexa, be a dear and pause the music."

"Pausing," a robotic female voice sounded.

"Thank you, Alexa." I saw the amused smirk on Max's face as Pop thanked the AI computer program.

"You're welcome," Alexa said.

Pop shook his head. "That Alexa is always so polite. Good manners are a lost art. Max! Ryla! Good to see you two again. Say Ryla," Pop said, a twinkle in his eye. "Susan's inside, making something that smells like waffles if you're interested."

As soon as he said waffles, Ryla was running up the concrete garage steps and barging into the house.

"Hiya, Maxy. I think she's got some fresh homemade sweet tea, too."

"I've never tried sweet tea."

Pop held a hand to his heart. "Son, you're missing the nectar of life. Why don't you follow your sister and bring out a glass for you and me." Pop looked over at me and startled, acting like he hadn't seen me. "Oh, and maybe this guy, too."

I was proud of Max when he went into the kitchen alone. I eyed Pop suspiciously, wondering why he'd wanted to get me alone.

"You taking those classics to sunny Florida soon?" I crossed my arms over my chest. His golf bag looked straight out of the 1970s and probably was a third hand-me-down. My parents weren't big on new things. Which, again, was why this supposed move to Florida was so out of left field.

"Ack, well, Kent and your uncle have been talking about golf and think I need new clubs. But I told them it was hard for me to do that much golf these days, and if I did, these work just fine"

He shuffled over to a folding chair, grunting as he sat. He inclined his head to the empty chair next to him.

"I'm glad you came over," Pop began as I sat down. "I've been meaning to talk to you about, uh, something. It's about Florida. Things aren't exactly as Kent described. I know we put an offer in on the condo and it's been accepted, and I know Kent made it seem like we're movin' any day."

I frowned, because that's *exactly* what Kent made it sound like.

"But we've barely started fixing this house to sell. Who knows if we'll actually be able to sell this place." He looked around the junky old garage like it was the Taj Mahal.

"Pop? You do want to move, right?"

In response, he picked an invisible speck of dust off his shirt. "I may not be as keen on it as your mother. And while the thought of being down there a few weeks at a time sounds nice, living there *full*-time . . ." He grimaced and looked over at me. "It sure would be nice to have this place to come home to."

"I thought you didn't have enough money to keep this place and buy the condo."

Pop shifted in his chair. "That's true. You know, son, and this is just a shot in the dark, but I'd always hoped that maybe you'd take this house on eventually, when your momma and I are too old to keep up with it. 'Course I wouldn't want you to feel any pressure, just throwing the idea out there."

I leaned forward. "I'm a little confused. Are you asking me if I have interest in buying this house from you and Momma?"

Pop nodded, shifting in his chair again. "I'm humble enough to admit that my arthritis is getting worse. Your mother, God love her, can only take so much. I know how hard you work and how much you save, Jace. I'm awfully proud. Proud as any father can be of their son. The house here is all paid off. If you were willing to live here, take care of all the upkeep like you've been doing and paying a portion of the utilities and taxes, I'd be happy to deed the house to you. Of course, if I get sick enough and you can't care for me, you can feel free to put my butt in a home. I know it's a lot to ask, what with your mother being how she is, but I think you movin' out has given her some perspective."

I looked over my shoulder, wondering when Max would be coming back with the tea. "This is a lot to process, Pop. And if you'd have asked me a few weeks ago, I probably would have taken you up on your offer. But, well, a lot's changed since then."

A helpless smile came over my face.

"You see, there's this girl—a woman. And she's a game-changer. I guess what I'm saying is, it's not just me anymore. I'd love to help you out, you and Momma both. And if you decide to stay here, regardless of where I'm living, I'll always come and help."

A knowing smile played over his lips. "Is it the kids' momma?"

I gave him a cautious nod.

"You know your Momma called that one a mile away. Ever since you drove away with those kids the first time you brought 'em over here, she's been pestering me on how to get y'all back over here. She wants to meet her something fierce."

I laughed, shaking my head. "Well, I'm thrilled to hear you say that, because she'll be here soon." I glanced at my watch just then and saw I'd missed a text from Polly.

Polly: I need to talk to you.

————

Worry tightened my insides as I drove to Daisy's ten minutes later. Pulling into the parking lot, I spotted Polly's father's Tesla near the back. After parking next to her, I cut the engine and climbed into her passenger seat.

Polly was sitting stiffly, facing the steering wheel, her hands splayed open on her knees. She'd obviously been crying, makeup from around her eyes had leaked in trails down her cheeks.

"Are you alright? What'd he do to you?" I put a hand on her forearm, needing to touch her.

She just shook her head, chest heaving. "My father . . ." she started, but her voice broke. I leaned over the center console the best I could, desperate to hold her in my arms.

"Whatever he's done. It doesn't matter, Polly. It doesn't. You have me. And you have two amazing kids who are funny and tough, just like you."

She turned to me with sad, swollen eyes. "My father's assistant, Jeffrey, has been spying on us. I haven't told you this as I didn't think much of it, but I've seen this black SUV behind me a few times and then again at Young Wills last Thursday. That was Jeffrey. He knows we're together and told my father God knows what."

I didn't want to worry Polly, so I rubbed her back soothingly as she spoke, unaware that I was counting how many favors I'd owe Sam when I gave him a call later. Someone's black SUV was about to get harmed. Or maybe I'd need to talk to him in person. Less evidence that way.

"And then he threatened some strange kind of public denouncement of me, threatening to tell everyone about you and I so I'll get fired and can't work as a doctor again. At least not around here."

I immediately started to shake my head. "That won't happen. No one will care, Polly. We're adults. Your father is trying to scare you. No one is going to care."

Her lips wobbled, voice breaking when she whispered, "That's not all."

I clenched my fists, hating how powerless I felt, and waited.

"He said he has a family from Green Valley that will claim that you acted inappropriately with their child at a school. He said that it doesn't matter if there isn't any proof, the damage to your reputation will be done. I can't do that to you, Jace. You are meant to work with kids. And you have your whole life ahead of you."

She looked down at her hands and took a deep breath.

"I love you. In my whole life, I've only ever felt this kind of love for four people: my mom, my two kids, and Leah. And now all of a sudden, you. Tell me Jace, how can I risk your future? I can't. I can't ruin your life."

I grabbed her face in my hands and kissed her, needing something to ground me. My mouth moved hard over hers, tasting the salt from her tears, the trembling sadness of her lips. I would not lose her. Not when I'd just found her.

I pulled back, continuing to hold her face, feeling tears in my own eyes.

"There is only one way you could ruin my life, Polly, and that's by leaving it. I've found the love of my life, and two kids I love with my whole heart in just a few short weeks. I couldn't believe it at first. But it's real. I used to be so angry at your ex, for leaving you and the kids like that, but now I'm thanking my lucky stars. He left, because I was coming. Someone, somewhere, knew that this—you, me, Max and Ryla—was it. We were meant to be a family."

Polly was full-on crying again, so I took a moment to brush my thumbs under her eyes.

"I want to be there on Max's first day of high school. I want to be there when Ryla loses her first tooth. I want to clap and cheer and embarrass the hell out of Max when he graduates college, and I want to scare the shit outta all of Ryla's boyfriends, then walk her down the aisle to the last one."

I continued to cradle Polly's face in my hands as I brought my forehead to hers. "It took me twenty-four years to find you. Don't cheat me out of the next seventy-six."

"Jace," she whispered roughly, burying her head in my neck until her sobs quieted and breathing calmed.

When she finally pulled back from me, eyes red and puffy, hair wild around her face, I still thought she was the most beautiful woman I'd ever seen.

"You really think you're going to live to be a hundred?" Her voice was hoarse and quaking, but she was teasing.

That was a good sign.

"Ryla may take a few years off," I teased back, my own voice thick with emotion.

Polly settled back into the driver's seat, looking utterly exhausted.

"What are we going to do? I asked him to give me a week to move out of the house, not that he agreed to it. If we moved out, I don't have a place to go. What if he makes good on his promise to tell everyone about us, people in town do care, and I lose my job? I need health insurance. I can't lose it."

A wild idea, one that didn't involve a black SUV, had been taking shape in the back of my mind. An idea that kept making itself louder in my head as Polly kept taking.

"Do you think your father will actually do this? It sounds an awful lot like a bluff. He's so worried about the court of public opinion, yet he's ready to throw his only daughter to the wolves? That doesn't sound likely."

Polly shrugged. "He certainly seemed serious."

I hesitated. "I have a wild idea."

Polly laughed mirthlessly, adjusting her dress. "Good, because I have none. Except for crying in Daisy's parking lot."

"Did you know that Tennessee doesn't have a waiting period for marriage licenses?"

Polly's head snapped up. "Waiting period for . . . no, I didn't know that," she said carefully, then scrunched her face. "Wait, how do you know that?"

"Sam tried to—" I stopped and held up a hand. "You know what? Never mind." I leaned closer to her, letting a wayward grin come across my face. "Think about it, Polly. If we're married, your father won't have a leg to stand on. We're only a dirty little secret to him if we continue to hide it. But if we get married, we're calling his bluff. And if it's a bluff, you'll be safe. Your job is safe. Your health insurance is safe."

Polly blinked. "And what about you? What if his threat to you isn't a bluff?"

"I know two county sheriffs, have pull with important people in town, and have the truth on my side." Was I happy about her father blackmailing me? No.

But was I worried? Also no.

Polly studied my face, then began to blink rapidly as she sat stock upright. "You're really serious."

I nodded, easygoing smile in place.

"You want to get married? To me?"

"Mmmhmm," I drawled lazily.

Polly shook her head. "But that's . . .well. I mean—that's insane!"

"Insane enough to work."

"What if it's a mistake?"

"What if it's not?" I leaned forward, grabbing her left hand and bringing it to my lips.

"Hold on, Romeo." Polly slid her hand out of mine. "This is all predicated on my father bluffing. What if he's not?"

I smiled and leaned back against the seat, inexplicably calm. "This morning, not five minutes before I got your text message, Pop asked if I had any interest in moving into their house. With his arthritis, my parents need someone to handle all the house upkeep, and eventually, he or both of them will need more care. He offered to deed the house to me in exchange."

Polly's eyes nearly bugged out of her head again.

"I said no. I told him if it was a few weeks earlier, I wouldn't have hesitated. I would have helped out and lived in that house as long as they needed me. But it wasn't up to just me anymore. You and the kids, that's where my home is now."

I could see her softening a bit but could still hear the gears turning in her head as she tried to puzzle her way around all of this.

"Polly, if you lose your job and can't find another one in town, I'll move anywhere you need to go with you and the kids."

I'd started inching closer to Polly as I talked, her face continuing to soften. She was moving closer to me, too, almost unknowingly. Like she knew the way forward but wasn't ready to go there. Not yet.

"Or we can stay in Green Valley and if you're game, we can live in my parents' house. We can start our life here, together, the four of us."

She startled at my words, eyes going soft then, looking mildly dazed, like she was finally starting to believe this was true.

"You have me," I continued. "So, you also have my family and my friends. You have Leah and the new friends you've made. And most importantly, we have Max and Ryla. Whatever is coming for us, we can get through it together."

We moved closer together still, our hands intertwining almost on their own accord.

"Say yes, Polly. I'll sign an iron-clad prenup where you can take me for all my money in the case of a divorce."

Our foreheads touched and I felt a little puff from her exhale on my cheek.

"Do you love me?" I whispered.

"Yes," she whispered back.

I closed my eyes briefly with relief, then opened them.

"Then say you'll marry me, Polly. We can face the future together."

CHAPTER
FIFTY-TWO

POLLY

Lehabah still pushed. Still shook with terror. Yet she did not stop. Not for one heartbeat.

"My friends are with me and I am not afraid."

Sarah J. Maas, *House of Earth and Blood*

The school board meeting the following Friday had an exceptional attendance . . . or so I was told. After all, this was my first one.

I'd arrived early to the high school auditorium with Jace, who gave my hand a little squeeze before Rose and I went to find our seats at the tables onstage.

Rose introduced me to school board members as they arrived. Most seemed nice and curious, until I saw the bottom dweller, himself, walk onstage. Brad stiffened when he saw me, then looked away, nose in the air.

Well.

A few minutes before the meeting started, nerves threatened to overtake me. I searched the audience, finding solace as I spotted Jace in the front row. He winked at me. Sitting on either side of him, were his parents. They both smiled and waved at me.

I'd met them for the first time last weekend, face blotchy and red, and engaged to their son. They took the news of our engagement remarkably well. On the other side of Jace's mom was a woman who looked like the female version of Jace. I'd been warned, before meeting Sarah, that she was a ball buster. True to form, within two minutes of meeting her, she threatened me with bodily harm should I hurt her brother. She could also execute one hell of a fast prenuptial agreement.

Jace's best friend, Sam, sat next to her. He kept giving Sarah puppy-dog eyes despite her shutting him down every time.

I gave a discrete wave back to Rae and Sienna who were sitting next to their very hunky, very bearded husbands, both of whom I'd met at my wedding earlier this week. In fact, Jace's entire guest list was more beard than not.

Butterflies danced in my stomach as I recalled wearing a white summer dress while someone I'd never met before but had curls that rivaled Jace's and an impressive bushy beard, played soft bluegrass guitar as I walked down the grassy aisle in Jace's parents' backyard, hand in hand with my children.

To the man that was now my husband.

As Jace and I recited our vows, my face hurt from smiling. We laughed and teased and cried our way through it, like we did everything. Like we would for the rest of our lives.

Sitting beside Rae and Sienna was Charlotte, who gave me a covert thumbs up. I'd gotten to talk to Charlotte during Young Wills practice this week, learning about her kids and her work in the school. She was incredibly knowledgeable about school accommodations and even helped Rose and I last night as we reviewed our materials for today.

I elbowed Rose, who was sitting nervously beside me onstage, as I spotted the three women who made up the majority of the bride's side at the wedding: Tiffany, Margo, and Eliza. They'd given me and Jace matching Kindles as wedding gifts. My matron of honor, Leah, protested when I asked her to watch Max and Ryla during the meeting. She reluctantly agreed when I told her I needed to focus, and I couldn't do that if my kids were here. I needed to know they were safe and happy, to do what I needed to do today. Before I left her house, she pulled me into a fierce hug, whispered how proud she was of me and to fight, then slapped me on the ass for good measure, before cackling and closing her front door.

And fight I shall.

"I call this Green Valley School Board meeting to order," the sniveling Mr. Goldenstein called out from his place at the center table. There were about fifteen of us in total, arranged at separate tables in a semi-circle on the auditorium stage.

"First item on the docket," a member next to Brad announced. "Approval of the new medical director of the school district, Dr. Polly Alberton. Welcome, Dr. Alberton." The member then smiled politely at me and nodded, and soon the other board members gave me professional nods and smiles, too.

"Thank you," I said into the microphone in front of me, fisting my trembling hands in my lap.

"I'm sorry to bring up an issue first thing," Brad cut off the member next to him as they were just opening their mouth to speak, an insincere smile on his face. "But I've been informed of a disturbing allegation about Dr. Alberton. Of course, I've emailed her repeatedly this week, urging her to step down to avoid discussing this in a public forum, but she has failed to do so. Thus, I have no choice but to bring these concerns to the board's attention now."

Reggie, who was sitting on my other side, stiffened. I felt a pang of guilt for not warning him; I wanted to save him from any backlash that may cost him his job if this went poorly. I'd been expecting what was about to happen, having been on the receiving end of several angry emails from Brad this week, making it clear what he was going to bring up today.

But that was Brad's mistake. I mean, he knew that my father was a judge, right? You don't announce your strategy to the opposing counsel before trial.

My father was a notable absence from my wedding. Of course, he also wasn't invited.

I'd emailed Jeffrey on Tuesday, informing him that the kids and I were moving out of the judge's house in one week, that I was marrying Jace, and that I would no longer be attending Sunday brunches or any future campaign events.

I hadn't heard anything from either of them since.

At Brad's declaration, I studied the faces of the school board members. Most looked shocked or confused, which gave me hope.

"Mr. Goldenstein, I don't think it's appropriate to discuss this in an open forum. We should bring this matter up at a closed school board meeting." That was from one of the few women on the board.

Glancing at Jace, he flashed a reassuring smile as I leaned forward into the mic.

"No, that's quite alright. I have no problem discussing this in public. Please proceed." I looked directly at Brad as I said this. My eyes silently communicating, *Bring. It. On.*

I could tell Brad lost some of his bravado, but he recovered quickly. "It has come to my attention that an inappropriate relationship has been discovered between Dr. Alberton and someone in her employ." I heard a few murmurs from the crowd as Brad continued, "She has been engaged in a sexual relationship with a young man who is the nanny for her children."

"Brad, can you tell us why it's inappropriate?" asked a male member of the board seated next to Brad.

"Certainly. The young man is only twenty-four years old, and she hired him to be her children's nanny." Brad looked from side to side, but the majority of the members were looking at him with persistently confused expressions.

"I'm sorry, Mr. Goldenstein. I still don't see how this is relevant to our proceedings today, nor appropriate on your part," the female member across from me said again.

Brad sneered. "She's thirty-eight years old. And clearly used her position of authority to seduce a subordinate. I do not think that someone like that should be entrusted to make sound decisions for our children."

I placed my hand over Rose's. She'd been fisting her pen so hard her knuckles were turning white. Yes, his words had a barb in them, but nothing compared to what I'd heard on a regular basis from my own father.

"How old did you say this young man was?" a member asked.

"Twenty-four." Brad leaned too close to the microphone, causing feedback that made everyone flinch. Silence descended as Brad craned his neck around him, likely realizing this was not going to be the easy win he anticipated.

Another member spoke up. "This seems to be a private matter. As long as it was a consensual relationship between two adults, I don't see how any of this is pertinent. It should have no bearing on our approval of Dr. Alberton today. We have all reviewed her impressive CV and personal statement. I propose we move to approve Dr. Alberton before Mr. Goldenstein embarrasses her, or himself, any further."

"Seconded."

I had to bite the insides of my cheeks to keep from smirking.

"Now, wait just a second," Brad thundered. "I also have it on good authority, that the only reason she wanted this position was because of her own son's mental health problems, which were so severe he was dismissed from his past school. That alone is a conflict of interest, and she should have no place on this board."

Metaphorically throwing down my gloves, I grabbed the microphone and spoke directly into it.

Loudly.

"Excuse me, members of the board, if you may allow me to speak?"

I was met with nods as Brad sneered at me.

"It's true that I hired Mr. Jace Vargas, who is twenty-four-years old, to be the nanny for my children when I moved to Green Valley. I was a single mother and took overnight call for my job. If I was called into the hospital, I couldn't bring my kids along with me, for obvious reasons. I needed someone to care for them. And while I am appalled that anyone would suggest that I would use a position of authority to pursue an inappropriate relationship with anyone, whether in my employ or not, I can appreciate that Mr. Goldenstein was working to uphold the principles of morality and fairness. Those are essential qualities for anyone in the community who works with children—"

"Or adults!" Rose piped up into the mic beside me, staring daggers at Brad.

I nodded at Rose and continued, emboldened by the few encouraging smiles as well as head nods from the surrounding tables. "The truth of the matter is that yes, Mr. Vargas and I started a relationship when he was in my employ. It was absolutely consensual," I looked to Jace and he winked, "and then we fell in love. I will also say that Mr. Vargas is no longer in my employ, but he does live with my children and I."

Brad sneered. "If he's no longer employed by you, why does he live with you and your children?"

"Because he's my husband," I answered calmly.

Gasps and murmurs, along with a loud piercing whistle, erupted from the crowd. Brad was practically seething, his face an alarming shade of red.

I leaned into the microphone once again, heart racing, palms starting to sweat. "As for the other matter. Yes, my son has an anxiety disorder. He was not dismissed from his last school, that was quite incorrect on Mr. Goldenstein's part, but he was forced to leave school because the special education programming at his school was inflexible and understaffed. I had no choice but to remove him from a school that was unable to meet his needs. When this position was offered to me, I was hesitant to take it. I was a single mother at the time, and caring for children with mental health challenges takes a fair amount of time. I couldn't help other children, at the expense of my own."

I took a deep breath, finding Jace's beaming face in the crowd, filling me with confidence.

"But I've found a family here. I've found friends. A community that supports us. Just like a school is the community that supports a child. I believe that with my expertise and personal experience, I am the exact right person to do this job. So that I can help as many children as I can, children like my son, who need help so they can succeed in school both socially and academically, but the backlogged and outdated systems don't allow him to get it."

I sat back, relief flooding me. Reggie clapped me on the back, a wide smile on his face. I studied each board member's face. Enthusiastic smiles and polite nods greeted me at every single seat.

Except of course, from the smarmy smarmerton sitting in the middle.

"Repeat motion to approve Dr. Alberton as the medical director of our school district."

This was quickly seconded, followed by a chorus of ayes from the board and one exuberant "Aye!" from Rose, next to me.

But it didn't stop there.

"Aye!" Jace shot up from the audience, followed almost immediately by three more ayes from Rae, Sienna, and Charlotte.

"Aye!" came Jace's parents and Sarah, who turned and glared at Sam, who shot up immediately with a high pitched, "Aye."

"Oh hell, I'm doing it too. Aye!" yelled Tiffany as my friends and family all stood up, one by one, to support me.

I glanced at Brad, who looked madder than a wet hen, but he leaned into the microphone and muttered, "Motion passed."

Heart bursting, the entire audience broke into applause, then quieted quickly because we were still at a meeting and had work to do. As I sat down, I let my gaze linger over my friends and my family, *my family,* feeling truly home for the first time.

EPILOGUE

POLLY

*I know at the moment what he's given me and it's not a chair. It's an invitation,
a welcome, the knowledge that I am accepted here. He hasn't given me a place
to sit. He's given me a place to belong.*

Katja Millay, *The Sea of Tranquility*

A few days later, it was our last night at my father's house. We'd spent the weekend moving our things out to Jace's parents' house. They were talking like they might be snowbirds, living part of the year in Green Valley and part of the year in Florida, though both Jace and Sarah have insisted that they'll believe it when they see it.

I still couldn't quite believe the turn my life had taken. I'd come to Green Valley desperate. My kids were miserable, I was miserable, having almost no friends and no family. And then Jace came waltzing into our lives, filling the house with laughter and magic, literally breathing life into us again.

Mr. Poppins, himself, was occupying the kids with ice pops, giving me time to move through the house slowly, somehow knowing that I needed a little time alone. I was thinking of my mother, working through memories from each room. But they were happy memories. Full of smiles and laughter. Like my father, the house no longer had any power over me. I lingered at the doorway of the library for a moment, and I could almost see the outline of a woman and her daughter snuggling on one of the leather chairs.

"I love you, Momma," I whispered, and shut the door.

———

I joined my family on the steps in the backyard a few minutes later. Pinks and yellows streaked across the sky as the sun set. I smiled down at my kids who were diligently licking and slurping away on their ice pops.

"It's a little melted." Jace held out a red one for me. I sat between Ryla and Jace, Max was on his other side.

"Thank you." I pressed my lips to his for a beat. He tasted like cherries.

"What were you, Rae, and Charlotte talking about for so long this afternoon?" Jace asked.

"Apparently, Brad Goldenstein stepped down today. Can you believe it?" I waggled my eyebrows, biting into my ice pop and crunching it with relish.

"I'm shocked." Jace smirked and shook his head slowly. "Couldn't happen to a nicer guy."

I dipped my head closer to Jace's ear, whispering, "And your sister called me today asking for my ex-husband's information. Any idea why she'd be calling me asking for that?"

Jace choked on his ice pop, then shook his head. "I swear I did not put her up to that. Did you give it to her?"

I lifted one eyebrow. "She's incredibly persuasive."

His lips quirked. "I'd have loved to see her face when you told her his last name."

"Brain freeze!" Max suddenly shouted, slapping a hand to his forehead.

"Put your tongue to the roof of your mouth," Jace explained, working Max through it.

"Why's his brain freezing?" Ryla had paused the eating of her blue raspberry ice pop to check on Max.

"It happens when you eat something cold too fast," I explained to her as something shiny on her shirt caught my eye. Leaning closer, I saw it was a Smash-Girl pin. "Where'd you get that Smash-Girl pin, sweetie?"

Ryla looked down, then pulled out her shirt to inspect the pin. "Miss Sienna gave it to me."

"Oh, that was nice of her."

I felt Jace shift next to me, having helped Max recover from his brain freeze. Jace's slid his arm around me, pulling me to his side, brushing a small kiss to my temple.

"Yep! She said she had a ton and didn't want them at her house anymore."

I frowned. "Why would she have so many Smash-Girl buttons at her house?"

Jace's body went rigid as Ryla replied, "Because she is Smash-Girl."

I laughed, shaking my head at Ryla. "You must be mistaken, sweet pea." What a cutie.

Jace's arm fell slowly, and he cleared his throat. "Actually . . ." he started.

I whipped my head to him. "Jace Vargas! Do you mean to tell me that nice woman you work with, who acts like she's your older sister, who helped us move and invited us and the kids for a playdate at the park with her three sons, is a bona fide *movie star*?"

"Surprise?" Jace tried to look contrite even as his shoulders shook in silent laughter.

Opening and closing my mouth, I looked back and forth between Jace and Ryla. "Any other secrets I should know?"

Ryla raised her hand. "Miss Rae is in the movies, too! What's her name again?" Ryla leaned forward, craning her neck to look at Jace, her little eyebrows furrowed together.

"Raquel Ezra," Max piped up.

I jumped up, spinning to face the three traitors. "You all knew?" Jace, Max, and Ryla were all giggling as I stood there, pointing at them in outrage.

"Treason! This is treason, I tell you!" I shouted dramatically. "I sentence you all to tickling!"

Ryla yelped and Max jumped up, each of them taking off in different directions.

"Run if you dare!" I shouted to them. "The Queen of Sheeba will always get the last laugh!"

I took off after my kids, but not before I turned back to see Jace, beaming with pride, as he watched us run and laugh and play in the late summer night.

The End

ACKNOWLEDGMENTS

To anyone who took a chance reading a new indie author and made it this far —thank you 😊

To my family, I would have no concept of what unconditional love would be without you.

To my husband and two kids, who gave me space and time and freedom to write. You are the loves of my life.

To my mom, to whom this book is dedicated. I won the lottery with you. Thank you for being with me during every step of this crazy reading and writing journey.

To my dad, thank you for demonstrating the importance of working hard and playing hard.

To my sister Jenny, every kick-ass sister I ever write will be a little bit you.

To my sister-in-law, Sonja, your support has been unreal. Thank you so much.

To Jess & Anna, you've both taught me what it means to be a friend. Jess, the day I almost pushed your bed off its frame was kismet. My life would be terrible without you in it. Thank you for eating carbs faster than anyone I've ever seen. Anna, thank you for loving me at every stage of my life. It's a rare gift that I will treasure always. Here's to Twister 3 when we can get the senior special.

To Penny Reid and Fiona. Getting this opportunity to work with you and join the SPRU family has been a dream come true. Penny, reading your books and being a part of the community you built has changed my life. The perspectives you share make me think and grow as a writer and person. Thank you doesn't seem adequate. I will forever be grateful.

To my incredible dev editor Nicole McCurdy. Thank you for encouraging me at every step of the way. You have an unparalleled breadth of knowledge and grasp of the romance genre that is invaluable to any writer working with you. You guide me to the exact reason why my story is stuck which reinvigorates me to continue writing—even when I'm pretty sure the story is shit. Your ability to blend constructive feedback with praise is a skill I wish all of my attendings had in residency. You make me a better writer with every edit we do.

To my very talented copy line editor, Briana Ozor. As my grammatical and proofreading skills are akin to a wheel of cheese, I can only imagine how painful this edit must have been for you and yet, your feedback wasn't anything but kind, encouraging, and helpful. Working with you made my work stronger. Thank you!

To my betas/friends.

Brittney – You are a beautiful example of what a friend should be. Thank you for your support, your ideas (YACHTSMAN), your time, and your willingness to placate me when I send you screenshots of my computer when I write something that makes me cackle. It's more appreciated than you know. I don't know how I could have done any of this without you. It would have really sucked.

Nikki – Sharing your experiences made this story stronger. You are amazing. Thank you for all of your feedback, your ideas, and continued support.

Kimberlee—The day you came into my life was special. Thank you for your enthusiastic support, your sense of humor, and your unparalleled book wrapping skills. The only problem with you is how far away you live, how dare you.

April – Thank you for your perspective, encouragement, and life lessons. If I ever need something, I know I can count on you—I'm so grateful to have you in my life.

Rose- Thank you for the gift of your name, your hugs, your friendship. . .and your Christmas trees. I love you.

The real book club- Tiffany, Claire, Sarah, Beth, Valerie. Thank you for the gift of your names, our conversations, your support and your humor. You are all amazing women.

To all of my book community friends/acquaintances/supporters. Your support and encouragement throughout this process has been unreal! I love being in this community with you.

To the intelligent, talented, funny and courageous romance authors whose quotes grace the beginning of each chapter. Thank you for writing stories about love that dare to end happily. I see you and how talented you are even if the rest of the world sometimes doesn't (those idiots).

Last but not least, thanks to Timothee Chalamet's hair stylist in *Dune: Part Two* which came out when I was brainstorming this book.

ABOUT THE AUTHOR

Krysta Dearson is a writer of romance with laughs, spice, and all the feels ——
if she's able to sprinkle in a little Midwest charm as well, the more the better.
A voracious reader of all types of romance herself, she loves a good HEA
along with angst, a strong heroine, and a swoon-worthy hero, but she's the
happiest when a book makes her laugh. In fact, she'd be supremely disappointed if she doesn't make you laugh multiple times when reading her books.
When she's not writing or working as a physician, she's juggling reading,
listening to audiobooks, watching law tube, and avoiding exercise and the sun
with her vampiric skin. Otherwise, she can usually be found with a can of Diet
Coke in hand while spending time with her two kids alongside her husband in
Wisconsin.

———

Find Krysta Dearson online:
Website: www.krystadearsonwrites.com
Facebook: https://www.facebook.com/profile.php?id=61554324157961
Instagram: https://www.instagram.com/krystadearson
Threads:https://www.threads.net/@krystadearson

Find Smartypants Romance online:
Website: www.smartypantsromance.com
Facebook: www.facebook.com/smartypantsromance/
Goodreads: www.goodreads.com/smartypantsromance
Twitter: @smartypantsrom
Instagram: @smartypantsromance

ALSO BY SMARTYPANTS ROMANCE

<u>Green Valley Chronicles</u>

<u>The Love at First Sight Series</u>

<u>Baking Me Crazy by Karla Sorensen (#1)</u>

<u>Batter of Wits by Karla Sorensen (#2)</u>

<u>Steal My Magnolia by Karla Sorensen (#3)</u>

<u>Worth the Wait by Karla Sorensen (#4)</u>

<u>Fighting For Love Series</u>

<u>Stud Muffin by Jiffy Kate (#1)</u>

<u>Beef Cake by Jiffy Kate (#2)</u>

<u>Eye Candy by Jiffy Kate (#3)</u>

<u>Knock Out by Jiffy Kate (#4)</u>

<u>The Donner Bakery Series</u>

<u>No Whisk, No Reward by Ellie Kay (#1)</u>

<u>Dough You Love Me? By Stacy Travis (#2)</u>

<u>Tough Cookie by Talia Hunter (#3)</u>

<u>Muffin But Trouble by Talia Hunter (#4)</u>

<u>*Oh Brother! Series*</u>

<u>Crime and Periodicals by Nora Everly (#1)</u>

<u>Carpentry and Cocktails by Nora Everly (#2)</u>

Hotshot and Hospitality by Nora Everly (#3)

<u>Architecture and Artistry by Nora Everly (#4)</u>

<u>*Small Town Silver Fox Series*</u>

<u>Love in Due Time by L.B. Dunbar (#1)</u>

<u>Love in Deed by L.B. Dunbar (#2)</u>

Love in a Pickle by L.B. Dunbar (#3)

Passing Notes by Nora Everly (#1)

Band Together by Piper Sheldon (#2)

Ex Marks the Spot by Hazel James (#3)

Past Tents by Stacy Travis (#4)

The Best Medicine by Krysta Dearson (#5)

Story of Us Collection

My Story of Us: Zach by Chris Brinkley (#1)

My Story of Us: Thomas by Chris Brinkley (#2)

My Story of Us: Grayson by Chris Brinkley (#3)

Seduction in the City

Cipher Security Series

Code of Conduct by April White (#1)

Code of Honor by April White (#2)

Code of Matrimony by April White (#2.5)

Code of Ethics by April White (#3)

Cipher Office Series

Weight Expectations by M.E. Carter (#1)

Sticking to the Script by Stella Weaver (#2)

Cutie and the Beast by M.E. Carter (#3)

Weights of Wrath by M.E. Carter (#4)

Common Threads Series

Mad About Ewe by Susannah Nix (#1)

Give Love a Chai by Nanxi Wen (#2)

Key Change by Heidi Hutchinson (#3)

Not Since Ewe by Susannah Nix (#4)

Lost Track by Heidi Hutchinson (#5)

Ewe Complete Me by Susannah Nix (#6)

Meet Your Matcha by Nanxi Wen (#7)

All Mixed Up by Heidi Hutchinson (#8)

Write or Wrong by Heidi Hutchinson (#9)